PRAISE FOR

THE GIRL OF FIRE AND THORNS

Morris Award Finalist

ALA Top Ten Best Fiction for Young Adults

"Elisa is a wonderful, believable hero, the kind that every reader can imagine as herself. I charged through the book in two days, savoring Elisa's realness and her unique, wonderful world! A unique and engrossing read!"
—Tamora Pierce

"Palace intrigues, desert rebellions, kidnappings, forbidden romance, and bloody betrayals, along with not a little time at the banquet table, make *The Girl of Fire and Thorns* a delicious debut."
—Paolo Bacigalupi, author of the Printz Medal–winning *Ship Breaker*

"Carson's mature writing style, thoughtful storytelling, appealing characters, and surprising twists add up to a page-turner with broad appeal."
—*Publishers Weekly* (starred review)

A "fast-moving and exciting novel."—*School Library Journal* (starred review)

"Romantic, lush, and thought provoking."—ALA *Booklist*

"It's wonderfully refreshing to see a heroine using her brain to win a war rather than strapping on a sword and charging into battle."—*Kirkus Reviews*

"Utterly fresh and compelling."—*Locus Magazine*

"A *Hunger Games* for fantasy fans."—*WhatchYAReading?*

"One of the most amazing YA fantasy novels I have ever read. Carson busts out of the debut gate guns a-blazin'."
—*Bookalicio.us*

"*The Girl of Fire and Thorns* is one of my Favorite Books Read in 2011."
—*A Chair, a Fireplace, & a Tea Cozy*

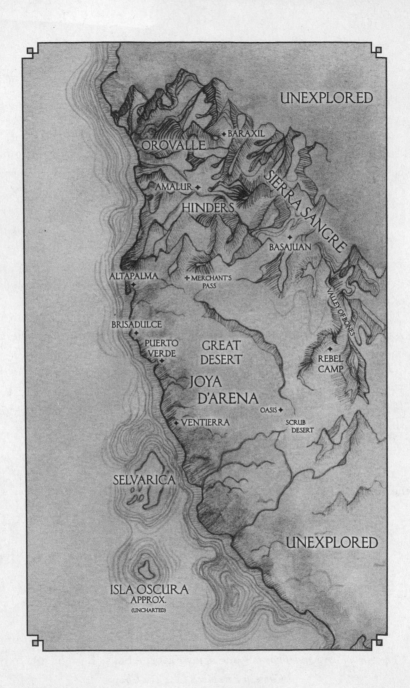

THE GIRL OF FIRE AND THORNS

RAE CARSON

GREENWILLOW BOOKS

An Imprint of HarperCollins *Publishers*

The Girl of Fire and Thorns
Copyright © 2011 by Rae Carson

First published in 2011 in hardcover; first paperback edition published in 2012. All rights reserved. No part of this book may be used or reproduced in any manner whatsoever without written permission except in the case of brief quotations embodied in critical articles and reviews. Printed in the United States of America. For information address HarperCollins Children's Books, a division of HarperCollins Publishers, 10 East 53rd Street, New York, NY 10022.
www.epicreads.com

The text of this book is set in 11-point Bell.
Book design by Paul Zakris

Library of Congress Cataloging-in-Publication Data
Carson, Rae.
The girl of fire and thorns / by Rae Carson.
p. cm.
"Greenwillow Books."
Summary: A fearful sixteen-year-old princess discovers her heroic destiny after being married off to the king of a neighboring country in turmoil and pursued by enemies seething with dark magic.
ISBN 978-0-06-202648-4 (trade bdg.)—ISBN 978-0-06-202650-7 (pbk.)
[1. Kings, queens, rulers, etc.—Fiction. 2. Prophecies—Fiction.
3. Magic—Fiction.] I. Title.
PZ7.C21677Gi 2011   [Fic]—dc22   2010042021

13 14 15 16 LP/RRDC 10 9 8 7 6 5 4
First Edition

 GREENWILLOW BOOKS

For Hannah Elise

PART I

1

PRAYER candles flicker in my bedroom. The *Scriptura Sancta* lies discarded, pages crumpled, on my bed. Bruises mark my knees from kneeling on the tiles, and the Godstone in my navel throbs. I have been praying—no, begging—that King Alejandro de Vega, my future husband, will be ugly and old and fat.

Today is the day of my wedding. It is also my sixteenth birthday.

I usually avoid mirrors, but the day is momentous enough that I risk a look. I can't see very well; the lead glass ripples, my head aches, and I am dizzy from hunger. But even blurred, the wedding *terno* is beautiful, made of silk like water with tiny glass beads that shimmer when I move. Embroidered roses circle the hem and the flared cuffs of my sleeves. It's a masterpiece, given its rushed stitching.

But I know the *terno*'s beauty will be much diminished when buttoned.

I sigh and motion for help. Nurse Ximena and Lady Aneaxi

creep toward me, armed with button hooks and apologetic smiles.

"Take a deep breath, my sky," Ximena instructs. "Now let it out. All of it, love."

I push air from my lungs, push and push until my head swims. The ladies jerk and loop with their flashing hooks; the gown tightens. The bodice in the mirror puckers. It digs into my skin just above my hips. A jagged pain shoots up my side, like the stitch I get walking up the stairs.

"Almost there, Elisa," Aneaxi assures, but I have a sickening hunch that when next I inhale, the gown's grip on my lungs will prove deadly. I want to rip it off. I want not to get married.

"Done!" they announce together, and step back, one on each side, to admire their handiwork. "What do you think?" Aneaxi asks in a tiny, faltering voice.

The *terno* only allows quick, shallow breaths. "I think . . ." I stare woozily at my breasts. The neckline presses a fleshy furrow into my skin. "Four!" I giggle anxiously. "Four breasts!"

My nurse gets a funny, choking look on her face. When my breasts overcame my chest last year, Ximena had been the one to assure me men would find them irresistible.

"It's a beautiful gown," Aneaxi says, looking pointedly at the skirt.

I shake my head. "I am a sausage," I gasp. "A big, bloated sausage in a white silk casing." I want to cry. Or laugh. It's hard to decide.

Laughing nearly wins out, but my two ladies surround me, wrinkled, graying mother hens clucking sympathy and assurance. "No, no, you are a lovely bride!" Aneaxi says. "You've had another growth spurt, is all. And such beautiful eyes! King Alejandro won't notice if the *terno* is a bit snug." So I cry, because I cannot bear sympathy and because Ximena won't look me in the eye when Aneaxi speaks her kindly false words. After a moment, though, the tears are because I don't want to wear the *terno* at all.

While I gulp and heave, Aneaxi kisses the top of my head and Ximena wipes at my tears. Crying requires breath. Great, heaping buckets of it. The silk strains, the puckers bite into my waist, the fabric rips. Crystal buttons tinkle against the glazed floor as air rushes into my famished lungs. My stomach responds with an angry growl.

My ladies drop to the floor and run their fingers through the hair of sheepskin rugs, along the crevices between clay tiles, seeking the liberated buttons. "I need another week," Ximena mutters from the floor. "Just one week to fit you properly. A royal wedding requires some notice!" It frightens me too, the suddenness of it all.

The bodice is loose enough now that I can reach back and undo the remaining buttons by myself. I shrug my arms from the sleeves and start to tug the gown below my hips, but the fabric rips again, so I pull it over my head instead. I toss the gown aside, not caring when the skirt misses my bed and crumples onto the floor. I pull on a rough woolen robe. It scratches my skin, but it is huge and comfortingly shapeless.

I turn my back on the ladies' scavenging and go downstairs to the kitchens. If my gown isn't going to fit anyway, I might as well soothe my pounding head and rumbling stomach with a warm pastry.

My older sister, Juana-Alodia, looks up when I enter. I expect her to wish me a happy birthday at least, but she just scowls at my robe. She sits on the hearth ledge, her back against the curving oven. Her legs are elegantly crossed, and she swings a slender ankle back and forth while she nibbles on her bread.

Why is she not the one getting married today?

When he sees me, the kitchen master grins beneath a flour-dusted mustache and shoves a plate at me. The pastry on it is flaky and golden, dusted with ground pistachios and glazed with honey. My mouth waters. I tell him I'll need two.

I settle next to Alodia, avoiding the hanging brassware near my head. She eyes my plate with distaste. She doesn't roll her eyes at me, but I *feel* like she does, and I glare at her. "Elisa . . . ," she begins, but she doesn't know what to say, and I make a point of ignoring her by shoving the flaky crust into my mouth. My headache lessens almost immediately.

My sister hates me. I've known it for years. Nurse Ximena says it's because I was chosen by God for an act of service and Juana-Alodia was not. God should have chosen her; she is athletic and sensible, elegant and strong. Better than two sons, Papá says. I study her as I chew my pastry, her shining black hair and chiseled cheeks, the arched eyebrows that frame confident eyes. I hate her right back.

When Papá dies, she will be queen of Orovalle. She wants to rule and I do not, so it is ironic that by marrying King Alejandro, I will be queen of a country twice as large, twice as rich. I don't know why I am the one marrying. Surely Joya d'Arena's king would have chosen the beautiful daughter, the queenly one. My mouth freezes, midchew, as I realize that he probably did.

I am the counteroffer.

Tears threaten again, and I clench my jaw until my face aches, because I'd rather be trampled by horses than cry in front of my sister. I imagine what they said to make him agree to this match. *She was chosen for service. No, no, nothing has happened yet, but soon, we are certain. Yes, she is fluent in the Lengua Classica. No, not beautiful, but she is clever. The servants love her. And she embroiders a lovely horse.*

He would have heard truer things by now. He will know that I am easily bored, that my dresses grow larger with every fitting, that I sweat like a beast during the desert summer. I pray we can be a match in some strange way. Maybe he had the pox when he was young. Maybe he can barely walk. I want a reason not to care when he turns away in disgust.

Alodia has finished her bread. She stands and stretches, flaunting her grace and her length. She gives me a strange look—I suspect it's pity—and says, "Let me know if . . . if you need any help today. Getting ready." And she hurries away before I can answer.

I take the second pastry. It doesn't taste like anything anymore, but it's something to do.

Hours later, I stand with Papá outside the basilica, steeling myself for my bridal walk. The arching doors tower above me;

the carved de Riqueza sunburst at their center winks balefully. Beyond the doors, the audience hall buzzes. I am surprised so many could attend on such short notice. Perhaps, though, it is the hurriedness of the whole affair that makes it irresistible. It speaks of secrets and desperation, of pregnant princesses or clandestine treaties. I don't care about any of this, just that King Alejandro is ugly.

My papá and I await a signal from the herald. It has not occurred to Papá to wish me a happy birthday. I'm shocked when his eyes suddenly shimmer with tears. Maybe he's sad to see me go. Or maybe he feels guilty.

I gasp with surprise when he pulls me to his chest and grips fiercely. It's suffocating, but I return his rare embrace eagerly. Papá is tall and lanky like Juana-Alodia. I know he can't feel my ribs, but I can feel his. He hasn't eaten much since Invierne began harassing our borders.

"I remember your dedication day," Papá whispers. I've heard the story a hundred times, but never from him. "You were lying in your cradle, swaddled in white silk with red bows. The high priest leaned over with a vial of holy water, ready to pour it on your forehead and name you Juana-Anica.

"But then heaven's light washed the receiving hall, and the priest sloshed it onto the blanket instead. I knew it was heaven's light because it was white, not yellow like torchlight, and because it was soft and warm. It made me want to laugh and pray at the same time." He is smiling at the memory; I can hear it in his voice. I hear pride too, and my chest tightens. "It focused into a tight beam that lit your cradle, and you laughed." He pats my head, then strokes the linen of my veil. I hear myself sigh. "Only seven days old, but you laughed and laughed.

"Juana-Alodia was the first to toddle over after it faded. Your sister peeled back the wet swaddling and we saw the Godstone lodged in your belly button, warm and alive but blue and faceted, hard as a diamond. That's when we decided to name you Lucero-Elisa." *Heavenly light, chosen of God.* His words suffocate me as surely as his embrace. All my life, I've been reminded that I am destined for service.

Trumpets blare, muffled by the doors. Papá releases me and pulls the linen veil over my head. I welcome it; I don't want anyone to see my terror or the sweat collecting on my upper lip. The doors open outward, revealing the massive chamber with its curved ceiling and painted adobe. It smells of roses and incense. Hundreds of shapes rise from their benches, dressed in bright wedding colors. Through my veil they look like Mamá's flower garden—orange clumps of bougainvillea dotted with yellow allamanda and pink hibiscus.

The herald calls, "His Majesty, Hitzedar de Riqueza, King of Orovalle! Her Highness, Lucero-Elisa de Riqueza, Princess of Orovalle!"

Papá takes my hand and holds it at shoulder level. His is as wet and fluttery as mine, but we manage a forward glide while a quartet of musicians strums the marriage blessing on their vihuelas. A man stands at the end of the aisle, black clad. His shape is blurred, but he is not short or stooped. Not fat.

We pass stone columns and oak benches. Out of the corner

of my eye, I notice a lady, a splotch of blue fabric, really. I notice her because she bends and whispers something as I pass. Her companion twitters. My face flushes hot. By the time I reach my tall, steady fiancé, I am praying for pockmarks.

Papá gives my slick hand to the man in black. His hand is large, larger than Papá's, and it grips with indifferent confidence, as if mine does not feel like a wet, dead fish in his. I want to wrench my fingers back to myself, wipe them on my dress maybe.

Behind me, a sniffle echoes through the hall; Lady Aneaxi's, no doubt, for she has been teary with nostalgia ever since the announcement. Before me, the priest warbles about marriage in the Lengua Classica. I love the language for its lyrical vowels and the way it feels against my teeth, but I can't pay attention.

There are things I have refused to consider in the days since the announcement. Things I have pushed deep inside with study and embroidery and pastries. And suddenly, standing here in my wedding *terno*, my hand in the iron grasp of this tall foreigner, I think about them, and my heart pounds.

Tomorrow I go to the desert country of Joya d'Arena to be its queen. I leave the jacaranda tree outside my bedroom window to bloom lilac without me. I leave my painted adobe walls and trickling fountains for a stone castle a millennium old. I leave a newer, vibrant nation for an enormous beast of a country—one scorched by the sun, and stale with the traditions that made my ancestors leave in the first place. I've not had the courage to ask Papá or Alodia *why*. I'm afraid to learn they are glad to be rid of me.

But the most frightening thing of all is I am about to be someone's wife.

I speak three languages. I've nearly memorized the *Belleza Guerra* and the *Scriptura Sancta*. I can embroider the hem of a *terno* in two days. But I feel like a little girl.

Juana-Alodia has always tended to palace affairs. She is the one who tours the country on horseback, who holds court with our papá and charms the nobility. I know nothing of these grown-up, wifelike things. And tonight . . . I still cannot think about tonight.

I wish my mother were alive.

The priest announces that we are now married, in the sight of God, the King of Orovalle, and the *nobleza d'oro*. He sprinkles us with holy water harvested from a deep cenote and then motions for us to face each other, saying something about my veil. I turn toward my new husband. My cheeks are hot; I know they will be blotchy and shining with sweat when he lifts the shield from my face.

He releases my hand. I clench it into a fist to keep from wiping it on my *terno*. I see his fingers on the hem of my veil. They are brown and thick with short, clean nails. Not scholar's hands, like Master Geraldo's. He lifts the veil, and I blink as cooler air floods my cheeks. I peer up at the face of my husband, at black hair that sweeps back and curls at his neck, at brown eyes warmer than cinnamon, at a mouth as strong as his fingers.

Something flits across his features—nervousness? Disappointment? But then he smiles at me—not a pitying smile, not a hungry smile, but friendly—and I gasp just a little, my heart a puddle of helpless warmth.

King Alejandro de Vega is the most beautiful person I've ever seen.

I ought to smile back, but my cheeks won't obey. He leans forward, and his lips brush mine—a chaste and gentle kiss. With the side of his thumb, he grazes my cheek and whispers, so that only I can hear, "Nice to meet you, Lucero-Elisa."

Platters of food cover the long table. We sit side by side on the bench, and at last I have something to do besides avoid his eyes. Our shoulders touch as I grab for the battered squid and a glass of wine. I chew quickly, already considering: Green chiles stuffed with cheese, or shredded pork in walnut sauce? Before us, on the floor below the dais, the *nobleza d'oro* swirls about, goblets in hand. Juana-Alodia drifts among them, slender and beautiful and smiling. They laugh easily with her. I notice surreptitious glances cast toward the man sitting beside me. Why don't they come and introduce themselves? It is unlike the golden horde to miss the opportunity to charm a king.

I feel his eyes on me. He has just watched me stuff a crisp-fried anchovy into my mouth. I am embarrassed, but I can't resist turning to meet his gaze.

He still wears that friendly smile. "Do you like fish?"

My mouth is full. "Ungh," I say.

The smile widens. He has beautiful teeth. "Me too." He reaches for an anchovy and tosses it into his mouth. His eyes crinkle at the edges while he chews, watching me. His mouth is still full, his voice muffled when he says, "We have much to discuss, you and I."

I swallow and nod. Hearing that ought to frighten me. Instead, a sweetness sparks in my stomach because the king of Joya d'Arena thinks I am a person one discusses things with.

Our banquet passes too quickly. We do talk, a little, but I am mostly a fool because all I can do is watch his lips as they move and listen to his voice.

He asks about my studies. I blurt to him about my hundred-year-old copy of the *Belleza Guerra*. His eyes flash with interest when he says, "Yes, your sister told me you are well versed in the art of war." I'm not sure what to say to this. I don't want to talk about Juana-Alodia, and I realize how ridiculous I must appear, a sausage child bride who never sits a horse and who wields a dagger only to cut meat. Yet I am fascinated by war and have studied every skirmish in my country's history.

A hush settles over the milling nobility. I follow their collective gaze toward the small wooden stage. The musicians have departed—I don't remember hearing the vihuelas cease—and in their place stand my father and sister. She raises a goblet, her arm bare and golden from the sun, and says in a loud, clear voice, "Today we are witness to the new union between Joya d'Arena and Orovalle. May God bless this union with peace and understanding, with prosperity and beauty, and"—she grins hugely—"with many, many children!" And the banquet hall fills with laughter, like it's the cleverest blessing in the world. My face burns, and I hate my sister more in this moment than ever in my life.

"Now, it's time to bid the happy couple good-night," she continues. I've attended hundreds of marriage feasts. Still, I jump when Lady Aneaxi's hand grabs my shoulder. A bevy of servants, dressed in white with garlands of paper flowers, has come with her to escort us to our nuptial chamber.

We rise, the king and I, though I'm not sure how, since my legs buzz with threatening numbness. My armpits feel sticky, my heart pounds. *Oh, God. I don't know what to do.* I blink rapidly, determined not to cry.

The servants, grinning and giggling, surround us and herd us from the banquet hall as the golden horde shouts blessings and encouragement. I steal a glance at my husband. For the first time since he lifted the veil from my face, he avoids my gaze.

2

OUR chamber is warm with the golden light and honeyed scent of beeswax candles. They flicker from all sides of the room, on the windowsill, on the stone hearth, on the mahogany tables that frame the curtained bed.

The bed . . .

On my right, my new husband is as much a statue as I, a dark pillar of shadow I dare not look at, so I stare at the bed's canopy, a breezy red-dyed cotton. Servants scurry forward to fold back the curtains and tie them to the bedposts. An enormous de Riqueza sunburst smiles at me from the quilt. I glare at the minimalist features, at the tongues of yellow fire that flare from its points, but Lady Aneaxi tosses a bucket of rose petals onto the quilt and spreads them around with her fingertips, and I find I am glaring at nothing.

The rose petals, blushed pink, offer their delicate floral scent to the air—a heady mix with the honeyed beeswax—which makes me think of our rose-tinged wedding ceremony and the way his lips brushed mine too quickly.

I want him to kiss me again.

His was not my first kiss. A tall, gangly boy had that dubious distinction, at a wedding feast when I was fourteen years old. I was hiding in an alcove, too shy to dance with everyone else, when he found me and confessed his love. His eyes flashed an intensity that made my face pulse with warmth. His lips pressed against mine, and I tasted the basil on his tongue, but he kissed me the way I would recite a passage from the *Common Man's Guide to Service*. By rote. Dispassionately.

I left the banquet flustered, and the next morning, while Juana-Alodia and I shared a breakfast of poached eggs with leeks, she spoke of a conde's son who had pulled her into an alcove the night before, a lanky boy who'd declared his love and tried to kiss her. She had pinched his nose and walked away laughing. She said he'd been trying to get into bed with a princess.

Now Aneaxi presses her lips to my forehead. "My Elisa," she whispers. Then she and the servants exit our chamber. Just before they close the door, I catch a glimpse of enormous sun-bronzed soldiers with steel chest plates. They wear the red silk banners of King Alejandro's personal guard, and I wonder if His Majesty feels unsafe. But when I look at him, at the black hair curling at his neck, the strength of his sun-darkened hands, I forget the guards.

I want more than a little kiss. But the thought is terrifying.

My husband says nothing, just stares unblinking at the petal-strewn quilt. I would love to know what he is thinking, but I can't bring myself to ask. Instead, I gaze at his profile and think of the passionless kiss of the conde's son. Blood throbs in my ears as finally I whisper, "I do not care to become intimate tonight."

His shoulders relax, and his lips betray a hint of a smile. He nods. "As you wish."

I turn and plop onto the bed, displacing pink petals that flutter to the clay floor. I am hugely relieved. But I'm also disappointed at his ready acceptance, because it would have been nice to feel a little bit wanted.

With his arms crossed, King Alejandro leans against a thick bedpost. He regards me easily now; I suspect he is as relieved as I am. In the candlelight, his hair has deep red tints, like the Sierra Sangre in the evening sun. "Well then," he says cheerfully. "I suppose we could talk."

He has such a nice voice. Dark and warm. "Talk?" I say cleverly.

The quirk of his lips widens into a huge smile, and it is like the moon has just risen on a summer night. "Unless you would prefer to be married to a stranger, of course."

Married . . .

Suddenly it all seems so preposterous, and I can't stop the giggles that bubble from my chest. I cover my mouth with a fist and laugh into my knuckles.

"I admit to feeling a certain awkwardness," he says, "but it hadn't occurred to me to laugh."

His words sober me. I look up, worried that I've angered him, but the smile remains, and his eyes hold a genuine crinkle.

I smile back. "I'm sorry, Your Majesty—"

"Alejandro."

I swallow. "Alejandro." The sympathy in his face breaks something inside me, and words tumble from my mouth. "Papá and Alodia always said I'd marry for the good of Orovalle. I accepted it years ago. Still, I'm only fif—sixteen. I'd hoped to have some time. . . . And I didn't expect . . . I mean, you're very . . ." I assure myself that his expression remains unmocking. "You're very kind," I finish lamely.

He moves to the window seat. "Hand me a pillow?"

I pull one from the bed, a round thing with a long red fringe, and I shake the petals off before tossing it at him. He catches it easily, then lifts long legs onto the seat and clutches the pillow at his abdomen. With his bent knees, his open gaze, he doesn't seem so much older.

"So," he says, looking at the ceiling. I'm glad he is willing to start the conversation. "Is there anything about me or about Joya d'Arena you would like to know?"

I think about this. I already know that his first wife died in childbirth, that his son is six years old, and that Invierne harries his borders more doggedly than our own with its need to acquire a seaport. Joya is mostly desert, but rich in silver and jewels, in cattle along the coastline. There isn't much I don't know. Except . . .

"What is it?" he prompts.

"Alejandro . . . what do you want? From me?"

His smile disappears. Briefly, I worry that I've irritated him, the way my questions always irritate Alodia, but then he moves his head and his jaw catches the light; it curves so perfectly into his hairline.

He sighs. "Our marriage is part of a treaty I made with your father. And there are things you can help me with. But mostly . . ." He runs his hand through thick black hair. "Mostly, I could use a friend." Alejandro looks me in the eye and waits for my response.

Friend. My tutor, Master Geraldo, is a friend, I suppose. Nurse Ximena and Lady Aneaxi, though they are more like mothers. I realize I could use one too. "Friend" is a comforting word, and a painful one, but it doesn't sound nearly so frightening as "wife."

I find it exhilarating that I can help him in some way, yet odd too. "It seems to me," I point out, feeling a little braver, "that the king of the richest country in the world would have no trouble making friends."

He looks up, startled. "Your sister says you have a way of getting to the soul of a matter."

I almost scowl, but I realize that Alodia's words may not have been criticism.

"Tell me, Lucero-Elisa." His lips curve into that gentle smile that already feels familiar. "Do you find it easy to make friends? As a princess? As the bearer of the only Godstone in a hundred years?"

I know exactly what he means. Remembering the conde's son who tried to kiss both my sister and I those years ago, I say, "You don't trust anyone, do you?"

He shakes his head. "Very few."

I nod. "I trust my nurse, Ximena, and my lady-in-waiting, Aneaxi. And Juana-Alodia too, in a way."

"What do you mean, in a way?"

I have to consider this before answering. "She's my sister. She wants what is best for Orovalle, but . . ." Something closes my mouth. Maybe it's the intensity of his eyes that darken from warm cinnamon to near black. I never hesitate to grumble about Juana-Alodia with my nurse. But with Alejandro . . .

"But?" he prompts.

His face is so intent on mine, so interested in what I have to say, that I blurt, "She hates me."

King Alejandro says nothing at first. I feel I have disappointed him, and I want to suck the words back into my mouth.

Then: "Why do you think that?"

I don't answer. Several candles have sputtered out, and I'm glad because it is easier to avoid his eyes in the flickering shadows.

"Elisa?"

Tell him about the Godstone, I say to myself. *Tell him that Alodia is envious. That she is angry because I am already sixteen but show no inclination to fulfill my destiny as God's chosen.* But his open gaze commands my honesty, and I say to him what I have told no one.

"I killed our mother."

His eyes narrow. "What do you mean?"

My lips tremble, but I inhale through my nose and distance myself from the words. "Alodia says Mamá miscarried twice. So when she became pregnant with me, she took to bed. She prayed to God for a son, a prince." I have to grit my teeth for a moment before I can continue. "It was a difficult pregnancy, and she was weak, and after I was born there was a lot of blood. Alodia says that when they placed me in her arms, Mamá saw that I was a girl. And dark skinned and fat." I feel the cold edges and aching hardness of my jaw. "And grief overcame her, and she breathed her last."

"Your sister said this? When? How long ago?" Though his questions are pressing, his voice remains kind, like he really cares.

But I can't quite remember.

He raises one eyebrow. "A year ago?" he prods. "A few years ago? Maybe when you were both very young?"

I frown, trying to place the moment. It was when Alodia and I still studied together. Our heads had nearly touched as we poured over a musty copy of the *Common Man's Guide to Service.* When Master Geraldo asked her to explain the history of the Godstone, I interrupted by reciting the passage word for word. It was after that tutoring session, while Alodia pursued me down the steps to the kitchens, that she told me the story of Mamá's death.

I don't want him to know how long I've harbored this memory, so I say nothing.

He just stares, and I want to slither beneath the sunburst quilt. "You think she still blames you for your mother's death?"

"She hasn't indicated otherwise." My voice is too sharp and hard, like a petulant child's, but I refuse to lower my gaze.

"I think you'd be surprised," he says.

"At what?"

"At a lot of things, Elisa."

Lots of things would surprise me, it's true. It's easy to be surprised when no one tells you anything. And with a start, I realize I still don't know what he wants from me. He could have found a "friend" in Alodia, or any number of young noble-women. The king brushed off my questions as if I were a child, just like Papá and Alodia always do, and like a twitterpated fool, I let him.

Before I can muster the courage to press the matter, he says, "I suppose we should sleep sometime tonight, since we're traveling tomorrow." He stands and begins flicking rose petals from the quilt.

I tell him, "You can have the bed; I'll take the window seat."

"The bed is large enough for us both. I'll sleep atop the quilt," he says.

I freeze. Then: "Fine." I sweep the remaining petals from the bed and pull the covers back. Sleep will be long in coming, I am sure. Not even the pulsing jewel in my belly can convince me to take off my wedding *terno* to get comfortable, and I don't imagine that sensing Alejandro beside me all night will help. I blow out the candles on my nightstand and slide between the sheets, my back toward my husband.

The mattress shudders as Alejandro settles his weight next to me. I hear his forced breath as he extinguishes the candles on his side. Suddenly I feel warm lips on my cheek. "I almost forgot. Happy birthday, Lucero-Elisa," he whispers.

I sigh into the dark. I thought the worst thing that could happen would be for my new husband to turn away from me in disgust. I was wrong. It is so much worse that he listens to me, sees me. That, in addition to being beautiful, he is kind.

It will be too, too easy to love him.

I am awake, eyes wide, heart fluttering, long after the last candle on the mantel flickers out, long after the man next to me settles into the steady, even breathing of sleep.

Our carriage heads a long procession that awaits beyond the cobbled courtyard. King Alejandro's personal guards stand tall beside it, their dark faces inscrutable. To reach them, we must pass the fountains and the jacaranda trees, through a gauntlet of nobles and servants armed with birdseed and rose petals. Alejandro reaches out to take my hand, but Papá grabs me first and enfolds me in an embrace.

"Elisa," he whispers into my hair. "I will miss you."

It nearly undoes me. In the last day or two, I have had more affection from my father than in the entire year previous. He is always so busy, so distant. Is it only by giving me up that he finds it in himself to care?

"I'll miss you too," I manage, and the words cut hard with their truth. I know I'll never be as dear to him as Alodia, but I love him just the same.

He releases me, and my sister glides forward. She wears a simple gown of blue silk layers that drop beautifully from slender shoulders, and her face is perfect and composed, like a sculpture. It nears mine—I smell her jasmine perfume—and I see tiny lines around her brown eyes. Worry lines. Strange that I have not noticed them before.

Alodia grips my shoulders with strong fingers. "Elisa," she whispers. "Listen well."

Something about her manner, the intensity of her gaze perhaps, causes me to block out the sounds of tinkling fountains and buzzing crowds to focus on her voice.

"Trust no one, Elisa, save Alejandro and Nurse Ximena and Aneaxi." Her voice is pitched so low, I doubt even our father can hear. I nod, feeling suddenly warm, and the Godstone flashes hot and hard. Is it a warning? "I'm sending pigeons with you," she continues. "Use them if you need to contact me quickly. When you arrive, do not be afraid to assert yourself. Do not be afraid to be queen."

She places her cheek against mine and strokes my hair, sighing. "Be well, Elisa, little sister."

I just stand there, stunned. My husband grips my hand and pulls me through the crowd of well-wishers toward our carriage. I know I should look up and smile. I should show the nobility a final, glorious view of their princess as she rides off into eternal happiness. It's what Alodia would do. But my vision is too blurred with tears, my face too hot, because my sister hasn't embraced me that way since we were children in the nursery together.

The carriage step is too high to navigate comfortably. The foreign guards look on as Alejandro steps in and then pulls me up beside him. I give him a grateful smile, noticing the birdseed and rose petals that have stuck in his black hair. I put a hand to my head and wonder how long it will take for Ximena to brush the mess from my own hair. My nurse is already ensconced with Lady Aneaxi in the rearmost carriage, and suddenly, I can't wait to see them again, to let them fuss over me. I resolve to seek them out at my earliest opportunity.

The seat is plush blue velvet, but it lurches hard against my rear as we set off. The *nobleza d'oro* cheers heartily, and for a moment, the air is a haze of seed and flowers and mad waving. The carriage window sits high enough that I can see across the courtyard, over the celebrating horde, to my father and sister. The morning sun is high now, casting a golden glow on the adobe of my sprawling palace, on the walls of beautiful Amalur. I drink in the sight of archways with their green creepers, of cobbled paths and tiled fountains. Mostly, though, I am transfixed by my sister. Her eyes are closed and her lips move as if in prayer. The sun shimmers against her cheeks, against the moisture there.

3

ALEJANDRO seems content to bear my company in silence. I fold my hands into my lap to keep them still and pretend to be indifferent while the carriage rattles away from my home. I imagine all the ways to start a conversation. Alodia always comments about shipyard construction, or the price of wool, but such topics would feel odd in my mouth. I should ask him about our marriage, and why my sister demands such caution, but I find it less frightening just to be silent.

The carriage lurches to a stop. The door swings open. Sunlight pours in around the enormous silhouette of a body-guard, and I raise my forearm against the glare. Confused, I turn to my husband.

"It's all right, Elisa," he says. "The guard will show you to your carriage."

My carriage? I try to puzzle this through. "My . . ."

"It would be foolish for my wife and me to travel in the same carriage."

My face tingles at his words—"my wife"—even as I parse

his meaning. I've read of such things. In times of war, important figureheads must never consolidate targets. I nod and take the guard's hand. A rough hand, strong and unkind.

"I'll check in on you when we stop to eat," my husband says.

We step down and away from the carriage, the unkind guard and I, and he leads me toward the back of our dusty procession. Plumeria trees, heavy with white blossoms, border the road, and I can no longer see the palace. My mind whirls with analysis, as if I were in Master Geraldo's study again, engrossed in the *Belleza Guerra*.

Never consolidate targets.

I freeze and look up at the guard. His face is youthful and handsome, in spite of its hard lines and sculpted mustache. Irritation flickers in dark eyes, but he composes himself quickly. "My lady, we must get you to your carriage." His voice is rough and strained, as if speech comes rarely.

Do not be afraid to be queen, Alodia had said. "You will address me as Your Highness." My voice is steady and confident, like my sister's. I feel ridiculous. "After the coronation, you will address me as Your Majesty."

He raises one brow. "Of course, Your Highness. Forgive me." But his look is skeptical, mocking.

"What is your name?"

"Lord Hector, of His Majesty's personal guard."

"I'm glad to meet you." I flash a courteous smile, the way Alodia would. "Lord Hector, what are we in danger from?"

My face warms and my heart drums in my chest. At any moment, he'll recognize this bluff of insane confidence.

But his brow softens, and he nods. "It is not my place to give details, Highness. But I will mention your question to His Majesty."

I can't bring myself to prod further. He ushers me toward the back, where my ladies have already opened their carriage door. It's covered in dust from being at the rear, but their arms are outstretched, waiting to help me step up.

They want to know why I do not travel with my husband. Awkwardness is common at first, they assure me. Don't worry. You'll adjust to each other soon enough. I grit my teeth, frustrated with their blind assurances but grateful for them just the same. I look down, unable to explain.

The carriage pitches as we set off again. It's hotter inside, and my skin becomes sticky. Were I athletic like Alodia, I'd get out and walk. I wonder if this is why my husband does not care to travel with me. Perhaps there is no danger at all.

I am married to a stranger, and no one has bothered to tell me why, other than to make vague references to a treaty. Surely the fact that I bear the Godstone has something to do with it. But since no one is forthcoming, I will have to find out for myself.

As Ximena wipes my damp forehead with her linen skirt, as Aneaxi pours me some cool wine from a traveling skin, I pray silently, asking God to make me a little stronger, a little braver.

Our route lies through the jungle of the Hinders, the mountains dividing our two countries. True to his word, the king checks on me regularly. At meal stops, he asks detailed questions about my comfort. Are your cushions thick enough? Would you prefer your carriage to take a turn at the head of the procession? Is the wine to your liking? He is sweetly attentive, always taking my hand and looking me in the eye, like he truly cares.

In response to the question I asked Lord Hector, my husband tells me the jungle is a dangerous place, crawling with the descendants of convicts who were tossed into the wild a century ago when Joya's prisons overflowed. But we cannot risk a sea voyage this near to the hurricane season.

Master Geraldo spoke of these Perditos, the lost ones of the jungle. My teacher said they stayed far away from the highway, so I'm not sure I believe Alejandro.

Sometimes our path is steep enough that my back rests comfortably against the boards of the carriage wall and I am able to doze in spite of the constant lurching. But after a while, desert cactuses and royal palms give way to golden rain trees, dripping yellow teardrops. The seed pods clunk onto the carriage roof at irregular intervals, making it impossible to nap. At night, I sleep fitfully in a large tent with my ladies.

The jungle rages with noise. Screaming birds, chittering spider monkeys, and buzzing insects all battle for attention. The wind cannot penetrate the foliage to cool us as we travel, but we hear it, whooshing through the canopy above. It is, truly, the most deafening place I've ever been.

On the morning of day four, the jungle goes silent. It happens so suddenly, so profoundly, that I peer around the curtain, expecting to find that God has whisked us to another time and place. But the silk-cotton trees still loom above me, their dark buttresses impenetrable in the filtered light. The same palm fronds twist desperately around them, seeking sunlight.

Two carriages ahead, Lord Hector drops from the roof to the ground, sword in hand.

Our procession has been large and clamorous with its carriage wheels, snorting horses, and clanking armor. Yet the jungle never saw fit to honor us with silent fear. Beside me, Lady Aneaxi mutters in prayer.

Then, far away at first, a drumbeat resounds. I can't pinpoint its direction, but the echoing thrum makes a cavern of my chest. It thunders again, closer.

The carriage jerks to a stop.

No.

Alejandro's guard has acted on instinct. They sensed danger and stopped the procession to establish a perimeter defense. The foliage hugs our path; were I to reach from the carriage window, my fingertips could flutter the drooping palm leaves. An unseen enemy could spear me just as easily.

Ahead is a slight clearing in the jungle where the trees retreat from the road.

"Lord Hector!" I call, heart pounding. He glances at me; his chest rises with a long, controlling breath. But I know I'm right in this. The *Belleza Guerra* devotes whole passages to sizing up an enemy's approach. "Make for the clearing ahead. We must be able to see them coming!"

He nods and shouts an order as another drumbeat thrums beneath my breastbone. The horses huff and prance in response, but they pull us forward, toward the clearing.

"Aneaxi. Ximena. We must get down, away from the windows." The carriage wobbles as they comply. We are an awkward threesome, barely able to squeeze into the floor space between benches.

"His Majesty's guard is the finest in the world," Aneaxi insists breathily. "We are in little danger." But her hand bruises mine with its grip.

With my free hand, I trace the line of the trapdoor until I can finger the latch. The thought of leaving the carriage frightens me, and I envision the three of us smacking the ground. I hope Aneaxi is right, that there is little danger.

The drums beat faster now, louder. My shoulder crashes into a bench as the carriage heaves. I don't dare lift myself to peer out the window, but I hope we've reached the clearing. I hear running footsteps and Lord Hector's muffled orders, then the metal-scraping-metal sound of drawn steel.

Something thunks against the carriage. And again. Soon it's like a rain of stones cracking against wooden walls. I hear a thud against the wall near my head. The shining black point of an arrowhead pokes through, a mere handsbreadth from my nose. My skin burns. The air is too hot, too stifling to breathe. The Godstone in my navel flashes ice cold, and I gasp, astonished. It has never gone cold before.

The paneling beneath my palms feels sun warmed. Too warm. The acrid scent of burning wood tingles in my nose as the Godstone continues to throb its icy warning.

Aneaxi whimpers, "Fire!" as our carriage fills with smoky haze and the shouting outside becomes frenzied.

"The princess!" someone yells. "To the princess!" But the voice is far off.

I search across the paneling for the latch to the trapdoor again. It opens downward, and we tumble through into the cooler, cleaner air beneath the carriage. I land on something that cracks beneath my weight. Aneaxi screams.

I don't have time to worry about how badly I've hurt her. The horses catch the scent of smoke and dance in their harnesses. We could be pinned beneath the wheels at any moment. I yearn for a knife to cut the horses free, to feel some kind of power in my hand. The carriage lurches forward. Behind me and to my left, I see Aneaxi's leg, cricked unnaturally, lying in the path of the wheel.

I feel sick. "Aneaxi, you must pull your leg in."

"I can't!" she sobs.

I hook her armpit and pull. Ximena does the same on the other side, but Aneaxi is large and I have never been strong. A horse rears. The carriage jerks. Panicked, Ximena and I wrench Aneaxi toward us, but we are at such an awkward angle, pressed against the ground, and oh, it is not enough.

Steel rings, and the carriage shudders. Someone has sliced through the harnesses, and tears of relief prick my eyes.

I'm not sure what to do next. The carriage provides cover, but it burns. Even now, smoke licks the floor above, curling around the panels like white snakes. Feet patter by at eye level. Our enemies are barefooted demons, nearly naked and painted in black-and-white swirls. Anklets of tiny bones clatter as one darts in and out of the jungle. Lunge, sidestep, disappear; then another takes his place. Their attack has no pattern. It is random, constant, indefensible.

A few paces away from our burning carriage gapes the opening of an enormous buttress, a cavern formed by the roots of a silk-cotton tree. I could reach it quickly, and Ximena, but I worry for Aneaxi and her broken leg.

I flip over to face my ladies. "We must get away before the carriage collapses."

They nod; Aneaxi's round cheeks are smeared with dirt made muddy by tears. My heart swells for a moment, for I'm not willing to lose either of them.

"Ximena and I will go first," I say to Aneaxi. "Then we will pull you out by the arms." I hope that by standing, we'll have the leverage to do what could not be done beneath the carriage. "Aneaxi, you must not scream, no matter how much it hurts."

She takes a few ragged breaths. Then she rips a strip of fabric from the hem of her traveling gown. My chest burns with pride when she wads it up and shoves it in her mouth. *I'm ready*, her eyes tell me.

Still we wait. The fighting is too close. From where we lie, we see pairings of naked, painted calves with boots and stiff hide. A man tumbles to the ground before me, and I scramble backward. His eyes are open and blinding white against the black paint of his face. His hair is as long as mine but twisted into thick clumps. He lies unmoving. Gingerly, heart pounding, I pry a stone knife from his still-warm hand and stuff it into my bodice.

At last I see a break in the fighting, and I gesture frantically to Ximena. We scramble from beneath the carriage on all fours. My foot tangles in my slip as I rise, but I rip right through it. Once clear, we turn and grasp Aneaxi's arms. She groans around the wad in her mouth as we pull. Her eyes clench tight; her face is bright red. Then she goes limp as unconsciousness takes her. As we pull her toward the dark cavity of the buttress, I expect to see an arrow impale her chest at any moment. Sweat slides down my back and across my stomach. Beside me, Ximena's gray bun has come loose and her hair swings below her shoulders. Little by little, we reach the line of the jungle. The ground slopes downward as we step beneath the roots. It's cooler here, and comfortingly dark. There is just enough room for the three of us in the little cavern. I catch my breath, holding tight to Aneaxi's shoulders, so relieved to have made it this far.

I have a better view of the battle now. My husband's guard seems to have found its footing against these strange savages. They fight back to back against the random attacks, shield arms at ready for incoming arrows. Bodies from both sides litter the ground, and my stomach roils at the scent of burning flesh. Our carriage is an inferno. Next to me, Ximena flinches when the flaming structure collapses to the ground, sending sparks in all directions. A few moments more, and we would have burned.

Beyond the ruined carriage, two savages have trapped one of our own against a tree. I cannot see his face, but his body is frozen in panic.

One of the savages leaps forward with a shriek, plunges a stone knife toward the man's chest. He lurches away just in time, and the knife jams into his forearm instead.

He fights weakly then, with left-handed strokes. When he hesitates yet again, I know he cannot last. The painted bodies sense the kill. They begin an odd movement, like a dance. Squat, pivot, creep. They are like jungle cats, all wild grace and hunting fury. Then I catch a glimpse of the doomed man's face.

Alejandro.

"No!" I clamber from our shelter. Ximena yells something indecipherable. She grasps my arm, but I wrench away. I feel so slow as I run toward my husband, my belly and breasts bouncing painfully with each step. As I pass the collapsed carriage, I pull the knife from my bodice. I don't know what I'm going to do, but I can't let Alejandro die. The painted men circle my husband, unaware of my approach. They move closer as Alejandro readies his sword with his good arm.

Desperate tears stream down my face as I launch at the nearest one. Together we plunge to the ground, and I'm crying and stabbing and stabbing until my arm is slick, until my shoulder burns from the impact of blade against bone.

Someone pulls me away. It's Alejandro. I blink to clear stinging vision and see two painted men lying at our feet. He must have dispatched the other. I should speak to him, and my mouth opens, but something bright draws my gaze downward. Crimson. So much of it, all down my bodice, soaking my skirt. Metallic saliva tingles against my tongue, and suddenly, I'm shaking so hard I feel like my teeth will rattle from my jaw.

Alejandro pulls me close against his chest and strokes my back, muttering words I can't take in. The battle is winding

down, and soon enough, I will fret about my burned posses-
sions, or Alejandro's injured arm, or Aneaxi's broken leg. But
for now I can't think beyond the warmth of Alejandro's chest.
He doesn't love me yet, but in this place of death, in this precious moment of shared relief, he holds me.

We lose fifteen men to the Perditos. Others, like Alejandro and
Aneaxi, are injured but will mend.

While Aneaxi sleeps, Lord Hector straightens her leg and
splints it. I walk a few paces away to breathe different air and to
wipe blood from my face with broad, waxy leaves. My dress is
filthy and soaked, the blood already turning brown and thick,
but most of my extra clothes burned with our carriage. My
stomach grumbles—I can't remember the last time I was this
hungry—but I'd feel ridiculous asking for food while others
tend to the wounded.

Lord Hector finds me later, sitting on a stump, staring at
the foliage around me.

"Your Highness, we have a prisoner."

I look up at him and notice that his mustache is matted and
sticky. "Oh?" I'm not sure why he'd bother to inform me.

"King Alejandro said that you would decide how to deal
with him."

Me? My heart thuds.

Perhaps it is a test, meant to appraise the girl who will be
queen. Or maybe Alejandro is busy with other matters. "The
man is a murderer," I say, for no other reason than to give
myself a moment to think.

"You have but to say the word, and I will dispatch him myself."

My throat constricts at the thought. It doesn't feel right that I should have the power of life and death.

I'd rather no one else died today.

"Does he speak?"

"Yes."

"Then I have some questions for him."

Lord Hector helps me to my feet. There is a glow of respect in his eyes that hadn't been there before. It warms me, but only for a moment. The cost of such respect has been too high.

The painted prisoner sits in a ring of swords. His hands are tied before him; his ankles are chained. He knows his situation is perilous. He glances around at his guards, white eyed, understanding that any one of them could stick a blade into his heart.

He sees me approach, and hope flickers in his eyes. Or cunning. There's something obscene about the paint swirls all over his body. They are ghostly, nauseating. Up close, I see hollow bones woven into his long, clumpy hair.

"My lady," he says. His voice is perfectly clear and crisp, incongruous coming from his savage mouth.

I almost correct his address, but I don't care to reveal who I am. "I've been tasked with deciding your fate. Is there a reason, any reason at all, why I should spare you?" I can think of a very good reason, but I need to know if he's amenable.

He is silent for a moment. Then: "I could help you."

"How?"

"I know the jungle. I know her secrets." His eyes are huge, like a cornered animal's.

"Will you answer any question asked of you? Truthfully? Without reservation?" Lord Hector nods his approval of my question. He thinks I am being strategic, but I simply do not have the courage to watch someone else die.

"I will," the Perdito says.

"Then I will spare you."

"Thank you, my lady." He leans forward, clutching the fabric of my waist, head down in veneration. It's the customary genuflection of a newly sworn vassal, and I find that I hate it. It's too intimate, too dangerous, even with the sword points now aimed at his neck.

Then he stiffens. His fingers have glanced across the Godstone beneath my bloody skirt. I know what he feels. A faceted surface, hard as diamonds but warm with life. He recoils.

"You!" he whispers. His eyes are wide and wet with frightened tears; his breath comes in gasps.

Someone lunges forward, a blur of gray hair and ruffled skirts. A gurgling sound, a body slapping the ground. Ximena! She backs away, and I see our prisoner lying flat on his back, my nurse's hairpin protruding from beneath his jaw.

I stare at the pin—so tiny—at the blood pooling around it, slipping across his skin into the jungle soil.

"So sorry, my sky. I thought he was about to attack you." She might have been telling me I was late for morning prayer.

I gaze unbelieving at my nurse, amazed at the speed with which she moved, wondering why recognizing the life in my navel would sentence a man to death.

4

THAT night, we sing a hymn of deliverance and light prayer candles for the dead. The candles are foolish. If the Perditos attack again, the tiny flames, floating like stars in thick jungle darkness, will make telling targets. But we light them anyway.

None of the fifteen were personally known to me, and as the king whispers each name, I cannot remember their faces. Still, everyone on this journey has been kind, and I mourn their loss because Alejandro does. While my husband speaks of them, I pray silently, thanking God for his life and for the lives of my ladies. The Godstone radiates gentle fingers of warmth throughout my body as it always does when my prayers are heartfelt. After a few moments, the strain in my back from dragging Aneaxi fades to a mild ache, and I feel deliciously sleepy.

As a little girl, my greatest fear was that the Godstone would stop living inside me, that it would grow cold and still like any ordinary jewel. I would know then that the moment to perform my service had gone, that I'd been too selfish or lazy or stupid to act. So I learned to welcome its tender responses to my prayers. They are signs that I am not a failure quite yet.

Alejandro finishes the ceremony with a muttered "Selah," and everyone breaks off to prepare for tomorrow's journey.

"Lucero-Elisa." His voice is so soft I think I've imagined it, but his eyes, sparking in the candlelight, fix on me as he approaches. His wounded right arm is pinned tight against his stomach, wrapped in a gray sling.

"Alejandro."

"I wanted to thank you, Elisa. Hector says you acted with remarkable courage throughout the attack." I don't remember courage. Just heat and fear. "And..." He avoids my gaze. "And you may have saved my life."

Alodia would deflect the praise, weak as it is. She'd turn it into a flattering treatise on how his mighty prowess would have won through in the end, even without help.

But he froze with panic, and if not for my interference, he would surely have died. Feeling bold, I say, "Yes, I did. And you're welcome." Perhaps this was my great service, to save the life of a king. But the jewel still thrums its portent.

He grins at me now, a boyish grin that warms me as much as the Godstone ever does, and my disquiet slips away. I smile back, feeling shy.

"Do you miss home, Elisa?"

My mouth opens to say yes, I miss it terribly, but I realize it's not true. "A little. I probably haven't been away long enough." It would be nice to feel safe again, to hug Papá, or even to study with Master Geraldo. But I don't yearn for those things. Not yet.

Just then, Ximena ambles toward me, so I excuse myself and hurry away. I'm not ready to face her. I don't know what questions to ask.

We endure the jungle five days more. Exhausted from double watches and stiff from cramming into too few carriages, we gradually leave the stifling growth of the rain shadow for the dry side of the mountains that overlooks the desert floor. Joya d'Arena, the Jewel of the Sand, stretches before us. Orange-red dunes roll along the horizon, soft with heat glare. I know Joya is a harsh, scorched place, but the wind-whipped sand and the fading light make it seem velvety and welcoming.

Lord Hector guides us west along the desert's edge, toward the sea. I see a line of deep green, perhaps days ahead, but in the shimmering heat it's hard to know. Beyond the palms awaits Brisadulce, Joya's capital. Alodia visited once, and she returned with stories of a marvelous oasis, beautiful sandstone buildings, and sparkling people who adored her on sight.

I'm eager to arrive, if only to change my clothes, order a bath, and lose myself in an enormous, multicourse meal. My head aches to think of fresh fruit and chilled wine.

We make camp along a stream that trickles from the mountains and heads west toward the city and the sea. In our borrowed carriage, Ximena orders me to take off my dress so she can wash it. She helps me with the buttons and I'm a little relieved, a little nervous, to have her so close by. She's been a mother to me as long as I can remember. But I think of her hairpin—something I've seen almost every day of my life—sticking out of a man's neck, and I marvel that I know so little about her. I've never asked. Where does Ximena come from? When did she begin working for my family? Why has she chosen to love me so? *"Spoiled girl,"* Alodia called me more than once as we were growing up. *"Coddled just because she's chosen."*

Alodia is right.

"Ximena."

"Yes, love?" Her fingers are busy at my back, loosening the stays.

"I'm sorry. So sorry."

The fingers pause. "Why do you say this, my sky?"

Tears prick at my eyes. "I don't know who you are or anything about you. I don't know who Aneaxi is. And it's my fault."

For once, my nurse doesn't brush off my objections with platitudes and weak praise. She just reaches around with her strong arms and hugs me close.

Ximena tells me that she is an orphan. As a little girl, she served priests in the refectory and laundered their robes. One man, Father Donatzine, noticed her quiet, hardworking spirit. He taught her to read and write well enough to scribe among the great historical documents of the Monastery-at-Amalur, where she took a special interest in the *Common Man's Guide to Service.* After years of engraving the precious words onto her heart, Father Donatzine recommended her for service to my father, who was a young prince at the time.

"I still visit Father Donatzine when I can," she says as she hangs my skirt to dry outside the carriage window. "He can't read anymore. So I read aloud for him. He loves the passages in the *Scriptura Sancta* about God's chosen." She has a lovely smile that makes happy lines around her small eyes. "He was so pleased when God chose you on your naming day. He'd made a special point of living long enough to see the next choosing."

I don't remember Father Donatzine. I should be flattered that a man I never knew attached such importance to my existence. But it feels intrusive.

It occurs to me to ask, "Will you miss him?"

Ximena nods. "Very much."

She pulls herself through the open door of the carriage and sits beside me on the bench. Her hands are sturdy and callused. I try to imagine them making careful brushstrokes on parchment. I've felt her rough fingertips against my back my whole life, watched how dexterous and capable they are. Capable of killing with a hairpin.

"You're looking at me strangely."

"That day. With the prisoner."

Her gaze softens. "I thought you might ask."

"You moved so quickly, Ximena! And you knew exactly where to stick that pin, and you knew he wasn't attacking me, and I . . ." It's coming out wrong, like I'm accusing her, which would be ridiculous since she's not the only one who killed that day.

But she looks at me the same way she always does, with endless patience and perfect love. "My sky, I wish I could tell you many things." She brushes my cheek with her knuckles. Then the carriage rocks as she descends the steps. "I need to check on Aneaxi."

Tiny bumps rise on my arms as I watch Ximena navigate the sleeping rolls and pit fires of our small camp. I realize I'm peering from the carriage clad only in my chemise and torn slip.

The next day I ride with Aneaxi, who needs extra space so her splinted leg can lie across the bench. Each time we hit a bump, she winces and sweat coalesces on her forehead. She fans herself while answering all the questions I should have asked long ago.

I learn that my lady-in-waiting is the bastard child of Conde Sirvano, of my father's court. Too controversial to make a good political match, too important to be shipped off to the monastery that raised Ximena, her status was a fluid thing, subject to the mood of her father. "Growing up in his household was dreadful," she says. "Whispers as I passed, dark glances. All my clothes were hand-me-downs from my older half-sister. But she would rip them or pour ink on them before giving them to me."

I am rapt as she remembers it all, because I know what it's like to have a favored sister, to bear the studied, condemning gaze of the court. All my life, Aneaxi has been the sympathetic one, wrapping me in a hug and saying how sorry she is for everything. Now I understand why.

"I started volunteering in the laundry. Just to get away and to feel useful. One day at court, my father noticed my hands—all cracked and peeling. He beat me." She shrugs, as if it doesn't bother her in the least. And it probably doesn't—not anymore. Aneaxi is never one to stay upset for long.

"But he also decided that if I wanted to work so badly, he would find something appropriate to my station, such as it is. He actually used those words, 'such as it is.' So he made me attend his latest wife, who was only a little older than I. He thought it would be a punishment, but we became friends. And when your mamá took pregnant with Alodia, my lady recommended me to Ximena, who was the queen's attendant at the time."

I ask, "Do you ever regret coming to the palace to serve my family?"

"Oh, dear, no. I loved your mamá. Alodia too, even though she is exasperatingly independent and stubborn. But you, Elisa. You are the delight of my life." She grins wickedly. "And besides, the food at the palace is so, so much better. The conde's cook should have been sent to the bull ring."

I giggle, remembering the night a year or so ago when we crept together to the kitchens for coconut pudding, right under Ximena's nose. Aneaxi has always been equal parts empathy, good cheer, and mischief—the perfect foil and partner for my earnest and careful nurse.

She stops fanning herself. Her eyelids are thin, near translucent like fine parchment. She has grown old recently, sometime when I wasn't watching. I lean over and kiss the wrinkles that cord her forehead.

She smiles, eyes still closed. "You're a good girl, Elisa. God was right to choose you."

I swallow. Her love for me has always been a foolish thing,

but I'm grateful for it. Maybe God sent her to me for a reason. Maybe he knew I'd need someone who could understand, even if only a little, what my life would be like. Gently I pry the fan from her fingers. As I wave it across her face, she sighs contentedly. I stay with her for a long time.

That night, Alejandro tells me we are only a few days away from my new home.

"Good!" I say. "I smell bad." Then my face flashes hotter than the desert summer. This miserable journey has made me too flippant.

But he just laughs. "You don't smell nearly so bad as Lord Hector." He glances to his right, where the royal guard sits polishing his sword. He looks up at the king's comment, and his mustache twitches, but his face remains properly stoic.

"How is Lady Aneaxi?" Alejandro asks.

I shrug. "She says the leg feels better, but she is determined to be cheerful, so I'm not sure. She's weaker than she admits."

"You love her very much." His gaze has softened, or maybe it's the firelight, but I can hardly breathe. He looks at me so intently, like I'm the only thing in the world.

"Elisa?"

"I . . . She is very dear to me."

"She is lucky to be alive. Hector told me how you and Lady Ximena pulled her from beneath the carriage."

I look down at the sandy shale that makes up our campsite, even though he's giving me the kind of tender smile a girl could think about for hours. Later, when I'm alone in my bedroll, I'll let the memory of this moment warm me to sleep. I will dare to hope that he is growing fond of me, that he is glad we are married.

Right now, I have questions.

"Alejandro. The Perditos. They didn't always attack travelers."

He runs fingers through black hair. "No. They didn't."

"Why now? Why us?" I clutch my skirt to keep from fidgeting. He will tell me not to worry, that these matters are not for little girls, the way Papá—

"We think they've allied with Invierne."

It's a moment before I can speak. "Why do you think this?"

"They have steel weapons now. Arrows made from a soft, light-colored wood we've never seen before. Also, a band of lost ones killed three merchants last year with a—a sharp tool used to break ice."

An ice pick. I've never seen ice or snow, though I've read about them. But why would Invierne ally with the Perditos? A thought occurs to me. "The highway is the only land route between Joya and Orovalle," I muse aloud.

He nods slowly, watching me with such interest that I feel I'm being tested. I realize we haven't met any other travelers on the road. During hurricane season, the highway should be overrun with merchants.

"It was a risky decision. To travel through the Hinders." I'm careful to keep my tone even, free of reproach.

"Yes, it was risky. But we kept our journey a secret. I don't know how they knew."

"Maybe the attack was random?"

He shrugs.

But my mind is stumbling over his words. *A secret.* "What do you mean? A secret?"

"The good people of Brisadulce don't expect their king to return for another month or so."

Their king. A secret.

And their queen? Something about my gaze sobers him.

I take a deep breath. "They don't expect me at all, do they?"

He shakes his head. "No. They don't know I'm bringing a wife home with me."

The road flattens, and our journey grows more comfortable. The air is hotter, but easier on the skin with its steady, quiet breeze. Blurry, brownish blots mar the horizon. Sandstorms, Lord Hector tells me when he catches me gazing at them. During hurricane season, the wind thrusts into the mainland from the ocean, and the resulting sandstorms can flay a man's skin from his bones. I'm glad we travel west toward the sea, keeping the dunes at a steady distance.

I miss Ximena. Maybe I shouldn't have asked about the man she killed. Now I feel this thing between us, huge and impenetrable and unspoken. She's as efficient as ever, helping me dress each morning, plaiting my hair, fluffing out my ruffled skirt each night. But her touch is brusque, her eyes distant and sad. Or maybe I imagine it.

Aneaxi grows weaker. Lord Hector thinks she's caught some kind of jungle fever, though no one else has fallen ill. Her skin, normally dark like mine, pales to ash gray. When she dozes, her dreams are fevered and strange. Something frightens her. She calls my name often, panicked, and I have to grip her sticky hand and whisper in her ear before she'll settle. When she wakes, she insists she holds no memory of her dreams, but I'm not sure I believe her.

Two days away from Brisadulce, our carriage begins to smell of rotting meat. I am no physician, and in spite of my royal education, I'm the least studied in the healing arts. Still, I know of no fever that would cause such stench.

I pull Ximena aside when we stop for a quick meal of nuts and dried mango strips.

"This isn't a jungle fever, Ximena. Or a broken leg. Why does she—"

Ximena looks down at my hand. I realize I'm gripping her arm too tightly, my fingertips deep in her flesh.

I pull my hand away, chagrined, but then I notice the tears pooling in Ximena's eyes.

"What is it, Ximena? There's something you haven't told me."

My nurse nods and swallows. "Aneaxi was injured more than we thought. She said nothing about it. Nothing at all." Her voice is a wavery whisper, and fear lodges like a heavy stone in my chest. I've never seen Ximena cry.

"More than just a broken leg, you mean."

"It's her other leg. There's a gash. Above her ankle. When we dragged her . . ."

A gash. Just a gash. That can't be too serious, can it?

Ximena continues to speak, but I hardly hear her for the

blood rushing past my ears. Something about an infection, about it being too late to amputate her leg.

I rush back to the carriage. Aneaxi lies sprawled across the bench. She moans with fever, even in her sleep. I reach for her leg, the unbroken one. Hidden beneath her skirt, the linens swaddling her calf are soaked and brownish as if tea stained. As I unwind them, the smell becomes unbearable. Like fish left too long in the sun, but sweeter, like rotting fruit. Aneaxi thrashes as I expose the wound to open air.

I recoil, hand over mouth. Purple and green streak pasty skin. Something black and viscous oozes from the gash; the skin at the edges peels back into a terrible sneer.

We did this, Ximena and I, when we dragged her from the carriage.

There is only one thing I know to do. I plunk onto the bench opposite my lady-in-waiting. The Godstone pulses warm beneath my fingertips as I close my eyes.

I am God's chosen. Surely he will hear my prayers.

The next morning, Aneaxi awakens from her fever. My heart pounds with hope. Throughout the night, the stone in my navel radiated such comfort that I know God heard me. I'm sure Aneaxi will be healed.

It takes her a moment to focus. She smiles when she realizes I'm beside her.

"Elisa," she whispers. Her brown eyes hold such serenity.

I stroke her forehead. "You should have told us, Aneaxi. You should have—"

"Listen to me."

My hand freezes midstroke.

"Elisa, you have a great destiny." Though soft, her voice rings with something fierce. The carriage rattles, my toes tingle.

She grabs my hand and squeezes. "You must not lose faith, child. No matter what. Do not doubt God or his choosing of you. He knows infinitely more than we can imagine."

I shake my head. This is not right. She's never spoken to me this way before. I open my mouth to tell her that she's going to be all right, that I've prayed—

"He loves you so much. As do I. Promise me you'll trust him."

I should promise. Anything to put her at ease. But I can't find the words.

She sighs, and her eyes grow distant. Her voice is so weak when she says, "You're the light of my life, Elisa. My special . . ." Her grip on my hand releases.

"Aneaxi?"

But she doesn't respond. She looks like a doll, her eyes glassy within a sculpture of frozen contentment, lips slightly parted. Gently, I reach forward and close her eyes with my fingertips, hoping it will make her seem merely asleep. But the stillness of sleep is nothing at all like the stillness of death.

5

I can't seem to clear my mind of haze, though I know Lord Hector is being gentle. I can tell by the way his voice deepens, the way the syllables come soft and slow. It's very kind of him.

"We'll take her with us into the city," Ximena says through tears. "She deserves a proper burial."

Lord Hector inclines his head. "Then I'll prepare her bod— the lady for travel."

I glance between them, realizing she responded to him because I could not.

"No." The word surprises me, but as it lingers in my mouth I understand how right the decision is. They wait for me to explain while I gaze across the desert expanse. It shimmers red-orange in the rising sun. Weeks ago, Aneaxi told me she'd always wanted to see the desert. She said she couldn't imagine land that rolled like waves, that stretched as far as the sea. "We'll bury her there. In the sand."

The guard's leathers creak as he bows acknowledgment. I lean against Ximena as she strokes my braid.

On the evening of the second day after God ignored my prayers, we reach Brisadulce. I don't notice the city as we approach, so seamlessly do the sandstone walls embrace the yellow desert floor. We pass through a line of coconut palms and suddenly it's there, rising three times the height of a man. Lord Hector rides beside my carriage as I crane my neck. He chuckles and tells me the walls were built to keep out sandstorms.

Brisadulce is nothing like the cities of Orovalle. I notice the stench first, like a privy that's run out of mulch. The streets are crooked and narrow. Merchants' shops and apartments tumble one upon another, like haphazard piles of children's blocks. I eye them with distrust. Everything is high and close and dim, and I don't know how people can live in such a place knowing that boundless sky and open desert lie steps away.

We receive indifferent glances as we pass—a woman beating a rough-woven blanket, two dirty-kneed boys who scamper into an adjoining alley, a tall bearded man selling coconuts—but we are travel worn, our carriages scarred by the battle with the Perditos. Nothing royal or noteworthy. I'm glad because I don't feel ready to be seen.

The ground slopes upward as we twist deeper into the city. Here the buildings stretch higher with cleaner lines, brighter curtains. Occasionally, twilight flashes against real glass panes. With the change in architecture, I expect my new home to be rich and spectacular.

It's not. Rising from a hill in the center of the city, Alejandro's monstrous palace is the ugliest structure I've seen. The history of Joya d'Arena shows in its patchwork of sandstone and river rock, of plaster and wood; the collective effort of a millennium of overzealous builders. The earth surrounding the walls is barren and gray, nearly indistinguishable from the stone in the fading light. The place desperately needs brightening. Maybe Alejandro will let me plant bougainvillea.

Torch lamps light our path as we steer around the palace toward the stables. We stop at guard intervals, and I hear voices ahead, though I can't make out the words. Perhaps Alejandro has identified himself. I imagine how he tells them about me. *I've brought the most wonderful, beautiful woman home with me for my bride!* Then servants scurry away to prepare feasts and flowers and singing for our arrival. I laugh aloud. I've had such ridiculous thoughts since my wedding.

I jump when Ximena's fingers squeeze my knee. It had grown dark enough for me to forget she rides just across from me. But I'm saved having to explain my laughter when Alejandro's head appears in the carriage window, backlit by torches.

"Elisa!" He grins like a little boy about to show off his favorite toy. "We're home."

Home. I manage a shaky smile in return.

"I told my seneschal we are weary from our journey and will do no receiving tonight. Also"—his smile turns apologetic—"I said you are a very special guest who should be given every courtesy. So let me know if anything is not to your liking."

A special guest. Is that all?

But he grasps my hand as I descend from the carriage.

When I look up to thank him, he doesn't let go, just clasps it tighter and says, "I'll show you to your suite."

I nod, swallowing. Ximena steps down behind me.

We're in a sandy carriage yard, the stables to our left. The darkness blurs details, but I hear nickering horses and smell manure tinged with the sharpness of fresh-cut hay. To our right, the monolith of the palace is heavy in the sky above me. My companions scurry about, unloading carriages and packhorses. I don't see anyone unfamiliar, which seems odd. Whenever Papá and Alodia return from a journey, the whole staff turns out in greeting.

Nighttime, no servants, a side entrance, a special guest.

For whatever reason, Alejandro has decided to keep me a secret.

It's hard to keep my hand in Alejandro's, because I'm not sure he cares. My pulse thumps in my throat, from exertion and maybe disgrace, as we enter the palace and maneuver through corridors and up a flight of stairs. Ximena follows behind. I've read the *Belleza Guerra* innumerable times, so I know I should concentrate on the route, get to know my surroundings. But I can't think past the humiliation that burns my face.

We stop at a mahogany door carved with vines and flowers. Alejandro opens it, and we step into a breezy chamber lit by beeswax candles. I don't have time to take in all the details because Alejandro pulls me toward him and takes my other hand.

"I'm going to ask you to keep a secret for me," he says as Ximena brushes past into the room. He looks the same as he did on our wedding night, his eyes cinnamon brown in the candlelight. "I'm not ready to reveal that I've married. It's something I must save for the proper time."

He is so intent on me as he pleads for understanding. Still, I say nothing.

"And I think it would be best," he continues, "if you didn't tell anyone about the Godstone just yet."

I suck my cheeks in and take a deep breath, refusing to cry in front of him.

"Elisa?"

As much as I want to help him, to win him over, I'm suddenly desperate to feel like I still belong to myself. So I fix him with my best approximation of Alodia's glare, the one she uses on lazy cooks and little sisters. "I will trust you, Alejandro. For now. Because my sister told me I should. But that is the *only* reason. I very much hope you will give me another."

I am shocked into silence when he wraps his arms around me and pulls me close. "Thank you," he says into my hair. Then he releases me, grabs my hand, and brings it gently to his lips.

I tremble at the warmth of his kiss, but when he bids me good-night, I am unable to return his smile with one of my own.

He closes the door behind him on the way out. I turn toward the bed, a high, thick thing with diaphanous curtains and a three-tiered stepstool. Ximena has already turned down the covers. She gazes at me with understanding, having missed nothing of my exchange with Alejandro. I can't help myself anymore. Sobs quake through my chest, my nose runs, and I just want to go to sleep and never wake up.

The Godstone is an icy fist in my stomach, twisting and grinding against my spine. I can't breath; my lungs are frozen in shock. Alejandro looms above me. He reaches for the stone. "Give it to me!" he shrieks. I scurry backward on the bed like a bug, curl against the headboard. Alejandro advances. He has the eyes of a hunter, sparking red and catlike. The way he moves, the way he smells—there's an animal inside him, squirming just under his skin. I don't remember grabbing the dagger, but it's cold and hard in my hand. I stab and stab at Alejandro until blood streams over my forearm and my palm aches from impact.

I blink. Lady Aneaxi smiles. "Trust," she says, reaching for the Godstone. Her nails prod the skin of my abdomen; they scrape around the stone. Fiery pain darts through my pelvis, down my legs. She digs deeper and pulls. It feels like my spine is coming out through my navel. The pain is too much to bear. I manage a breath. Quick and shallow, but it's enough that I can scream. Aneaxi draws back, startled. Her fingertips, swollen and black with infection, drip crimson. She grins. "You must wake up, my Elisa."

"Elisa! Someone is at the door."

I open my eyes to a silk canopy of orange and coral, trimmed in glass beads that catch the gentle morning light. Ximena nudges my shoulder as a thump sounds at the door.

"I think you were dreaming, my sky."

My muscles melt into the silk covers; I unclench my jaw and catch my breath. The bed is yielding and soft. The kind a girl can sink into if she doesn't want to face the day. But the knocking continues.

I pull the covers up to my chin. Ximena smiles in sympathy as I call out, "Come!"

A girl about my age enters. She is petite and beautiful with elegant cheekbones, graceful and dainty even in her homespun wool. She curtsies low; it looks like a dance step, like she's about to twirl away. I stare at the shimmering black hair poking from beneath her maid's cap. Finally I realize she's awaiting permission to address me.

"Speak."

She stands and smiles. One of her front teeth folds in slightly. I focus on the flaw as her gaze follows the form of my body beneath the covers, comes to rest on my face. Black eyes flash, like she has learned something valuable. She raises an eyebrow just slightly; then her expression becomes vacant, and she lowers her head.

"I was sent to help you prepare for breakfast."

My stomach growls, and I imagine fresh baked bread with honey, fig cakes with sweetened coconut milk.

"Your name?" I ask.

"Cosmé." She has the odd, lilting accent of the desert people.

I flip back the covers and sit up. The floor is a long way down, and I scoot over the edge until my toes touch the sheepskin rug. "Cosmé, my clothes are a disaster from my journey. Could you find a blouse and skirt for me?"

Her brow knits in confusion. "I could find a corset and a dress maybe . . ." Then she gasps. "You're from Orovalle!"

Dread fills my gut. A corset would make me look like a stuffed pig, and except for my false wedding, I've never worn anything so restrictive. Do the women of Joya only wear corsets?

"Yes, I am visiting from Orovalle. You may address me as Lady Elisa." I catch an approving look from my nurse.

She curtsies again. "I'll see what I can find, Lady Elisa." And she glides away as if she were the princess and I a dumpy maid in a sooty dress.

While she is gone, Ximena and I explore the suite a bit. There are three rooms. My bedroom with the huge bed has a dressing table, a tiny balcony overlooking a dry garden, sheep-skin rugs, and large, tasseled cushions. The smaller maid's room has bunked beds and a wardrobe. A cool atrium with a garderobe and bathing pool connects the two. The pool is square shaped and marvelously tiled with tiny, hand-painted designs in blue and yellow. A glowing skylight suffuses the atrium with hazy gold. The entire suite contains not a single chair. I remember Alodia recounting how the people of Joya d'Arena use cushions for sitting.

Another door leads from my bedroom, but it is locked.

The suite is no larger than my chambers at home, but it's rich with deeper colors, finer fabrics. I love the silk and gauze that canopy my bed and swathe my walls. But I miss the tinkle of fountains, the creeping allamanda that sneaks tendrils of green through my window.

Ximena brushes and plaits my hair as we wait. It's my favorite time of morning because I love the feel of her fingers against my scalp, the gentle tugging. My hair is shining and black, with waves that fall to my waist. Ximena usually creates two braids, one atop the other, because there is so much of it. Aneaxi used to tell me I had pretty lips and eyes, too. She was wrong, of course; my lips look like fat slugs and my eyes are far too small, overwhelmed as they are by cheeks like pomegranates. But it's nice to have one lovely thing.

Cosmé returns with an armful of clothing. She spreads everything out on the bed and I can hardly breathe for the beauty of it all. So many colors, so many fabrics and trims. Glass beads sewn into panels, gem-encrusted bodices, the tiniest, most detailed lace. I run my fingers along the skirt of one dress. It's a soft coral, like my canopy, with a light fringe at the hem. But everything is petite. Made for a dainty person like Cosmé.

". . . that Queen Rosaura was about your height," she is saying, "so I thought one of these might fit."

Of course they won't fit. They are so obviously too small that I stare at the tiny maid. She has insulted me on purpose, and I don't know why.

Ximena's hand rests on my shoulder, and it's all I can do not to cry. I stare at the tile floor, at a sheepskin rug that curls up on one end. Softly, she whispers in my ear, "I washed your blouse and skirt in the atrium last night. They are nearly dry."

I almost choke with relief. "Thank you."

Cosmé guides us downstairs to a vast, loftily ceilinged dining hall. Light streams blue from high stained windows. People are already seated on cushions when we enter, a row of steaming dishes between them, and they look up in mild interest. The men are clean shaven, the women corseted. Everyone wears bright colors, blank expressions. No one speaks. I don't see my husband anywhere.

A woman stands to greet us, smiling, and I smile back gratefully. She glides forward, golden arms outstretched. Her eyes, shimmering honey brown beneath black lashes, are startling in her tanned face.

"You must be Alejandro's special guest!" she says. Her voice is soft and high like a girl's. Only faint lines and slight weariness around her eyes reveal that she is older than I, maybe late twenties.

I nod, unsure what to say. I wish the king was here so I could follow his lead.

"Come, sit with me." She grabs my arm, and I let myself be pulled along. "I'm Condesa Ariña. I'll introduce you to everyone after you've had something to eat."

As Ximena and I settle beside her, the damp ruffles of my skirt stick cold against my legs. It is odd that the condesa has not asked my name, that she speaks of my husband with such familiarity.

I try not to be too interested in the food as she fills a wooden platter for me, selecting from various dishes before us. I look at the people seated around me; they eat daintily, glancing away as soon as my gaze catches theirs. The chamber is stone-cold gray and huge, too huge for two handfuls of people. I miss my cozy adobe.

Condesa Ariña sets the platter in my lap. "Here you are, Lady Elisa." So she already knows my name. I've told no one to address me that way save Cosmé. I glance toward the curtained doorway we entered through, but the maid is gone.

I attack the food. It's a bit bland, but so much nicer than traveling fare. I bite into a puffed pastry, remembering an almond glaze that would contrast beautifully with the mild egg flavor. Maybe Alejandro's kitchen master will be willing to experiment with some of Orovalle's finer dishes.

Then I remember Ximena. Ariña hadn't bothered to serve her. I hand her my platter, smiling in apology. She winks at me and grabs a tiny quiche. As I settle the platter between us, I notice several of my companions looking at me strangely. I wonder what I've done wrong. Maybe they're not used to seeing a servant treated with respect. Or maybe I don't eat daintily enough for them. I stuff another pastry into my mouth and stare right back.

Attention shifts toward the doorway. The curtain moves aside, and Lord Hector enters, followed by Alejandro. I'm so relieved to see them both. Everyone stands and bows low, and I sit there like a fool, not sure what to do. Does a wife bow to her husband in Joya d'Arena? Does a princess bow to a king? I only bowed to my father on formal occasions.

I clamber to my feet, and my face flushes hot when I realize my damp skirt is stuck to the backs of my legs. Alejandro can't see, but I'm sure Condesa Ariña is making a careful study of my ample rear. I don't dare yank my skirt from behind.

Alejandro strides toward me, smiling like he's glad to see

me. His skin is fresh scrubbed; his hair sweeps away from his forehead in soft, black waves. I'm caught by the way it curls behind his ears, by the strength of his jaw that frames otherwise delicate features. He grabs my shoulders and leans in to kiss my hot cheek.

"I trust you slept well, Highness?" he asks loudly.

Highness. I feel the collective gaze of my breakfast companions hammer me with silent surprise.

He turns to face them. "Have you met everyone yet, Elisa?"

"Only Condesa Ariña, who has been most kind." To our left, Lord Hector's mustache twitches.

Alejandro looks over the top of my head toward the beautiful lady. "Yes, I'm sure she has been." His gaze travels around the room. "I'd like to introduce Lucero-Elisa de Riqueza, princess of Orovalle. She is visiting us indefinitely on behalf of her father, King Hitzedar."

I almost laugh when all those who have been so carefully indifferent bow to me. So, I do get to be a princess of Orovalle. At least I'll have that. But by revealing who I am, surely they will know about the Godstone I carry. In Orovalle, everyone knows the name of the bearer. Perhaps things are different in Joya d'Arena. Centuries ago, when my ancestors left Joya to colonize our little valley, few remained who followed the path of God.

Alejandro gestures for me to sit. "Please. I didn't mean to interrupt your breakfast." I do so gladly, giving a worried thought toward plucking the plastered skirt from my rear when next I stand. He settles between me and Ariña. Lord Hector stands guard behind him.

I can hardly bear the polite nonsense from the others that ensues. Did you sleep well? How is breakfast? Let me know if you need anything! And of course there are inquiries about my journey, which I answer in monosyllables, not wishing to discuss Aneaxi's horrifying death or the jungle battle. Alejandro introduces me to each of them, but they all blur in my mind. I only remember a conde Eduardo, a general Luz-Manuel, and of course, the condesa Ariña. I'm good at memorizing things, and I should note everyone's name, but it's hard to care. I'm still so tired, so alone.

I find myself leaning toward Alejandro. It would be nice to feel his arms around me, like the day of the Perditos' attack, or last night when I told him I'd trust him. But I stop myself. I'm not really his wife in this stifling place, and in spite of our conversation on our wedding night, hardly even his friend.

Maybe he senses my sudden sorrow, because I see a question in his eyes. I manage a slight smile. Beyond him, the lovely Ariña watches us. Her face wears a child's pout, like she might cry. She catches my gaze and looks down at her platter. I study her profile, intrigued. Something about her eyes, wide with hurt, about the way she swallows hard.

"What is it?" Alejandro whispers.

Is there something between you and Ariña? "Er . . . thank you for sending Cosmé to help me this morning."

"Cosmé came to you? I didn't send the girl." His whisper rings with alarm. "I didn't send anyone. I was going to have breakfast brought to your room." He lowers his voice further. "Cosmé is Ariña's maid."

"I see." And I certainly do. Ariña wanted to find out about Alejandro's "special guest." What will she do when she learns about our marriage?

"I can forbid her to attend you again."

I start to nod, then think better of it. "No. But thank you." Then I grin. *"Don't be afraid to be queen,"* Alodia had said. I am not the queen yet, but I intend to be.

I lean across him, toward Ariña. "Condesa?"

"Highness?" Such a lovely, innocuous voice.

"Thank you for lending me the use of your maid. I tragically lost my lady-in-waiting on our journey and found Cosmé's presence such a comfort."

Ariña smiles, catlike. "You're quite welcome."

"I was wondering if you wouldn't mind lending her to me for the duration of my stay? She does excellent work."

Her face freezes for such a quick instant that I'm almost sure I imagine it. "Of course, Highness." She inclines her head in perfect acquiescence.

"Thank you."

The *Belleza Guerra* devotes several lengthy passages to the art of keeping one's enemies close and intimate, and I know Alodia would approve. I finish my breakfast with genuine pleasure, savoring the tiny quiches and spicy sausage.

6

AFTER breakfast, Lord Hector pulls me aside. I look up at dark eyes—darker even than Alejandro's—and a rugged, mustached face. His skin is too weathered and crisscrossed with scars for one so young, but I should not have thought him unkind. Hard, perhaps, but not unkind.

"Your Highness, Alejandro told me to warn you." He talks fast and low. "You may go anywhere in the palace or the city of Brisadulce. But you must always be accompanied by Ximena. It is not safe otherwise."

I nod, wide-eyed at both his warning and the implication that Ximena is indeed capable of protecting me.

"In fact," he continues, "if you have no plans for the day, His Majesty would like for me to show you around."

Of course I don't have plans. "Thank you, Lord Hector. I'd like that." Were I home in Orovalle, I'd be making my way to Master Geraldo's study by now. What will I do with my days here?

"In an hour, then." He bows low and returns to Alejandro's side.

I return to my suite to write a letter.

Dear Alodia,

Ximena and I arrived safely in Brisadulce. I'm sorry to report that we lost Aneaxi to a jungle infection.

I need your counsel. Alejandro does not wish to acknowledge me as his wife. He says the time is not right. He also does not wish to reveal that I bear the Godstone. Did you know this would happen? Should I continue to trust him?

I am sending a more detailed letter by post, but I don't expect it to reach you for some time. Please respond with your thoughts soon.

Give my love to Papá.

Elisa

I copy it three times, hoping my sister will read the anger and frustration in my harsh pen strokes. "We lost Aneaxi to a jungle infection." Such a huge and horrible thing reduced to a single, pathetic phrase, but I can only send so much on a pigeon's leg. I roll the tiny parchments to fit inside casings no longer than the first joint of my forefinger. Ximena takes them — all three fit easily into the palm of one hand—and leaves our suite for the dovecote. I offer a quick prayer of thanks that my sister's pigeons survived our jungle ordeal.

Then I laugh wryly. How quickly and unbidden the prayer came. It is such a habit to attribute all of life's good things to God. For the first time I can remember, I wonder if I should be thanking someone else. Alejandro's soldiers, maybe. Or even myself. We are the ones who won through that day, not God.

I put my fingertips to my abdomen. The stone is smooth and

warm even through the cotton weave of my skirt, proof that God—or someone—is there. Someone placed this thing in my navel with its burning affirmations, its icy warnings. And through it, someone responds to my prayers with tangible comfort.

But that same someone ignored my prayers and allowed my lady-in-waiting to die. It makes no sense, but Aneaxi's dying wish was that I not lose faith. I'm trusting a lot of people on faith. My sister, Ximena, Alejandro, and now God himself. *I will need more than this, O God. If you love me as Aneaxi said, please send me something to go on. Something soon.* Tender heat blossoms in my belly, spreads into my chest and down my arms until they tingle delightfully. It is the same as that night by Aneaxi's bed, the night I pleaded with God for her life, so I'm afraid it means nothing.

Cosmé arrives before Ximena returns. She curtsies, but I catch her sullen look. I don't release her from her curtsy until I'm certain she is uncomfortable.

"Hello, Cosmé."

She rises. "Highness, the condesa says you sent for me." Her short black hair curls so appealingly from under her maid's cap, and her black eyes are wide with virtue. I want to pinch her.

I swallow guiltily. "Yes. I'll need a maid for my stay, and I'm quite taken with you." I wonder if it sounds as silly to her as it does to me. "Ariña was kind enough to lend you to me."

"What would you have me do?"

I hadn't thought this far. She will need to be kept busy. Too busy to spy or gossip.

"Er . . ." I look around my suite, searching for ideas. Like all the rooms I've seen in this monstrosity of a palace, it is far too large for so few furnishings. It feels open and gaping and altogether unhomelike. "I need a chair. Two chairs. If you can't find any, I trust you to commission them. Also, I need plants. Large plants in pots. Anything green and alive. I want two for the balcony, at least two for the bedroom, one for Ximena's room."

Cosmé gapes at me like I've swallowed a scorpion. I try not to look too smug. Not only will such a task take her all day in this empty, barren place, it will give her something harmless to blather passionately about.

I'm still congratulating myself when Ximena appears.

"It's nice to see you smile," she says.

I don't want to talk about the things that have stolen my smile lately. "You released the pigeons?"

She nods. "The handler was quite curious. It was wise to write in the Lengua Classica." The holy language. Ximena scribed copies of the scriptures for years and is probably as fluent, if not more so, than I.

"When Lord Hector comes," I say, trying to sound offhand, "let's see if he'll take us to the monastery."

Longing widens her eyes. "I would like that very much," she whispers.

We don't wait long. Lord Hector appears in the doorway dressed in light armor—rawhide instead of steel, a brown walking cloak instead of the crimson drape of the Royal Guard—and bows from the waist.

"Ready, Highness?" I take the offered arm and step into the hall, Ximena following behind.

Lord Hector's knowledge of the palace and its history astounds me. He guides us through the armory, the reception hall, the grand ballroom, the library. Know your environment, the *Belleza Guerra* says. So I focus carefully on what he tells us. I repeat words and phrases in my mind and create pictures to accompany them, the way Master Geraldo taught me. And tomorrow, I will retrace this walk and try to remember everything I learned. It won't be difficult; Lord Hector's enthusiasm is contagious.

In the portrait room, he points out Alejandro's father, a thickset and graying version of my husband. King Nicolao, the guard tells us, beat back the forces of Invierne to save the hill villages east of the desert. He was killed by a stray arrow during battle.

Something about Nicolao, or maybe about the last war with Invierne, silences the guard.

"You served Alejandro's father?"

He nods, his eyes fixed on the painting. "Indirectly. When I was twelve years old, I became Prince Alejandro's page. We often kept company with the king. He was a good man." I don't know him well enough to determine if it's wistfulness that softens his voice.

But something makes me ask, "And Alejandro?"

He finally looks away from the face of King Nicolao to stare at me. "His Majesty is . . . different from his father. But he is also a good man."

"You are young to have made Royal Guard."

"I grew up here in the palace, and Alejandro was like an older brother to me. When the position became available, it gave him comfort to assign it to me."

It's hard not to fidget under his gaze. Lord Hector is formidable and stern in the space beside me, and so intent that it's possible he's trying to communicate something different. He has the look of one with a mighty mind, whose thoughts spin hidden beneath the impassive surface.

Master Geraldo would like Lord Hector.

The guard raises an eyebrow, and I realize I'm grinning. "You remind me of someone," I explain.

He smiles back. Years of soldiering drop from his face, and I realized he's even younger than I thought. His teeth are startling; so white beneath his mustache and so rarely displayed. He says, "Someone whose company you enjoy, I hope."

The words feel strangely out of character for him. "Of course," I manage.

But I sense him stiffen, and a sudden cushion of awkwardness makes him feel far away.

He gestures toward the portrait next to King Nicolao's. It's of a woman with silk-smooth skin and obsidian hair. She wears a cream-colored gown and fingers a matching string of pearls with a delicate, tapered hand. She reminds me of my sister, with the same subtle grace and serene composure that elevates a pretty woman to true beauty.

"That is Queen Rosaura, Alejandro's first wife and mother to Prince Rosario."

My heart drops into my stomach and warmth floods my cheeks. I hadn't truly understood, until this moment, how impossible it would be for Alejandro to love me.

"Highness?" the guard asks. "Do you feel unwell?"

I put my hand to my stomach. "Did you hear that growl?" I give a nervous laugh as Ximena catches my eye. I wish she didn't know me so well. "Lord Hector, why don't you show us to the kitchens next?" And I offer him my arm. It's a trick of Alodia's I've observed hundreds of times, whenever she needs to distract or confound.

He takes my arm and we turn to go, but not before I glimpse a crack in his composure. It's fleeting, but I'm struck by how the lines around his eyes and mouth settle into sorrow with comfortable familiarity.

The kitchen master is delighted to fill me with honey and coconut scones. By the time we reach the monastery, I'm miserable from stuffing myself and from walking so much.

The monastery attaches gracelessly to the north wing of Alejandro's palace. One moment we walk beneath wood-beam braces, along sandstone hallways trimmed in the same blue-gold tile as my atrium; the next, we are surrounded by low-ceilinged adobe, curving walls, and clay tile floors. It's as if we've stepped from Joya d'Arena into Papá's palace hacienda, and I feel a pang of desire for home.

A tiny, aged man draped in undyed wool hobbles toward us, pointed features twitching. Ximena surprises me by asking, "You are Father Nicandro?"

He claps and grins wide. "Lady Ximena! I received word from Father Donatzine to expect you." He embraces her while Lord Hector and I look on, invisible.

I close my eyes while they chatter, inhaling the poignant scent of roses and prayer candles. I know I will return to this place often, to pray or merely to be silent and alone. The Godstone responds to my thoughts with warm, soft comfort.

Father Nicandro breaks off midsentence. He turns his head to study me. "Donatzine did not tell me," he whispers. "Ximena, you are guardian to the bearer!"

Lord Hector steps closer, as if to shield me, while wariness clouds Ximena's eyes. My heart beats faster. The priest sensed the Godstone living within me. And this displeases my nurse.

"Are you certain it was wise to bring her here?" Nicandro asks.

I'm right here! I want to scream. *I am not a small child to be discussed over, the way Papá and Alodia always do.*

Ximena doesn't answer him right away. I watch her consider for a moment, eyes narrowed. "We thought it best." Her voice is soft, meant to not carry. "In Orovalle, the bearer is well known and closely watched. She'll be safer here, where few people still follow the path of God."

Safer. Is this why they married me off so quickly? Because the Godstone puts me in danger? I flash back to the painted savage who lay dead in jungle trash for recognizing what I bear in my navel. I glance at Ximena, relieved to note her long, gray, pinless braid.

Of course she probably knows many ways to kill a man.

I hurry forward, placing my body between Ximena and the priest. For once, I'm glad for my girth. "Father Nicandro." I smile with my mouth, though I cannot force pleasure into my eyes. "I'm Elisa, and I'm very glad to meet you."

I am not a tall girl, but I tower over him by half a head. He smiles up at me, delighted. "Welcome to the Monastery-at-Brisadulce. Ours is the first, you know. Built only a few years after God carried our ancestors from the dying world in his righteous right hand."

I nod. "I hear you have the oldest known copy of the *Belleza Guerra*."

"Yes, yes. Several centuries old. Sadly, the vellum cannot last much longer."

I feel Ximena behind me, watching, but I ignore her. "I'd dearly love to compare it to my own copy. There are a few places where I fear the text may have been altered a bit."

His smile widens, his pointed features twitch with excitement, and I know I've found a friend at last. "Please, come by anytime. I take it you are adept in the Lengua Classica?"

"It's the most beautiful language in the world."

I could not have chosen a better response, for he claps me on the back and ushers me into a thorough tour of the monastery and its accompanying library of sacred documents. Ximena and Lord Hector follow behind in silence.

Much later, Lord Hector guides us back to our suite. We thank him and bid him good-bye, then I collapse onto my bed. I haven't walked so much in years.

Ximena draws a bath while I rest. A breeze flutters the curtain of my balcony and rustles the fronds of a large palm. A palm! I sit straight up and look around the room. Two chairs, simple but sturdy, rest beside the strange, locked door. Several potted plants sit against the opposite wall: another palm, a tree with coin-size leaves, a tiny rose bush with soft pink buds. I lie back, smiling, not at all displeased at the prospect of thanking Cosmé.

My nurse calls me into the atrium. I worry for my new friend, Father Nicandro, and I cannot meet her gaze as I undress. She grabs my arm to support me as I step across slippery tiles into the bath. The water is delightful against my sore feet and smells faintly of cloves.

Ximena begins to knead my shoulders after I settle in, but I stop her.

"Ximena?"

"Yes, my sky?"

"Will you . . ." It's so hard to ask, and the words feel like stones in my throat. "I mean, are you going to kill Father Nicandro?"

She gasps a little, as if catching on a sob. "Oh, Elisa." I feel her lips press against my hair. They linger there for a long time. "No, I will not."

I sigh and close my eyes, able to relax at last. "Thank you."

7

CANDLES sputter in the breeze from my open balcony, and the words of the *Scriptura Sancta* blur on their pages. I am reaching over to snuff the flames when someone knocks on the mysterious door.

Ximena tumbles into my room through the atrium, her hair mussed, her face alert. I shrug in answer to her unasked question. The knock sounds again.

"Come," I call as my nurse sidles close to my bed.

The door opens silently. Alejandro stands in the doorway, straight and tall and wonderful.

"Hello, Lucero-Elisa. Ximena."

Ximena relaxes into a graceful curtsy. "Your Majesty." She straightens and smiles. "If you'll excuse me, I'll return to bed."

The king and I haven't been alone together since our wedding night.

"How was your first day in Brisadulce?" He leans against the wall; the distance between us is disappointing but safe.

"Fine." I search for something clever to say. "Your kitchen

master makes excellent honey and coconut scones."

At his raised eyebrow, I consider pulling the covers over my head. Queen Rosaura's delicate face and slender neck swim before me. I doubt she spent much time in the kitchens.

But his pleased smile holds no contempt; he's taking the compliment to heart. "I'm just sorry I wasn't able to show you around myself."

I'm sorry too. I would have liked the excuse to cling to his arm all day. "Lord Hector was pleasant company."

"Lord Hector is a good friend," he says carefully. "He became my page when he was a boy. As he grew older, I took him more and more into my confidence."

I nod politely, wondering what the point is. I haven't known Alejandro long, but he does not seem one for idle conversation. To fill the space, I say, "He spoke highly of you." It's not the exact truth, but it seems appropriate.

"He speaks highly of you also."

"Oh?" I hope the dim candlelight hides my blush.

"Indeed. He says you've got steel in you, that you are wise beyond your years. He wouldn't say more, which is odd because, as I've said, we're very close." It bothers him that Hector would keep something from him. And it bothers me to see how deeply aware of my "years" Alejandro is.

"I have no idea what he means," I lie. Lord Hector watched me intervene on Father Nicandro's behalf. I don't know why the guard chose not to relate the incident to Alejandro, but I don't mind having this harmless secret together.

Alejandro shrugs and looks away, and I find the gesture so

vulnerable, so endearing, that I almost blurt the day's events. I wish he would sit next to me on the bed. I imagine what it would be like to feel his cheek against mine, my fingers in his hair.

Finally he says, "I need your help, Elisa."

"My help?"

"Please. I'm leaving tomorrow for Puerto Verde, to visit my mother and retrieve my son. He's been fostering there the last three years."

"Oh." I look down to hide my disappointment. "How long will you be gone?"

"A month."

A whole month! I'm proud of the evenness in my voice when I say, "And how do you want me to help?"

He grabs one of my new chairs and swings a long leg around to straddle it backward. His arms hug the chair back, and he cocks his head. "Yours is the newest presence in Brisadulce, and a royal one, no less. While I'm gone, some of the others will approach you to take your measure. Maybe to see how useful or important you can be to them."

I nod along with him. I understand these subtle battles, this understated leveraging for power. I've observed it my whole life, my response always one of stunning disinterest. At home, Juana-Alodia is the virtuoso, and Orovalle's *nobleza d'oro* dances enthralled by her melody.

"You can help me so much, Elisa," he continues. "Just by paying attention. Write it down if you must. Write down who seeks you out, what they offer, anything you think may be important. And then, when I return . . ."

He wants a spy in his own household. Perhaps he worries that some in his court are preparing to move against him. Or maybe, like Alodia, he simply uses every available pawn to play the game. They would have been well matched, my husband and my sister.

He takes my silence for hesitation. His gaze is unwavering as he rises from the chair and approaches my bed. "Please, Elisa," he whispers.

My heart pounds in my throat as he takes my hand. It's shapeless against his straight, strong fingers. But he leans closer, and I smell the spicy wildness of him.

"This is what we discussed," he whispers. "That night. When I said I could use a friend."

Our *wedding* night. Why can't he say it? But I nod anyway. I'd agree to anything, with his lips so near mine.

He leans back, the intensity gone, replaced by that easy, boyish grin. Now that he no longer hovers next to me, my mind begins to clear.

"The door you came through. Where does it lead?"

If he is taken aback by the change in subject, he does not show it. "My suite. It attaches to this one, of course."

Of course. These rooms must have belonged to Queen Rosaura. He has given me that, at least.

"You will bring the prince back with you, then?"

"Oh, yes! He's a bright boy. Already a skilled horseman. I'd like very much for you to meet him."

"I'd like that too." But it's not true. I feel even less ready to be a mother than a wife.

He turns to go. Once in the doorway that connects our suites, he glances over his shoulder and says, "Lord Hector was right. There's steel in you."

The days following Alejandro's departure pass interminably. Though I've agreed to be his eyes and ears, I avoid the dining hall and its maneuvering nobility as often as possible, preferring to take my meals alone with the kitchen master. He's a kind fellow, thin and flour dusted, and he seems glad for the company.

During the afternoons, I seek out Father Nicandro. Together, we pour over the *Belleza Guerra*, spotting contextual inaccuracies in my own copy. His study is so like Master Geraldo's, with its haphazard scrolls and dusty vellum and close-in adobe walls. It smells of candles and age and drying ink, and I have but to close my eyes to imagine myself home in Orovalle, in the one place where I don't feel useless.

Questions tumble around in my head about the Godstone, about its history, about what Nicandro meant when he called Ximena my "guardian." But my nurse is always hovering about, guarding me from myself, and I'm afraid to ask lest she change her mind about sparing the priest. One morning I rise early and creep from our suite to seek him out, but he is not there. When I return, Ximena scolds me for venturing out without protection, and the fear in her eyes, true and fierce, frightens me.

Cosmé is in constant attendance. Though no one will take Aneaxi's place, Cosmé is the most efficient maid I've ever had.

I tell her so, frequently, and it gives me such a twist of pleasure to watch her react to praise from someone she despises. The *Scriptura Sancta* calls it "the fire of kindness."

She is cleaning out my fireplace one day, her hands and arms black with soot up to her elbows, when I invite her to move her things into Ximena's room.

"There is plenty of room," I assure her. "And I know the servants' quarters are cramped."

"Thank you, Highness," she says without looking up. "But I have my mistress's suite to myself right now."

"You do?" I realize I haven't seen Condesa Ariña in days, maybe weeks.

"She went to Puerto Verde with the king, of course."

She says it so flippantly, between shovelfuls, but her words are like fists in my stomach.

My voice is tight and wavery. "Does she accompany His Majesty often?"

Cosmé stands, the bucket of soot weighing her shoulder down. A gray-black smear streaks her lovely forehead. "They get away together as often as possible. She accompanies him almost as often as Lord Hector. Would you like a fire tonight, now that it's all clear?"

"No, thank you," I whisper. Who would need a fire in this place? I can hardly breathe for the strangulating heat around my neck.

That night, after Ximena has gone to sleep, I sneak down to the kitchens. The kitchen master is there, getting a head start on tomorrow's batch of bread. He says nothing when he sees my unshed tears, just gestures toward a bench near the round oven and hands me a platter of cheeses. A pungent variety with tiny bits of pepper tingles on my tongue. I eat until my belly aches, until I can no longer distinguish the spice of the peppers. I wash it all down with two glasses of wine and lurch back to my suite.

The next day, General Luz-Manuel, a man I've only seen from across a cluster of food platters, calls on me. My head aches from lack of sleep, so I feel justified turning him away with apologies, pleading illness. I know I've failed Alejandro by denying a member of his household. Married to him less than a month, and already I've failed. But it's hard to care.

My husband has a mistress. I know it with certainty. "Mistress" has always felt like such a naughty word, but not a serious one. I am a naive child, so out of my depth.

I lie in bed all day. Condesa Ariña's face flutters in the canopy above me—the coral of her gently flushed cheeks, the softness of her skin. She has a part of my husband that I don't even begin to understand. I try not to think of them together, but I can't help it. Then, without meaning to, I start imagining his warm hands on my bare skin. It's exciting and terrifying, and part of me is glad that I may never know. I'm not sure I could bear to be naked before him.

Late in the afternoon, a pageboy brings a message from the dovecote. Ximena grabs it and sends him away before he can ask questions. She breaks the canister's seal and hands it to me. I recognize Alodia's hurried script.

⁜ ⁜ ⁜

Dearest Elisa,

My condolences regarding Aneaxi.

Your status in Joya d'Arena was not part of our negotiation. He agreed to marry you in the sight of Orovalle's nobility and take you safely to his country. In return, Papá will commit troops for the upcoming war with Invierne.

Elisa, little sister, if you wish to be Joya's queen in spirit as well as name, you can make it happen, but you must make your own decisions regarding your place there. I cannot counsel you.

I do believe you have it in you to be a great queen.

Papá sends his love.

Alodia

I read the letter over and over, imagining my sister's exasperated face. When we were children together, she would huff away, rolling her eyes. The Lucero-Elisa of a month ago would have seen this letter as but a grown-up version of that same contempt, that same frustration at my inability to meet hers and Papá's expectations. But I feel the truth of it now. Alodia thinks I could play the game if I chose to, and play it well.

She thinks I could be a great queen.

It's heady stuff. I begin to wonder, hesitantly, if she is right. I've never wished to rule. Ruling is tedious and exhausting, but better, perhaps, than being useless. And it might be the only way to make Alejandro mine in some way, to matter to him. I toy with the idea for hours, asking what Alodia would do in my place, remembering applicable passages in the *Belleza Guerra*.

I make a mental list of my advantages. Alejandro is housing

me in the queen's suite. I'm not sure what it means, but it's significant enough that his mistress sent her maid to spy on me the day after I arrived. I have Ximena, a woman I don't begin to understand, but whose loyalty to me is unquestioned. I've made a friend in the head priest of the Monastery-at-Brisadulce. I am a princess of Orovalle and therefore outrank everyone save Alejandro and his young son.

But the hugest advantage of all is that I bear the Godstone. A tremendous honor, I've always been told, bestowed by God only once every hundred years, a sign that I am destined for greatness.

But I've had several perplexing hints that I don't know much about it at all: Alodia's warning that I should trust no one. The execution of a man who recognized my Godstone. The way Father Nicandro reverently referred to my nurse as my guardian. And now Alodia's letter, which says I was to be taken *safely* away.

The *Belleza Guerra* says to beware of power, for it is the sparking stone of fear. What is it about my Godstone that sparks so much fear?

I place my fingertips against the smooth surface. Even through my nightgown, it pulses soft and warm. If I decide to play this terrifying game, my first move must be to discover what it truly means to be the bearer. And I will have to sneak around Ximena to do it.

I close my eyes and pray. *Did you place your stone inside me to help me become queen?* I can't decide how I want God to answer.

A warm hand presses against my forehead, and I open my

eyes. Ximena looks down at me with an affectionate smile. "You look better," she says. "More color to your cheeks."

I smile back. "I feel much better."

"Are you ready to eat more? I could get some pastries for you, some chilled juice?"

"No, thank you." My mind whirls with planning, for I may have thought up a way to speak with Father Nicandro in secret. "I'm not hungry."

8

THE *Scriptura Sancta* says that all men are equal in the sight of God, and once every week servants sit shoulder to shoulder with merchants and nobles. The first time Ximena and I attended weekly services at the Monastery-at-Brisadulce, we sat on our rough bench surrounded by the merest handful of strangers. Each week the crowd grew, and today, every seat on every bench is taken, and the air is hot with bodies.

I suspect I am the cause of their renewed devotion. Everyone wishes a glimpse of this reclusive princess of puzzling status, this large, foreign-clad girl who frequents the sacred library and prays with such piety. I'm glad for the throng. So many people will make it easier to slip my note to Father Nicandro, right under Ximena's guardian gaze.

I bow my head as the priests, led by Father Nicandro, guide us through the "Glorifica." Translated into the Lengua Plebeya, it lacks the lyrical beauty of the original language. Still, the words burn my heart with their richness, and the Godstone responds to our chanting with joyous warmth.

My soul glorifies God; let it rejoice in my Savior
For he has been mindful of his humble servant
Blessed am I among generations
For he lifted me from the dying world
Yea, with his righteous right hand he lifted me
He has redeemed his people, given them new life abundant
My soul glorifies God; let it rejoice in my Savior.

The altar blazes with a spread of prayer candles. Behind it, Father Nicandro lifts a single rose toward the ceiling. It's the holy variety—I can see the thorns even at this distance—chosen and consecrated because of its bloodred sheen and sharp spikes. He intones about this perfect symbol of the beauty and pain of faith, and we echo our response.

After a hymn of deliverance, Father Nicandro asks those who wish to be blessed to make their way forward with quiet decorum. It was for this reason I chose a seat on the edge of the bench. The ruffles of my skirt trail into the aisle, and I tug them closer to clear the way.

A scattered handful of people rise and begin edging center and front, toward the altar. My head is bowed, but my eyes are open, and I sense someone approach from behind in the aisle. My timing must be perfect. A quick glance over my shoulder reveals a tall, middle-aged woman in a gray maid's frock. I wait until she is nearly to the edge of my bench.

I launch to my feet and step out in front of her. I hear a gasp as her knees impact, just slightly, the backs of my thighs. I turn my head and smile apologetically; her return grin is shy but genuine.

Ximena rises to follow, but it is too late. At least one person will stand between us, and my nurse will not be able to see what transpires as I ask my blessing.

One by one, each petitioner whispers to Father Nicandro. He prays, then pricks a fingertip with a rose's thorn. Together, they hold the bleeding finger above the altar until the stone receives a single drop of sacrifice. Father Nicandro makes the cupping sign of the righteous right hand beneath the supplicant's chin, then passes him or her off to another priest, who awaits with a cleansing cloth and water with witch hazel.

When the young boy in line before me begins whispering to the priest, I reach, so slowly, beneath the waistband of my skirt for the message I prepared. The success of my plan depends on the priest, on his willingness to receive my message during a holy sacrament, on his ability to seem unfazed.

Perhaps I've made a mistake. Father Nicandro will be angry with me. What if he interrupts the ceremony? What if Ximena sees? His life could be forfeit after all.

I change my mind. My hand reaches for my waistband again, to shove the message away, but I am not quick enough. The boy has stepped aside to cleanse his finger and Father Nicandro's gaze has lowered, briefly, to the tiny roll of parchment pinched between my thumb and forefinger.

I step forward to take the boy's place, holding the roll tight against my breast. Father Nicandro's left hand cups the back of my neck and pulls my head downward until we are forehead to forehead.

"Your Highness," he whispers. "What do you seek from God today?" With his other hand, the one that holds the rose, he reaches out and grasps the parchment between his middle and index fingers. With one quick, smooth motion, my message disappears into his voluminous sleeve, as if he is well practiced at intrigue.

He waits calmly for my answer. I give him the truth. "Wisdom," I whisper back. "I need so much more than I have."

I sense approval in his voice when he intones the blessing. The prick is fast and deep; I suspect the priest is nonplussed after all, for it is deeper than usual. It throbs as we hold it over the altar, the ensuing drop welling fat. It sizzles and browns when it lands on the hot stone. A smaller drop follows immediately.

Nicandro jerks my hand away and gives me an apologetic smile. I smile back, happy to leave this place with nothing worse than a too-deep thorn prick.

I retreat to the corner to have my finger bathed and bandaged, and the tall maid takes my place. My heart pounds with what I've just done. I pray Ximena did not see our exchange, and that Father Nicandro reads the note soon. *Meet me tonight*, it says. *At the first morning hour, next to the ancient texts.*

After services, I plead exhaustion and take a nap. I will need the extra sleep to stay quietly awake well after Ximena retires to her room. Like me, she reads from the *Scriptura Sancta* every night, and it could be hours before she blows out her candles to sleep.

I'm awakened from my nap by a knock at the door. Ximena sets down her sewing—she has been constructing looser-fitting skirts and blouses for me from the material at hand—and moves to the door.

She opens it a crack, but the male voice on the other side is muffled. "She's resting," Ximena says.

"Who is it?" I whisper from the bed.

"One moment," she says to the visitor, then turns to me. "It's General Luz-Manuel. Again."

I mouth the words, "I can't turn him away twice." I'm glad Cosmé has the day off and won't be here to spy on me as I receive the general. I tumble from my bed as Ximena tosses me a dressing robe. I whisk it around my shoulders and tie it at my neck.

Ximena rolls her eyes conspiratorially, then opens the door. "Please come in, General."

He rushes in, as if afraid I'll change my mind. He's thin and stooped, balding at the top, and he wears the same sculpted mustache as Lord Hector and the rest of the Royal Guard.

Thinking of Lord Hector makes me smile. I'll be glad to see him again, one of the few who have been truly kind to me since I came here.

"Highness." He bows low.

"General Luz-Manuel. I apologize for not being more prepared for visitors."

He waves off my apology. "Do you often feel poorly, Highness?" His eyes are so full with concern.

"I'm always tired after services," I respond evenly. "Don't you find the sacrament of pain emotionally exhausting?"

He just shrugs. "The reason I came . . ." He looks down at the floor. "I've been elected to invite you, er, officially, to the next Quorum meeting."

Joya d'Arena's Quorum of Five. Alejandro's council, consisting of top-ranking nobles and officers. I must be cautious here, lest they use me to maneuver during his absence.

"Naturally, I'd be happy to attend. I'm not sure what I could offer, though."

He clears his throat. Perhaps he resents his task as errand boy, or disagrees with the Quorum's decision to include a child in their meeting. "We are beginning preparations for the war with Invierne." Like my sister's letter, he treats war as a foregone conclusion. "We'd like our next discussion to include representation from Orovalle."

It makes sense. If the people of Joya don't know about my marriage to Alejandro, then they probably don't know my father has already committed troops. But this is exactly the kind of thing Alejandro told me to expect, so I know I must play along.

"When is the next meeting?"

"One week from yesterday, directly following the noon meal."

I give him my most confident smile. "I'll be there."

After he leaves, Ximena looks up from her sewing. It always

amazes me how invisible she is to visitors. They are foolish to ignore my nurse, for she misses nothing.

"Be careful with the Five, my sky. By reputation, they are clever enough to give even Juana-Alodia a turn."

I glare at her. Even she measures me against my sister. "I can handle them," I snap.

"I didn't say you couldn't. Just be careful. Be *smarter* than Alodia."

I look down at my coverlet, feeling guilty for doubting her. "I'll try."

Ximena stays up late to finish my skirt. I read from the *Scriptura Sancta*, but even my favorite passages are lifeless on the page. I keep glancing at my nurse. Irritation wars with affection as I watch her bow over the fabric long into the night, wrestling with buttons and ruffled silk. She works so hard on my behalf, and tonight, I betray her.

At long last, she gathers the fabric together and stands, yawning. "I'm so sorry, my sky, but I can hardly see the stitches anymore. I'll have to finish tomorrow."

I fix her face in my mind, the round cheeks, the worry lines at her temples. I wish I'd had more time with Aneaxi, wish I'd known to memorize her features. Already her laughing eyes blur and I can't remember if she stood eye level with me or a little taller. "Thank you, Ximena. The skirt is lovely."

She lumbers over to my bed and bends down to kiss my forehead. "Sleep well, my Elisa."

Thankfully, the glow seeping through the atrium from her

bedroom flickers out almost immediately, and I'm left wide-eyed in the cool dark.

I wait.

My eyes grow heavy, but nervousness keeps me awake. I dare not light a candle to read. After a while, I rise from the bed to pace silently on slippered feet.

The sound of monastery bells, distant but pure, drifts through my open balcony and strikes midnight. Still I wait, listening at the atrium's edge for movement from Ximena's room. Finally I wrap myself in a long robe and creep out the door.

The hallways are silent and glowing. Sparse torches make odd light patterns against sparkling sandstone, and I almost laugh, for Alejandro's monstrous palace is nearly beautiful at night. I'm terrified that I'll be seen. The shape of my body is nothing if not recognizable, and even a fleeting glance would give me away.

I chide myself for cowardice. I've as much right to walk the halls late at night as anyone else. A clever excuse would not be so hard to come by. Still, my thighs burn from stepping with quiet precision, and when I finally reach the wooden monastery doors, my jaw aches from clenching my teeth.

I hurry inside and tiptoe to the library to await Father Nicandro. Just enough moonlight filters in through the long windows for me to find my way into the archive where the oldest documents are stored. I settle on a scribing stool.

I don't wait long. A pool of candlelight announces his presence. I look up, startled, marveling at his stealth.

"Your Highness," he whispers. "You used our most sacred ceremony to summon me here. I trust you had good reason?"

My shoulders slump. "I'm sorry, Father. I thought it best, but . . ." I shrug, unable to look him in the face.

He settles next to me, placing the candleholder on the table between us. In its flickering light, I see ancient scrolls on shelves, piles of parchment ready for copying, wooden cupboards that house the oldest, most light-sensitive documents, and I realize I've forced him to bend yet another tenet of his occupation. "I'm so sorry." I gesture lamely at the candle. "I wasn't thinking. I know candles don't belong in scribing rooms." Sunlight only was the rule back home, for it became too easy to knock over a lamp or candle after hours of scribing. My neck is hot with embarrassment.

"Elisa. What is it? Why this secret meeting?"

I look up, and his eyes are so full of compassion that I blurt, "I need help. I need to know about the Godstone."

A grin splits his face. "I suspected as much. I will help in any way I can."

My relief is so great, it's hard to keep my lower lip from quivering. "Really?" It's overwhelming, this feeling that someone will help me.

"Really. Had you been born here, in Brisadulce, it would have been my task to instruct you in all things pertaining to the Godstone. So we shall discuss it thoroughly while keeping an eye on this candle." His tone is one of gentle teasing. "Now tell me, what *do* you know of it?" In the candlelight, his eyes are more piercing than ever, his nose beakish. I warm to his zeal, so like my old tutor's.

I take a deep breath. "I know all the passages in the *Scriptura Sancta* relating to the Godstone and the bearer by heart. So I know God chooses one child each century for an act of service." I realize my fingers have traveled to the stone in my navel from habit. "I know God stuck this thing in me during my naming ceremony. I can feel it living there, pulsing like a second heartbeat. It responds to things sometimes, things I don't always understand. Mostly, it responds to my prayers."

He nods along with me. "And the Godstone's history? What do you know?"

"Besides myself, only one bearer has been chosen from Orovalle. That was four centuries ago, soon after our valley was colonized. All the others have been from Joya."

"Do you know anything about the nature of this service?"

I shrug. "Just that it's something big and wonderful and . . ." I'm gesturing with my hands, trying to explain a concept that feels so huge, but remains vague in my mind. "I guess I don't know much about it at all. I grew up hearing about my destiny. People seem to think I'm going to be some kind of . . . hero." I feel the blush creeping into my cheeks. It's ludicrous, and I peer through the dimness, expecting to find those sharp eyes mocking me.

But it's too dark to tell. "And the first bearer from Orovalle. Do you know what act of service he performed?"

"Of course. Hitzedar the bowman. My father is named for him. During my country's first skirmish with Invierne, he killed thirty-four men, including the animagus leading the attack. He was . . ." I look down at my hands. "He was sixteen years old."

He is silent for a moment, thoughtful. "Have you read Homer's *Afflatus*?"

My blank look is answer enough.

Father Nicandro sighs deeply. "It is as I feared."

"Feared? What did you fear? What is Homer's *Afflatus*?"

"Homer was the first bearer. Tradition places him among the first generation born to the new world."

I've never heard of Homer. How could I have been kept ignorant of something so important as the first bearer? "And this . . . *Afflatus*?" The Godstone warms to the word.

"It was his act of service. The spirit of God possessed him and he wrote the *Afflatus*, a collection of prophecies. About the Godstone, among other things."

My hands are ice cold, my breathing tight and hard. The Godstone aches with such pulsing warmth that nausea coils just underneath. "Prophecies," I whisper. "A sacred text. I never knew. I never . . ." I rise from the stool. "The people of Orovalle. They don't know about this." I pace toward the shelves and back.

"Your Highness—"

"They should know. Do you have it here? I can have Ximena scribe a copy for the Monastery-at-Amalur. Master Geraldo would love to see—"

"Elisa!"

I look up, startled by the edge in his voice.

"Your Highness," he says, gently now. "They already know."

It takes a moment for his words to sink in. When they do, pain like fire blossoms in my chest. "Who, exactly, already knows?" I think I know the answer, but I need him to say it.

"Everyone." His lips press into a thin line before he says, "I'm sorry, Highness. Everyone knows but you."

9

I see my life in sudden clarity. The hush whenever I walked into a room. Glances exchanged between my tutor and my sister. Hand-guarded whispers. Reassuring platitudes delivered from behind worried countenances. I thought it was because the world holds me in contempt, because I am so unlike my sister. Because I am fat.

This creeping, wormy feeling is humiliation. I've excelled as a student; noticing details, solving logic puzzles, memorizing information. It's the one thing I've taken pride in.

But how easily I was fooled. A stupid, stupid child.

"Highness?" His tone is cautious, worried.

"Why?" I whisper. "Why keep this from me?"

"Sit down." He waves toward the stool. "Your pacing makes this old man dizzy." He glances toward the candle as I comply, then says merrily, "We might need another one of these."

I don't appreciate his good cheer. "Tell me."

He leans forward onto the table. "When the Vía-Reformas left Joya to colonize Orovalle, they had one very important goal."

I already know this. "To pursue God."

He nods. "They believed—still believe—that man's highest aspiration should be the study of sacred texts, that the increasingly godless world had blurred divine truths that waited to be rediscovered. Man's second highest aspiration is—"

"Service."

He nods. "Yes, service. So they left, and several years later, when the next bearer was chosen in Orovalle, they took it as God's mark of approval."

"What does this have to do with Homer's *Afflatus*?"

"Patience. I take it the royal family remains staunchly Vía-Reforma?"

"Of course." It has always been a source of pride that my ancestors were not afraid to seek truth.

"As with all good movements, it started well. The need to return to the path of God was real. But it grew. It gained such momentum, and it became . . . something else."

Though I'm angry at my sister, at Master Geraldo, especially at Ximena, for keeping things from me, I'm not sure I'm ready to hear my faith has been misplaced. "Explain." The warning in my voice is unmistakable.

"They studied. Oh, they studied. It became about pride—they understood the sacred texts better than anyone, and they knew it. A cultural obsession formed, based on this investigation of scripture. They found truths that were . . . hidden from lesser eyes."

I am quick to defend. "That is perfectly reasonable. It's much easier to understand the *Scriptura Sancta* or the *Common Man's*

Guide to Service with intense study. As the *Sancta* says, "'Much study leads to much understanding.'"

"True," he agrees with an indulgent smile. "But it also says, 'The mind of God is a mystery and none can understand it.' You see, they went too far. They shunned the obvious, natural reading of the text for the hidden, unnatural one. Their precious truth was eclipsed by snobbery and elitism."

"I need an example."

He rises from the table and disappears into the gloom of bookshelves. I hear him rifling through scrolls, mumbling to himself, then footsteps as he returns. A smell precedes him, the musty, animal-skin scent of deep secrets.

"This," he announces, spreading a scroll across the table, "is Homer's *Afflatus.*" The edges try to curl back into their scroll form; Nicandro uses his forearm to hold them down. With his free hand, he points to a passage in the middle. "Here. Read this."

The candlelight is too dim, the script eddies and churns across soft vellum, and I am so weary. I rub my eyes and lean closer.

And God raised up for himself a champion. Yea, once in every four generations He raised him up to bear His mark.

(The champion must not fear.)

But the world did not know him and his worth was hidden away; like the desert oasis of Barea it was concealed. Many sought the champion; from evil intent they sought him.

(The champion must not waver.)

He could not know what awaited at the gates of the enemy, and he was led, like a pig to the slaughter, into the realm of sorcery. But the righteous right hand of God is mighty.

(His mercy extends to His people.)

I sit back and consider. The passage rings true in my heart; the Godstone vibrates softly in response. But there is newness here too, and I let it seep into my mind a moment. The realm of sorcery. The gates of the enemy.

"Why did my Vía-Reforma family hide this from me?"

Father Nicandro leans forward and smiles. Like all good teachers, he loves the moment of revelation, when the light of knowledge passes to his pupil. "It's all about this word right here." He points to the passage that reads, *He could not know what awaited at the gates of the enemy . . .* "'Could.' One tiny word. The natural reading of the text indicates that the champion is ignorant, for whatever reason, of the danger that awaits him."

I nod. That is exactly how I interpreted it.

"But!" He waggles a finger at me. "There is another passage. 'He who serves must not lose purity of intent.'"

I'm familiar with those words. They're from the *Common Man's Guide to Service.* A favorite quote of Ximena's.

"Two different meanings," he continues. "'Could not' and 'must not.' In the original language, however, it's the same word: 'Né puder.' Our forefathers, for whatever reason, translated them differently. The Vía-Reformas believe the first instance is in error. Where it says 'He could not know what awaited,' it should read, 'He *must* not know what awaited.'"

"So they believe it means that the bearer should not be told about the danger. It became a mandate rather than an observation."

"Precisely."

"So I have been kept in ignorance."

"Yes."

"Because of one word."

He shrugs. "There are other similar passages they use to bolster their claim, but this is the main one."

"The other bearers, the ones from Joya. Were they kept ignorant?"

"No. Just you and Hitzedar the bowman."

I put my face in my hands, trying to understand it all. Father Nicandro hasn't answered all my questions, but I'm too tired to remember them right now. I worry what Ximena will do when she finds out I know about Homer's *Afflatus*. Maybe it would be best not to tell her. And what if the Vía-Reformas are correct? What if I'm not supposed to know any of this?

"Father." I despise the quaver in my voice, but I'm helpless to stop it. "What awaits me at the gates of the enemy?"

"My dear girl, that I cannot tell you. No one knows. We only know that great danger awaits the bearer."

"But I will win through in the end, right? I mean, it says, 'The righteous right hand of God is mighty.'"

"Again, I don't know. I don't wish to alarm you, but I'm more concerned with what it doesn't say. It doesn't say the champion prevails." He reaches across the table and flips the scroll over. "Look at this."

It's a list of names with corresponding dates. One name every hundred years, with a few astonishing gaps in between. Toward the bottom, I see my own name. *Lucero-Elisa de Riqueza.* It's been newly added, for the ink is darker and the letters do not bleed into the page. I stare at them in wonder. Homer leads the list. Hitzedar the bowman is only a few slots above me.

The bearers before me. Real names, real people.

"There are gaps." I give Nicandro a questioning look.

"Yes. Our record is incomplete. Either we've lost the history, or some of the bearers were never recognized."

A startling thought. "How can that be?"

He shrugs. "Maybe they lived far from a monastery, raised in superstition, ignorant of their destiny. Maybe they died—or were killed—before they could complete their service. Who really knows?"

"So it is possible." My greatest fear realized. Destiny is too fluid a thing to ensure with a mere stone. "It's possible to die before completing the service."

"Oh, yes. Of these names"—he waves an arm above the list—"fewer than half performed recognizable acts of service. And most of them died young. And brutally. Like Hitzeder the bowman, who died with an arrow in his heart."

Not very good odds.

A sharp ache is forming behind my eyes, the ache of worry and unshed tears. I pinch the bridge of my nose and say, "Why are you telling me this? My nurse . . . she is, that is—"

"She's your guardian. The lady Ximena would give her life for you."

"She's my *nurse.*" She's more than that, of course, but I'm tired and surly.

"A guardian is selected by the nearest monastery to watch over the bearer. In Orovalle, I'm sure her job included seeing to your ignorance on certain prophetic matters. Actually—" He looks away, into the dark. "I'd prefer she not know about this conversation. As head priest of the Monastery-at-Brisadulce, it's my duty to instruct you, to prepare you in any way I can. But a Vía-Reforma would see things very differently."

She's done more than watch over me. "She killed a man once. Because he learned I bear the stone." I watch him closely for a response, but his sharp face is stolid. "With a hairpin," I add, and am satisfied with a telltale twitch.

"Lady Ximena is a formidable woman." His voice holds both respect and fear.

It was very kind of him to meet me at this horrid hour and instruct me at risk to himself. I reach forward and take his hand. "My nurse will not know of this meeting."

He squeezes back, needing assurance as much as giving it. In spite of the night's revelations, I am filled with the warmth of knowing I have a friend.

"God always chooses well, my child. I will help you any way I can."

I take a deep breath to still the fear that vibrates in my chest. "If he chooses so well, why have so many bearers failed? Why does he sometimes ignore my prayers?"

"I don't know, Elisa. There are many things about the Godstone and its bearers that we do not understand. But God knows. He knows more than we can imagine."

Aneaxi's words, before God let her die. Though I have enough control to keep from rolling my eyes at him, I can't force the proper platitudes to my lips. Would he still believe me a worthy bearer if he knew of the doubts always sneaking into my thoughts?

The stool creaks as I rise. "Thank you, Father. I have more questions, but I'm tired, and I . . . well, I need to think about all this for a bit."

He stands and grabs my upper arm. "I have something for you, before you go."

As he disappears again into the dark, I stretch and yawn. I hope it's a copy of Homer's *Afflatus*. I'd dearly love to study it myself. Ximena could not know I possessed it, of course, and different hiding places compete in my mind for viability while I wait.

He's gone a long time. I hear ruffled parchment, the click of a key and lock, a grating sound. When he reenters our meager pool of candlelight, he holds a fist-size leather pouch with long drawstrings that dangle between his fingers.

Not the *Afflatus*. I try not to seem disappointed. "What is it?"

He upends the pouch. Three small, sparkling items clatter onto the table. I lean closer. They are faceted jewels the size of my thumbnail, mostly dull in the dark but with hints of fire where the candlelight catches them just right. Deep blue. Familiar. I pick one up; it's cold and hard in my palm.

"Godstones," Father Nicandro says.

I catch my breath. It's so different outside of the body, heavy and lifeless.

"This monastery had the privilege of overseeing three bearers. When they died, their Godstones detached. That one"—he points to one on the table—"is twelve hundred years old."

It's a strange feeling to hold my history in my hand. And as the stone in my navel pulses a warm greeting in contrast to the cold thing in my palm, I realize it's my future too. My death.

I drop it next to the others and wipe my hand on my robe.

Nicandro gathers them into the leather pouch and pulls the drawstrings tight. "No one but a bearer can harness the power of a Godstone. I don't know if any power remains in the old ones, but you might find them useful." He hands it over with a shrug.

I'm not ready to take it from him just yet. "And if I die? Before doing some kind of service?"

"Then I'll take them back. Along with your own stone."

It's his candor that convinces me to grab the little bag. He has frightened me with his forthrightness, but it makes me feel as though I can trust him. I shove it in the pocket of my dressing robe.

"Anything else I can do for you tonight, Highness?"

My stomach growls just then, and I flinch, embarrassed.

He chuckles. "We priests keep odd hours, and our kitchen is never closed."

So it is laden with two pomegranate scones—one in my

pocket, one in hand—that I creep back to my suite. I'm buzzing with new knowledge as I walk the quiet, torchlit corridors, nibbling on a scone: Homer's *Afflatus*, the failed bearers before me, the guardian in the guise of a nurse.

The gates of the enemy.

I went to the priest seeking an advantage, something that would help me play the game of power here in Joya d'Arena and make me significant to Alejandro. Instead, my path is more shadowy than ever.

Like a pig to the slaughter.

Now, it would be enough simply to survive.

I round the corner that leads to my suite and stop short, just quick enough to keep crumbs from getting on the rough cotton robe that looms before me.

"Elisa!" Ximena wraps me in an embrace, and I mash crumbs all over her robe anyway. She grabs my shoulders and thrusts me backward. "Where were you?" Her voice is harsh with anger and fear.

I hold up the half-eaten scone. "I was hungry."

"Oh, Elisa. My sky. I woke up and thought I'd try and finish your skirt and I went to the atrium to get everything and I couldn't hear you breathing and . . ." She takes a ragged breath. "You should have awakened me. I'd have gone with you."

My guardian.

I know that watching over me is her duty, that her passion is fueled by centuries of a religious fervor I'm only beginning to understand. But the way her eyes caress my face and the way her hands rub up and down my arms with desperate relief are testament to something deeper.

My nurse.

"I'm sorry." I reach into my pocket for the second scone, and my fingertips brush the leather pouch. It feels so huge and bulky there, and I worry that Ximena will see its shape through the fabric. "I . . . um . . . brought you a scone."

She takes it from me, a soft smile curving thin lips. "Thank you." She turns and links a companionable arm in mine to escort me back.

Ximena is tall and sturdy and strong. As we walk together, arm in arm, I lean my head against her shoulder, taking comfort in her solid familiarity.

Later that night, when I am certain Ximena again sleeps, I creep out to the balcony and bury my dead Godstones at the root of my potted palm tree.

10

DAYS later, Ximena and I are in the kitchens—avoiding the dining hall yet again—lunching on soft venison with piquant currant sauce. The kitchen master is more ragged than usual, hardly acknowledging me in his rush to get a huge batch of pollo pibil just right. I chew contentedly and watch him spice the chicken breast with garlic and cumin, then drizzle it with soured orange juice and wrap it in packets of banana leaves.

"Are we expecting guests?" I ask through a mouthful of meat.

He jumps. "It's the king's favorite. He requested it especially for tonight."

I swallow half-chewed food and wince at the lump in my chest. "You mean he's back?"

He carries packets of meat to the coals for burying. "Got back last night."

The venison weighs in my gut like a rock. Alejandro returned. And he didn't even tell me.

I drag my nurse back to our suite so I can freshen up and don my new skirt. Ximena crafted it to flow around my legs rather than stick to them like a wet blanket. I want to brush my hair, rub a little carmine onto my lips, maybe.

Cosmé is out on the balcony when we arrive. She's hanging my sheepskin rug over the edge and beating it with a wooden club. She doesn't look up as we enter, but calls out, "His Majesty came by while you were out."

"Oh?" I don't want to gratify her with too much interest.

"He wants you to attend the prince's reception tonight."

I don't know of any reception.

It's odd. I've never been one to enjoy a feast or ball or even the yearly Deliverance gala. Still, it rankles to know a celebration is being planned that I knew nothing about. I feel so disjointed and out of place. My undefined status here is partly my fault, I know. Perhaps if I dined with the rest of Alejandro's household, or showed a tiny interest in palace affairs, things would be different.

Cosmé pushes the potted palm aside to give herself more room to flip the rug. I wince, thinking of the Godstones now buried in the soft soil.

"Where will the reception be held?" I ask to distract her from the palm.

"The king said there will be an official grand entrance in the receiving hall. You're to stand on the dais with the Quorum of Five. I'll show you where to go."

Standing on a dais sounds frightfully conspicuous. "Thank you, Cosmé."

"Hmph." She curtsies, her face expressionless.

Alejandro's receiving hall shines with gaudiness. It's long and rectangular, with a high arched ceiling painted in curling roses and exaggerated thorn spikes. Chandeliers drip an even line of crystal from dais to double doors. The thrones are especially excessive with their gilded lines and plump velvet and backs that reach twice the height of a man.

The king does not rise to greet me, but he smiles and kisses my hand, and my face flames. I take my place on the dais along with the members of the Quorum, slightly behind Alejandro's throne, looking over his dark head at the milling nobility. A favored position, I assume, until I see Condesa Ariña reach out and rest a casual hand against the empty throne beside him. Her claim looks real and right somehow. Maybe because she is the only thing of true beauty in this repellent place, with her corsetless gown of simple ivory that hangs like gossamer from a gather beneath her breasts. She gazes down at the king, her eyes soft and luminous. It's the look of someone pleasantly drowsy after eating an enormous piece of mango pie.

Alejandro ignores her, just stares out across his buzzing throng of subjects.

Lord Hector is a tall pillar beside me. I feel his soft breath against my ear. "As a princess of Orovalle," he whispers, "you needn't kneel when His Highness comes through the doors."

I smile up at him gratefully.

A hush settles over the swarm, and it seems as though a wave passes through the people as bodies turn toward the towering double doors. Faintly at first, I hear the first chords of Vieira's "Entrada Triunfal." The vihuelas crescendo, the doors open.

A group of people enters, backlit and indistinct at this distance, and the multitude drops to one knee en masse. The music intensifies as they approach. A boy leads them. He's small and sulky and profoundly interested in the tassels that flutter with each step of his pertly red-dyed slippers. I fight the urge to giggle.

He makes his way forward in an approximation of a straight line. A skinny, pinched-faced woman offers encouragement by way of regular nudging. At last, he draws near enough that I can see his face clearly; little Rosario is a model of his father, with the same cinnamon eyes, the same dark, curling hair. But there is a cast to his features, something delicate in his chin and cheekbones that speaks of other blood. I wonder what Alejandro sees when he looks at his son, whether it's a shadow of himself, or a reminder of the woman he loved and lost.

A movement catches my attention. Next to the empty queen's throne, Condesa Ariña has risen from her kneeling position. She clasps her hands to her breast and gazes at the boy with such maternal longing that I want to smack her.

Rosario is nearly to the dais when Alejandro reaches out his arms. In a flash, the little boy tumbles up the steps and launches onto the king's lap. The reception hall echoes with soft amusement as they embrace. Alejandro rises, the boy's arms hooked firmly about his neck, and intones, "My son, Prince Rosario de Vega, heir to the throne of our great nation."

As the crowd roars, I try to remember if Papá ever made such a fuss over me, or even Alodia. If so, I was too young to recall. Or maybe fuss is reserved for sons.

Alejandro introduces the boy to the members of the Quorum sharing his dais: General Luz-Manuel, Condesa Ariña, Lord Hector, Conde Eduardo. At last it's my turn. Alejandro balances the boy on one knee as he twists to face me. "And this is Princess Elisa. She is here on behalf of her father, King Hitzedar of Orovalle." A simple introduction for a child.

Prince Rosario looks up from his father's lap. Such a sweet face with gentle lines, wide eyes, and spider-leg lashes. He looks me over, his eyes grow rounder, and he says in a high voice clear as monastery bells, "You're fat."

Sharp intakes of breath. Then silence, taut and heavy. Alejandro's face is frozen, and the hand clutching his son's tiny shoulder whitens. Surely the entire nobility can hear my heart beating, my every breath. For a brief moment, I consider fleeing, but even in my shocked state, I know things would be worse for me if I did.

So I do the only thing I can.

I laugh. I laugh like it's the funniest thing I've ever heard. The sound is too loud, too forced, but after a moment it doesn't matter because the dam of silence bursts and the crowd's relieved laughter joins mine.

⊹ ⊹ ⊹

The sitting cushions are absent from the dining hall that night, for there is room only for standing. Everyone mills about, pinching bits of the kitchen master's pollo pibil from blackened banana leaves and drinking sweet late-harvest wine.

Several people approach me, smiling and at ease, to chatter and inquire about my well-being. They've never taken an interest before, and I realize a barrier between us is gone, ripped away by the words of a child. I can't decide whether or not I'm glad for it.

I'm blissfully chewing on shredded chicken, savoring the tang of cumin and garlic across my tongue, when Condesa Ariña sidles next to me, wineglass in hand.

"Highness." Her voice is as high and clear as Rosario's.

"Condesa."

"Are you enjoying yourself?"

Alejandro's court eddies around us. I want to flee to my suite and bury myself in blankets. "Oh, yes. I'm having a lovely time. Prince Rosario is quite charming."

"He is." She lifts the wineglass to pink lips but only pretends to sip. Does she ever eat anything?

"And of course, the pollo pibil is excellent," I say. "Alejandro chose well. You should have some." I'm deeply satisfied by the hint of a question in her brow. Maybe she knows nothing about the king's food preferences. Maybe she doesn't like hearing me refer to him with such familiarity.

"I had some earlier. It was delicious." Of course I don't believe her. "You know," she continues, and the way she looks at me with those startling honey-gold eyes makes me feel like a mouse in a trap. "What Rosario said. In front of everyone. No one really thinks that about you."

I stare at her, a little disappointed at her lack of subtlety. I know I'm just a girl, but I expected better from her. I shrug and say, "'From the mouths of innocents flows truth . . .'"

She looks at me blankly. "Oh. You're quoting something. Everyone just adores how devout you are. I've considered studying the scriptures more. So much wisdom to be gained. If only I had more time."

It's possible that her words are a peace offering, however slight. But her benevolent gaze is too self-aware, her wineglass too full. "I highly recommend it, even for those not suited to the complexity of in-depth scriptural study."

I see the precise moment she extracts the poorly veiled insult from my words. She curtsies, graceful as always. "Well, enjoy the rest of the evening, Highness."

As she drifts away in her gossamer gown, a deep voice at my ear says, "Don't underestimate her, Princess." Startled, I look up at Lord Hector. His handsome face is very close, and as always, the wheel of thought spins beneath his placid surface. "She is more formidable, more intelligent, than she seems."

I nod, swallowing the unexpected lump in my throat as he slips away.

I continue to graze while performing the parrying dance of polite conversation. My eyes never stray far from Alejandro's lanky form. He circulates among his guests with captivating ease. After a while, I can eat no more.

The light shafts slipping through high windows narrow,

then disappear. Servants bring torches and sconce them at regular intervals along the sandstone walls. They clear the serving tables of pollo pibil and replace it with platters of iced melon and peeled grapes.

I catch a glimpse of Ximena. She leans against the wall, her face shadowed. She has been close by since the prince's grand entry, a silent companion. It would be nice to be invisible like she is, and I wonder what she has observed this night.

I follow the focus of her gaze, across the heads of over-dressed nobles to where Alejandro stands, his arm linked in Ariña's. They chat with General Luz-Manuel. The king laughs at something he says; the sound carries over the general din and makes me shiver. Ariña rises on tiptoes and kisses his cheek. He leans into the kiss.

The spicy meat churns in my stomach, telling me I'll have trouble sleeping tonight. Still, the iced melons, golden with honey glaze, are too delightful to resist. Their chilly sweetness bursts across my tongue. I eat another, and another.

I'm not sure how long I stand there, joined to the serving table as if by design. Eventually, I feel Ximena's gentle hand on my upper arm.

"Let's go, my sky."

I don't resist when she pulls me away, and I stumble after her, so full I can hardly breathe.

I lie awake a long time, unable to relax. Sharp pains shoot across my abdomen and down my legs. The food I've eaten burns in my chest. Worse, I can't stop wondering how many people watched as I consoled myself. I imagine Alejandro shaking his head at the indignity, while Ariña clings to his arm, smirking. I imagine Lord Hector turning away in disappointment.

Hot tears of shame dribble down my cheek and onto my pillow. I miss Aneaxi more than ever. She wouldn't have cared that I am unfit to be queen, that Alodia was wrong about me. She would have wrapped me in her arms and told me God was right to choose me.

I reach down for the Godstone and press my fingertips against the cool surface. It's been strangely restful all day. *I don't understand why I'm here, God. Maybe you made a mistake.*

It warms to my prayer and vibrates gently. The added sensation in my belly is too much, and I launch from the bed and dash for the atrium. There's no chance I'll make it to the garderobe at the far wall. I clutch the tiled edge of the bathing pool and heave the contents of my stomach over the rim. I retch until my nose and throat burn, until my stomach aches from the spasms.

Breathless, I slide down to the floor and lean my cheek against the blessedly cool tile of the pool. The taste in my mouth is abominable, but I feel too weak to rise. After a while, I realize the pains in my abdomen are gone.

I feel for the Godstone again. *Help me,* I plead. The stone responds, hot and sharp, but this time, it doesn't make me queasy. From desperation, I pray like I haven't prayed in weeks. I tell God about Father Nicandro and the dead Godstones buried next to my palm tree. I tell him about Condesa Ariña, Cosmé, and Lord Hector. I ask him if the Vía-Reformas who kept me in ignorance were misguided and pray for his protection should I encounter the gates of the enemy.

I ask his forgiveness for doubting him. I tell him I want Alejandro to love me.

Ximena shakes me awake some time later. I open my eyes to find my cheek pressed hard against the grout. A stabbing crick in my neck makes it hard to turn my head. Dawn's light has hit the skylight just so. It streams down in dusty orange around me. Ximena steps back, into the shadows, and I'm alone for a moment, bathed in God's radiance. I hold up my hands and watch the light play across my fingers. Warmth suffuses my body, flowing into my extremities from the soft buzz in my navel. I wriggle my toes, delighted.

"My sky." Her voice is soft and filled with wonder. "You should try to get some real sleep. In your bed. You have your first Quorum meeting this afternoon."

I had forgotten. I clamber to my feet and step reluctantly from my sunbeam, but it begins fading, or spreading, until the atrium is diffused in mere daylight.

The warm glow stays with me, pulsing like blood through my body, long after I sink into bed and drift into easy sleep.

11

I prepare carefully for my first meeting with the Five. Still a little queasy from the night before, I send Ximena to fetch a simple meal of bread and fresh fruit. I soak in the now-clean pool while I wait for her, breathing deeply.

Perhaps the Quorum is the enemy referred to in Homer's *Afflatus*. But after a night spent praying, smooshed against the tile of my atrium, I feel strangely at peace. I am God's chosen, I tell myself. The bearer.

When Ximena returns, she helps me dry and dress. She has completed a new blouse to match my skirt. It's loose fitting and shimmering red with a thick sash of black velvet. Draped over the white, ruffled skirt, it makes me feel taller, maybe even slimmer.

"Thank you, Ximena. It's beautiful." She grins at my praise, and my heart tumbles just a bit. It takes so little to make her happy.

"Black boots," she says, and I nod. I hate the boots, with their heels and pinching stays, but they'll add half a handspan to my height. I don't know what garb is appropriate for a Quorum meeting, but it's right, somehow, for me to wear the traditional dress of Orovalle. General Luz-Manuel said I would be representing my home country, and so I shall.

Ximena braids only the top section of my hair and loops it around my skull, letting the rest dry in soft curls down my back. With gentle fingers, she applies a touch of kohl to the tips of my eyelashes, a dab of carmine to my lips.

"I have some jasmine perfume," she suggests.

The scent of jasmine reminds me of home, of the creeper that wraps around the trellis in Mamá's flower garden. It also reminds me of my sister. I remember her last embrace that day in the courtyard, and the way her perfume flowed around us.

"Be smarter than Alodia," my nurse had warned.

"No, thank you, Ximena. I'd prefer the freesia."

The meeting chamber is low ceilinged and windowless, and I duck reflexively when I enter. It's like a treasure house, buried deep in the center of the palace with torchlit walls of river rock and bolted double doors. I feel the pressure of history bearing down on me, centuries of power struggles and hushed meetings, secret assignations and war councils.

We sit on cushions of red velvet that surround a huge oaken table, low to the ground and worn smooth by countless fingers and elbows. Alejandro folds his legs and sits proud at the head. I'm sure it's no accident that he's framed by the golden crown seal emblazoned on the tapestry behind him. I'm on his right, the guest of honor. General Luz-Manuel sulks across from me on Alejandro's left. Next to him, Lord Hector gives me a wink of encouragement.

Condesa Ariña glides in just as everyone else has settled, smiling apology. She is tightly corseted and beautiful, with shining hair and a silk gown of soft green that flutters with each step. It's hard to look away from the tiny curve of her waist.

Conde Eduardo, a thickset man with black hair trimmed in gray, calls the meeting to order. To my delight, he quotes the *Scriptura Sancta.* "'Wherever five are gathered, there am I in their midst.'" Five. The holy number of perfection.

He introduces me formally—a redundant gesture, but it makes me feel welcome—and the meeting of the Quorum of Five begins.

The first topic is construction of Puerto Verde's shipyard. I force myself to pay attention to the tedious details of acquiring timber and builders, of devising a system to charge merchants and traders for berth.

Alodia would jump right in with cleverly phrased opinions and flattering manipulation, but I am not Alodia. Instead, I listen for the ebb and flow of emotion in their words, mentally cataloguing when certain matters incite passion or indifference. Conde Eduardo has a vested interest in the lumber trade, though he says nothing of his holdings, and General Luz-Manuel would dearly love to leave Brisadulce for a post elsewhere.

At last we segue into matters of war. Conde Eduardo waves a parchment at us, the broken seal a bright splash of red. "We have yet another request from Conde Treviño to send troops into the hill country. He says their situation is tenuous, that thousands of the enemy are pouring from the Sierra Sangre into the foothills."

Ariña's face goes blank at his words, her brow smooth as butter.

I'm suddenly very alert, very interested.

Alejandro leans forward, and his elbow almost touches mine. "Any casualties?"

Eduardo shakes his head. "As yet, none. But several sheep have gone missing, and the nearest encampment is a mere day's journey from the outer villages."

General Luz-Manuel's fist cracks the table. "Majesty! We cannot wait for the enemy to strike. Every moment we delay allows Invierne to gain strength."

A chorus of mutterings. Alejandro stares straight ahead at nothing; Ariña shifts on her cushion and looks down at her lap. This discussion seems to be familiar territory for the Quorum, with painful, predictable results.

Conde Eduardo takes a controlling breath. "We cannot engage," he says in a clipped voice, "until we know their intent. Would you have us attack blindly?"

"It must be so convenient for you," Ariña snaps, "to plan my war from your seaside holdings on the other side of the desert."

"Your war?" Eduardo scoffs.

"My people. My land. My war." I'm surprised at the steel in her voice. I'm more surprised to find she's from the hill country across the desert. I'd thought her sea bred, with her light skin and golden eyes.

The general watches me from across the table. "Perhaps our representative from Orovalle has something to say about this." He smiles at me indulgently, as if to a small child.

The air is suddenly hot, the chamber walls so near. I inhale slowly through my nose, feeling the heaviness of Alejandro's gaze. Lord Hector nods, almost imperceptibly.

I begin slowly. "In Orovalle, our biggest concern is our complete ignorance of Invierne's aim." Affirming nods all around. "Invierne's ambassador campaigned for port rights in my father's court for three years, but never disclosed his country's purpose, other than to make vague mention of trading. Last year, the ambassador left in the dead of night without saying a word. Given the history between our countries, we've anticipated war ever since."

"It was the same here, " Alejandro says softly. It's disconcerting to see the fear in his eyes. Looking at him now, I find it unsurprising that he froze in panic during our fight against the jungle Perditos.

My gaze lingers on him as I say, "But why? Why do they need a seaport so desperately? And why were they not forthcoming about the details? The *Belleza Guerra* devotes lengthy passages to understanding one's enemy. I think it should be our highest priority."

"No one is going to contest that," Ariña says. "But my people don't have time for us to educate ourselves about the enemy. They need help now."

She is right, of course.

Tears shimmer in her eyes. "I'm tired of waiting, waiting,

waiting for Invierne to strike. Why not take the war to them? Drive them out once and for all."

But she's terribly mistaken about that.

Lord Hector gazes at me steadily, measuring me with that enigmatic mind of his. "You disagree, Highness." A statement, not a question.

I know my next words will ensure Ariña's everlasting enmity, but I must say them anyway. "I do. I disagree."

"There!" cries Conde Eduardo. "Even the princess advises caution."

My eyes narrow before I think to school my expression. "Your pardon, my lord, but I'm quite sure I've advised nothing as yet." Lord Hector's brief nod encourages me to continue. "I think we should let Invierne come to us."

"Why?" Alejandro asks. His face is intent, but with interest rather than challenge.

My husband values my counsel. It's exhilarating. I say, "Our army will not fare as well in the hills. Three hundred fifty years ago, my country routed Invierne in the Battle of Baraxil, in large part because the hot jungle was unfamiliar to the enemy. Why give them the advantage? We should force them to fight in shale and sand and heat, instead of the forested mountains they're accustomed to." I warm to the topic, gaining confidence with each word. "If Invierne brings the war to us, they'll provision their army long distance. That means guarding their backs. Leaving a vulnerable supply train. It makes them weaker. They want a seaport. I say, make them spend the resources to come and get it. The desert nomads will know how to avoid them. We make our stand here, in Brisadulce. We use the time to prepare. We build layers of fortifications extending outward, into the desert. We set traps—"

"And what about my people?" Ariña's voice is dangerously level.

I regard her steadily, certain of my logic. "Give them the order to evacuate."

Her body is tighter than a vihuela string. I half expect her to launch at me from across the table. "You expect them to give up their homes. Their livelihoods."

I nod. "Until that territory is clear, yes." I turn to Alejandro. "If you allow the hill country to be your war front, you risk *all* of Joya d'Arena."

Lord Hector's warning about Ariña being more formidable than she appears echoes in my mind, but Alejandro looks at me with such gratitude. Hope, even. I realize I've said exactly what he wished I would.

"Do you think," says General Luz-Manuel, "that your father, King Hitzedar, would be willing to lend troops?"

Alejandro stiffens but says nothing.

I'm not sure how to respond. According to Alodia's letter, Papá has already committed troops as a condition of our marriage, but it is clear the king has not shared this arrangement with even his top general. I search Alejandro's face for a clue, but find nothing.

"I think it likely," I say finally. "Invierne is our enemy too. I'd be glad to speak to him on your behalf."

Alejandro's brow relaxes. He nods, just slightly, but I don't know what it means. *Well done.* Or perhaps, *We'll talk later.*

From across the huge table, Ariña glowers. She looks back and forth between the king and me, trying to understand our exchange. After a moment, she settles back on her cushion, eyes narrowed. For some reason, I don't think the hill villages are forefront in her mind.

The king sends for a map of the city, and the tiny chamber grows thickly hot as we discuss fortifications and provisioning. Alejandro speaks with a marked lack of resolve that aggravates Eduardo and the general. He wants to know how we would establish our perimeter *if* we let Invierne come. How we would store foodstuff for the city *if* there were a siege. I wish he would commit to a course of action.

At last, Conde Eduardo stands and stretches. "You'll have to excuse me, Majesty. Our meeting has gone overlong, and I am expected elsewhere."

Alejandro looks up from the map. "Of course, Eduardo. Thank you for your counsel today."

As the conde takes his leave, Lord Hector bends toward the king's ear. "Majesty. The prince is waiting for you by now."

Alejandro's eyes widen. "Oh." We look at him questioningly and get a jumpy smile in return. "I promised the boy I'd take him into the city today." He puts his hand to his chin and rubs. "Hector, would you mind taking him for me? Tell him I got detained in a meeting?"

The guard's face is stony, but he nods and rises from his cushion.

"Lord Hector," I say, quickly before Ariña can react. "I was planning a trip into the city today, anyway." It's not true, of course, but I can't let the opportunity pass. I force a laugh. "Here more than a month, and I've yet to have a proper tour! I'd be happy to take Rosario with me."

The king brightens. "Thank you, Elisa. I'd appreciate it. Lord Hector will accompany you." He winks at me; my chest goes hot. "Let's give Lady Ximena the afternoon off, shall we?"

I nod, unable to speak. Lord Hector heads for the door. As I stagger to my feet to follow, Ariña turns to Alejandro, confusion and hurt on her face, as if she suspects there is something between us.

The king ignores her, bows over the map again, asking General Luz-Manuel where he'd like to station bowmen *if* Invierne makes it all the way to the city walls. I know, like I know my own name, that Alejandro has not told his mistress about his wife.

Ximena is delighted to have some free time. After assuring herself of my commitment to caution and giving Lord Hector a portentous look, she hurries off to the monastery to immerse herself in decaying documents.

The guard escorts me to Rosario's suite on the next level. It's a short walk. Still, I regret my offer when my stiff legs contend with the stairs.

The pinched-face woman opens the door and scowls. "Where's the king?" She peers into the corridor and looks each way.

"His Majesty will be unable to accompany His Highness on

today's outing," Lord Hector says. His voice is even lower than usual, his syllables crisp. "Her Highness, the princess Elisa, will be going in his stead."

She looks me up and down, then calls inside, "Rosario, dear. Time for your outing."

Moments later, a dark head thrusts around her narrow hips into the doorway. Rosario's brown eyes are huge with hope, but when he sees me, his face melts into disappointment. "Where's Papá?"

"Your Papá is doing something very important for the kingdom," I tell him. I know nothing about children, but I soldier on. "I'm going into the city today, and you may come with me."

He narrows his eyes and his bottom lip sticks out. "Get Papá," he snaps.

I wait for the woman—I assume she's his nurse—to correct his behavior. I wouldn't have been allowed to speak to someone that way, even at six years old. But she just pats his head, waiting for my response.

So I respond as a mistress to a servant; it's the only way I know how. "Rosario, you will address me as 'Your Highness.' You will not command me in anything. Rather, you will ask politely and with deep respect. Is that clear?"

His nurse pulls him close and stares at me in defiance. "He is barely six years old. You can't expect—"

"You are dismissed."

Her jaw twitches. She opens her mouth to protest, but Lord Hector's glare makes her think better of it. After a quick curtsy, she flees.

Rosario stands alone, dwarfed by the wood frame doorway, his brown eyes enormous.

I can't help but smile. "Do you like coconut pie?"

"Yes," he whispers. "And coconut milk."

"Yes, what?"

"Yes . . . Your Highness."

"Me too. I eat it as often as I can. And I've heard the very best coconut pie is right here, in Brisadulce. I'd really like to find some."

He nods solemnly. "Is that why you're so fat?"

I'm not sure why his observation doesn't bother me this time. Maybe it's the innocent delivery. Or maybe it's because I finally realize I'm not the only person in this place to suffer the king's neglect.

I grin at him with genuine cheer. "Yes. That's definitely part of it." I reach out my hand. "Want some pie?"

He grasps it, shyly, and I'm surprised at how sweet and warm his fingers feel in mine.

12

ALODIA visited Brisadulce once before and returned with descriptions of sparkling buildings and exotic people. As we meander through the merchants' market south of Alejandro's palace, I realize her account was much exaggerated. Houses and shops certainly sparkle, for they are mostly of sandstone with a smattering of adobe. But it's hard to breathe in their tall, constricted shadow. The city was built around a seaside oasis, but we see little of it as we wander outside the palace walls, blocks from the ocean. Still, the people of Brisadulce exude a unique vivacity, in spite of the dry heat and dusty streets. I see it in the coconut seller who cheerfully chucks his wares at the heads of scampering children, in the laundress who accepts five full loads from different patrons and promises to have them back, pressed, the next day. It's a city of people who aren't afraid to greet strangers in the street, who laugh at every opportunity.

It's nearly a perfect afternoon. Hector is again enlightening company, with an admirable grasp of history and detail. I could wander the city with him for hours, in spite of my aching legs.

But little Rosario is a demon child. He flits here and there, interested in everything he notices for the space of a breath. We find coconut pie at a teetering booth of sweets, but even this cannot hold his attention. After a few bites, he tears off after a scrawny creature of dubious canine origin, the remaining pie a forgotten, whitish lump in the sand.

His behavior is not only maddening, it's dangerous. Though we wear simple clothes without identifying marks, we cannot risk losing the heir to Joya's throne to his own scampering abandon. I shudder to consider Alejandro's reaction should something happen to the boy.

When Hector pulls him, thrashing, from a nearby alley, I make a great show of reluctance at having to cut our outing short. The prince glowers at me, but I remain firm.

When I was younger, I used to yearn for a little brother or sister, someone I could take charge of the way Alodia did me. I told myself I would be a good big sister, not like her at all. But now I wonder if I was as exasperating to her as this young boy is to me.

"I'm thirsty," Rosario says as I grasp his hand again, determined to hold tight.

"I'm sure we can find some water."

"I want coconut milk."

"I don't believe that is the correct address."

He expels a frustrated breath. "Could I have some coconut milk? Your Highness?"

I remember what Ximena used to tell me every time I asked

for a pastry. "If you behave, I will bring you coconut milk myself. But if you don't behave, no milk." I imagine I'll join him for a cupful. I love the way the kitchen master stirs in a bit of honey and cinnamon and chills it in the cellar.

But Rosario does not behave. He slips my grip twice, and I send a prayer of gratitude for Lord Hector, who nabs the boy each time.

At last we come to the palace via the side entrance, and I place myself on Rosario's left, a bodily barrier between him and his milk. Sure enough, just as the arched entrance to the kitchens comes into view, Rosario begins to lag behind. Just a little.

He tries to pull away, but I grip tighter.

"Milk!"

"No."

"Coconut milk!"

I squat down and look him in the eye. He looks so much like Alejandro, with black hair that curls at the nape and brown eyes with red tints like rich mahogany. But where Alejandro has smile lines and lips that always laugh, Rosario is angry and unpredictable as a coiled cobra. It saddens me. He is too young to be so fiercely desperate.

"I promised you there would be no milk if you misbehaved. I always keep my promises."

He glares at me. I glare back. At my side, I feel the quiet, comforting weight of Lord Hector's approval.

"Papá doesn't keep promises."

"I do."

Suddenly the prince's face flows into soft, cherubic lines, and his hand in mine relaxes. But I see the telltale twitchings in those devious pupils, and I relax my grip not at all as we walk the interminable corridor to his suite.

His nurse is there when we arrive, changing the sheets on his bed. She gives me a wary glance when we open the door.

Prince Rosario gazes up at me. "Will you come see me again? Your Highness?"

I raise my brows. "Will you try to behave?"

He nods emphatically.

"Then yes. I think we should have another outing sometime soon."

He grins. "Promise?"

"I promise." The entire day was such a struggle. I find it hard to believe he would desire a recurrence. I'm not sure *I* do.

But his smile is like the sun rising huge and bright over the Sierra Sangre. All of a sudden he lunges forward and wraps his arms around my hips. I pat his head, awkwardly, while Lord Hector's mustache twitches. When at last he disengages, I feel strangely empty and cold.

I give his nurse strict orders to refuse any requests for coconut milk, but I don't feel I can trust her. After the door closes, I turn to Lord Hector.

"My lord, would you mind doing me a favor?"

"Ask."

"Could you stop in the kitchens? The staff should know about the terrible nausea His Highness suffered today. Naturally, all requests for coconut milk should be met with water and mild tea." Maybe I'm being too hard on the boy. And it feels unfair to forbid him something that I myself learned to find comfort in when I was about his age.

"Of course, Highness. You've made a powerful friend today, Highness."

I'm not sure if he refers to himself or Rosario. "Elisa," I say, exasperated. "Please call me Elisa. 'Highness' is for errant servants and lonely children."

At last he grins, true and real, and the sorrow lines in his face transform into undeniable proof that the man laughs on occasion. He offers me his very large, very muscled arm and escorts me back to my suite.

Cosmé is using my bed for temporary laundry storage when I arrive. I stand for a moment in the doorway, footsore, watching her. Such deft fingers slide across the fabric in a whipping motion, folds appearing beneath them as if by magic. I recognize one of my curtains, the golden gauze ashine with cleanness, tossed haphazardly across one corner of the bed. Bath towels, all variations on a blue theme, lie neatly stacked nearby. So much work to keep my suite beautiful. I hadn't even realized the curtain needed washing.

Cosmé hums while she works, a cheery hymn I recognize from last week's services. It's strange to see her so unguarded. For the first time, I realize the stoic expression I see every day is not the natural one. I watch her for a long time, trying to understand this other Cosmé, to puzzle out how a maid could feel more warmth for a bath towel than for a princess.

But then, it's not my goal to be popular with Ariña's maid.

"Ximena has not yet returned?"

She jumps; a towel flutters to the stone. "I'm sorry, Highness. You startled me." Her face is blandly beautiful once again.

"I'm sure the towel is uninjured. My nurse?"

"Stopped by to get some supplies, then went to visit Father Nicandro in the monastery."

I can't help but smile. "She used to be a scribe."

Her black eyes open wide. "Lady Ximena?"

I'm wickedly pleased to surprise her, and I want to brag about Ximena. I want to tell this pert girl that my nurse is one of the smartest, most educated people I've ever met, that she can kill a man with nothing but a hairpin. Of course, I say nothing.

"I don't think Ximena expected you back for some time," she says, needing to fill the silent space.

I sigh and lean against a bedpost. "His Royal Unruliness proved difficult. We've returned well before dinnertime, yet I am exhausted."

Cosmé steps forward in that gliding way of hers. "Since Ximena is gone, I'll help you change. Then I can draw a bath if you like."

It takes a split second for my tired, fuzzy head to realize she's reaching for the thin sash at my waist. I take a panicked, violent step backward, but it is too late. I've already felt her clever fingers glance across malleable flesh to obstinate stone.

Though I've stepped away, her arm remains raised, and she stares at her fingertips like they are ugly, foreign things that suddenly attached to her wrist by chance. When she finally looks up to meet my gaze, tears stream down her face.

"You!" she whispers. Her lips curl in disgust. "How can it be *you*?"

The gem flashes hot in my abdomen. Nausea worms beneath it.

Cosmé shakes her head and mutters. "It makes no sense. No sense at all. Maybe it's a mistake." She wipes at tears with the backs of her knuckles.

"Cosmé."

"It can't be you. It can't be. The bearer is supposed to be—"

"Cosmé!" She goes silent and studies me: my face, my hands, especially my stomach. I see the exact moment when she remembers herself again. A flicker of horror, followed by her usual veil of calm.

"May I be dismissed?" Her face may be calm, but her voice is still tight.

"No." I step toward her. "Cosmé, you must tell no one about this."

"Of course not, Your Highness. A good lady's maid is always discreet."

"Yes, I'm sure." I smile humorlessly. It is, I hope, a decent approximation of the dangerous smile I've seen Alodia wear to good advantage. "I shall strive to be clearer. Not too long ago, someone—a seasoned warrior—discovered the stone I carry. Moments later, Ximena killed him with nothing but a hairpin." I feel the smile turn more dangerous. No longer Alodia's but fully my own, because I get to brag about my nurse after all.

I don't dismiss the maid until I'm sure I detect understanding in her eyes.

⁜ ⁜ ⁜

I do not tell Ximena about the exchange with Cosmé. Though I hold no affection for the maid, I've no wish to see her die. Still, she reacted with such passion to discovering the stone. I need to tell someone. Maybe Father Nicandro. I resolve to seek him out tomorrow.

We begin our nightly routine. Ximena brings me a glass of chilled wine and a candle for my dressing table, then unbraids my hair while I sit, reading from the *Scriptura Sancta*. The lyrical quality of the language, the calming truth in the words, usually lull me into dream-readiness. But not tonight. The swirling script blurs on the page, becoming dark, probing eyes. Alejandro's eyes. I remember the way he looked at me during council, the way the lines of his face softened as he studied me. Ariña noticed, too.

I close the *Scriptura*. "Ximena."

"Yes, my sky?"

"I want to look . . . nice. Tonight."

I catch a hint of her smile in the mirror. "You think he will visit?"

"Maybe." I do think he will. But I'm afraid to say it, as if saying it would make it not happen, and then she would know how disappointed I was.

"Well, just in case, then." Her thumb caresses my jawline.

My hair, free of the braids, falls crimped past my waist. Ximena pulls some of it back from my forehead and fastens it loosely with a pearl comb. It makes my face look longer, thinner, and my eyes are suddenly noticeable. My nurse dabs a bit of carmine on my lips. She picks up the kohl but changes her mind. "No need," she mutters. I'm not sure I agree.

Ximena helps me into my nightgown. She chooses a fawn-colored silk that warms the brown of my eyes and makes my skin glow. I stand before the mirror for a moment, half in approval, half in despair. I'll never be dainty or fair or beautiful like Ariña. Even now, stretching as tall as I can, my stomach and breasts swell against the fabric. But my dark skin is unusual, uniquely me, and my hair shimmers.

This is Lucero-Elisa, I think to myself. *Bearer of the Godstone.*

Ximena reaches forward and loosens the ties of my neckline a little. Just enough to draw attention. Then I climb into my huge bed, where she arranges the blankets around me, drapes my hair across my shoulders, and hands me the *Scriptura* so I can pretend to read while I wait for Alejandro to knock.

I wait for a very long time, heart pounding in my throat, feeling foolish. I'm glad Cosmé does not attend me in the evenings, that only Ximena will know I took such pains. After a while, I give up reading and pray instead, and the Godstone sends massaging fingers of warmth in response. I doze.

He knocks.

I jump, confused for a moment. The candle has burned halfway down, and a dollop of wax has cooled on my nightstand. On the second knock, I call for him to enter. As the knob turns, I worry that I might have drool on my cheek, that my gown has fallen too low, but I forget such things as soon as I see his face.

"I hope I'm not too late," he whispers. "General Luz-Manuel kept me almost all day."

"No, of course not. I was just—" The *Scriptura Sancta* lies skewed to the side, one corner floating over the edge of my bed. I giggle. "I guess I fell asleep reading."

Alejandro settles before me on the bed. He is tall enough to climb up without the stool. "You have always been so devout?"

I shrug. "I've been studying the sacred texts since I was a little girl." All but Homer's *Afflatus*, anyway. "Seemed necessary, bearing the Godstone." Yet it has not been enough. God remains inscrutable to me, and I feel no closer to my divine appointment with heroism than the day he stuck the thing in my navel sixteen years ago.

He reaches forward and grasps my hand. His thumb sweeps gently across my knuckles and my whole arm tingles. It is always so hard to breathe when he is near.

"Elisa." His voice is lower than usual. "Thank you for your help with Rosario today. It gave me the opportunity to take care of some very important things." He smiles, his eyelids heavy with exhaustion. "My son adores you."

Thinking of the little brat helps me find my voice. "I'm not sure about that."

"He spoke of nothing but you tonight."

"He did?"

"He did."

"Well, I like him too." It's true, oddly.

"You'll make a great queen."

My mouth opens. I stare at him like a dead rock cod.

He just nods, oblivious to my surprise. "I'll announce our engagement soon." He leans forward and kisses me on the cheek, lingering a moment. His lips are warm, slightly moist. I wish he would move them lower, toward my lips.

I mutter unintelligible politeness as he takes his leave, then I watch his long legs patter away. The door to Alejandro's suite closes and the lock clicks before I truly realize what he said.

Engagement.

He doesn't intend to tell the people of Joya d'Arena that we are already married.

I have been strong three times today, holding my ground with the Quorum, with Rosario, with Cosmé. But with Alejandro, I always dissolve into a pool of weak helplessness. He is a good man, I'm sure of it. And so beautiful as to be dazzling. But I don't like the person I am when I'm around him.

I am sick of being treated like a child. Weary of secrets. Disgusted with myself for letting it all happen. Anger begins to boil inside me, and it makes me feel daring. Daring enough to call out, "Ximena!"

She rushes through the atrium, her bun in disarray. "What is it? Are you all right?"

"Ximena, what am I in danger from? Why am I safer here than in Orovalle?"

She leans into the archway, her shoulders slumped. I see conflict on her face—the furrowed brow, lips pressed into a thin line. Her Vía-Reforma beliefs make it difficult to discuss the Godstone with me. But she wants to. I know she does.

I say, softly, "Don't you think I would be safer if I knew what I was facing?"

Her features settle into resignation, and she takes a deep

breath. "There were . . . incidents. Most recently, your taster. She died. Poisoned."

"My taster? When?"

"A few months before you married the king."

"I had a taster?"

She says nothing.

My heart thumps wildly. Someone tried to kill me. "Because I am a princess? Or because I am the bearer?"

"There was nothing to be gained by the death of the second princess. Unless someone wanted to leave the ascendancy open. But there were no attempts on your sister's life."

"I had a taster." Someone risked her life every day for me. Died for me. Someone I never knew. "No wonder you were always so incensed when Aneaxi and I sneaked down to the kitchens."

"Yes. Surely you noticed how she always fetched the food and served you herself? That's because, during those late-night forays, Aneaxi had to taste instead."

I can't breathe for the sudden weight on my chest. Ximena hurries to the bedside, wraps me in her arms. "I'm so sorry, my sky. We all wanted to keep this from you, give you as normal an upbringing as possible. You are safer here, where few follow God's path and most never learn the name of the bearer."

"Why? Why would bearing the Godstone make someone want to kill me?"

Her hands rub up and down my upper arms. "Oh, lots of reasons. Because you are a political symbol, even to those who don't believe in God's power. Because religious zealotry makes some people do strange things."

She should know.

"And, to be perfectly frank, because your flawless stone, ripped from your dead body, would fetch an astonishing price on the black market."

I gasp, as stunned by her bluntness as I am the crude idea that the Godstone could be an ordinary object of commerce.

"Oh, my sky, I never wanted to frighten you this way, but you see now why you must be cautious, yes? Please tell me you understand."

I choke out the words. "I understand."

It is a long time before I'm ready to snuff the candles and close my eyes.

I'm not sure what awakens me. Ximena left the door to the balcony open at my request, and the light breeze flutters the curtains. But the whipping sound is gentle, nothing I don't usually sleep through. It is mostly dark, for there is no moon. I see the barest outlines of my dressing table and bedposts in the coppery glow that seeps into my chamber from a city that never quite sleeps.

I smell cinnamon, sharp and sweet. It's strong enough that my nose tickles. I sense a human presence in the dimness, and I think it's Ximena until a rough cloth covers my mouth. I try to jerk my head to the side, but the cloth is heavy and grips my face. This is what Ximena warned me of, what everyone feared. I need to scream, to alert my nurse.

"Unnng!" I manage through my nose. The effort expends all the air in my lungs, and my heartbeat fills the empty space.

Tears trickle from the corners of my eyes, and I'm dizzy with the need to breathe. I suck air right through the cloth in spite of the hand holding it there. I feel a moment of victory, knowing the attempt at suffocation will fail. Maybe if I kick my bedposts, or twist around . . . but the cinnamon scent becomes tiny prickles in my throat, in my chest. My head whirls; I'm sinking farther and farther into my mattress. Something closes around me, something darker than mere dimness and hotter than desert summer. The copper glow from my balcony winks out.

I'm rocking from side to side, gently. My arms are pinned tight, swaddled like a child's. Or maybe I'm in a coffin. My eyelids flutter, but they are stuck together and crusty. I can't force them open. After a moment, I don't even try, because I sense that the glare would be too harsh. I always imagined the afterworld would be a bright place, but without the desert heat. Without the taste in my mouth of meat gone sour.

I hear conversation. Easy, comfortable, mundane. Something about stopping to rest, about our water supply, a joke about camels that I don't understand though everyone laughs. One of the voices is feminine and familiar. I can't place it, but muddled recognition clamps my teeth tightly together.

"The princess will awaken soon," someone says.

"We are too far away for it to matter," responds the familiar voice.

I try to squirm or cry out or kick something, but my body won't obey. Desperation swells my lungs, hot and thick. *You can't take me away*, I sob, somewhere deep inside the unresponsive carcass that is my body. *You can't! Alejandro is finally going to marry me.*

Someone mutters something about an oasis, and the voices break into laughter again. It has a giddy ring to it, a ring of triumph.

PART II

13

I don't know how much time has passed. My awareness is strange, full of heat and shimmering, and I cannot tell whether I'm awake or dreaming. Perhaps I float along in the bizarre vividness that divides the two.

Darkness slides over me like a curtain, blessedly cool against my eyelids. All at once, the gentle rocking motion stops. I hear murmurings. Gradually they crystallize into voices: a woman, two men. "We'll need to feed her soon. No, I don't know when she last ate. Yes, you're right, water first." My stomach aches with emptiness, but any thought of food sends curls of nausea through my stomach and dry phlegm to the back of my throat.

A hand caresses my cheek, large and warm. Gentle.

"Are you hungry, Princess?" A young, male voice. Very close. He holds the syllables back in his throat, then springs off of them in the lilt of the desert people.

I strain to open my eyes, but something seals them shut.

"Ah, poor thing. Let me . . ." Cool, dripping cloth smoothes across my eyelids. I realize I'm desperately thirsty. My eyes flutter open.

I gasp, for his face is only a handspan above mine. I notice his eyes first, huge and glimmering brown like polished breadnuts. They are framed by more hair than I've ever seen on a boy. It parts in the middle and hangs in black waves well past his shoulders. Soft stubble can't hide his youthfulness. It's a pleasant face.

The face of my captor, I remind myself. "What do you want?" My tongue is thick in my mouth, like a dry pillow, and the words sound muffled and round.

"We want *you*, Princess." He stands and steps out of my vision, revealing a ceiling of strange fabric held in place by wooden posts. It's dense like wool, but variegated and rough as unfinished parchment.

He returns with a wooden cup. He reaches under my shoulders and lifts me easily with one broad hand. With the other, he puts the edge of the cup to my lips.

"Drink. If this settles well, we'll try some food." The water is warm and bitter, but I slurp it eagerly. The cup empties too quickly, and he lowers me back. "Now we wait a bit." He settles back, like a stray dog on his haunches, and looks me over with interest.

"Who are you?" I ask, and my voice works better this time, though it wavers with fear. I hope Ximena is all right. I hope Alejandro is searching for me.

My captor smiles shyly, and his teeth are shocking white

against dark desert skin. "I'm Humberto," he says. "Traveling escort, by profession."

I try to shift onto my side to see him better, but my body is stiff and my hips won't obey. "Humberto. Why can't I move?"

"Oh, that's the duerma leaf. You breathed in a good lot of it. It will go away in a day or two."

A day or two? "How long have I— That is, how long since you *kidnapped* me?" I'm gratified to see him wince.

His smile disappears. "Awhile, Princess. Long enough."

"The king will find me."

"He will look," he says solemnly, then changes the subject. "You have nice eyes. Very pretty."

I close those eyes tight. Even so, tears squeeze from the outside corners and dribble down my cheeks.

"Oh, Princess, I'm so sorry. I hope I didn't say anything . . . And you'll be treated well, I swear!"

I open my eyes. The concern in his face is plain, even through tear-blurred vision. "What do you want? Why did you take me?"

He shifts uncomfortably. "We'll talk about that later. Hungry yet?"

"A little."

"Wonderful!" He launches to his feet. "I'll be back."

I'm left alone to stare at the strange ceiling, finally understanding that I'm in a tent. Thick blankets swaddle me, pinning my arms to my sides. By the smell, I guess they're made of goat hair. My exposed face and neck are chilly, the drying tears on my cheeks icy.

Muffled voices trickle in from outside. Three at least. My enemy must be powerful, or at least very clever, to sneak into the royal wing of Alejandro's palace and then escape with an enormous bundle of a person.

My enemy. I remember the words of Homer's *Afflatus* about the enemy's gates. About the realm of sorcery.

I hear the flap of heavy fabric followed by shuffling footsteps, and Humberto hovers over me again. He puts the cup of meaty broth to my lips, and I sniff it suspiciously.

"It's not poisoned," he says. "If we wanted to poison you, we could have done so when we dosed you with duerma leaf."

"Taste it for me."

He shrugs and tips the cup against his mouth. I watch closely to make sure he ingests a good bit.

When he returns the cup to my lips, I sip eagerly. It's delicious and hot, with an unfamiliar, gamey meat spiced with garlic and green onions. He pulls the cup away to let me swallow and catch my breath.

"Thank you. What is it?"

"My sister makes the best jerboa soup in Joya."

"Jerboa?"

"Little sand rat." He makes a tight fist. "About so big."

I recoil into my blankets. "I'm sipping rat soup?"

He laughs. "Well, jerboas are very different creatures, really. Cleaner, for one. A lot more appealing too, with nice tawny fur and tufted tails."

I am not reassured.

"Ready for more?"

Though he said I would be well treated, I am certain of nothing and cannot know when next I'll eat. I force myself to slurp the rest.

When I finish, Humberto stretches. "Try to sleep, Princess. We leave in the morning." Leave and go where? But he is gone, the torch with him, before I can ask my question, leaving me alone in the frigid dark.

I have never felt so frightened and powerless. Closing my eyes again is a relief. In spite of everything, I drift into natural sleep.

I'm awakened by an intense need to relieve myself. Golden light and pleasant warmth creep into my tent, but the pressure in my lower abdomen is ferocious. I flex my toes and bend my knees to test them. They're heavy and weak, but they do respond. Quietly, I wriggle my arms from their stiff swaddling.

A light wind batters the tent walls, but I hear no voices, no movement outside. Nothing ties me down. Perhaps they didn't expect the duerma leaf to wear off so soon. Just maybe, I can escape.

I twist away from the goat-hair blankets and clamber to my feet, then I freeze for a moment, listening. Nothing. I tiptoe across canvaslike material to the tent flap and put my hand to the light-edged crack. I hesitate, realizing I'm still clad in my nightgown and bed slippers. But I cannot afford time for modesty. My heart patters as I peel aside the fabric.

Light blinds me. I turn my face to the side and wait for my

vision to adjust. It does, slowly, as a hot breeze ruffles hair that has escaped Ximena's clip. I step outside, into fine sand that warms my feet even through my slippers.

Another step, and I know, definitively, that there will be no escape. I hug myself, sickened by hopelessness and feeling very tiny. The swooping dunes of Joya's desert are everywhere, in every direction, burnished red in the shadowed side, bright like molten gold in the sunrise, to the very edge of the world. The breeze stirs little eddies along the top sides, and I see how fluid this place is, how unpredictable and dangerous. The sun is at my back, already merciless. I stand on a rise such that my shadow stretches into the distance, curling and plunging across the scalloped sand.

"Going somewhere, Highness?"

I jump at her mocking voice. It's the familiar one I couldn't place while fighting my duerma-leaf coma. I close my eyes and take a deep, controlling breath before turning to face her.

"Hello, Cosmé."

She stands straight, arms crossed, short hair curling and loose in the desert breeze. Her black eyes and delicate features are the same, but she seems different without the maid's apron and cap. Or maybe it's because her stoicism has been replaced by open hostility.

"It's so nice to see you," I lie. "I hope you're well."

"I see the duerma leaf is wearing off quickly."

"What did you do to Ximena? Did you kill her to steal me away?"

She shifts in the sand, a tiny crack in her callous bearing, perhaps. "Your nurse is fine. I put a pinch of duerma leaf in her tea so she would sleep soundly; that is all."

The relief is overpowering, but I will not cry in front of Cosmé. The only weapon I have right now is unpredictability, so I shower her with polite respect. "Thank you. And thank you for the soup last night."

Her brows furrow in annoyance. "Don't thank me. My brother has taken a liking to you and insists we treat you well, so thank him."

"Humberto is your brother?" I can't imagine how two such different people could come from the same blood. Though looking at her now, I see they share the same curling black hair, the same cast to brow and nose.

She doesn't deign to answer. "I have traveling clothes for you. We must set off right away. Humberto will teach you to pack your tent. You'll be responsible for it from now on. Also"—she gives me a disgusted look—"if I catch you stealing food or water from the stores, I will kill you, understand?"

I nod coolly, though my pulse is a drum at my temples, and say, "You have nothing to worry about. I'm not the kind who sneaks around in the night taking things that don't belong to me."

Her face twitches. "Just get dressed." She whirls and marches away before I can ask her where we're going.

It was foolish to aggravate someone who just threatened to kill me. I will have to be so much wiser if I am to survive whatever is to come.

The pressure to relieve myself is fierce. I take a deep breath to still my panicked heart, then I trudge through the sand, looking for Humberto.

We break camp quickly. Besides myself, Cosmé, and Humberto, there are three other boys about my age, who regard me guiltily every time they pass. My maid—my former maid—hands me a pile of clothing, leaving Humberto to explain how everything is worn. It's light in color and thickly woven. A shawl goes over my head to protect me from the sun. Ties tickle my left cheek, and I resist the urge to scratch. Humberto explains that I can tie my shawl around my face if the wind picks up, to keep the sand out.

The most important item is a pair of stiff boots. "Sand and shale will wear through an ordinary pair of boots in days," he explains. These are stiffly soled and knee high, with chaps made of camel hair that wrap around several times. Humberto shows me how to tuck the edges in below my knees and fasten them with ties. "It's the season for sandstorms," he says. "And the sand is most violent near the ground. I know they're hot, but they'll protect your legs."

Sandstorms. I remember Hector telling me about them as we gazed from a place of safety over distant dunes. He told me they could flay a man's skin from his bones.

What has made these people so desperate that they would risk the desert during sandstorm season?

We leave the packhorses behind with one of the young men and set off walking, while two camels carry our tents and our food and water. I stare after the man who rides in the opposite direction. There is a way out of this desert, for those who know it.

"He'll be fine," Humberto says. "He's a traveling escort, like me."

"Why can't we ride horses?" Horses have always frightened me, but riding would be better than slogging through sand on foot.

He nearly chokes. "Oh, Princess. Horses need too much water to last in the deep desert. We rode them this far so we could get you quickly away. But only camels from here. It's many days to the next water source."

My stomach does a little flip. Though my hope of escape fled this morning, I'd harbored thoughts of Alejandro rescuing me. Surely he is ransacking the palace in search of his missing wife. Maybe even sending runners into the surrounding desert. But the farther we travel, the harder it will be to find me.

"Where are you taking me?"

"Far away, Princess." He holds up a hand to forestall further questions. "Don't bother asking more. I won't tell you. At least not yet."

"I'm not . . . that is, I've never been an athletic person. I will walk as long as I can, but . . ."

"Oh, I have that figured out already." He's wearing that grin of his, like he's perpetually on the brink of laughter. "We brought you here on a travois. Did you think we could carry you the whole way?"

No, of course not. The strongest man alive couldn't carry me for any distance.

"I mean," he continues. "You can ride in the travois if you need to, but try to walk for a while? It puts a strain on the camels. They'd need more food and water, see, and my sister . . ." His voice trails off.

What was he about to say? My sister wants an excuse to kill you? "I'll do the best I can."

He nods. "I know you will."

Walking through desert sand is the hardest thing I've done in my life. It only takes moments for my ankles and calves to burn with effort, for my breath to come in dry heaves, for sweat to soak through the first layer of clothing. But I press forward, nearly gasping with relief each time our small group crests a dune. Inevitably, I lag behind.

I take some comfort in the fact that I've been outfitted with great care. My captors mean for me to arrive somewhere, and safely. But getting left behind in this wasteland would be certain death. Cosmé looks over her shoulder from time to time, as if expecting to find that I've given up or collapsed in the sand, and each time she does, a fire burns in my gut and I put one leg in front of the other in grim mutiny.

As I wade through the sand, I have plenty of time to think about why I've been kidnapped. By stealing me, they have stolen a Godstone, and I dread the moment when they realize how useless I am. What will they do then?

My only hope is that Alejandro searches for me. That, in spite of the slim odds of finding me in this vast place, he cares about me enough to not give up.

At last, we stop for rest and water. Cosmé passes a goatskin bag around. I watch to see how much each person drinks, and I'm careful to take only my share. The bag goes around twice, and Cosmé moves to reattach it to the camel's pack.

"Cosmé." Humberto gestures toward me with his chin. "A little more for the princess." She glares at him, but her brother smiles in return. "She's not accustomed to this, and she's perspiring a lot. Please."

She grunts, but tosses him the bag. He catches it easily and hands it to me. "Drink deep, little princess."

I hesitate, not sure what to do. One of the other boys, the darkly quiet one, glares at me. The other, slender as a tree even in his desert robes, winks over his crooked nose. I raise the goatskin to them both. "Thank you." And I take a single, deep draft. Oh, it is not enough, but I hand it back to Humberto.

We set off again, and my legs are wobbly as date pudding. I fall behind even sooner this time, but I keep moving, teeth gritted with resolve. The heat is unbearable, my lungs burn, and the air shimmers before me. After a while, I don't even try to keep an eye on my companions, finding it easier to look down, following the sandy indentations left by their feet.

My walking turns to sliding, then stumbling. I walk right into a camel's rear.

"Oomph," I say. I look up, blinking. The others have stopped to wait. They're staring at me, but I cannot discern their expressions through stinging eyes.

"Humberto." It's Cosmé's voice, and it's unusually soft. "Rig the travois."

I want to hug her.

Humberto rushes around while I sway on my feet. At last he takes my hand and guides me to his makeshift sand-sled. I lie down and cover my face with the shawl, and we set off. The camel's gait is strange and jerky, but after a while, I adjust to the odd rhythm. I am exhausted, and my eyes drift closed, but I cannot sleep for overhearing snatches of relaxed chatter and easy laughter. It is clear that my captors do not feel there is any danger of being pursued.

14

THAT night, Humberto shows me how to erect my tent. The poles aren't heavy, but managing their awkwardness requires strength and balance. He assures me I'll get the trick of it, but I don't see how.

After the tents are pitched and the camels tended to, Cosmé builds a fire and makes a batch of jerboa soup. I walk away from the hot flames to watch the sun set across the desert. It's a beautiful place, vast and shimmering, red as blood in the fading light. The dunes fascinate me. Though rippled on the windward side, leeward they are smooth as cream and dishonestly soft, like a favorite rug. It's an astonishing place, and terrifyingly powerful, and I find I'm resting my fingertips against the Godstone in wonder.

"Does it talk to you?" Humberto stands beside me. I didn't notice his approach. He shifts on his feet; his brown eyes are black in the twilight, like his sister's.

"Why? What do you think the Godstone can do for you?"

He looks down, his face grave. "It can save us."

My mouth opens to protest, but I stop myself just in time. My survival may depend on their belief that I can actually do what they hope.

His next words come in a singsong chant, "'And God raised up for Himself a champion. Yea, once in every four generations He raised him up to bear His mark.'"

"That's Homer's *Afflatus*!" I grasp his upper arm. "You know of it!"

His face is puzzled. "Of course."

Cosmé calls us to dinner at that inopportune moment.

"More soup!" Humberto says, then rushes away. I plod after him, preparing myself to appear confident, like one who can save others.

I settle across the fire from Cosmé, amazed at the sudden drop in temperature and grateful for the flames. There are five of us, including myself. The divine number of perfection. From my studies with Master Geraldo, I know the desert nomads always travel in multiples of five, for luck and blessing.

Cosmé passes a bowl to each of us. After watching the others, I understand not to expect a utensil, to tip the rim to my lips and scrape at the shreds of meat with my dusty fingers. I scour every drop from my bowl, and my stomach gurgles in response. The soup has chased away my hunger, but I am far from full. I set down my bowl, disappointed. Cosmé stares at me from across the fire ring. The sun has long since disappeared, and the wavering flames make ghastly shadows of her face.

"Highness," she says, soft and low. "You get the same ration as everyone else."

I meet her gaze steadily. "I did not ask for more."

She stands and brushes sand from her legs, then kicks a bucketful into the fire to smother it. Our camp is now lit by only two small torches and the faintest smear of stars. The desert feels huge, surrounding us with deepest black.

We head off to our tents. I wrap myself tightly against the cold, already deriving comfort from the biting musk of my blankets. My last thoughts are of Homer's *Afflatus* and the gates of the enemy.

Early the next morning, after a too-small breakfast of jerky and dried dates, I pack my tent by myself. It takes me longer than everyone else, and my arms shake from the effort, but I do it. Then I discover that I'm expected to walk again. My legs ache so badly, especially above my ankles, that tears prick at my eyes when we set out. Humberto's thick form wavers far ahead. He guides us on this hot journey, so there will be no chance to discuss Homer's prophecy or ask more questions until we rest.

I push through the sand with agonizing slowness, and before long, my captors are dark motes on the yellow-orange horizon. I should wonder if they've given up on me and left me to the desert's cruelty. I should worry about dying here, about my body becoming a dried husk. My stomach is a gaping hole beneath my rib cage, burning with hunger. Worse, my head pulses behind my eyes and I feel nauseatingly dizzy. I need to eat something sweet to make the headache go away, but I know I'll get nothing of the sort.

The wind picks up, flinging sand into my face. Without stopping, I pull the shawl across my nose and fasten it, the way Humberto showed me. I press on.

I don't know how much time passes, but all at once I feel an urgent grip on my arm. I look up, blinking through my headache, into Humberto's face.

The Godstone sends ice up my spine and into my chest.

"You must hurry," he says into the wind. "Sandstorm."

Oh, God.

"The others are erecting the tents ahead. Can you run?"

I nod, though I don't know how my legs will manage it.

He wraps my arm around his shoulder for support, and together we hurry through the sand. Humberto is very strong, lugging me along at a pace much faster than I could have managed on my own and yanking me back up each time I trip over my feet. Swirls of sand gust against our legs. Humberto's panic is unmistakable. He pulls relentlessly, calling, "Faster, Princess. We must move faster!" So I churn my legs as fast as I am able, sucking air through my shawl, my heartbeat a drum in my throat.

At last we crest a rise. Just ahead, the camels are lying side by side, huge lumps in the sand. Cosmé hurries to erect a tent of sorts around them while they grunt and toss their heads.

Another tent squats next to them. The crooked-nosed man beckons us frantically from the opening.

But my legs plant in the sand, hard and stiff as stone pillars, for in the distance, a wall of darkness races our way. It rages black along the ground, tossing sand high enough to cast the entire sky in shades of brown.

"Princess!" Humberto yanks me forward, but my legs remain frozen, and he mostly drags me toward the tent. The storm's *whoosh* is deafening. I don't know how we can survive such a thing. Our tents look so inconsequential, so fragile, and I know I will die here, my flesh ripped from my bones, the Godstone buried in a mountain of sand.

We plunge inside the tent. Cosmé tumbles in after us. She pulls the flap closed and ties it down. As I catch my breath, I stare at my four captors, dismayed by the wideness of their eyes. Camels moan in the distance.

"The camels?" I gasp. They are strange creatures, but less frightening than horses, with their long soft lashes and perpetual smiles. I can't bear the thought of the sandstorm shredding their hides. "Will they—"

"They're better suited to the desert than we are," Cosmé says. "They know to lie down during the storm. They'll be fine." She shrugs. "Unless they're buried for too long."

Buried? Humberto is tying a rope around my waist. "Buried?" I whisper.

Humberto leans close. "Princess, if the tent falls apart, find a piece of it to wrap yourself in." He ties a section of rope around his own waist, then tosses it to Cosmé to do the same. "Make a space for air, like this." He demonstrates with a blanket, wrapping it halfway around his head and forearm.

He doesn't see my nod of understanding, for the space inside our tent is suddenly blacker than night as the sandstorm's roar overtakes us. I no longer hear the camels, or the flapping of the outside tent layer, or even the breathing of my companions.

Were it not for the rope connecting me to the others, I could imagine myself completely alone. The tumultuous snarl of sand is so huge and steady, so pure, that it is almost like quiet. I sit for a long time, feeling my heartbeat slow and my breathing steady.

Silence crashes around us. True silence, as if the world has died.

"Is it over?" I ask, jumping at the sound of my own strange voice.

"Hush." It's Cosmé. "Do not waste air with your prattle."

Waste air? Understanding dawns: The sand has buried us.

A moment later, the thrashing storm of sound resumes, followed by another unsettling hush. The terrifying afternoon stretches on in darkness while we are buried and unburied several times. Even more terrifying is the sure knowledge that the storm will erase all trace of our passing, that Alejandro will never find me now.

At long last, the silence remains. From the center of the darkness, Cosmé says, "Try it now, Belén."

I hear rustling, the rub of fabric; then sand and light pour in from a hole near the top. I blink at the crooked-nosed man as he thrusts a long pole upward. Through it, I see blue, beautiful sky. I put my fingertips to the Godstone and send a prayer of thanks.

Cosmé and Belén dig us out of our tent. The outside layer is ripped in places, but Humberto says it will hold with a good mending. The camels were only half buried. All five of us get down on our knees and scoop sand away until we can lift the heavy material from them. Grunting and moaning, they sway to their feet and shake their heads around. The largest, a brown-near-to-black creature, chews his cud, while the tawny one paws at the sand. Such common behavior for camels, already familiar to me, and I marvel at their smiling acceptance of the day.

The sun is low in the sky, smearing copper across newly formed dunes by the time we dig the tents out and pitch them properly.

We let the fire burn longer tonight, thanks to a fresh supply of camel dung. Over another measly repast of jerboa soup, I ask, "Are sandstorms always like that?"

Humberto's mouth is full, so it is Belén who answers me. "We get one or two bad ones like that each year," he says. "Usually they're mild and quick."

I slurp my soup, savoring it, dreading the moment when my bowl is empty. The eyes of my companions fix on me, taking my measure. One pair—Cosmé's—finds me wanting, the contemptuous curl of her lips apparent in the firelight. Ah, but the others. Their eyes hold questions, perhaps even reluctant respect. Even the quiet boy studies me carefully. I know what Alodia would do.

I say, "You all knew exactly what to do. To survive."

Humberto shrugs. "We're traveling escorts. It's our job."

Cosmé is a maid, not a traveling escort, but now is not the time to bicker the point. I nod to myself, as if deep in thought. "The desert produces strong people." I hope my words don't come across as fawning.

But Belén lifts his chin with pride. "We've survived worse than sandstorms."

"I don't doubt it." I scrape the rest of my soup from the bowl, then lick my fingers. As I set down my bowl, I say, "But something else is coming. Or has already come. Something you're not sure you can survive."

None of them meet my gaze. Cosmé crosses her legs and studies her knuckles.

I dare to ask, "What is it? Why haul a fat, useless girl across the desert? Why am I so important that you would send Humberto back for me in the face of a deadly sandstorm?"

"We didn't send Humberto back for you," Cosmé snaps. "We sent him back for the Godstone."

Of course. "Why not just pry it from my navel, then?" I know it's a mistake as soon as the words leave my mouth.

Cosmé's grin is predatory. "I'm still considering it."

"Cosmé!" It's the first time I've heard the quiet boy speak. "We can't risk it yet. The prophecy is not clear. We can kill her later if she proves ineffective."

Humberto's eyes narrow, and he glares at the boy. "No one will kill her, Jacián. Not ever."

Jacián just shrugs, then settles back into silence.

That night, Humberto creeps into my tent and quietly settles his bedroll beside mine. I'm relieved to see him, for I know why he's here. He's afraid of what the others might do.

The days are interminable and hot, but I use the time to think. I resolve to appear cooperative and unthreatening, for my survival depends on remaining with my captors for now, on giving them no reason to kill me.

We leave the dunes for a low plateau. The sand no longer sucks away my every step, so I keep pace with only a bit of struggle. Humberto leads us, never hesitating to choose our direction, though I don't know how he manages this. Our water runs low and our rations are restricted. My skin longs for the cool water of my bathing pool. No, that's wrong. The water in my pool was always warm. But I imagine it cool, as vividly as I imagine Ximena's strong fingers kneading my shoulders.

My lips crack and sting. The camels' arching humps shrivel, then list to one side. Humberto assures me this is to be expected, that they'll recover with water and grazing, but I can't help feeling sorry for them. After a while, though, my mind holds nothing but maddening thoughts of water.

After days of traveling across the plateau, Humberto guides us into a deep gully. The camels snort and groan, kicking their knees up and rolling their heads as we pass between cavernous cliff walls. We turn a corner, and the gully opens into an oasis of clumped palms and yellow-feathered acacia trees, of green grass and a pond of sparkling blue water. It's the most beautiful thing I've ever seen.

We all rush forward, five humans and two camels, until we are hip deep in water. "Don't drink too much right away!" Humberto hollers. "It will make you sick." I take a couple of large gulps, then sink down until the water covers my head, reveling in the coolness, the *wetness*. When I surface, the others are splashing one another, cackling like children. Humberto thrusts a tiny wave my way with his huge hand, and without thinking, I join their game, laughing and splashing. I pretend that I've known them all forever. That I am safe.

Much later, our outer layers of clothing swing from the branches of a large acacia that overhangs the tiny lake. Our tents are pitched, the camels calmly grazing on wheatlike grass that waves on the opposite bank. I sit with my bare legs dangling in the water, admiring the new calluses on my feet. I'm strangely proud of them.

Humberto drops beside me and spreads his head shawl between us. Inside is a large handful of fresh dates, gathered from a nearby clump of squat palms. I squeal in delight and pop one into my mouth. It's sweeter than honey, sweeter than a street vendor's coconut pie. Or maybe it just seems that way after a steady diet of jerky and jerboa soup. I spit out the pit and grab another. "Thank you so much!" I say with my mouth full.

He studies me while I chew, and it's a look of curiosity, maybe respect. I don't feel disconcerted as I did under Alejandro's demanding gaze.

We camp there for two wondrous days before setting off, rested and water-plump and cool. Walking is less difficult now, though by no means easy, and over the next several days, I'm able to talk with the others as we travel. Jacián remains taciturn, but Humberto and Belén are happy to regale me with stories of foolish travelers and camel races. I learn that each of my companions has crossed the desert several times, even though they are young to be so well traveled. Jacián is the oldest at nineteen, and Humberto the youngest at sixteen, like me.

Even Cosmé joins our conversation at times, though she is guarded. There are so many things I want to know, about the Godstone, about the prophecy she spoke of, about her service to Condesa Ariña. But I dare not ask. Her desire to rip the stone from my belly is never far from my thoughts, so I'm careful to keep our discourse light and unprovoking.

Because of the way the afternoon sun blazes at my back, I know we travel east, toward the outer holdings and the amassing army of Inviernos. But the fastest way to silence the group is to ask about our destination. On my third attempt, Humberto finally says, "It's a secret place, Princess, and you'll not learn more than that."

We leave the plateau and enter a rocky desert of squat bushes and occasional cactuses. The camels graze as they walk, chewing on dry grass and rigid thorns with equal enthusiasm. I'm delighted to hear the cry of vultures. And everywhere are unblinking lizards, too brave or lazy to scatter from our path until the last instant.

Our incline steepens; the way grows jagged with deep fissures and buttes that spring from the earth to dizzying heights. I could wander the maze of this desert for a lifetime and never find my way home. My only hope is that our secret destination will provide some means of getting a message to my husband.

At long last, after nearly a month of hot travel, we skirt a monolithic butte layered in smears of orange and yellow. On the leeward side, a village cozies up to the mountain in a series of giant stair steps, near invisible with its matching orange-hued brick. People scurry about and wave like mad when they spot us.

My heart pounds and my throat tightens. Not long now until they realize they were wrong to take me, that I cannot help them at all.

Cosmé rushes forward to greet an older man coming toward us. He wears the same generous desert robes as my companions, so it's a moment before I notice that one sleeve lies flat against the side, empty. Other villagers come into view. They are ragged. Wounded. Several faces bear burn scars, rippling like the windy side of a sand dune. Others, like the man clinging to Cosmé, are missing limbs. One young boy, not much older than Rosario, wears a wad of wool shoved into his eye socket, tied down with a strip of dirty fabric.

Most of them are children.

I remember back, a lifetime ago, to the meeting of the Quorum of Five. We'd just received a dispatch from Conde Treviño that requested aid but assured us there had been no casualties yet. Perhaps news travels slowly.

"Oh, Humberto," I whisper, frantic. "We didn't know—*I* didn't know—that the war had started already." I place my fingertips to my Godstone and send a quick prayer for warm comfort.

Humberto reaches down and gently lifts my chin with his forefinger. The hopelessness in his eyes frightens me. "Princess. The war with Invierne never ended."

15

I don't understand. The last war was a skirmish, really. It ended after only two years of fighting, when Alejandro's father drove Invierne high into the Sierra Sangre.

The older man releases Cosmé from a one-armed embrace and hobbles toward me, staring. "Cosmé," he whispers. "You have brought me the champion."

She snorts. "She bears the Godstone, anyway."

He ignores her, his black eyes fixed on my abdomen. "It sings to me," he murmurs. "They said it would, should I ever encounter it, but I did not believe."

"Who?" I demand. "Who said that?" Father Nicandro sensed it too, but I didn't have the chance to ask him about it.

"The priests, of course. At seminary." His face twitches beneath a short gray beard.

Humberto steps forward. "Princess, this is my uncle, Father Alentín, formerly of Conde Treviño's holding."

"You're a priest?" I've never seen one like him before, ragged and filthy and mutilated.

He blinks. "So sorry, my child. Or . . . Princess? I'm not being very welcoming, am I? It's just I never expected . . . I mean . . . yes, a priest. Ordained at the Monastery-at-Brisadulce, and"—shaking fingers press against his lips as he closes his eyes—"I cannot believe we found the bearer at last."

The Godstone is quiet within me, neither warning nor approving, but his hopeful desperation disturbs me. From behind him, tattered children creep toward us, eyeing me with a mix of awe and suspicion. I resist the urge to hide behind Humberto.

Humberto settles a protective arm across my shoulders and says, "We've traveled a great distance, Uncle. We desperately need baths and something to eat. Fresh meat, maybe. Some fruit would be nice. Anything not dried."

My mouth waters at his words, and I lean into him gratefully.

The children surround us and herd us toward the clinging adobe buildings. Even exhaustion and thirst cannot overcome my wariness, for some in the crowd—like Cosmé—regard me with such predatory hunger, as if I am a juicy pig roast garnished with pepper sauce.

The buildings are merely a front for a cool cavern system that worms through the great butte. Fresh springs provide drinking water, even a wide, shallow pool for bathing and laundry. Cosmé shows me where I can undress and bathe in private, a little alcove tucked away with a rock shelf for my clothes. She thrusts a dirt-encrusted bulb at me—it's layered and crisp like an onion—and tells me it will lather against my skin. The water is cold and reaches midthigh, but it's clear as crystal, and my toes wriggling in the sand seem closer, like I could reach down and grab them without bending.

As soon as I'm alone, I try to remember how Lady Aneaxi, and later Ximena, laundered my clothes. We had servants for that purpose, so my ladies laundered rarely. I recall soaking and rubbing, a little soap. Unsure how much time I'll have, I hurry out of the robes and dunk them. After much swirling and wringing, I apply the onionlike bulb and get a light lather. It smells tartly of broken leaves but seems to work well enough, as grime and oily sweat and a few stray hairs swirl away in the circulating water. I also wash my nightgown, the one I wore when Cosmé and the others wrested me from my bed. It's made of creamy silk and fine lace with tiny glass buttons along the front, and it might be valuable enough to trade, valuable enough to bribe an escort back to Brisadulce.

I wring it out gingerly. Then, holding it at the shoulder seams, I give it a light flip to pull the fabric taut, the way Ximena would. And I freeze, looking at the thing in my hands. It feels foreign, from another life. So delicate and lovely. So . . . huge.

I gasp. Shaking, I pull the soaking garment against my torso, hold it at shoulder level, let the hem swim in the water. It's more than huge. It's a tent of a gown, with armholes that scoop halfway down my rib cage, with extra gathers to allow a bust of mountainous proportion.

I let it drop into the water.

I've been wrapped in shapeless robes and camel-hair chaps

for nearly a month. Breathing hard, I peer—hesitatingly—at my navel. I'm shocked to see the winking blue of my Godstone peering back. I raise an arm and admire the curving shape of it, the way my upper arm tapers so naturally into my forearm, like they were meant to live together. I run my hands across my breasts, down my sides, over my buttocks, around to my thighs. Then tears spring to my eyes as I do it again.

I am not even close to thin. Certainly not beautiful like Alodia or Cosmé. But I don't have to part my breasts or press into my stomach to see my Godstone. I still crave honey pastries, but my head doesn't pound to think of them. I can walk all day without getting a rash.

I can walk all day.

I lie back in the water and float, smiling up at sparkling stalactites, at shafts of aquamarine light that pour through clefts in the rock. When Cosmé returns to fetch me, I tell her I need more time.

I'm not done being naked.

That night, everyone gathers beneath a monolithic overhang. It's as if the cupped hand of God swept along the base of the rock, leaving a vast half-cavern with a canopy that is part rock, part star-pricked sky. A cooking pit glows red in the center, surrounded by too few people. No more than forty, and at least two-thirds of them are younger than me.

Father Alentín presides over a feast of lamb braised with turnips, fresh parsley, and marjoram. He pats the sandy ground in invitation, and I settle next to him, cross-legged. The others give us wide distance, glancing over their bowls. I eye them warily.

As I eat, I hold each bite in my mouth, savoring the moist richness, the zing of just-warmed turnip. He tells me flocks of sheep are hidden in a nearby valley, along with fields of potatoes and turnips and carrots. He encourages me to eat as much as I want, assuring me that although people lose their lives daily in this time of war, food, at least, is plentiful.

"Father," I mumble around a mouthful of meat. "Alejandro, the king. He does not know you are at war."

Speaking my husband's name makes my throat twinge with sadness. I hope he is well. I hope he searches for me.

Alentín is shaking his head. "Of course he doesn't, dear girl. No one has told him."

I chew and swallow. "I don't understand."

"We don't dare tell him we already fight, that we've already lost more battles than we can count. His Majesty, may he live forever and prosper greatly, bears no great love for the hill country. He'd just as soon give us up for lost than send help. He'd *rather* give us up. He's already so short on troops from the last war, you see, and we've been such trouble. So difficult to govern from across the desert, with little of value to offer the crown. Our sheep and cattle are the finest in the kingdom, but are poor stock indeed after a forced march across wasteland. He is better served to take inferior tithes from the coastal holdings." I nod, remembering my studies with Master Geraldo. Joya d'Arena's greatest weakness, he always said, was its sheer size.

A girl no more than eight years old approaches shyly with a tray of date balls. I decline, already full, but Alentín grabs one and pops it into his mouth. He chews as he talks. "The one thing we have is gold. The hills vomit a bit of the stuff every year during the flash floods, but His Majesty, may multitudinous sons spring from his loins, does not have an exceeding passion for it. Still, it's *something* to keep his interest. We got word a few years ago, from someone highly placed in his court, that if full fighting broke out in the hills, he might declare us a casualty and simply surrender the land."

Oh, he definitely would. My heart thuds, as I recall how glad Alejandro was when I advised evacuation of the villages. I was foolish enough to think his gladness was for me, for my wise counsel. Now I see that he was looking for an excuse to turn his back on these people. "You do not dare tell him how nearly lost the hill folk already are."

"We do not dare. By all accounts, he is a good man but a weak king. He always chooses the surest, easiest path, if he chooses any path at all."

Though his words ring with disappointing truth, I doubt he would say such things if he knew I was the king's wife. "So he must be made to believe there is still hope, lest he refuse any aid."

"Yes."

But the king will never send aid. I cannot look at the priest's face for wondering what part I have played. I close my eyes for a moment and imagine meeting with the Five all over again. If I knew then what I know now, would my counsel have been different? If I had seen these ragged orphans in the flesh, seen how they suffered, would I have found a way to justify a distant war front? It's so hard to know.

"Father Alentín, what exactly do you think I can do for you?"

He wipes his mouth with the hem of his robe and belches happily. "We hope you can save us, of course. For nearly twenty years, we searched for the bearer. These last few, while the fighting has been most intense, we sent people to every part of Joya d'Arena looking for you."

Anger rumbles in my chest like an avalanche. Even here, so far from home, the expectation for my service is a yoke around my neck. I say through gritted teeth, "How can I save you? I'm just a girl. I eat too much. I hate the idea of ruling things. There is nothing I can . . . Well, I'm good at embroidery. Shall I embroider you a lovely victory tapestry?" I want to hit something. I eye Cosmé, talking to Belén in the distance.

"My dear girl, you have something none of us have."

I sigh. "The Godstone."

"Sorcery."

"What?" Sorcery is such an archaic term, used only in classical study. "No, I don't. The *Scriptura Sancta* forbids sorcery."

He smiles. "Ah, little princess, humans were never meant for this place, you know. But the First World died and God brought us here with his righteous right hand anyway." He leans forward, black eyes intent. "Homer's *Afflatus* tells us that magic crawls beneath the skin of this world, desperate to squirm free. To combat it, God selects a champion every century, someone who can fight magic with magic."

He settles back and crosses his legs while I reflect on my midnight meeting with Father Nicandro in the monastery library. . . . *He was led, like a pig to the slaughter, into the realm of sorcery.*

"Invierne!" I gasp. "That's the realm of sorcery!"

He nods. "My niece tells me you are from Orovalle, a Vía-Reforma kept in ignorance of bearer lore."

I bow my head, unsure whether or not to feel ashamed.

"Foolish cultists," he spits. "His Majesty, may sun finches warble sweet melodies in his ear, was wise to steal you away."

Steal me away. As Alentín scrambles to his feet, it occurs to me that maybe Alejandro agreed to our sham of a marriage only in part because Papá promised troops. Maybe he needed a savior too.

Alentín asks, "Would you like to borrow my copy of the *Afflatus*?"

"Oh, yes," I breathe. "Very much."

I'm given two beeswax candles—precious commodities, Father Alentín tells me—and a squat box of an adobe hut. After hanging my nightgown on a peg, I flip my bedroll across hard-packed clay and settle onto my stomach to read the *Afflatus*. I shiver at the introductory paragraph, knowing I read God's history, hoping I'll discover something of my own destiny.

It is I, Homer the mason, chosen of God to bear His Stone. To the families survived of God's righteous right hand, now scattered to the edge of the sand: Greetings.

Homer tells his own story first. Like me, he received the Godstone on his naming day when a shaft of light thrust into his navel. Growing up, he was feared. Sometimes ridiculed. The priests took an interest in the boy, for they sensed something about the stone, something that made them want to sing hymns or pray or maybe laugh aloud. So they took him into the monastery and taught him to read and write the Lengua Classica. Then, when he turned sixteen, they sponsored his apprenticeship to a local mason.

He was tending the brick ovens one day when God smote him with a vision and demanded he write down every word. Homer fell against the oven door, comatose, and his arm sizzled there while God spoke to him. When he came to, he rushed to the monastery. His left arm was charred and oozing, but he refused all aid until he sat upon a scribing stool with ink, quill, and vellum before him.

Homer bore the burn scars proudly for the rest of his life, but I wonder about a god who would allow such a thing. Surely this man held a special place in God's heart. Yet he suffered greatly.

And he was not the only one. According to Father Nicandro, some of the bearers died during their acts of service. Many did not complete them at all. I wonder which would be worse.

I'm just beginning Homer's account of the actual vision when a presence fills the doorway behind me. I turn over.

Humberto stands there, eyes wide, bedroll under one arm. He cuts a slimmer figure than when we first met—like it did me, the desert sucked all the water out of him—and the candlelight accentuates new hollows beneath his cheekbones. I'm glad to see him.

"Hello, Humberto."

"Princess." But he doesn't move to enter.

"You still think I'm in danger? That someone could murder me for the stone I carry?"

He shifts on his feet. "I can't say. My people are not murderers. But they are desperate. And hardened."

"Then it would help me sleep soundly tonight to know you were nearby."

He grins and enters, then lays his bedroll before the threshold. As he unlaces his boots, I see him eye the hanging nightgown.

It's the loveliest thing in the village, its tiny weave and shimmering folds so obviously out of place. "It doesn't fit anymore," I say casually. "But it's the only thing I have left from . . . from before. I can't bear to part with it." It's not true, of course. I hope it will be my way out of this remote village.

He stretches out onto his side and props his head up with a forearm. "Don't worry, Princess." He nods solemnly toward the gown. "A few weeks of regular food and water will set you right."

He closes his eyes and sighs, too quickly to see my perplexed look. Does he think I want to fit into the nightgown again?

The dripping candle reminds me I have little time to read, so I return to Homer's prophecy.

Yea, once in every four generations He raised him up to bear His mark . . . He could not know what awaited at the gates of the enemy, and he was led, like a pig to the slaughter, into the realm of sorcery.

Do all of God's chosen enter the realm of sorcery? Or some? Or just one? Maybe, even, just me?

My gut quivers each time the Godstone is mentioned in the same passage as "sorcery." But it quickly becomes apparent that Father Alentín was correct. Homer believed future Godstones would combat the danger magic poses to humanity.

The manuscript is not long. I read through it three times before setting it aside and blowing out my candle. Sleep is a long time coming.

I wake to shouting and pattering feet. Humberto and I thrust from our bedrolls and dash outside. Everyone rushes in a unified direction, down the side of the butte and around it. Their faces hold excitement, and maybe concern. We follow, arms raised against morning glare. People line the ridge above, and Humberto helps me as we scramble up the rocky rise.

When we gain the top, the foothills stretch before us. They dip and zag, ever inclining, until they disappear into the mighty shadow of the Sierra Sangre. The mountains are blue-black and white capped, the sun a giant orb peaking over their edge. Tonight, when the sun sets, they'll glow red as blood.

Humberto points downward, into a ragged gulch lined with mesquite and crippled juniper. Heads bob through breaks in the brush. Twelve, at least. A few horses with large packs.

As they draw near, I suck in breath. The packs are bundles of humanity, bloodied and broken. Those lucky enough to be on their feet stumble forward in exhaustion, faces streaked with sweat and dirt, maybe blood.

"That's my cousin," Humberto says, his voice wavery. "Reynaldo, the boy in the front. His village is large. Hundreds of people. If Invierne attacked, if these are the only ones who escaped . . ." He can say no more, and I reach up to clasp his fingers.

He squeezes the bones in my hand together. His lower lip quivers as children pour into the gulch to help the refugees. Their little faces are so hopeful, and they chatter at the newcomers with eager abandon. It takes me a moment to realize they are asking after relatives—parents, siblings, cousins who have gone missing.

Father Alentín comforts a young woman, supporting her up and over the ridge with his good arm. They pass close enough for me to see the bruise pillowing across her forehead, the bald spots and scabs from hair ripped out at the roots, her mangled earlobe. The priest whispers something as they pass, and she looks up at me, startled, with hopeful tears in her eyes.

"I'm Mara," she whispers. "Thank you for coming."

While she and Alentín slip down the rise, I stare at her back, at the grass stains on her robe.

16

COSMÉ tends the wounded and directs everyone to help with decisive efficiency. I sit curled against the wall of the huge half-cavern, unable to look away. Many of them wear charred robes over burned flesh. One of the men bundled across a horse's back is already dead when they untie him and lower his body to the ground. The other three thrash with infection and fever. I remember Aneaxi's leg, the smell of rotten meat, the edges of a wound that scalloped around black ooze, and I cannot bring myself to help or even get close. But I stay because it's oddly comforting to watch my former maid. There's a familiarity to the way she cuts their clothes away and cleans their wounds, the way she stitches flesh together and launders bandages. Her face is just as impassive, her hands as economical and capable as if she were still in my suite cleaning and folding curtains.

I envy Cosmé her usefulness.

In Brisadulce, I was the secret virgin-wife of the king, the visitor from a foreign land, a guest staying in the former queen's suite. But I never understood my purpose there. Now, because of the Godstone, I've been forced across the desert to meet a supposedly great destiny. And yet nothing has changed. I cower in my corner, unable to act.

Just like Alejandro, I realize with a start. I, too, could let myself be paralyzed into indecision, into weakness.

Cosmé's curling hair falls forward as she leans over to wipe blood from a man's neck. Her hair has grown a little and falls just past her shoulders. She hollers for a strip of cloth. A tiny, barefoot boy with a crutch limps over with a bandage. Cosmé uses it to wrap her hair into a quick ponytail. I stare at her messy curls, the way black strands lie sweat-slicked against her ear, and I realize that, young as she is, no matter where Cosmé goes, no matter what situation she is in, she will always make a place for herself.

My heart pounds as I stand. I step among the wounded, and I approach Cosmé, refusing to look down at them. I grit my teeth with determination, trying to make a stone of the revulsion and fear in my chest.

"Cosmé."

She doesn't look up. "I'm very busy. If you need something, ask someone else."

I take a deep breath. "Can I help?"

She rings a dirty rag out onto the ground, then dips it into the bucket beside her. "There is nothing you can do. Go eat something."

I almost walk away. Instead, I say, "I know you hate me. But don't let that make you stupid."

Her head whips up.

"Let me get you some fresh water," I continue before she can respond.

Slowly her gaze moves to the bucket next to her. She nods. "Actually, that would help. Here." She lifts it toward me. "Don't dump it anywhere near our drinking water."

It's heavy, and the handle digs into my fingers, but I hurry away, glad to do something besides touch infected flesh.

I fetch water all morning. Once the others see what I'm doing, buckets appear out of nowhere. I dump the smelly, brownish, sometimes viscous stuff against the sunny side of the butte, then hurry into the caverns for a fresh refill. I can hardly keep up with demand, though I move as fast as I can. By the time the last wound has been cleaned and stitched and bandaged, my thighs and shoulders burn and I can no longer feel my fingers.

I collapse against the wall and close my eyes, trying to relax my cramping forearms.

"Highness."

I look up. Cosmé stands over me with a water skin and a plate of steamed trout on a bed of greens. My mouth waters. "You haven't eaten anything all day," she says.

I reach up. "Thank you, Cosmé."

She turns to go, hesitates, turns back around. "I don't hate you."

I'm not sure what to say, so I just nod acknowledgment.

That night, I sit cross-legged in my hut, Alentín's copy of Homer's *Afflatus* in my lap. I delve deeper this time, studying it sentence by sentence, as if I were in Master Geraldo's study pouring over the *Scriptura Sancta*.

My candle is half burned when Humberto enters. He grins at me before laying his bedroll out in front of the door.

"I thought you might spend the night with your cousin instead," I say, glad to see him.

"Plenty of time to catch up with him later. And he needs the rest." He sits and pulls his boots off with a grunt. "Studying the *Afflatus* again?"

"Yes." I roll my shoulders to relieve the ache there. "I'm hoping to find some kind of clue."

He scoots onto my bedroll and sits beside me. He stares at my face. "You seem . . . that is . . . I mean . . ."

I don't understand why he's so flustered. "Humberto?"

He shakes his head. "Your eyes. They do something to me."

I blush furiously, but I'm saved having to reply when he says, "What I meant to say is that you seem worried. Frightened."

I gape at him. "Of course I'm frightened. I was kidnapped, remember? Dragged across the desert on some vague hope that I can save you. I *want* to help. In spite of everything, I really do. But I don't know how. There was one other bearer from Orovalle. Hitzedar the bowman. He killed thirty-four men, including an animagus. My country was saved that day. In my whole life, I've killed one person in battle, and I hardly knew what I was doing—"

"What? You killed someone?"

"Yes. And I don't care to discuss it. But my point is, I'm not a warrior. I don't know how I can possibly save you." I put my face in my hands. "Hitzedar was lucky. He completed his service. So many others never completed theirs. Many of them died." I look up at him finally, but it's hard not to cry. "Humberto. I don't want to die."

He puts an arm around me and pulls me to his chest. "I don't want you to either." As he strokes my back, I let the tears fall. "You are braver than you know, Princess. And smart. I think you can help. I truly believe that."

"How do you know?" I whimper into his robe.

"Have you heard of Damián the shepherd?"

"No." But it sounds familiar.

"He was my great-grandfather. He bore the Godstone."

I look up at him, amazed, and I remember where I've heard it before. "I've seen the name. On a list of bearers kept in the Monastery-at-Brisadulce."

His smile beams pride. "Damián was a hardworking man. He lived in a village many days' journey from here, closer to the Invierne border. He used to stay out all night with his sheep. He wasn't very comfortable around people, you see. One day he discovered a tiny spring, a damp spot, really. It was in a small valley that got lots of shade and had plenty of grass for grazing. A water source made it a perfect location for a village. So he set himself the task of digging a well where the little spring was, all by himself. He told his wife about it, very excited. I think it was an excuse to stay away from home longer. She was a shrew. But he never finished."

"What happened?"

"He dug down a ways, nearly the height of a man, but not far enough to get more than a trickle of water. Then when a sheep slipped down an incline and got tangled in a bramble, Damián went after it, but he slid on the scree and tumbled to his death."

I glare at him. "I thought this was going to be an encouraging story."

He smiles. "It's not over. His well was forgotten, overgrown by mesquite. Almost twenty years later, a large scouting party from Invierne came through that little valley led by an animagus. The men of Damián's village lined up on the ridge with spears and bows, only slightly outnumbered. But the animagus sent his fire against them, and they began to burn. The villagers were just about to turn and run for their lives, when the animagus suddenly disappeared. At first they thought it was new magic, something they'd never seen before, but then the enemy panicked. The villagers took advantage of the confusion and slaughtered them from the ridge above." He leans closer and his eyes spark with amusement. "Later, they discovered the animagus had fallen into Damián's well and broken his neck."

I frown up at him. "So you are saying that Damián's act of service was to dig a well? *Part* of a well?" Could it be true? Could an act of service be something this subtle? This inglorious?

Humberto shrugs. "When the men returned to the village, they told Damián's widow about the part her long-dead husband had played. She showed them his Godstone, something she had kept since his death. She said she knew something important had happened because it had cracked right down the middle."

"His Godstone cracked?"

"It did."

"That makes no sense."

"What do you mean?"

"I've seen Godstones. Old ones whose bearers have been dead many centuries. They weren't cracked." I wish I had thought to ask Father Nicandro if the Godstones came from bearers who had completed recognizable acts of service.

"Well, I don't know much about Godstones, but I do know my great-grandfather saved the village that day. It was a big scouting party, and the fact that it was led by an animagus means it had significance. Up until that point, the inhuman ones were mere legend, never sighted. It's possible Damián's well delayed Invierne's invasion for years."

"It's possible. And Damián never knew he completed his service."

"He never knew."

I lean my head against his shoulder. Strange how the presence of this boy is so much more comforting than my husband's ever was. Near Alejandro, I was too dazzled to be at ease. "You think I will complete my service," I say, "even if I never understand how?"

"Yes."

But I could still die inanely, like Damián, or suffer grave injury, like Homer. *Like a pig to the slaughter . . .*

"You know, Princess." Humberto's thumb grazes my chin. "My grandfather, Damián's son, was one of the men on the ridge that day. If he had died, Cosmé and I, my cousin Reynaldo, even Uncle Alentín . . . none of us would be here today."

And suddenly I understand why Homer accepted his injury. I understand why it is better to die from my service than never complete it at all. Far, far better. Homer and Damián never profited from their acts of heroism; everyone who followed did. In the same way, I may never reap the benefits of mine, should I complete it. But that doesn't matter, because God placing his stone in my belly was never about me.

The next day, I set the *Afflatus* aside in favor of my old favorite, the *Belleza Guerra*. Every passage inspires more questions. I spend the whole day running back and forth between my borrowed copy of the manuscript and the people who have survived the war thus far.

Father Alentín tells me the warriors of Invierne are unskilled but numerous as the stars in the sky. They pour from the snowy heights of the Sierra Sangre, led by animagi who wield amulets of fire. Though five of Invierne's warriors perish for every one of ours, it is not enough. Once an animagus enters the battle, our people must flee or die.

"How many exactly?" I ask him. "Is their army nearby? Do they seem ready to march?"

"There are two armies," he says. "One within a few days' travel by horse. Another much farther north, a stone's throw from Conde Treviño's holdings."

"Two armies. With quite a distance between them."

He nods, rubbing the stump of his shoulder.

"How many?" I ask again.

"My girl, there are thousands. Ten thousand at least, and their numbers swell daily."

Two enormous armies. Even the combined might of Joya d'Arena and Orovalle could not compare. "One will skirt the desert to the south," I muse aloud. "The other will follow the jungle line to the north. They'll advance on Brisadulce and the costal holdings from opposite directions. A giant pincer."

Alentín leans closer. "I think so too. But I doubt that His Majesty, may orchids bloom in the wake of his passing, is prepared to fight a war on two fronts."

"I fear you are correct." Alejandro, with his inability to make decisions or commit to anything, is prepared for nothing. I glance at the priest's maimed shoulder. Tentatively, I say, "Do you mind telling me how you lost your arm?" It feels rude to ask, but I must learn all I can.

"An arrow shattered my arm just above the elbow. In the days it took me to travel to this hiding place, it sickened with disease. I passed out soon after I arrived. When I woke up, the arm was gone." He shrugs. "An arm for a life. Not such a bad trade."

"So they use arrows." Like the Perditos of the jungle. "What other weapons?"

"For questions about weapons, my girl, you should ask Belén."

I thank him and hurry away in search of the tall boy. I find him outside an adobe hut, scraping a fresh sheepskin with a half-circle blade whose handle fits neatly into his palm. We haven't spoken much since our journey across the desert, and I'm wary as I approach. But he greets me with more warmth than I expect, even brightens with interest at my question.

"They use the bow and arrow mostly," he says. "Their bows are much larger than ours. The height of a man or longer. They don't shoot with the same accuracy as our bowmen, but their arrows fly much farther."

"Could we make a similar weapon?"

"No." He looks up from the sheepskin. "We'd need trees. Lots of very tall trees with wood that hardens just the right amount as it dries."

"What other weapons?"

"Some spears. Most carry short swords. We have the advantage there, with our long blades. You don't ever want to wrestle one, though." He sets the knife atop the skin and pushes up the sleeve of his robe. Four parallel lines of raised, whitened flesh streak down his forearm.

I shudder. "They look like claw marks. Really large claw marks."

He retrieves the scraping blade. "I don't think they have claws. More like gloves with something sharp rigged into the fingertips. They fight like animals. Like mountain lions, but without the cunning."

Again, I think of the Perditos. My stomach flips a little as I remember their random attack patterns, the slinking grace with which they moved.

"But the weapon you need to watch for," he says, punctuating the syllables with flicks of the knife, "is the amulet of an animagus. They wear them around their necks on heavy chains or leather ties. They never use them during the first part of the battle, something I've always wondered about, but after a while, that amulet starts to glow. Then light comes out of it, pure and white hot, fast as an arrow. It burns everything it touches." He shakes his head sadly. "We've won a few skirmishes against Invierne, even outnumbered as we are. But whenever an animagus leads them, we lose. Quickly and badly. We've learned to call retreat as soon as we see that amulet smolder."

I know I must learn more about the animagi; they seem to be the key to Invierne's strength. The first documented instance of an animagus in battle is the account of Hitzedar the bowman. Since then, they've shown themselves infrequently, but to hear Alentín and Belén talk, encountering one of Invierne's reclusive sorcerers is commonplace.

"Belén, I need to find out more about the animagi. What do they eat? What do they wear? What do they *want*? Maybe someone has infiltrated their camp. Maybe Conde Treviño—"

"You need to talk to Cosmé."

"What?"

"Cosmé. If you want to talk to someone about sneaky things"—he waggles an eyebrow at me—"talk to her. She's a spy."

I allow my head to fall into my hands. Of course she is. She's probably as efficient a spy as she is a laundress. I thank him and dash away in search of the travel escort/maid/healer/spy.

She's in the half-cavern, tending the wounded. Another man

died during the night, she tells me before I have a chance to say anything. But the others might heal. It will be a few days before we know for certain.

"Can I ask you some questions?" I expect her to brush me away, but I have to try.

"About?"

"Er . . . sneaky things."

She raises an eyebrow.

"I'm trying to learn about Invierne. Especially the animagi. If my father or my sister were ruling in Conde Treviño's place, we'd have infiltrated the enemy camp by now. We'd know who leads them, what their plans are, what they eat for breakfast, what they—"

"Treviño knows nothing."

My disappointment is like a stone in my gullet. "You're sure?"

"I'm sure." She stands stiffly and faces me. "I suggested it when I was in his court. I thought we should send spies with the supplies. But the conde and his daughter felt it too risky."

That makes no sense. "Supplies?"

Cosmé's face wrinkles with disgust. "The good conde made a deal with Invierne, you see. They don't attack his holdings, he sends them sheep and foodstuffs."

My heart beats against the base of my skull. "This is a jest."

"No."

"The conde is a traitor."

"Yes."

"Does the king know?"

She shakes her head. "Ariña would never tell him."

Ariña? What does my husband's mistress have to do with . . . then I understand, and I roll my eyes at myself for not having seen it sooner. "Ariña is Conde Treviño's daughter."

"Yes. She represents her father in the Quorum of Five."

"So you were sent to spy. As Ariña's maid. Spy on what?"

She shrugs. "Officially, to glean palace gossip. To help Ariña in her bid to become the next queen. But by then, Humberto and I had connected with Uncle Alentín's group." She snorts derisively. "I guess we're revolutionaries of sorts, rebelling against the conde's betrayal, against the king's useless passivity. So I went to Brisadulce, hoping to find the bearer. I found you." She looks around the cavern floor, at the sprinkling of injured villagers. She chuckles, but her eyes are devoid of humor. "What a fearsome group we make, don't you think, Highness? A bunch of children, playing at revolution."

"Call me Elisa." I look around too, but instead of seeing hopelessness, I see wounded survivors. I see a lovely, hidden village that prospers in spite of the war. "Cosmé, how serious are you about continuing the fight? I mean, why not just walk away? If you fled, north of Orovalle maybe, you could live."

Her lips press together as her black eyes widen. Even angry and sad and streaked with dirt, she is a beautiful girl. "I will never give up," she spits, stepping forward until her forehead is inches from mine. "They killed my parents. They killed most of my friends. I'm going to kill as many of them as I can before they finally stick an arrow in my gut or burn me to ashes."

I resist the urge to step back. "And the others? Do they feel as you do? Will they keep fighting?"

"Most of them, yes."

We stare at each other for a long moment. "Good," I say.

Surprise flickers in her eyes before I turn and walk away. The threads of a battle strategy are patterning together in my mind. It's an insane plan, like nothing the warriors of Joya d'Arena have ever tried before.

It will never work.

17

THE ceiling of our hut glows rich ochre in the candlelight. I stare at it, unable to sleep for the ideas buzzing in my head. Humberto's breathing is steady and regular. He's probably asleep already. I blurt, "I want to call a meeting. Of the whole village."

Humberto starts, then rolls onto his side. "You do?" he yawns.

"I do." I study his face, looking for disapproval or misgiving. He is quite handsome, I realize suddenly, with his desert-bred cheekbones and glorious hair.

He blinks, eyes lidded with sleepiness, and rubs the stubble on his chin. "A meeting for what?"

"To talk about the war. I have some ideas."

"You should have Uncle Alentín call it. He's been thinking of holding worship services for us all. The children look up to him."

"Good idea."

Humberto yawns again, then rolls onto his back and shields his eyes with a forearm.

"Do you think they'll listen to me?" I ask.

He lifts his chin and looks at me upside down. "Yes, Princess. You are the bearer. They will listen to you." He settles back and closes his eyes.

"You don't still think someone will try to rip the stone from my body, do you?"

"I might," he mumbles.

"What?"

"If you don't let me sleep, I might rip it out myself."

I'm much relieved to see the grin spread across his face. "Oh."

"Good night, Princess."

"Call me Elisa."

He growls.

"Sorry. Good night."

Alentín agrees to call a meeting, but suggests we wait. "We just sent scouts to look for more survivors," he explains. "We'll wait for them to return."

I can't argue, though I'm not happy at the prospect of growing sick with nervousness over the next several days. Alodia was always the one to address the court. Except for a few minor toasts, I managed to hide quietly in the background. This should feel different. Fifty or so orphaned children shouldn't frighten me. It's not like I'll be standing before the golden horde of Orovalle while they study the puckered fabric at my waist or twitter about how much I ate.

I am the bearer, I tell myself. I represent hope for these people.

I find I can no longer sit still for such long periods of time, so I ask Cosmé to teach me about duerma leaf. She narrows her eyes in distrust as she ponders my request. For a moment, I'm reminded of Lord Hector, of the way his busy mind spun beneath his careful countenance. It saddens me to think of him and Alejandro and Ximena searching for me, worried about what has befallen me. I wish there was a way to get a message to Brisadulce.

"I'll teach you."

I step back in surprise. "Thank you."

She guides me over the north ridge into a small twisting valley. The day is particularly hot, and grit fills my mouth with each sharp breeze.

"It grows in the shade," she says. "Usually in soft soil, but not always. Look for it on the sunrise side of boulders." She points to a low shrub with broad leaves of velvety sea green. "It produces small yellow berries twice a year. The berries are poisonous, but the leaves are very useful. I've been giving the wounded a mild tea to help them sleep." She strips several leaves in a smooth, gripping motion. "Don't pull it up at the root. If you strip the leaves, they'll grow back next year."

I copy her motion and end up with several, moist where they broke off from the stem. They smell faintly of cinnamon. "What did you use on me?" I ask. "It wasn't a tea. And it worked quickly."

Cosmé nods. "Duerma leaf holds a lot of water. If you take the fattest leaves and squeeze the moisture from them"—she plucks a larger leaf and waves it in front of my nose—"then let it dry into a powder, you get something that will make a person sleep for days if inhaled."

"Like me."

"Like you."

"Could someone die from this?"

She shrugs. "Sometimes. A very concentrated dose would do it, maybe. If we harvested the berries, I'm sure I could concoct an effective poison. And sometimes people just react strangely to it."

"So there was a chance I would die."

She smiles, and I'm startled at the genuine humor in her black eyes. "A very small chance. At the time, you were quite . . . large. It would have taken an enormous amount."

I glare at her, even though I don't mean it. "And the tea you gave Ximena. How effective do you think that was?"

"She probably awakened late morning with a pounding headache."

"Interesting. Very interesting." I look around the tiny valley. It's dry mostly, and rimmed in cactuses, but duerma leaf and mesquite huddle together in shady places. "Is there a lot of it around?"

She lifts her chin. "What exactly are you planning . . . Elisa?"

"Not sure yet. But I think we'll need lots of duerma leaf. And—" I raise an eyebrow at her. "Sneaky people."

The half-cavern fills quickly. We don't usually light torches for fear of discovery, but tonight is the exception. Everyone has come, even the limping wounded. One of the scouts—a young man no older than seventeen—brought back five survivors, half starved but uninjured, so a hint of celebration buzzes in the chatter as we wait for Father Alentín to begin services. As I look out over the congregating people, my palms begin to sweat, and I regret eating so much jackrabbit stew for dinner. Our number nears sixty now. I try to think of something else.

I helped prepare dinner tonight, even skinned a rabbit under careful supervision. Rabbits, I learned, part from their skin with disturbing ease. My clumsy knife produced a ripped and useless hide, but I'm confident I can do it again if the need arises.

Alentín steps onto a boulder and holds his good arm at shoulder height until everyone is silent and attentive. He clutches a rose in his hand. I hope he either has another one stashed away, or doesn't expect many petitioners. If he intends to officiate the sacrament of pain, a single rose will not remain sharp of thorn for so many prickings.

Together we recite the "Glorifica," then he begins to sing. I recognize the words, though the melody is a bit different, more minor and haunting than I'm used to, but the combined voice of the children is as high and clear as bells. I catch on quickly and sing my hope to God.

We finish our hymn and line up for the sacrament. In Brisadulce, when Father Nicandro officiated, only a scattered few sought the pain of devotion. But here, in this place of desperate hope and brutal reality, every single person, adult and child, lines up to be pricked by the rose and receive a blessing.

Father Alentín prays, asking God's favor on the ceremony, then quotes the *Scriptura Sancta*: "Has not God chosen those who are pained in this world to inherit his paradise? For it is through suffering we understand our need for his righteous right hand. Indeed, our spiritual needs outweigh our physical ones. Blessed be the name of God." One by one they are pierced and blessed and tended to. Belén acts as the priest's assistant, anointing their tiny prick wounds with ointment, wrapping them in bandages, giving the occasional cryer a quick hug.

When it's my turn, Father Alentín smiles sadly, even as he grasps my neck and pulls my forehead against his own.

"What is it you seek, child?"

Last time, I prayed for wisdom. God must have answered my prayer, for I certainly feel wiser now. Older. Different. But I still don't understand what God wants from me. I sigh. "Alentín, I need faith. I have so many doubts about God and His will."

His lips, moist and warm, press against my forehead. "Everyone has doubts," he whispers. "Pray through them. God will show you what to do when the time comes."

He pricks my finger, and it throbs faintly. He holds my hand over the cooking pit—no glorious altar in this remote place—until a single drop of blood browns on the hissing coals. He nudges me toward Belén, who cleanses and wraps my finger with reverent care. Then I take a seat against the wall and close my eyes, breathing deep to calm my churning stomach.

The sacrament is over too soon. A hand grips my shoulder. I look up into Alentín's kind face. "It's time, Elisa."

I can't move.

"If you want to address everyone, you must do it now."

"What if they don't listen to me?"

He doesn't answer. I put my fingertips to the Godstone and take a ragged breath. "God," I whisper. But I am unable to finish my prayer for the sudden power that courses from my navel, up my spine, down my arms, like soft lightning. My eyes widen, my mouth hangs open, my fingers twitch.

"Elisa?"

I look around at the assembly. They sit cross-legged, mostly young faces shimmering with firelight and with hope. They stare at me, waiting. "I'm supposed to do this," I murmur in wonder. The terror is still there. My legs are stone pillars as Alentín helps me to my feet, but there is rightness in my gut too, mixing with the fear. He leads me to the boulder. I don't step up, knowing I'll never be able to balance on the thing.

Alentín sits before me, and I am the only one left standing.

"Um, hello," I say eloquently.

A few mutters and nods.

"I am Lucero-Elisa de Riqueza, Princess of Orovalle. And I, uh, bear the Godstone." Some raised eyebrows, a few gasps—probably from the newcomers. "I was a guest of His Majesty, King Alejandro de Vega, in the city of Brisadulce for a time." With a start, I realize I've been in the desert longer than I was with the king. "There, I was privy to a war council of the Quorum of Five. I know what is coming and what the king plans, and I can tell you it will not be enough. Alejandro has no intention of sending aid. We are on our own to defend the hill country." I dare not tell of my part in Alejandro's decision, but my face burns with the truth.

"You're certain?" a man yells.

I look in the general direction of his voice. "I'm certain. He may send a small contingent to force evacuation, though."

The place erupts with panic. Bile fills my throat at the hurt in their faces, at their sense of betrayal. But I need them to be angry. I clasp my hands behind my back and wait as the initial shock wears to a general din, then silence.

"We cannot look to the king for help," I say when I have their attention again. "And we cannot depend on Conde Treviño to protect us. From what I understand, two vast armies prepare to march on Joya d'Arena. King Alejandro could defeat one of these armies perhaps, but two? And I know of no defense against the fire of the animagi." I shake my head. "They are many, we are few. We are wounded and tired. They are grown men and women. We are mostly children. We can expect no aid. In short, we cannot war with Invierne and live." I have practiced these words for days, yet I fear they are coming too fast.

"Then we die honorable deaths!" someone hollers. A buzz of agreement follows, though some stare at the cavern's chalky floor in silence.

"Honor from death," I snap, "is a myth. Invented by the war torn to make sense of the horrific. If we die, it will be so that others may live. Truly honorable death, the *only* honorable death, is one that enables life."

"Are you suggesting retreat?" It's Humberto's soft voice.

Even in the firelight I can see the disappointment on his face.

"Not exactly." I smile at him, taking comfort in his presence. My own personal guard, like Lord Hector is to Alejandro. Humberto can't help himself; he smiles back.

The crowd shifts uncomfortably. I must make my case quickly before I lose their confidence.

"I've thought long and hard these last few days about how we could defeat Invierne. But of course, defeating them here in the hill country is impossible. We cannot defeat Invierne; therefore we should not try. This does not mean"—I hold up my hand to forestall the grumbling disagreement—"that we will not fight. I believe we can and we should."

My words are right and true, and I pace back and forth with the energy that buzzes in my limbs. "But we will never engage in an all-out battle. Our goal will be to harass them. Weaken them. Terrorize them. We will be the spirit of death that visits them in the night, the hidden viper in their path. We will be the Malficio, the curse on their existence. Yes, they will eventually cut a wide path through our hills, and they will reach King Alejandro and the costal holdings. But by the time they do, they will be exhausted from triple watches, starving from interrupted supply trains, and fearing for their lives, for they cannot know when next the Malficio will strike." My smile is wickedly genuine when I say, "If we are very clever, very careful, I think we can give the king a huge advantage. I think we can help him win this war. But there can be no heroes, no honor in senseless death. Our goal will be to sting them only, and live to sting again."

They nod to one another, murmuring assent. I almost have them.

"There are only fifty of us!" a young man yells. It's Jacián, the silent companion on our desert journey. "And so many of us are wounded. Crippled, even. Most are far too young to hold a weapon."

"Yes, and those who can't fight will have even more important tasks." At this, several heads perk up, eyes widen. I suddenly understand that the littlest ones, the ones who have suffered the most, could be my greatest adherents. I need only convince them they are needed. "I'm sure some among you are cunning gossips. You are to take refuge in the larger villages and begin spreading rumors of the Malficio, the spirit of vengeance that rises in the hills against Invierne. You will have no firsthand knowledge, naturally, but you will encourage speculation. The rumors should make their way to the enemy quickly. Then you will return.

"Others will harvest duerma leaf. As much of it as we can find. Still others will make garments to closely match those of our enemy. There is so much work ahead of us that every hand, every mouth, every mind will be needed."

I scan the crowd, gauging their reactions. Most sit forward, attentive. Others narrow their eyes as they consider my words. Even Jacián nods a grudging accord.

"Since there are two armies," Belén calls from his place beside Cosmé, "they must be talking to each other. If we can figure out how to stop them from communicating—"

"Yes!" I almost jump in excitement. I hadn't made that connection yet. "Belén, that is exactly the kind of thinking we need."

"You said something about a viper?" A shy, feminine voice. It's Mara, the young woman with the mangled ear who thanked me for coming those days ago. "I know you didn't mean it this way, but my cousin in the village of Altavilla actually has some."

I nod, thinking of the possibilities. "Good. That's very good."

And suddenly ideas fly at me from all sides. Many of them are ludicrous, but some are not. I encourage them all. It goes on for a long time, until someone yells, "Why should we help the king fight his war? He's never helped us!"

I shake my head. "No, we are not helping the king. We are using him to fight *our* war."

"But these are his lands." It's Jacián again. "Say the war is over. Say Joya d'Arena is victorious. Then we go right back to paying taxes to a man who can't be bothered by us. If we help him, we should be honored in some way. Rewarded."

And now we come to the crux of the matter. I can't control the smile that spreads across my face. "Do you want to be free of Joya d'Arena? Would you prefer to govern yourselves?" It's a radical thought. Treasonous. I see shock in the faces around me. And interest. "Because if you do, I think I can make it happen. I think I can convince the king to give this land to you. No rebellion. No sedition. If you help him win this war, you can be your own nation."

They are so quiet, so still. It's a huge claim, preposterous even. But I have yet to play my last trick.

"How?" It's Cosmé. She steps out of the shadows, and her eyes shimmer with tears. "How could you do this?"

I take a deep breath. I'm about to betray a confidence, betray Alejandro, but the rightness still sparks in my chest. "I am not merely Alejandro's guest visiting from afar. I am secretly his wife. And he still owes me a wedding gift."

I hear indrawn breaths. Cosmé's jaw hangs open. A movement catches my eye, and I turn just in time to see Humberto's back as he hurries out of the cavern and into the night.

"His wife," Cosmé mutters. "But he doesn't know what has become of you! What if he marries . . . someone else?"

For the briefest moment, I dare to ask myself: *What if he married someone else in the wake of my disappearance? Would it be so bad?*

I shove the thought away.

I say, "My father agreed to commit troops as a condition of our marriage. Joya's army never recovered from the last war, and Alejandro is desperate to fill his ranks. He won't jeopardize their agreement. He can't wait forever, but he will wait."

Alentín asks, "Would your father withhold troops if he learned you are missing?"

"He might," I admit. "And if he did, I'm afraid this plan would fall apart." Trying not to sound too eager, I suggest,

"Maybe it would be best to send Alejandro a message? To let him know I am safe and well?"

Jacián shakes his head. "We would all hang!"

"Not Alejandro, then," I say. "I'll write to my nurse instead, saying nothing about your identities or our location. Just a quick note to assure her that I live. Ximena will tell my husband only what he needs to know, and she can vouch for my safety to Papá if necessary. Ximena has served my family a long time, and her word will carry more weight with my father than even Alejandro's."

They all agree, with some reluctance. I will write the message in the morning, and someone will carry it to the pigeon post at Basajuan. Though it may take weeks to reach Brisadulce, I feel such relief. I hope Ximena writes back.

Briefly, I wonder if I ought to miss my husband more. I've thought of him constantly these last few days, but only in the context of making plans for our war. I don't yearn for his company the way I do Ximena's.

Cosmé says, "Just tell us, please, that you can do as you say. That when the war is over, you will convince the king to hand over this territory."

A blanket of stillness settles over the crowd. They regard me with expectant hope.

"I will do it," I say with conviction.

They break into excited chatter. We huddle together in the half-cavern late into the night, making plans. They are with me now, mind and heart. I still don't know the purpose of the Godstone living inside me. I have no idea how to fight the animagi. But I've given them a chance. Something to fight for. It will have to be enough.

When I finally stumble to my hut, exhausted, Humberto is not there. It feels strange to close my eyes without saying good night to him first. I lie awake a long time, keenly aware of the empty space at my threshold.

18

IN the morning, I use the village's last bit of parchment to pen a brief note to Ximena in the Lengua Classica. I sign it "Tuciela"—"your sky," and I hand it over to the young boy appointed courier.

Father Alentín and I spend the rest of the morning navigating the steep levels of the village, interviewing each inhabitant. I write their names on thick sheep's hide. My wrist aches and I'm frustrated from forcing the ink into even, readable letters. We question them thoroughly, and I note where each person is from, along with any skills they may have. Even the youngest among them are remarkably self-sufficient, able to prepare food, make clothing, herd sheep, carve wood.

They view me with wide-eyed adoration and nervousness. Alentín is a huge help, thinking of questions I never would and treating each person, especially the children, with such easy, comfortable compassion. Soon I have a list of fifty-six names, and I've spoken with everyone except Humberto. Cosmé tells me he was tired of eating nothing but mutton and left early to hunt.

Late in the afternoon, Cosmé and Belén join me in my hut. We sit cross-legged, pouring over the list while we dine on leg of lamb stuffed with white beans and mushrooms.

"Only fifteen can use a bow and arrow," Belén points out.

"How quickly could we train the others?" I ask. "Not to be expert marksmen, but to just shoot at something?"

"Quickly. But that's not the problem. We don't have enough weapons."

"Could we get more?"

He shrugs. "We could make more, but it would take a while. We don't have much timber in the area."

"Nine know how to use a sling," Cosmé points out. "To make more of those, we just need leather. And rocks. Boys love to sling rocks."

"Yes!" Belén raises his fist in a victory gesture. "We shall save the world from Invierne with slings!"

Cosmé shrugs. "Anyone who can kill a rabbit at twenty paces could kill an Invierno at ten."

"Well." I take a deep breath. It feels ludicrous, like we're little children playing at war, which, of course, most of us are. "Then everyone will try their hand at the sling while we figure out how to make more bows and arrows."

According to our list, we have a blacksmith among us, but no iron. Seamstresses, but we don't know how the enemy costume themselves. We have a journeyman midwife who helped Cosmé stitch the wounded, and two trappers whose traplines snaked deep into the foothills, before Invierne came. Mara is a

cook of some renown. Everyone else is a child, possessing useful general knowledge but little in terms of specialized skills.
So many people, so many abilities. I just don't know what to do
with them all.

A headache throbs behind my eye sockets. I pinch the bridge
of my nose and murmur, "I need more information."

"About the people?" asks Cosmé. "All you have to do is ask."

"No. About Invierne. About their army. How close could
someone get to them without being seen?"

Cosmé chuckles. "If it were me or Belén, or even my brother,
very close."

"Close enough to observe them for a few days?"

Cosmé and Belén exchange a glance. It's the comfortable,
intimate look of people who have known each other a long
time. "We could," Belén says. "There's a cave nearby. High on a
ridge. It was . . ." He looks down for a moment. "It was a favorite hideout when we were younger."

If it's true, this could be exactly what we need. "I want a map
of their encampment," I say. "I want to know where they eat,
where they sleep, how the place is organized. Do the animagi
mingle with the others or keep to themselves? What do they
wear? How are they supplying the army from over the mountains? How do—"

"Elisa," Cosmé snaps. "We'll do it. The five of us will leave
tomorrow."

"The . . . five?"

She nods. "You, me, Belén, Jacián, Humberto. We jour-
neyed successfully through the desert during the sandstorm

season. Surely you wouldn't risk sundering a divinely blessed grouping."

And he was led, like a pig to the slaughter, into the realm of sorcery. I smile weakly. "I guess I saw my function here as more . . . organizational."

Cosmé snorts. "Eat well tonight, Princess. For tomorrow's journey will bring fond memories of jerboa soup." She stands and stretches.

Belén grabs my arm. "Elisa, you have a potent mind. If anyone needs to observe this army, it is you." His smile cannot mask the seriousness in his eyes. "Just try not to slow us down."

They leave to make preparations. I stare after them, my stomach in my throat, my hands clammy in my lap. They are right, of course; I need to observe the encampment myself. It's a small comfort that I will likely fulfill my act of service someday, even without realizing it. And I know this is necessary. The will of God. Because maybe I am the one the prophecy spoke of, the one who would enter the gates of the enemy.

But I want to live. I want to see Ximena again. And Alejandro. I want time to figure out what I feel for my husband.

Everyone will have something to do in our absence. A few will travel to the conde's holdings to spread rumors of the mysterious Malficio. Some are tasked with building our arsenal and training in the use of sling and of bow and arrow. Still others will dig pits throughout all the major approaches, to be covered later by tent canvas and a shallow layer of dirt. The littlest are tasked with harvesting duerma leaf.

I dread the journey. Heat, aching feet, tiny tasteless meals. This time, since we travel in stealth, we cannot take the camels and must carry our own packs.

The whole village sees us off. They wave as we climb the rise, their hopeful faces grinning absurdly above frayed robes and bandaged limbs. Humberto leads us again, silent and unsmiling, shoulders hunched forward as if plowing our path through the air. He has not spoken to me in nearly two days.

The straps of my pack bury themselves in my shoulders, weighed down by my bedroll, dried food, a water skin, ink and hide to map the army.

Humberto sets a vigorous pace. As before, I struggle to keep up. I'm not the same fat princess who was kidnapped from her bed in Brisadulce, but compared to my nimble companions, I am slow and lumbering. Our journey through the desert was brisk but steady and straight. Here in the hill country, my knees and ankles throb from maneuvering around boulders and mesquite, from huffing up a rise only to skid down the other side. I'm easily the noisiest of our group, and I can't imagine how I'll sneak close to Invierne's army undetected.

By the time we break for a quick lunch of jerky and dried dates, my robes stick against my chest and the skin beneath the shoulder straps stings like an open sunburn. I drop my pack to the ground and make a point of sitting next to Humberto on a boulder. He stares straight ahead, nibbling on his jerky.

"Humberto?"

"Hmm," he grunts.

I keep my voice low. "Why are you angry with me?"

He casts me a darting glance. "I'm not angry."

"You're ignoring me."

"Yes."

I sigh with exasperation. "I've never had a friend before. Just tutors and nurses and servants and . . . a sister. So I'm not very good at being a friend. I don't know why I upset you and I don't know what to do about it."

"His Majesty is not your friend?" His voice is wry and startling.

Is Alejandro really my friend? I shake my head. "I honestly don't know. He said he wanted me to be, but now I wonder if those were just words to placate a child. We never spent time together or got acquainted. He has a personal guard, Lord Hector, and I think he and I could have been friends given time."

"You didn't tell me you were married."

"I'm not in the habit of revealing state secrets to kidnappers," I snap. "Of course I said nothing. And see? You're angry."

"No. I just feel . . . foolish."

I stare at his profile. "Why? I don't think you're foolish."

He finally returns my gaze. "I thought that maybe, when this was all over, maybe you and I could . . . which is stupid, because you're a princess and I'm a traveling escort. See? I'm foolish." He jumps up from our boulder, shoving the rest of his jerky into the sash at his waist.

I'm too stunned to follow. Heat crawls up my arms and into my neck. I am the one who is foolish for not having understood his desire to protect me, his easy chatter, the way his eyes always linger on my face. It's heady and wonderful and frightening. My first coherent thought is: *I wish Alejandro had been the one to feel such things.* But my next is: *I'm glad it was Humberto*, and I want to keep the memory of him fresh and unique in my head, completely separate from Alejandro's.

I don't notice the pain in my shoulders for the rest of the day. I glide along in a daze, wondering at this miracle of someone caring for me in such a way. That night, as we set up camp on a ledge above a dry wash, Humberto ignores me again. But I sidle close to him in the dark while he gathers firewood. I whisper, "I still don't think you're foolish."

The smell of the earth changes with the cooling temperature. It prickles against my nose, citrusy and moist. The cactuses and tumbleweed gradually cede to piñon and juniper. We cross shallow creeks on occasion, and Humberto supplements our jerky and jerboa soup with mottled trout. After a few days, the risk of being sighted is too great, so we leave the ridgelines in favor of gulches and small valleys. Each night I crawl into my bedroll exhausted, a different kind of exhaustion than when we traversed the desert. This time, my very bones ache from impact.

My companions flash me irritated looks as we travel. I manage to collide with more branches and dislodge more stones than a team of carriage horses. I'm desperately aware of the need for stealth, but the harder I try to be silent, the clumsier I become. Belén lags behind the others to instruct me on how and where to step, but after a while, he snaps with impatience.

I've always been graceless, my feet tending to thump down wherever I can plant them. Here, though, it is not enough to merely avoid a sprained ankle.

I'm near to tears when Belén calls to Humberto in exasperation, "You help her for a while!" Up ahead, Humberto nods. Cosmé and Jacián look on in usual silence as the two boys trade places.

Humberto is far more patient than Belén. He shows me how to place my feet just so, explains how to support each step with my thighs and calves. He's careful not to touch me, though I wish he would.

It feels like a dance lesson—something I never excelled in—all precision and hidden energy. By the end of the day my muscles buzz, half numb with the effort, but I'm snapping fewer branches, and I'm glad for having spent hours with him.

That evening we light a small, smokeless fire to heat our soup, but stomp it out as soon as the sun disappears. My companions are less talkative than usual. Every sound or shadow sends them into suspicious alertness. They schedule rotating watches throughout the night. I offer to do a stint, but Cosmé shakes her head and tells me to sleep well. "You slow us down enough as it is," she says.

She is right, of course. I need the extra coddling; prefer it, even. I just hope that if we're able to observe Invierne's army, I'll prove myself worth the trouble.

We break camp in hurried silence the next morning. Humberto leads us with his usual unerring confidence, though we follow no trail that I can see. We travel along a graveled ravine, surrounded on both sides by bluish clumps of stunted juniper and dry buckwheat. The sun is high and angry. I'm pulling my shawl over my burning scalp when the Godstone turns to ice. I gasp in frozen shock. So cold. So piercing.

"Belén!" My voice is like a rodent's squeak. His tall form is closest to me; the others are too far ahead to hear.

He whirls and glares down his hooked nose, but his face softens when his eyes latch onto mine. "What is it?"

My fingers, numb with cold, press against my navel. "The Godstone. Something is wrong." I'm near to tears. The stone has turned my blood to ice only twice—to herald the Perditos' attack and to warn of the sandstorm. "It only does this when danger is near. Very near."

Belén doesn't hesitate. He sprints forward and grabs Jacián and Cosmé by their robes. Far ahead, Humberto turns to see what the commotion is about. Belén waves him back frantically. They scan the area around us even as they hurry toward me.

Humberto grips my upper arm. "What is it, Elisa? What's wrong?"

"I don't know. I never know, but the Godstone— I think we should hide."

Jacián is already crawling up the rise toward a thick clump of juniper. "Up here!" he gestures. "Enter through the back of the bramble. I'll cover our trail."

Cosmé and Belén dart up the slope. Humberto and I follow more slowly. It's slippery and steep, and I grab on to jutting roots to pull myself up. The clump is hard to penetrate, the trees dense and tightly possessive of the ground around them.

Humberto yanks on the branches so I can scoot inside, but they still scrape against my back and shoulders. I prop myself against a twisted trunk to remain level on the steep slope. Next to me, the others are in similar positions. Moist tartness seeps from the leaves, or perhaps the bluish berries, making the air acrid but cool. Spiderwebs tickle my cheeks. I don't know how long we'll have to hide here, crouched in this awkward manner, our scalps brushing the canopy.

A moment later, Jacián joins us, breathless. "Any idea what we're waiting for, Princess?" he whispers.

I shake my head. "But the Godstone did this right before the sandstorm hit."

"So it could be anything?"

I nod, just as Cosmé slaps a hand over his mouth. Silently, she points downward into the ravine we just left. The trees are too dense to catch more than the barest glimpses of ochre-thick dust and rough rock, and I'm not sure what she's pointing at.

I hear them first. Pattering footsteps across gravel. A clattering sound, like wooden wind chimes. Or hollow bones.

Suddenly I can't get enough air. I'm too close to the ground, swathed in darkness. I expect arrows to pierce my side at any moment, for flames to engulf our carriage, and I won't be able to get my ladies out in time—

A hand on my shoulder startles me. I look up to find Humberto leaning toward me, his eyes very close and bright. I swallow. The Perditos' attack is long over, I know, but I peer through the branches into the ravine, expecting to see men painted in black-and-white swirls, creeping like animals, wearing tiny bones around their ankles and in their hair.

I catch a glimpse of fur. A long quiver of arrows. Waist-length hair that grows in clumps. I don't dare breathe as they creep past on bare feet. A hunting party perhaps? Scouts? Their flesh is so pale. Red and blotchy in places from the sun. I wait for a sign that we've been spotted, but it's too hard to tell through the trees. They are a marvel of silence, their footsteps and clattering bones only audible at this close range. Were it not for the Godstone, we would have stumbled right into them. I don't see paint swirls. Still, the resemblance to the Perditos is uncanny.

Inviernos. At last I gaze at my enemy, albeit in the mere glimpses allowed by dense branches. They are smaller than I imagined, paler, but more savage looking. Like the Perditos, they slink along with animal grace.

We wait in tense silence. My feet cramp and my neck itches madly, but I dare not move. The Godstone continues to pump ice through my veins. Humberto's hand is heavy and hot on my shoulder, and I'm glad for it. There are so many below, travel-ing in a long line of at least three abreast. What would they do if they discovered us? Would they kill us instantly? I haven't heard of anyone being captured. What if an animagus is with them? He could burn our clump of trees to ash if he wanted.

At last the way below is clear. Still we wait, as dust from their passing settles. Then Cosmé puts a finger to her lips and motions for us to stay put. She creeps from the shelter of our trees with astonishing stealth. My legs tremble with the effort of keeping my body still and upright against the slope, and sweat trickles down my temples as we await her signal to move.

She returns a moment later. "They travel west," she whispers breathlessly. "They don't seem to have noticed us, but we need to get away in case they catch our trail or discover our campsite. The way east is clear. For now."

We scramble out from under the trees. Humberto helps me down the slope. I hold on to his hands a little tighter, a little longer than necessary. At the bottom, we pause to catch our breath.

"Elisa, from now on, you lead with Humberto," Cosmé says. "Even if you slow us down. If that thing inside you tells you"—she makes a vague gesture with one hand—"then wave your arms or something, so we can head for cover."

I nod, even though the prospect of leading the group into enemy territory terrifies me. What if we can't find cover next time? What if I'm too slow to react? But as I hurry ahead with Humberto, I find myself smiling. Just a little. Because I may prove useful after all.

19

WE travel in silence for two days, rejecting easy gulches and soft inclines in favor of deer trails that cling, near invisible, to steep slopes, camouflaged by thorny shrubs and gnarled juniper. Humberto leads us decisively, with me right behind him.

The Godstone stilled and warmed again to my body as soon as we were out of reach of the enemy's scouting party. But since then, it has gradually cooled in increased warning. So I am not surprised when we top a ridge as the sun sets and look toward the Sierra Sangre to discover a diffuse glow, orange-red in the fading light, spreading like a blanket along the base of the mountains.

"The army of Invierne," Humberto whispers at my side. "Still more than a day's travel away. Yet their cook fires shine like a small city."

I gulp and grasp for his hand. "The gates of the enemy," I whisper back.

"Perhaps," he says, and his thumb caresses the back of my knuckles. "Elisa, I won't let anything happen to you."

It's a sweet sentiment, and I'm grateful for it, but not even Humberto can protect me from a whole army. I look up at his profile and say, "Thank you."

He drops my hand as the others crest the rise behind us. "We must camp before all our light is gone," he says, then scurries down the other side, and I am hard pressed to keep up.

We dare not light a fire that night. We sit in a circle on our bedrolls in a tiny, sheltered hollow and gnaw on dried venison and shriveled dates. I will be hungry again too soon, but at least I don't get the headaches anymore. Looking around, I realize I'm not the only one who is unhappy. I giggle.

Cosmé leans forward while the others raise their brows. "Something funny, Highness?"

I grin at her. "I think we actually miss your jerboa soup."

Belén and Humberto chuckle while Cosmé pretends to be offended. Jacián gazes toward the mountains, uncaring. He is always so quiet, so disconnected. In spite of a month's journey together across the desert, he remains a stranger to me. Sometimes I forget he's there.

"Everyone to bed," Cosmé orders. "I'll take first watch."

For once, Cosmé lets us sleep late. "They do most of their traveling early in the day. They don't like the heat," she explains. "Since we're so close, we stay put until the sun is high."

I find stillness more repugnant than traveling. When I walk, I have things to keep my mind busy, like where to place my feet and how badly my shoulders ache. Hiding in relative comfort, I remember to be terrified. I can't decide if I'm relieved or not when we finally shoulder our packs and follow Humberto out of the hollow and into the shadow of the Sierra Sangre.

The Godstone grows ever colder. I pay close attention to it, uncertain that an icy warning would provide enough contrast to alert me. My stomach tightens in response, and my muscles stiffen. By the time Cosmé calls a halt, I'm trembling from the chill.

We shelter in a copse of pines. I drop my bedroll twice trying to flip it out onto a carpet of pine needles.

"Elisa?" It's Humberto's concerned voice. "You're shaking."

I nod and take a shivery breath. "So cold."

He puts his hand to my cheek, and I lean into its warmth. "God! Elisa, your skin is like ice." He rushes to his pack and withdraws his tinderbox.

"What are you doing?" Cosmé asks as he squats down with flint and steel.

"We need a fire. Quickly, before the sun goes down."

"No fire!"

"It's Elisa. We need to get her warm."

Cosmé turns to me. "Is it the Godstone?"

I nod.

"Is someone approaching?" Belén asks.

"I—I don't know. Don't think so. Just getting colder. As we get closer."

Cosmé closes her eyes and pinches the bridge of her nose. "What if we can't get her near the army?"

The others look at me in dismay. Even through my frosty

fever I can read the thought in their eyes. *What if we've dragged her all this way for nothing?*

"Almost got a fire going," Humberto says. "Another moment."

We've come so far. The thought of returning to our village unsuccessful fills me with dread. And now my companions risk discovery, just to keep me warm.

I place my fingertips to the Godstone. The chill of it seeps through my robes. *God*, I pray silently. *What should I do?* As always, the stone responds with vibrating comfort. My belly begins to warm.

"Humberto!" I hiss. "Put out the fire!" I close my eyes and smile. *Thank you, God. If I have to pray all night and all day tomorrow, that's what I'll do.* Tendrils of warmth creep up my back, down my legs, into my arms and fingertips. I hear snapping branches as Humberto stomps out the fire.

I look up, feeling loose and relaxed. "I have to keep praying," I explain. "I need each of you to wake me when you take watch, so I can warm myself."

Humberto places his hand on my cheek again, under the guise of checking for warmth. "This Godstone is a strange thing," he says, but I see the relief in his face. The others stare at me with a mix of awe and alarm.

After we flip out our bedrolls, Belén surprises us by pulling a loaf of bread from his pack. "Been saving it," he says. "For our last night before reaching the army. Probably dry now."

Humberto slaps him on the back. "You're a good man, Belén."

I pray over our meal, aloud, then continue praying in silence as we eat. The bread is indeed dry and squished, but rich with figs and nuts. I fall asleep asking God for courage and stealth, and thanking Him for giving me one more chance to be truly and satisfyingly stuffed with dinner.

We sleep late again. After we roll up our beds, I pull Cosmé aside.

"If I don't make it back," I say, "and you do, will you promise to continue with our plan?"

She studies my face a moment, then nods once. "The Malficio will become a living thing. I promise."

"Thank you."

"You think you're going to die."

I shrug with purposed nonchalance. "The *Afflatus* is unclear on that point. And all bearers die eventually."

"Then why did you agree to come?"

So many reasons. Because I was done with being useless. Because I decided it was better to die, if that meant completing my service. Because Alodia or Ximena or Lord Hector wouldn't hesitate in my place. Because it was time to grow up.

"It is the will of God," I tell her. A weak answer, and a hypocritical one, for I am as lost as a lamb in a bramble when it comes to God's will. But giving voice to the real reasons would be too hard.

Humberto tosses his pack over one shoulder as he approaches. "We should reach the cave today," he says. "Jacián will move ahead and make sure it remains undiscovered. If not,

I have another place in mind, but the cave would be ideal."

He turns eastward, and as we move to follow, a stiffening chill slithers down the bones of my legs. I pray fast and fervently, until my muscles relax and walking becomes a natural, fluid motion. Father Alentín said I should pray through my doubts, and that's exactly what I do. I chatter at God without ceasing, telling him about my fears, about the ache in the arches of my feet, even about the lizards that scuttle across my path and the hawks that scream overhead. I wonder if he laughs at my mindless prattle, or if he even cares. The Godstone continues to spread warmth, though, so long as I keep it up.

Moving with stealth while carrying on a perpetual one-sided conversation is not easy, especially for me. My mind is busy enough with the task that the afternoon slips away. I'm surprised to look up and see Jacián stopped ahead of us, an unlikely grin on his face. "The cave is clear," he announces. "And the entrance is nicely overgrown."

Humberto's body loosens visibly. I hadn't realized he was so concerned. He guides us into a narrow dry wash. It's dusty and tight and overgrown with thorns, so I'm dismayed to learn we must wait here for dark. At my grimace, Humberto smiles and says, "And be sure to watch for vipers."

I glare at him, then lean against the uneven wall and close my eyes. I tell God I long for a bath in the cavern pool of the village, followed by a meal of juicy lamb chops and stewed carrots.

We don't wait long, for the sun disappears sooner in the hills than in the desert. The need for stealth is greater than ever, but in the red haze of fading light, I can't see well enough to plant my feet. Every snap beneath my boots, every scuff against shale sends a vast echo of announcement. My desperate prayer leaks from my mind to my lips, and I find I'm muttering as we scurry along. Oddly, the others don't shush me.

Night falls as we navigate through brambles and around boulders, switching back at increasingly higher levels. At last, the shadowy black of clumped juniper breaks wide to reveal deepest, star-pricked blue, smudged along the bottom edge with the orange-red glow of Invierne's army. Jacián beckons us forward to the rim of a great cliff, and we look down, not nearly far enough, into an enormous valley. Campfires dot the rolling expanse like candle flames in velvet, as far north and south as I can see, and eastward to trickle up the slopes of the Sierra Sangre.

"Oh, my God," I whisper.

Jacián leads us over the lip and down a narrow deer trail. We inch along sideways, our backs tight against the cliff face. In the dark, it is the most dangerous part of our journey. I hardly notice. All I can think about is the size of Invierne's army and the strange, manic faith my companions must possess to bring someone like me across the continent to save them against such a thing. I hear rustling as Jacián pushes brush aside to reveal the cave opening; it's small and deeper black than the darkness around us. One by one, we crawl inside. The air instantly cools and moistens my skin. I feel a hand in mine and recognize Humberto's touch.

"Step carefully, Elisa," he whispers as he pulls me forward

and around a corner. I can see nothing, but I follow without question, my mind in a daze as icy creepers shoot through my abdomen. I've forgotten to pray.

The sonorous strike of flint and steel is near instantaneous, with a spark that blazes behind my eyes long after it fades to mere candlelight. Cosmé holds the candle aloft, revealing a high ceiling dripping stalactites. "I haven't been here in years," she says softly.

"We used to play here," Humberto explains in my ear. "When we were little. In springtime, a shallow stream, perfect for splashing, runs through this chamber."

"The candlelight?" I ask. "Is it safe?"

"It's safe. In the next chamber over, we can even have a small fire."

The chamber he speaks of is tiny and round, with a soft sand floor. More important, its entrance is camouflaged by an immense limestone pillar that juts from the ground. The entire cavern system is sprinkled with dead branches, whorled and worn smooth from spring's flash flooding, so we have no trouble collecting enough wood for a cheery cook fire. We lay out our bedrolls, then sip pine-needle tea.

Belén takes the first watch at the cavern's cliffside entrance. I pray warmth into my body before fading into uneasy sleep.

Morning brings dim light. Like in the bathing caverns behind our hideaway village, the sun finds its way even into the depths of the earth. Already I am alone in our tiny limestone chamber. After praying to warm my numb limbs, I rise to retrieve ink, hide, and quill from my pack. I'm eager to be done with this task.

Cosmé enters just as I stand to go. She holds a jackrabbit upside down by its feet; long, veined ears trail in the sand. "Getting started already?" she asks, indicating the hide with a lift of her chin.

"I don't care to linger here."

Her eyes are bright, and there's something remarkable about her easy, relaxed humor. A different kind of girl sparkles just beneath that perfect skin, a girl with a ready smile and kind eyes. Perhaps revisiting her childhood haunt brought it out. Or maybe she's just glad we arrived safely. Whatever the reason, I realize that Cosmé, already lovely, could be stunningly beautiful if she chose.

She frowns. "What are you staring at?"

"Um . . . the rabbit. How did you . . . ?"

"Humberto got it with a sling. He's always accommodating when I threaten to make soup for breakfast."

I chuckle. "He's very capable, isn't he?"

"Like you, my brother appreciates food only if it can be served in large quantities."

I choose to believe her teasing the friendly sort, and I grin right back. "Your brother is a wise boy."

"He's at the entrance on watch if you want to join him. I'll bring you both breakfast when it's ready."

"Thank you."

I retrace last night's journey through the twisting cavern. It's not difficult; all I do is follow the brightest path of sunlight.

Humberto is there in silhouette, his back against the rim of the opening. A spiky tangle of mesquite obscures the view. When I step forward, I feel Humberto's hand on my knee.

"No farther, Elisa," he whispers. "Stay out of the sun. Morning lights the cliff face like a torch. You'll observe in the afternoon, when the sun is behind us."

I swallow hard at the reminder of the peril we've put ourselves in.

Our thighs brush as I settle next to him. I don't move at all, perfectly happy to be so aware of his body next to mine, to listen to his soft breathing.

I see our enemy clearly through tiny breaks in the bramble. This cave is an excellent observation post. Though I can't discern the layout of their camp, I can make out individuals as they scurry about at unknown tasks, clothed in leather and furs, barefoot, pale skinned, lively. The most striking thing is their hair. I see shades of black like mine, some with red tints like Alejandro's. But others have hair the rich brown of coconut shells, or even lighter—the yellow-gold of honey or straw.

"They are strange looking," I whisper. "So savage. So colorful."

Humberto grunts. "Wait till you see an animagus."

I pray to ward off the sudden chill beneath my breast. Then I change the subject. "Where are Belén and Jacián?"

"Belén hunts. We have a bet as to who can get a bigger rabbit. Jacián is exploring the area to see if anyone has passed by recently. They won't be back until the afternoon. The sun is too high for them to slip down the cliff unnoticed."

I shake my head, in awe of my companions. I can't fathom leaving the sanctuary of our cavern. But I travel with people who move across the land the way a gull skims the water. They are so at home in this place, even with the enemy a stone's throw away.

Humberto's profile is golden in the glow of morning. The soft fuzz of his beard-to-come curls around his jawline, blending seamlessly into a mess of hair that waves down his back. Sitting next to him makes me feel less afraid, somehow.

"I'm glad you're here," I say.

He whips his head around. I almost flinch as his steady gaze travels down my face to my lips, and even though no prayer fills my heart, the pit of my stomach buzzes with warmth. My lips part. I lean closer.

A movement catches my attention, and I gasp as the Godstone shoots cold fire through my veins. "Humberto," I whisper, frantic. "Those Inviernos! Are they coming this way?"

He peeks at the group gathering below. His brow furrows with alarm, but he shakes his head. "They can't possibly see us," he mutters. But the Inviernos continue to mill about at the base of our cliff. A few look up in our direction. Humberto swears and turns a fierce gaze on me. "Run back, Elisa. Tell Cosmé to bury the fire. I'll cover our tracks."

Even more than the cold, I'm frozen by the sadness in his beautiful eyes, deep and true. He squeezes them closed a moment and breathes deeply through his nose. Then, with one swift movement, he cups the back of my neck with a strong hand, pulls my head forward, and presses his lips to mine. He wastes precious moments kissing me, his tongue gliding across my lips, darting at my teeth. I open my mouth and kiss back just as eagerly.

His other arm snakes around my waist and he stands, pulling me against his body, pulling me to my feet. Then he thrusts me away, but not before I see the wetness glistening in his eyes. "Go, Elisa! Run, now!"

I back into the cavern, away from him, my knees shaking and my lips barren. Then terror overtakes me, and I flee toward Cosmé.

20

Cᴏsᴍᴇ́ reacts instantly to my breathless exclamation by kicking sand onto the fire. She looks around our chamber.

"Jacián's pack is still here," she says in a clipped voice. "Bury it while I dump breakfast."

I drop to my knees and scoop furiously, glad for something to do. *This is it,* I think, as I fling sand in all directions. *What I feared.* I dig and dig, mumbling senseless prayers, until I reach dampness.

Cosmé returns and tosses the pack into the hole. Together we cover it up, then Cosmé stomps around to level the area. A presence darkens the entry.

"They climb the cliff," Humberto says in disbelief. "They know we're here."

Cosmé's face is a stone. Humberto looks at the ground as though ashamed. They've been so strong since I've known them. So decisive. I suddenly feel lost and small.

"At least Belén is safe. And Jacián." Cosmé whispers.

Safe. My mind begins to clear of fear-fog. "There is no other way out of the cave?" I ask.

"No," Humberto says.

I would never scurry up the cliff quickly enough, and even if I did, there is no way I could avoid pursuers in a footrace through the hills.

"Could you two make it out and escape? I mean, without me?"

They say nothing. Which is answer enough.

"Show me the best place to hide. Leave me with food and water and get away from here."

I see denial in Humberto's eyes, acceptance in Cosmé's.

"Look for me in a few days," I add. "If I can escape the cave and head west, I will." No such thing will happen, of course, but it might convince Humberto to go. "I bear the Godstone. If anyone has a chance to survive, it's me. Now, go! Lead them away from me."

Though Humberto continues to hesitate, Cosmé yanks me forward. "There is a place at the end of the other corridor," she says as I hurry after her. "A wedge of sorts. It will be uncomfortable, but you will be out of sight."

We're there too soon. I wish the cavern was larger, easier to get lost in. Cosmé shows me a crevice. It inclines upward in a series of scallops and drips, a waterfall of sparkling limestone.

"Climb up," Cosmé orders. "Once in the shadows, you'll see an impression on your left. Crawl inside as far as you can fit."

I comply quickly, using all fours to scramble up stone that is too smooth for purchase. I feel her hands on my rear, shoving me forward. The impression is dark on my left; I cannot tell how deeply it penetrates. I twist awkwardly and scoot inside, scraping my knees. It's a cavern within a cavern, with a depressed area guarded by a lip of stone. I scoot as far back as I can, well into darkness.

"That will have to do," Cosmé says. "Hold tight. I'll bring food and water."

It's cooler here, almost chilly. Or maybe that's the Godstone. *Please keep me safe, somehow*, I mouth. The floor is sandy and comfortable, but I have to hunch my head and shoulders and fold my legs tight to keep them in shadow.

Humberto's head peeks into the opening. He tosses my pack inside, to land next to me in the sand. "I put all our food and water inside. Also, your ink. I suggest smearing your face and all the light parts of your clothing with it. If there is a flash flood, the water will come through this chamber. Let it sweep you back into the cavern. The water will stay shallow there."

Flash flood?

"Humberto!" It's Cosmé's voice, distant now. "I hear them!"

His eyes are huge and sad. Apologetic.

"Go, Humberto," I say softly. "I don't want anything to happen to you."

"I'll come back for you. No matter what."

"I know."

He reaches inside, squeezes my ankle. And then he's gone, leaving me alone in the tight, chilly dark. A moment later, I hear shouting. They've been spotted leaving the cavern, and pursuit begins. I'm torn between hoping my enemy chases after my companions and wanting them to come after me instead, giving Humberto and Cosmé a chance to escape.

I listen closely, holding my body tight in painful stillness.

The shouting fades. Perhaps they move away from me. I can't decide whether or not to feel relieved.

Then I hear soft, sliding footsteps in the sand.

My heartbeat thunders in my ears. I'm afraid to breathe. Surely they will see this crevice. They will peer up its length and glare into my obvious hiding place. I think of the ink in my pack, wishing I'd had time to smear my face and clothes with its concealing black. But then maybe the smell would have given me away.

The smell . . . the cavern still reeks of sizzling rabbit meat. My eyes tear up. Humberto and Cosmé and I should be sharing a meal together right now. And then I think: *What a strange thought to have when capture or even death looms so near.*

The footsteps draw closer. Hushed male voices speak a language I don't understand.

But suddenly I do understand. It's similar to the Lengua Classica, though the syllables are more clipped and guttural than I'm used to. I'm so stunned that for a brief instant, I forget to be afraid. The people of Invierne speak the Lengua Classica?

"Né hay ninguno iqui," someone says. There is no one here.

"Lo Chato né sería feliz si alquino nos escapría." The Cat will be displeased if someone eludes us.

The guttural voices seem louder, nearer. Before me, an arm's length away, a hand settles on the limestone waterfall, lit by sun streaming through fissures in the earth above. A thick, pale hand. Crisscrossed with scars the puckering white of bread dough.

Please, God. Make him go away.

I wait for an arm to follow. Maybe a pale face. I close my eyes, refusing to look. Finally I hear, "Né vieo nado." I see nothing. The sound of slithering footsteps fades. I sense my aloneness, and it is an empty, sorrowful thing.

I refuse to move, afraid it's a trick, afraid they stand guard at the entrance, waiting for me to reveal myself. I wish I had duerma leaf with me, so I could sleep through this nightmare. Then, days from now, I would wake, either captured or free. Or I would be dead and I wouldn't wake at all. Either way, I would escape this terror of not knowing what would befall me, not knowing if my enemy lurked just around the corner.

My stomach aches with emptiness. I need to relieve myself. But I refuse to twitch a finger, even to breathe too deeply. My lower back aches with the need for release and from holding my legs so tight against my torso. Still, I manage to doze off, infused with the warmth of my life's most earnest prayers. *Please watch over Humberto and Cosmé and Jacián and Belén. Let them escape. Let them live.*

When I wake, my back is rigid as stone and my stomach is a hole in my gut, throbbing with hunger. It's impenetrably dark, so I know I've slept at least until late afternoon, maybe longer. I reach, quietly, for my pack and manipulate the ties, surprised at how naturally my fingers decipher the knots, and reach inside for my packet of jerky. The meat—dried strips of mutton cured in salt and then sweetened with honey—is comforting, though it sticks in my teeth as I tear it apart. Afterward, I sip from the water skin, wondering if I should conserve, wondering how long I'll be stuck in this hole. I feel around in my pack to see what Humberto left me. Another packet of food, a second water skin, a candle, a knife, a tinderbox. I've never lit a fire myself, though I've watched the others do it. It can't be that difficult.

I sheath the knife against the hide of my boots, shoving it under the camel-hair wrapping. Before I do anything else, I must relieve myself. I consider digging a hole right here in my tiny cavern, but then I'd be forced to sit atop my own waste. Better to sneak down the incline now and crawl back up before morning.

Gradually, silently, I force my leg over the stone lip, then grasp it with my hands as the other leg follows. I slide down the incline on my belly and let go at the last instant, breathing a too-loud sigh of relief when my boots contact the sand floor. I straighten and listen a moment. Nothing. I take a few experimental steps forward. Still no sound.

I don't dare go too far, for I've no assurance I'll find my way back in the dark. Sitting on my heels relieves the pressure in my abdomen a bit. I scoop sand away, stopping at intervals to listen. Then I pat at the ground, feeling for the depression, and mark the deepest spot with a toe while I lift my robes and fiddle with the drawstring of my pants. The urge to go is overwhelming, and I barely settle into a squat in time.

I hear voices, then sliding footsteps.

I don't have time to finish. I yank up my pants and scramble toward the incline while warm urine pours down my leg. The limestone is too slick, too soft. I climb partway up, clawing at the stone, ignoring the burning rawness of my fingertips, but my legs tangle in pants that were left loose and untied. The voices approach. My scrambling becomes frantic, but each time my fingers find purchase, my foot slips. Tears of panic run down my face. Then the Godstone turns to ice, and I gasp in shock. My fingertips freeze. I lose my grip and slide down. My rear slams into the cavern floor; the breath in my lungs flees in a single, violent gale.

Torchlight burns my eyes. Rough hands seize my shoulder. They yank me to my feet, spin me around. I see pale faces, matted clumps of hair, angry eyes.

One turns away in disgust, wrinkling his nose. I smell my own urine then, robustly sharp. For a brief moment, the humiliation overpowers my fear. Until one of them says, in the Lengua Classica, "Take her to the Cat."

A shorter, powerful man holds a dagger to my throat as they shove me forward. I think of my own knife, stashed against my boot, even as I shuffle ahead surrounded by Inviernos. For the first time, I let myself remember the Perdito I killed, the way the knife rebounded against bone, how it slid between his ribs the way a needle slides into thick tapestry. The blood soaking my skirt cooled so quickly. Could I kill again?

"This girl is no warrior," one says. He is right, of course. When I killed the Perdito, it was mostly by accident.

"Where are your companions?" another demands.

I open my mouth to say, *What companions?* But then I remember that most of the hill folk do not speak the Lengua Classica. So instead, I say in the Plebeya, "I don't understand you."

The blow is so sudden, I don't even have time to be afraid. My lip splits wide and throbs with pain as he leans closer, his eyes fiery orange in the torchlight. "You barbarians are all filthy," he spits. "Urinating on yourselves. Speaking such a filthy language." He turns to the others. My eyes have adjusted now, and I see five of them, all men dressed in undyed leather with fur trim. "Take her down the cliff," he orders. "If she can't keep up, throw her over the side."

They rush me through the cavern to the entrance and force my legs to dangle over the edge. It's too dark to see where to place my feet and hands, but a spear in my face inspires me. I slither along, feeling for brush or niches. It's not as difficult as it seemed during the day. With my body pressed against the ground, I realize it's not perfectly vertical. I consider sliding down and out of reach of my captors. I'd risk a broken leg, or worse, but it would be unexpected. A quick glance downward changes my mind. The campfires of Invierne's army stretch forever. Once on the ground, there will be no escape. So I take my time—as much time as the spear pointed at my eyes allows—and I climb down with careful precision.

My arms burn by the time we reach the valley floor, but I am oddly energized. I consider dashing away, but I'm not quick enough or strong enough to evade my captors. I imagine what it would feel like to have that spear crush its way into my back. Right now, for whatever reason, I am alive. As they lead me toward a large, bleached-white tent, the only outward sign of resistance I dare is a head held high.

Others look up from their fire pits as we pass, eyes wide with curiosity. One hunches over a skewered rabbit, and her posture pushes the outline of breasts against a fur-trimmed leather vest. I stare right back at her as my captors prod me forward. I realize I cannot distinguish the men from the women from a distance. They all wear the same clothes, have the same clumpy hair, the same pale skin.

A small brass bell dangles from the tent wall. One of the Inviernos gives it a shake.

"Enter," someone calls, and ice clutches at my abdomen once again. I pray for warmth and safety as one of my captors sweeps aside the tent flap and thrusts me inside.

Spicy incense curls around my head, beckoning me toward a stone altar covered in candles, all in varying stages of melting. I blink to clear my eyes of smoke and light.

"You've brought me another barbarian," the same voice sneers. It is deep and as cold as the ice in my stomach. "Why didn't you just kill her?"

The squat man to my right bows. "Forgive me, my lord. I thought it strange that someone who is clearly not a warrior would be hiding in the cave above our camp. But if you'd like me to take her away and bother you no more—"

"Not a warrior, eh?" A figure steps closer. He is of medium height, my height, and thin as the trunk of a coconut palm, blinding in robes as white as quartz. His face is pale and slick, as if a sculptor carved it with an artist's attention to beauty. A long braid of white hair curls across his shoulder like a snake. No, it's lightest yellow, like the innermost edge of the sunrise. Most disconcerting of all are his eyes. Never have I seen such eyes, for they are blue, as blue as my Godstone. How can he see?

He leans forward until his bloated lips are a handsbreadth from my brow. "You are a soft little thing, aren't you. Are you a warrior?"

Is this the Cat? An animagus, perhaps? Is this one of those responsible for burning the flesh of my people? For sending both my father's and husband's countries to war? Staring into his unnatural eyes, something sparks in my gut. Something altogether different from the stone there. My body begins to pulse with it; my cheeks feel hot. I realize it's rage.

I narrow my eyes and say, loud and clear in the Lengua Plebeya, "I'm sorry. I don't understand a word you're saying."

He studies my face a moment; then his eyes flash, wild and dangerous, and he turns his back and glides away. The way he moves makes my skin crawl. He's as graceful as the smoke curling around us, smooth and effortless.

From a wooden stand next to the bright altar, he grabs a wineskin and pours a shimmering dark red liquid—wine, I hope—into a ceramic mug. As he sips, he regards us thoughtfully from over his shoulder. "You never found the three that escaped?" he asks.

"No, my lord," says the short man.

He sips again. With his free hand, he reaches forward and flicks his fingers with irritated nonchalance. My companions freeze. I stare at them, at eyes wide with terror, as they choke and wheeze, unable to move. This is sorcery, I realize, and my Godstone flares in response.

The blue-eyed man glares at me. "You still move!" he says. He flicks his fingers again. I'm not supposed to be able to move. I'm supposed to be paralyzed like the others. So I go very, very still, even though the rage still thrums through my skin. I hear Alodia's voice in my head. *Sometimes it's best*, she used to say smugly, *to let your opponent think he has control.*

"If they are not found tomorrow, they will have passed from our reach," he says.

My mind trips on his earlier words. *The three that escaped* . . . But I have four companions. Maybe one is also prisoner in this camp. Or dead. It's hard to maintain my false stillness while thinking of Humberto. I imagine him facedown on the rocks, a spear protruding from his back, or maybe an arrow. My cheek twitches.

"Find the others," the blue-eyed man says, his voice quiet now, conversational. He flicks his fingers again, and the others flee. He advances on me.

I'm still terrified, but it's a thinking kind of fear, and different possibilities tumble through my head in fierce competition.

The candlelight sparks against something hanging on a brown leather tie around his neck. A tiny cage dangles at the midpoint of his chest, small enough to wrap in the palm of my hand, with black, ironlike bars and a tiny latch at the top. There's something bright inside.

"Soft thing," he whispers, looming closer, and the little cage swings against his chest. "I see the intelligence in you.

There is something about your face. Something strange."

I hear his words, but they don't make sense. I can only stare at his amulet, at the shimmering blue stone locked in its tiny cage. I've seen such a thing before, in Father Nicandro's study, in my own navel.

It's a Godstone.

21

I'M stunned, truly frozen, though not by the animagus's sorcery. Can this be the amulet spoken of? The one that leaves rippling burn scars on the bodies of my people? If so, how could God allow something so sacred to be used in such a way?

It cannot be the animagus's own Godstone, unless he ripped it from his own belly. More likely he found it some other way. Father Nicandro gave me only three, but nearly twenty centuries have passed since God brought us to this world. Nearly twenty bearers. And then comes the most dreadful thought of all: *Is it possible, then, that God would choose bearers among the enemy?*

He studies me as these thoughts race through my mind. I hope my face hasn't given away too much.

He smiles. His teeth are yellow and sickly, at odds with the perfect planes of his face. "You've made me late for dinner," he croons. "But don't worry. I'm a reasonable man." He cocks his head to one side, then rotates it to the other, and I feel like a small rodent facing down a mountain lion. "You don't understand the holy language, do you? Don't worry, don't worry. When I return, the earth shall have a bit of your blood, and then we shall see." He caresses my cheek, and I barely suppress a shudder at his touch, cool and dry like snakeskin. "I'll bring you something to eat. Be a good girl and don't move while I'm gone." He chortles at the joke.

And he leaves me alone in the tent.

I look around frantically, wondering how much time I'll have. This could be my only chance to escape, but I must think quickly. I consider running, but there are too many Inviernos between me and the hills. It would be best to wait for the animagus to return. To kill him. Maybe I could take his Godstone and hold it before me like a weapon as I flee the tent. I don't know how to use it, of course, but maybe it would buy me time. Maybe not. At least I would die knowing I'd rid the world of one of Invierne's sorcerers. Hitzedar the bowman killed one. And Humberto's grandfather, Damián. Now, it's my turn.

I feel ridiculous reaching for the knife at my boot, even more so when I feel the urine that sogs my pants beneath my robe. I decide to not think about it.

I don't know if I can make myself stab someone again. Killing with a knife is so personal, an intimacy I never thought to endure. Besides, as my captors so aptly pointed out, I am no warrior.

So, to be successful, I must catch him by surprise. I hide the knife in my sash so that the handle pokes my back. I'm just as likely to stab myself with a sudden twist of my torso, for nothing stands between the blade and my skin but a worn robe. But

I don't know where else to hide it that is within easy reach.

I glance around the tent, looking for anything else that might aid me. A sleeping roll lies against one wall, thick with yellowing wool. The ground is worn down and smooth, empty but for the stone altar shimmering with candles, the wooden stand with a wineskin, and a few gray-brown plants stunted from lack of sun. I peer at the plants. There's something familiar about their velvety texture, about the withered, brownish berries. I move closer to where they wilt at the base of the altar, realizing the thing was built around a natural boulder. And the plants are indeed familiar. The color is all wrong, from being deprived of sun and fresh air, but they are certainly duerma plants.

There cannot be much time left. I flick several berries into my palm, dismayed at how dry they are, how easily they separate from their stems. I wince when the wineskin's stopper comes unplugged with a slight pop. I drop a berry inside, then hesitate, thinking. The rest, I separate with my fingernail to expose the insides before letting them tumble inside.

I hear footsteps, and I take a moment, stupidly, to glance toward the tent flap. He must find me in the exact position he left me. Where was I standing? Were my arms at my sides or slightly forward? I rush back to the spot I was in and turn to face the altar. No, not quite right; the candles were hotter against my skin. The tent flap opens as I shift slightly to my left. The hidden knife blade pokes at my back as cooler air flushes my face and flutters the candles like an invisible, sweeping hand.

The animagus enters, chuckling. "Ah, you are such an obedient thing. You did not move at all. Not even to wet yourself again." He carries two wooden bowls, and in spite of my predicament, my mouth waters at the rich smell of venison with basil and garlic. "You will find that I am a kind man. See? I have brought you something wonderful to eat." He sets a bowl on the ground before me, and sits cross-legged. "Sit."

I stare at him.

"Sit, sit, sit," he says, flicking at the air, then patting the ground in front of him.

I comply, slowly, watching him for a sudden movement.

He scoops a chunk of meat toward his mouth. His teeth clamp down on it so that bits of grizzle and stringy flesh dangle from his thick lips. He shakes his head around, flinging meat across his cheek, before jutting out his chin and gulping it down. He didn't bother to chew.

I look down at my own bowl, devoid of appetite.

"Eat!" he orders, indicating the bowl.

I hesitate. What if he poisons me?

"Eat, eat, eat!"

I dip a finger into the sauce and lift it to my lips. After a tentative taste, I suck it off eagerly.

"Now, as we dine . . ." He lobs another chunk into his mouth and swallows it whole. "You will tell me about your companions, the ones who fled the cave before we found you."

I just gape at him, trying to look like an imbecile.

"I shall rephrase." And he says, in the Lengua Plebeya, "Tell me about your companions."

I gasp.

He smiles. "It is distasteful for me to speak your language. It is like dirt in my mouth. Therefore, you will tell me what I want to know. Quickly, so I do not have to sully myself with too many barbarian words."

My heart pounds. It would have been so much easier to pretend ignorance. Now, I must choose my words with exceeding care.

"What are you going to do to me?" I ask, not bothering to disguise the tremor in my voice. I need to stall him long enough that he takes a solid draft of wine. Or gets close enough that I can stab him after all.

"I'm going to dine with you while you tell me about your companions. If you do not tell me, I will feed the earth a bit of your blood and use magic to open your mouth. Then you will decide."

"Me?" I whisper. "I will decide?"

"Whether you live or die."

There will be a cost, a choice. I don't know what it is, and I don't care. If I can kill him, it won't matter.

"I want to live," I say, pretending to be more afraid than I am. Suddenly, I realize I'm no longer cold. No longer in a state of perpetual prayer to keep my limbs from freezing. Maybe because whatever happens next will be my act of service? Or maybe it's the presence of the foreign Godstone.

Ah, the Godstone. This could be my only chance to understand.

"That . . . thing around your neck," I say, pointing. "My people fear it greatly."

"Eat, eat!"

I stick a finger in the bowl again while he settles back, the beautiful blue of his eyes flashing in arrogance. "It is something to be feared. This, and the stones of my brothers, will deliver your land into our hands. It is God's will."

I almost stab him right then. What would this man know of God's will? He is insane, hardly human with his wild eyes and predatory hunger. My hands shake with rage, though I'm not sure whom it's directed at. The Vía-Reformas kept me in ignorance according to the will of God. Father Nicandro told me about my heritage for the same reason. Cosmé and Humberto kidnapped me to bring about His will. Now, even my enemy presumes to know the mind of God.

Alentín assured me that everyone has doubts. But it seems as though I am the only one without a single idea about what God wants from me. I am His bearer, and I understand nothing.

"Why?" I whisper. "Why are you doing this?"

"I think a little wine with dinner would be perfect, don't you?" He shoots me a feral grin, then rises to his feet. I can hardly breathe for watching him approach the stand with its wineskin.

God, please let him drink.

He glides across the ground with leonine grace, and it's as if something else squirms beneath his taut skin. A creature within a creature. Alodia would seem oafish next to him.

He fills two mugs.

I don't know enough about duerma leaf. I don't know how long it takes for the poison to kill someone, or whether or not raw berries will even do the trick. I lean back as he approaches, seeking comfort in the feel of the knife point pricking my rear.

He settles back down. "Tell me about your companions," he says, "and I will give you some wine."

As if wine were such a treasure. There is something simple and ingenuous about him. Or maybe it's insanity. I pretend to consider.

"What do you want to know?" I ask. My breath catches in my throat as he sips.

"Why did you come?"

The *Belleza Guerra* says the best deceptions are born of truth. "We wanted to see your army," I tell him.

"I don't believe you are that stupid." He takes another sip.

I gaze at the other mug, as if longing for it. "We were sent," I say.

His eyes widen. "By whom?"

"I cannot tell you."

He leans forward, close enough for me to see his black irises. They are oblong, like a cat's. "You will tell me, or you will bleed."

I make a careful study of the food in my bowl, pretending to deliberate. "It was the conde," I say at last. "Conde Treviño." The man who supplies our enemy with food. The traitor. "There are many in the conde's court who do not believe your army to be so large. He needed confirmation and sent us to find out."

He sits back, considering, and brings the mug to his lips again. "I don't believe you."

God, please let the poison work. "Why not?" I try to look confused.

"Because you are no warrior. The conde is a great fool, but he would not send a child who wets herself to spy on an army."

He is right, of course, and my heart pounds out the truth. I bear the Godstone! It screams. But I know, as sure as I've known anything, that this animagus must never know about it.

"I'm not sure why he sent me," I say, my head bowed in mock shame. *Keep him talking,* I tell myself.

"You are a very poor liar."

He moves so fast, I hardly see. I only notice the pain, bright and bursting along my forearm. I look down at the blood welling there in two parallel streaks.

He flicks two fingertips at me, and I see the sharp objects embedded there, sticking from beneath his fingernails, dripping with my blood.

My pulse hammers in my arm, crimson streams over the edge, drips onto the ground. The hazy air wavers before me and I feel myself swaying.

He sips again. "Now, once the earth has tasted your blood, maybe we will know the truth of this."

Bright drops fall onto the hard-packed ground. They spread on impact, flattening, blurring into the ground, browning. The Godstone turns to fire, and I nearly choke as the burn gushes up my spine.

"The earth loves your blood," he sings. "Oh, yes, yours in particular, it loves, loves, loves. My stone warms already." He lifts the mug to smiling lips.

The amulet swaying against his chest begins to glow, white-blue like predawn stars. He is going to burn me. He will force the truth from me by sizzling my skin one wet bit at a time. I am not a strong person. I know I will say anything to make the pain stop.

He is much quicker than I am, so I know I must do this exactly right. While my left forearm continues to feed the earth my life's blood, I reach with my right, slowly, to the knife that bruises my back. I hold it there in hesitation. This could be the moment I die. He could slice me with those manufactured claws and rip out my throat if he chose.

"I don't want to die," I tell him, truthfully.

He smiles like a father fawning over his favorite daughter, the way my father used to look with such fond tolerance at my sister. "All you have to do is tell me . . ."

He doesn't finish. He looks at me strangely, squinting his unlikely eyes. "You can't disappear on me, girl," he says, slipping back into the Lengua Classica. "It is too late. The earth has already tasted you."

My gaze does not move from his too-lovely face, but I pull the knife from my sash.

"I'm so tired. So tired, tired, tired." He looks around the tent, unable to focus. Then his eyes widen with understanding. "What have you done to me?"

I want to tell him he is a fool. I want to show him my own Godstone, alive and real. I say nothing.

He grasps for his caged Godstone and thrusts it toward me,

but the glow already fades. "Why does it not burn you?" he demands, his voice garbled. "Why?"

I respond in the Lengua Classica. "Because it is not the will of God."

His blue eyes widen. He opens his mouth, but no sound comes out. He topples backward and lies there, his head at the base of the altar, his ear brushing the leaves of the dying duerma plant.

"Thank you, God," I breathe aloud. "Thank you."

I put a hand to his chest. A pulse flutters beneath his ribs, faint but true. Not dead. Maybe the duerma berries lose potency when dried. But if my own experience with duerma leaf is any indication, he will sleep a long time.

With the knife, I cut a strip from the hem of my robe and use it to bind my bleeding forearm.

Inexplicably, I am alive. There must be a way to escape, to warn the others, for I have learned much. The animagi can freeze a person's muscles with a flick of their fingers. They arm themselves with Godstones. They've found a way to bring forth fire by "feeding the earth" with blood. My tiny army of children, my Malficio, must know of these things.

So, I curl my knees to my chest, and I think.

I'll never make it past the perimeter of the camp dressed as I am. I must disguise myself. The bleached-white robes of the animagus beckon to me, and I almost laugh aloud at the idea. I could take his robes. His amulet.

I reach for his head with distaste. His white-yellow hair slithers against my palm as I pull the amulet over his head.

When I drop it around my own, the Godstone in my navel jumps with joyous greeting. "Stop that," I mumble.

Getting him out of his robe is more difficult. In spite of his slenderness, he is very heavy. I roll him back and forth, releasing first one arm, then the other, then push him onto his stomach. Without his robe, he seems fragile, the blue of his veins spidering across the pale flesh of hairless legs. His long braid glitters in the candlelight like liquid gold. In a flash of pique, I grab it and saw it off at the nape.

The smell of incense almost makes me gag as the robe settles across my shoulders. It's made of hide I've never seen before, thick and heavy, but pliant and flowing as fine silk. I tie it closed and pull out the amulet so its dark cage shows against the robe's whiteness. The cowl fits neatly over my head. I weave the frayed end of his braid into the ties of the robe and let it dangle down my chest. Within the robe, I hold tight to the knife.

I look down at the animagus. So delicate. So beautiful. He will awaken eventually. Maybe I should put the knife into his heart while he sleeps so he does not live to burn again. But the thought of using a knife again repulses me.

I get a better idea.

His bedding lies flush against the side of the tent. I yank at one end, pulling it toward the center. The wool is soft and very dry. I lift a candle from the altar, carefully, so the hot wax does not splash onto my skin. I grab the edge of a sheepskin and hold it to the flame until it catches. As the wool curls and blackens, I avert my head to avoid the acrid smell. It burns slowly. It will be several minutes before flames hit the tent walls. Enough time for me to reach the edge of the camp. I refuse to think about the man lying at my feet.

I'm ready, but I can't make my feet move toward the tent flap. *Please, God. Let this work.* I must walk with confidence. Gracefully. Head down so no one sees the dark cast of my skin. I inhale deeply and wait for my heart to still. Behind me, the bedding pops; a glowing spark bounces at my feet, then blackens into dust.

I force my mind to stillness. *Do not think, Elisa. Just do.* I part the tent flap and stride into the firelit night. The flap falls shut, disguising the growing conflagration inside. I quick-step forward, placing my legs just so, the way Humberto taught me. It's the best approximation of grace I'll ever manage, and I hope it is enough. Inviernos look up at me as I pass, but I ignore them, striding with purpose. I feel their wild eyes on my back. The Godstone goes cold.

"My lord," someone says in acknowledgment. I give the briefest nod, keeping the cowl tight, and continue on. Surely he will see that I am not slender. Not graceful.

I weave through fire pits, around bedrolls, toward the comforting blackness of the hills, listening for someone to cry out in warning. I am almost there.

Something odd catches my attention, off to my left. Something out of place. I allow the slightest turn of my head. It's a man. Dressed not in furs, but in the robes of the desert people. His hair is black and unclumped, his skin is dark. He scrapes food from a bowl, and I cannot see his face, but my chest burns with the implication. One of Joya's own, eating with the enemy. There are no ropes or chains that I can see. No animagus nearby to force him into magical paralysis. One of the others, a pale, muddy-haired Invierno, pats him on the back. He looks up and smiles. My legs turn to water; I gasp out a sob.

It is Belén.

22

WE were not discovered. Belén told them where to find us. The animagus's words return to me: "The three who escaped . . ." I had worried that someone had been captured or killed.

The hand grasping the knife shivers with rage. If I kill anyone tonight, it should be Belén. Maybe, dressed as I am, I could walk right up to him.

But I reject the idea as soon as it comes. He would recognize me, of course, and I would never escape. The things I have learned must be shared. I do not have the luxury of vengeance.

"My lord?" someone says at my elbow.

I have tarried too long. Maybe they heard my gasp of surprise. Hands still shaking, I move away from the one who spoke, hoping he attributes my action to the arrogance of an animagus.

A few more steps to reach the dark. I will have to feel my way up the cliff, but after climbing down from the cave at spear point, I think I can do it. I must do it. The robe should be discarded. It will be too bright against the cliff face. Maybe I should aim for the cave again. I think longingly of my pack, with its food and water. But the cave is probably under guard now that it's been discovered, and I have no way of finding it in the dark anyway. I will have to do without.

I step quietly out of the firelight. The cliff face looms before me, gradually inclining at the base, then steepening into darkness. I brush against a juniper branch, feel its whispering needles against my cheek, smell its tangy pine scent. I duck behind it to remove the robe.

Shouting rings through the valley, hurried and fierce. I peer through the branches. In the distance, one of the fires flares brighter, higher than the others. It's the animagus's tent. The Inviernos closest to my hiding place scramble to their feet and run toward it.

I must move now.

I drop the robe, but the last thing I want to do is leave a marker of my escape route. Even if I climb the cliff unnoticed, it won't take long for them to figure out what happened and give chase. I pause long enough to yank the white braid free of the robe and shove it into my waistband. Then I cover the robe as best I can with dirt and pine needles.

While the enemy scrambles to put out the fire, I sprint for the cliff. Climbing is easy at first, and I only use my hands occasionally, but the incline steepens, and soon I'm on all fours, my fingers sliding around, searching the dark for handholds. A root here, a ledge there. The skin of my legs burns from chafing against urine-soaked pants. My fingernails fill with dirt, my shoulders burn, the fleshy areas beneath my thumbs harden with cramping until I can hardly grip. Something scuttles across my hand. I wrench it back. Breath-stealing pain shoots up my finger; warm liquid oozes over the webbing of my fingers, across my palm. I've ripped off a fingernail.

I try to ignore the pain, to keep climbing. It's too dark to see how far I've left to go, and I dare not take time to gauge my progress. My grip is slippery with blood now, the muscles in my forearms spasm. Reaching above my head, I feel the cliff face curve back on itself into an overhang, and my heart pounds in dismay. Climbing over it is impossible. My muscles already threaten to betray me. I scrape to the side, looking for another way up.

The overhang stretches a long way. Spiderwebs stick against my face as I scoot along, but I resist the urge to bat at them. I pray as I travel, desperate for the Godstone's warmth to breathe life into my stiffening limbs.

At last I feel a break in the overhang. I clamber upward eagerly, expecting to be spotted any moment. My right fore-arm hooks around a large ledge. No, it's the top of the cliff. I'm almost sobbing in relief as I yank my body over the top. Unable to trust my shaky legs, I roll away from the edge.

I shouldn't rest. I should launch to my feet and run west, my back to the glow of Invierne's massive army. But my limbs won't move. I lie on my back, catching my breath, staring at the star-pricked sky. Away from the campfires, the stars are brilliant. White sparkles in a quilt of black.

The beauty of the night sky offers strange comfort. It is

unchanging. Immune to the wars of this world. Something to count on. I scramble to my feet and run.

I should have thought to steal some food. Or water, at least. I stumble along as dawn breaks against my back, finally understanding how precarious my situation is. I'm too exhausted to outrun pursuers. I'm thirsty. And I have no idea where I'm going.

The fear in my head beckons me to continue, no matter what. But another voice—one that has become familiar in these last months—reasons that I will soon be useless without water and rest. I need to drink, to sleep. Otherwise, I'm likely to stumble from sheer exhaustion. And in this harsh land of jagged rocks and steep ravines, a stumble could lead to death, as it did for Damián the shepherd.

I decide to travel until I find a stream; then I will look for a place to hide and sleep. But how to find water? I close my eyes, thinking of Humberto, wishing he were here to guide me. I think of the kiss we shared, imagine his lips against mine. The possibility of never seeing him again makes my chest hurt.

Then my eyes snap open, and I force myself to remember our journeys together. What would Humberto do? I scan the horizon, looking for ravines coupled with vegetation that is thicker, greener, than the rest. An area ahead and slightly south looks promising. I step forward with renewed energy.

It's a dry wash, worn smooth from spring flash flooding, cracked from the heat. But rich vegetation lines the edge, and I know I'm on the right track. I hike up a gravelly rise to survey the land, and try again.

I see a depression rimmed in thick piñon. Its southward direction dismays me, but I must have water. My ankles shake as I trudge toward it; my tongue is thick with dryness. When I reach the edge, the trees are too thick to see, but I hear a gurgling sound. Or maybe that's just wind in the branches. I grab at trunks, at outcroppings, as I slither haphazardly down the scree, into the dusty hollow. The branches break wide. A tiny brook snakes along the bottom, no wider than my leg, but clear as crystal. Gasping, I fall to my stomach and lap at the water. I drink until my stomach can hold no more.

I want nothing more than to sleep. But I force myself to remove my boots and pants and soak the dried urine from them in the stream. With the edge of my desert robe, I wipe down my legs. They are red and bumpy, and the water stings even as it cools my skin. I hang my pants to dry on a branch, giving a quick glance to my surroundings to make sure they'll not be easily spotted from above. I crawl beneath the shady boughs of a sprawling piñon pine. I curl my bare legs under my robe and rest my head on a bed of pine needles. Sleep comes easy.

The sun is low when I wake. Though my back and arms ache from climbing, I rise immediately to take advantage of the remaining light. I have nothing for carrying water, but I must keep moving, as far away from Invierne's army as I am able, so I dare not travel along the southward-running brook. I drink as much as I can, which makes the hunger fade a bit. Wincing, I peel the bloody strip from my forearm, wash it as best I can, and rewrap it tightly. The welts sting, and I know I must find a village before infection sets in. I study my finger carefully. Only half of my nail ripped off, and the tender part has scabbed nicely. I tear another strip from my robe and bandage my finger. Remembering our desert journey from Brisadulce, I soak my clothes through before setting off, to protect my body from the heat.

Lizards scatter from my path as I walk; a squealing turkey vulture circles wide to the north, against a backdrop of roiling clouds. I step along with renewed energy. The cuts in my forearm sting, and my finger throbs, but I can't help smiling as I travel. I escaped the army of Invierne. I faced capture, sorcery, even the beginnings of torture, yet I escaped. It is in no small part due to my Godstone. I should have been paralyzed by the animagus's sorcery, burned by the amulet I now wear around my own neck. But his magic didn't affect me, and I can only suppose my Godstone protected me. Homer's *Afflatus* says that the purpose of the bearer is to fight sorcery with sorcery. Maybe this strange immunity to magic is what he referred to.

I wish I could discuss it with Humberto. Or Father Alentín. With a pang, I realize I want more than anything to talk it over with Ximena. I'm desperate to see her again, to feel her strong arms holding me tight. I hope she does not receive my message that I am well, only to learn later that I died here in the scrub desert.

I crest a rocky bluff and gaze across the cracked wilderness. Razorback ridges snake eastward, separated by deep canyons, dotted with mesquite and juniper trees that are starving and broken like crippled old men. I'm so small standing here, the land before me so vast and stark. My aloneness hits me like a kick in the gut. My smile fades, and I shiver with cold. From habit, I pray to warm myself. But the cold isn't coming from the Godstone anymore. A bright flash to the north catches my eye. Blue-black clouds plunge toward me, heralded by a frigid wind.

I curse myself for a fool for soaking my clothing before setting off. Cosmé or Humberto would have known better. The wind strengthens; wet robes slap, stinging, against my skin. I hope it rains. The water might wash away my trail, and the wet clothes wouldn't matter so much. But thinking of the trail I've left brings another uncomfortable realization: I'm standing high on a ridge in full view of potential pursuers.

My skidding descent sends me into a dry wash. But dry for how long? I remember Humberto's warning about flash floods and jog along the wash, scanning the sides for a place to shelter. The sun has set and colors have muted to gray before I find a large boulder with a slight overhang, nestled beneath a spreading juniper. I climb up, shivering with cold, and huddle against the smooth stone. I wish I had my tinderbox with flint and cutting steel. Or even Cosmé's jerboa soup. As the first fat drops plop against the ground at my knees, I begin to wonder if, in spite of my unlikely escape, I'm destined to die out here after all.

It rains all night, alternating between soaking sheets of water and icy drizzle. It's too dark to see the bottom of the ravine, but water rushes by, as deafening as the wind. I pray continuously, and the Godstone overcomes the worst of the chill, but I'm far too uncomfortable to sleep. And I'm afraid that if I doze, I'll lose my perch and tumble into the water rising some unknown distance below me. When the rain finally abates, I decide to wait out the night instead of trying to climb in the dark. I'm dizzy from hunger, chilled and sore, and I know I'd never make it. It's the longest night of my life.

Dawn brings pinkish light, a crisper, crystalline world, and rekindled determination. It is true that I am no warrior, that I am ill suited to wilderness survival. But I can find a way. *"You have a first-rate mind,"* the traitor, Belén, told me. Thinking of Belén steels me further. I must get back to Father Alentín's village somehow, to warn them.

The ravine is filled with water now, muddy and brambled. I refuse to look at it as I scramble from my ineffectual shelter and up the rise. My robes aren't as soaked as they could be, but they are damp enough to chill me thoroughly. I pray as I walk along the ridge, knowing I'm in plain sight but not daring to travel where a wall of water could wash me away. Hunger gnaws at my stomach. At least I won't lack water sources for a while.

The sun warms my back as it rises, bringing a smidge of comfort. And an idea.

I stop in my tracks, turning the thought over in my mind. On the journey to Invierne's camped army, my Godstone grew colder with increasing danger. As I travel away, it warms again to my body. Over the years it has always warmed to my prayers, even to certain people. Just maybe, it can be my beacon to safety.

Placing my feet carefully while minding the stone is arduous. I head westward, sloping ever downward, hoping to feel a pulse of increased warmth or a little tug. Hours pass before I notice something, and when I do, it's only a faint itch. A ghost sensation, perhaps, created by my desperate hope. But when I twist a little to my right, it tickles again. Only a tiny buzz of warmth at my navel, but I'm so excited I plunge down the embankment. At the muddy bottom I pause again and pivot around until the sensation is strongest. My hands shake with exhilaration. Maybe, just maybe, I'll live through this.

I hunch my shoulders and push forward determinedly, stopping at intervals to drink from sinkholes in the rock or to concentrate on the Godstone, trotting headlong when I get a surge of warmth. I travel in this way for hours. But my ongoing hunger and the increasing throb from my forearm exact a toll. I feel myself weakening. My legs plunk down with each step as if made of lead; my vision shimmers with dizziness and maybe fever. My body is desperate to rest, but if I don't find food and treatment for the infection that swells my arm, it won't matter. I push on.

The Godstone's telling tickle strengthens, a good thing since my mind is too hazy to pay attention otherwise. As afternoon hangs the sun in my path, blazing and blurring, my feet begin to stumble. I trip along a soft ridge, a winding wrinkle of ochre earth. Something thin and twisted catches my ankle, and I pitch forward into the air. My shoulder cracks on gravel, then my hip. I can't breathe for the impact as I tumble down the ravine; my vision narrows. Then the sounds of sliding scree and cracking bones fade. I still hear them, but remotely, with indistinct curiosity. Then I don't hear them at all.

My eyelids flutter. Light and pain burst across my body, sharp as daggers, bone deep. I cry out, but the breath in my lungs spreads like fire beneath my right breast.

"Elisa? Are you awake?"

That voice! That precious voice. "Humberto?"

He's laughing, giddily, and kissing my cheek, caressing my forehead, saying my name over and over again. "I went back for you, but I couldn't find you anywhere, and the whole army was in such a panic for some reason, and then it rained and I couldn't even pick up a trail—"

"Humberto. I'm very hungry." When I open my mouth, pain zings from my jaw to the back of my neck. I don't know how I'll manage food.

"Oh! Of course. I have jerky, and—"

"Need . . . soft . . ."

I hear eager rummaging. Water poured from a skin. "I'll make some soup," he says. "Mine isn't as good as Cosmé's, but it'll do."

I close my eyes, content to let him take care of me, happy and amazed to be alive. I flex my toes and wriggle my arms to assess the pain. It's everywhere constant, but worse along my ribs and at my left temple. I lie prone, a bundle of softness stuffed beneath my neck, a sling pinning my right arm against my side. A fire crackles beside me. For the first time in days, I'm blissfully warm.

"Humberto? My arm . . ."

The fire pops as he rearranges the kindling. "I think you cracked a couple of ribs when you fell down that hill. I put your arm in a sling so you wouldn't move it while you slept."

"You saw me fall?"

"Elisa, you tumbled right into my carefully hidden camp."

My shocked sob brings piercing pain to my ribs. Tears leak from my eyes, and my breathing comes faster. It was Humberto I tracked. My Godstone led me to Humberto.

The pain from trying not to cry is too much. My vision dims.

"Humberto," I whisper.

"Are you all right, Elisa?"

I see his shadow looming, growing darker. "While you make soup, I—I've decided to pass out again."

I sink into a lovely place, dark and soft. But something tugs at the edge of my mind. Something I must tell Humberto right away. About a traitor.

I sleep.

23

IT'S nearly dark when I wake. I open my eyes and flinch away from the grin hovering over my face.

"I thought I heard you waking up. Still hungry?"

I mutter something. Humberto lifts my head and spoons soup between my lips. It's plain and watery and amazing. I giggle.

"What? Why are you laughing?"

"This is just like before. After you kidnapped me. Except the soup isn't as good."

He sits back on his heels, his smile fading. "I'm sorry about that, Elisa."

"No, the soup is fine!"

"I mean about the kidnapping."

"Oh." I take a deep breath, then catch myself as pain punches my chest.

"It was a bad fall." He spoons more soup into my mouth. "You were lucky. You could be coughing blood, or you could have broken a leg, or—"

"I don't feel lucky. I think it's getting worse."

"Cracked ribs hurt the worst on the second day. It will feel better after that."

"Humberto!" A wave of nausea ripples from my head to my stomach as I struggle to sit up. "We have to go now. We have to warn everyone." I'm so dizzy, but I must stand somehow.

"We're not going anywhere." He puts a hand to my chest and forces me back down. "You shouldn't travel for at least two weeks."

"Two weeks! Humberto, we were betrayed. We must warn Father Alentín."

The spoon freezes in the air above me as his eyes narrow. "Betrayed?" he whispers. "What do you mean?"

I look longingly at the spoon. "It was Belén. I saw him in the camp, eating with the Inviernos like they were lifelong friends."

The spoon shakes. I reach my chin toward it, my mouth open, hunger still gnawing at my spine.

"Belén would never—"

I lie back, sighing through the pain in my lower chest. "How else did they find us? They didn't stumble onto us, remember? They didn't spot us from below. They came straight for us. *They already knew.*"

He is silent for so long. My stomach growls. Then: "Are you sure it was Belén you saw? Absolutely sure?"

"I'm sure. I walked right past him."

"Did he see you?"

"Maybe. I don't think he recognized me."

He stares past me. "Belén," he murmurs. "Why would you do this?"

I can't bear the hurt in his face. "I'm so sorry."

"You're right. We have to warn everyone."

"Maybe there's another explanation. Maybe he came to find me."

"Hmm. Maybe." But his voice lacks sincerity. "Here, finish your soup."

I slurp it eagerly, and I'm almost done before I notice the prickle at the back of my throat, the faint taste like cinnamon. "You put duerma leaf in my soup."

"I did. Just enough to help you sleep through the pain tonight. Tomorrow you will tell me what you were doing in Invierne's camp. And we'll figure out what to do next."

My eyelids grow heavy as the world begins to swallow my body. "Humberto. I'm so glad you're here."

"Me too, Princess."

"You mean you walked right out of his tent in his own robe?" His voice is incredulous, and laughter crinkles the corners of his eyes.

"Yes. I wish I could have taken the robe with me, but I was afraid it would show up against the cliff."

"You climbed the cliff? In the dark?"

I reach my hand toward him, showing off the wet, brown-stained bandage wrapped around my finger. "I don't recommend it. I ripped off a fingernail. Oh, and also . . ." I lift my other arm and peel away the fabric. It throbs where the animagus clawed me, but the pain is not so fierce as the ache in my ribs, and I had nearly forgotten it. The bandage has dried against my skin, and I have to yank on it to unwrap it. "I think this is infected."

He holds my wrist and rotates the forearm, his eyes moving along the length of the parallel welts. "It's not too bad," he says. "I'll need to open them up and squeeze the infection out, then let it drain for a day or two." His look intensifies. "It will hurt. But the skin around it looks healthy. If we do it now, I'll think it will heal nicely."

I swallow. "Let's do it."

He holds his knife blade in the flames for a moment, then lets it cool. He chatters to distract me while he slices me open, and I'm surprised at how little it hurts. I feel mostly pressure, like he's cutting into a very close layer of clothing. But when he starts to squeeze, black spots flash and swirl just behind my eyelids. I sneak a glimpse, just once. The fluid oozing from my arm is viscous and greenish, tinged with blood. I turn my head away and grit my teeth as Humberto pinches down the length of my forearm. When he flushes it with icy water, tears spring to my eyes.

The fire flares as he tosses the bandage atop the burning branches. For a brief moment, the air smells of rotting meat. I lie still, collecting my breath.

"I should make you wait weeks before traveling," Humberto muses aloud. "But we need to get back to the village as soon as possible."

Humberto could go without me, but I'm afraid to suggest it. I don't ever want to be alone again. Instead, I ask, "What happened to Cosmé and Jacián?"

"My sister and I found Jacián a few hours later. Or he found us, rather. He'd been watching the camp and saw us being pursued." His face tightens. "We split up to avoid them. I don't know if either of them made it. If they did, they're far away by now."

"But you came back."

"I couldn't leave you."

We stare at each other. I want him to kiss me again. Maybe I ought to say something about it.

Finally I manage, "We're still very close to the army."

His gaze shifts to my lips. "Yes."

"You shouldn't keep the fire going."

"Um . . . no."

"Then put it out, Humberto. I'll live without it. Tomorrow, we leave."

He shakes his head as if to clear it. "You can't possibly walk."

"I most certainly can. I'll start slow, I promise. You can scout ahead in the morning. Find a secluded campsite just a few hours ahead, then come back and get me. If that works, maybe I can go a little farther the next day."

He starts to protest but goes silent. I know he's desperate to find out about the others and warn the village. "We'll try it," he concedes. He smiles softly. "And see? I told you that you're braver than you know."

His face is so intent on mine that I have to look away.

Every step sends pain jolting into my ribs and back. Walking is both worse and better, though, for the motion chases some of the stiffness away. Breathing is near impossible, but my head clears, my neck relaxes, and the bruises on my arms and legs turn from purple to sickly yellow. The Godstone no longer flares in icy warning, but I continue to pray as I walk.

The next day, we do the same, traveling only a few hours. The day after that, my breakfast tea sends spicy tingles to the back of my throat.

"Did you put duerma leaf in this?"

He just stands there, looking smug.

I sway backward, into the bedroll he gave up for me. My eyelids are too heavy for a decent glare. ". . . hate you," I say.

"You can tell me all about it tomorrow." He leans forward, and I'm only vaguely aware of his lips pressing against my forehead.

As we travel, I'm delighted to see the vegetation disappear, to feel the air warm, hailing the encroaching desert. When the soil turns red and buttes reach for the sky in fiery layers, I even feel a pang of homesickness.

A sentry meets us while we are yet a half-day's walk from the secret village, then hurries ahead to warn everyone not to kill us on sight. After exchanging a questioning look, Humberto and I quicken our steps. He strides ahead unerringly, and I thank God for leading me to him. This dry hill country is a maze of twisting ravines and identical buttes, and I never would have found my way without help.

At last our mountain rises before us, the huge overhang of the half-cavern embracing the village tight within its shelter.

Everyone is there to greet us, smiling, and my eyes fill with tears. It is so different from my first suspicious reception here. Alentín hobbles toward me, his one arm outstretched. I rush forward, ignoring the residual pain in my ribs, and wrap my arms around his skinny frame.

So many faces I recognize, this time open and hopeful. They try to grab my hands and hug my thighs, but Humberto pushes them away. "She is injured!" he hollers. "Don't squeeze too hard."

My face burns with humiliation. For some reason, I hate feeling coddled in this particular moment. Then I spot Cosmé elbowing her way mercilessly through the crowd. She slows upon seeing Humberto, her relief apparent. They exchange an acknowledgment; then she approaches me and I notice, unaccountably, that she's cut her hair short again. Her jaw twitches, her eyes widen. She leans forward—for a moment I think she's going to hug me—then she whacks my shoulder and grins. "I didn't think you'd make it back."

I sigh. "I didn't either."

"She killed an animagus," Humberto announces.

Everyone stares at me in silence.

"Well, we don't *know* that," I protest, shifting on my feet. "I never saw the body."

"But you gave him duerma berries and burned his tent to the ground."

I shrug.

Cosmé peers at my face. "I don't believe you."

"Can we talk about this later? I really need a bath. And food. Anything but jerky or dates."

But she won't let it go. "Lying isn't going to make you into a hero."

The spark of anger in my gut quickly fades to sadness and exhaustion. I have nothing to say, so I turn away, thinking only bathing thoughts. Then, I get an idea. I stop.

"Cosmé," I say over my shoulder. "I brought a gift for you." I reach into my sash and pull out the animagus's yellow-white braid. I toss it at her feet. "For being such a good friend."

I feel eyes boring into my back as I hurry into the cavern.

The story of my escape has already spread by the time I finish bathing. Everyone pats me on the back, asking questions, offering congratulations. And everyone has their own story to tell. My Malficio was very busy while we were away.

At night, Alentín sits cross-legged beside me in the sand of our half-cavern while we wait for dinner to be prepared. He tells me of a group of five older boys who quietly stumbled upon an enemy scouting party while hunting. They tracked the party for a day, waited for the right opportunity; then, early in the morning, they attacked with bows and arrows from the ridge above. The scouting party was much larger, easily fifteen men, so each of our hunters killed a single man and then retreated. Two days later, they did the same. They left the remaining handful to spread the word of their defeat. Since then, the village rallying cry has been, "Each one kill one."

Alentín tells me, "It is as you said. We sting, and then live to sting again."

"Each one kill one," I echo. "That's perfect." I push away my discomfort at the thought that we are encouraging children even younger than me to kill.

"We found another group northeast of here. Probably traveling between armies. They were camped next to a brook. One girl took an enormous batch of duerma leaf powder and poured it into the water a ways upstream. Half of them passed out. The rest panicked." His face hardens when he says, "We slaughtered them in their sleep, then took their clothes and weapons. Burned the bodies." He looks away.

"You did well." But my belly squirms.

"This idea of yours. Inflicting harm with little loss of life. Terrorizing the enemy. It's a good one, the best one, but it still hurts my heart." He looks down and draws swirls in the dust with his fingertip. "I just hope His Majesty, may minstrels compose epics at the sound of his glorious name, will do as you say and give this land to its people."

I whisper, "I will do everything I can."

"I know you will."

"Father, I need to show you something." I glance around to make sure no one is looking, then pull the animagus's amulet from beneath my woolen blouse. I'm not sure how Alentín will react to seeing the cause of so much suffering, but I'm desperate to talk to someone about it. I lean forward, the caged Godstone cool and dead in my palm.

Alentín's eyes fly wide. "Did you take that from your animagus?" he whispers.

"I did."

He starts to reach for it, then yanks his hand back. "Are

you sure it was a good idea to bring it here, Elisa? This is an instrument of evil. What if it starts to burn—"

"It won't."

"How can you be sure?"

"It's not evil. It's a Godstone."

His face freezes. "That's not possible. God would never allow such a thing."

"I don't understand it either, Alentín. But I know a Godstone when I see one. This is the fourth one I've seen, besides my own. There is no doubt."

Alentín's voice drops to a whisper. "How did he acquire such a thing?"

"I don't know. Godstones detach from their bearers at the moment of death. So maybe the animagi steal them. Or maybe—"

"Maybe what?"

I lean in. "Maybe some bearers have been selected from Invierne."

His eyes narrow. "Inviernos are evil. They do not walk the path of God."

I shrug. "But they have Godstones, and they do sorcery with them. If I could learn how to use it the way they do . . ."

His tone is dark and cutting when he says, "That would be a very dangerous game."

I smile humorlessly. "No more dangerous than what we already do. You were the one who said the bearer was to fight magic with magic."

He sighs. "Yes. It's why we brought you here, after all, but that doesn't mean I'm happy about it. Promise an old man you'll be careful?"

I reach forward on impulse and hug him. "I promise."

We're interrupted by Mara, who bears steaming plates of spiced lamb shanks with buttered spinach. I breathe in through my nose, savoring the rich moistness. Not jerky, not dates. We take our plates, and Mara squeezes my shoulder before stepping away.

I hold the first bite in my mouth, letting the juice from the meat burst across my tongue. I almost shudder. I remember our last loaf of bread the night before we found Invierne's army, squashed from riding in Belén's pack. *Belén.*

"Father, I must tell you something else. Belén . . . has he returned?"

He swallows a mouthful. "He has not. Jacián returned—he's hunting now—but not Belén. Cosmé is worried for him."

I take a deep breath. "He may have betrayed us."

He leans forward, eyes sharp. "What do you mean?"

I describe what happened, what I saw in the camp of our enemy.

"You're certain?"

"I've asked myself every hour of every day if there is a way I could be wrong, Father. He was not being held against his will. He moved freely in the camp. I saw . . . camaraderie between him and the Inviernos. And there's no other explanation for how they knew where to find us. My companions are all highly skilled. I'm certain we didn't give our location away by accident."

He ponders, searching my eyes. "If we take this to the village, it will be your word against his."

"Yes."

"The village might listen to you, though Belén is one of their own. You are the bearer. And you have slain an animagus."

"I didn't actually see the body—"

"If you called for it, he would be executed."

I swallow. "I don't want that. I want to give him an opportunity to help. To tell us what he knows."

Alentín nods. "Then I will spread the word, quietly, that Belén is to be held for questioning if he returns. And we will double our perimeter guard. We are prepared to flee this place at the earliest sign of attack."

It's as good a plan as any. I turn my full attention to my plate.

We all work hard during the next weeks, for we can't be sure how much time we have before Invierne begins its march. Our "gossips" return from the villages with news that rumors of the Malficio are at full strength. Some of them bring trusted friends and family members with them. A village nearby is razed to the ground by animagi, and we rally to collect the survivors. Our number swells to more than eighty, and I am relieved to add a solid contingent of adults to our group.

Then something happens that I hadn't anticipated: Word trickles in of attacks upon the enemy that were not orchestrated by our group. Other villages, other hidden camps of refugees, have adopted our strategy. They harry the army all along its formidable length, striking and retreating only to strike again. The curse of the Malficio has fed on itself, become a living thing all its own.

But there is no sign of Belén. Humberto finally confides that Belén and Cosmé had promised to marry, should they survive the war. My former maid is more distant than ever, and my heart aches for her.

Then one day a shout rings out from the perimeter, and moments later a sentry hauls a blindfolded captive into our village. He's a thin-boned, younger man wearing the same desert robes I've grown accustomed to. But a closer look reveals a fine weave, a brighter white, and a sash with embroidered gold threads. He claims to have a message for the leader of the Malficio.

We drag him deep into the cavern where he cannot see the village and its surroundings. A small group of onlookers gathers around us, blocking any escape. While Jacián and the sentry hold him by the shoulders, I rip off the blindfold.

"You have a message?" I ask. My voice has acquired a dangerous edge, born of responsibility and worry. It's a voice I'm not sure I like.

"I am to give it only to the leader of the Malficio," he says, and I have to credit him for his unflinching gaze and a head held high.

"You do not speak with the accent of the desert people," I say.

"I am not from the desert."

"How did you come here?"

He deflates just a little. I well understand that feeling of utter exhaustion barely held in check. "I have traveled for almost three weeks, asking for the Malficio. I heard in the villages that I should seek southward, nearer the desert. Please tell me I've finally arrived. I thought, maybe, with the blindfold—"

"You have reached the Malficio."

"Oh, thank God. Are *you* their leader?" He peers at me in dismay.

"I am."

Jacián growls in warning as the messenger reaches beneath his sash. "It's not a weapon," he says, smiling shakily. He retrieves a leather pouch, squashed flat, and fumbles with the ties. From inside, he pulls out a roll of parchment, also flattened but still sealed in bright red wax.

The people around me gasp in recognition of the seal. My fingers shake as I slide my thumbnail through the wax and unroll the parchment. I read. Then I read it again to be sure. My heart pounds as I raise my eyes.

"It's from Conde Treviño," I tell them. The traitor. Condesa Ariña's father. "He wishes to discuss an alliance."

24

"IT's a trap," Humberto growls, staring at the earthen floor.

"I have to agree," Jacián says.

We are gathered in my adobe hut with Cosmé and Father Alentín to discuss the conde's mysterious summons. Mara has made my favorite dish tonight—lamb shanks roasted in coals and sliced thin, then rolled with a batter of bread and onions, garlic and pine nuts. I eat slowly.

Father Alentín is nodding. "The conde has proven treacherous," he says. "He gives the fruit of his people's labor into the hands of Invierne. He refuses to defend the villages. He may have promised to deliver you to the enemy."

"Why?" I ask. "What does he have to gain?"

"Who knows?" Humberto says, throwing up his hands. "Promise of amnesty. A place in the new government, perhaps."

I narrow my eyes, thinking. "But it is possible, just *possible*, that he truly wishes to discuss an alliance." When I look around for confirmation, only Cosmé does not meet my gaze.

Humberto's face twitches. "Elisa, please don't go."

"If there is a chance the conde is willing to aid us, don't you think it worth the risk?" I'd like to go to Basajuan for other reasons too. A city that size would have news of Brisadulce and Alejandro, maybe even a reply from Ximena. But I keep that to myself.

"The conde thinks he's doing the right thing," Cosmé whispers. She's been silent most of the evening. "He thinks he is saving the lives of his people by treating with the enemy." There is something depthless about her eyes in the candlelight. We stare at her collectively, but her delicate features remain frozen.

Humberto reaches forward and clasps his sister's hand. A pang of envy shoots through my chest and leaves me feeling empty. "Cosmé," Humberto says gently. "Would the conde betray Elisa if he thought it would help his people?"

"Absolutely."

Jacián rocks back on his heels, sighing. "It concerns me that his messenger found us so easily."

"The messenger says he is merely one of many who were sent," Alentín points out. "Maybe he was luckier than the others."

"Or someone told him where to find us," Jacián counters.

"What do you mean, someone?" Cosmé asks, her voice dark and silvery.

Jacián leans toward her, unintimidated. "I mean Belén. He's still out there. He probably told the conde all about us. Two traitors working together."

"Belén would never—"

"He already has."

They glare at each other a long while. I can't begin to understand how they feel. Though his treachery nearly resulted in my death, Belén was not a child playmate of mine. Not a future husband. For the hundredth time, I hope I am wrong. I put my fingertips to the Godstone and pray that I was misled, and that Belén, wherever he is, remains loyal to his friends and to our cause.

Father Alentín breaks the tense silence. "We need to add to our numbers. As it stands, we can only harass one army. To be successful, we must make our presence known on both fronts."

"Do you think the conde can help us? That he can be swayed?" I ask.

He rubs the stump of his shoulder in thought, then shakes his head. "I don't know, Elisa. But His Majesty, may his magnificent sword shatter the breasts of his enemies, must encounter *two* weakened armies to have a chance at victory."

I chew on a meat roll and ponder his words while Cosmé and Jacián continue their mutual glare.

When the idea comes, I almost choke. "What if . . ." I hold up a hand to forestall talk while I chew and swallow as quickly as I can. "What if we *force* the conde into an alliance?" The meat roll is a lump in my chest. I hit my sternum with my fist.

"What do you mean?" Humberto asks.

"I mean we can force him to ally with us. If Invierne believes he has violated their agreement, he will have no choice."

Cosmé's black eyes narrow as a huge smile lights Jacián's face. "The supply train," Cosmé says.

I nod. "The supply train. If we go to Basajuan and figure

out how and when Condé Treviño pays his tribute, we can interfere. We'll poison the food, lace the water with duerma leaf, anything we can think of. Invierne will think themselves betrayed. When Conde Treviño is most desperate, the Malficio will offer to aid him."

"You're mad," Humberto says, but I see the resigned admiration in his face. "It just might work."

"I hear a lot of 'if' in that plan," the priest says. "If you can find out the details of the supply train. If you can infiltrate it. If you are not caught. If Invierne even gives the conde a chance to seek your aid rather than destroying him utterly at the first sign of betrayal."

His words sober me. We no longer play games of war, and this is no small prank. Hundreds of Inviernos could die. Maybe more. And there is no way to anticipate the level of retaliation our people would face.

"This is a war, Father," Jacián says in that quiet voice, his face dark. I'm glad he is not my enemy. "The information we've gathered indicates Invierne will begin their march any day. When that happens, thousands will die. It is inevitable. Elisa's plan gives us an opportunity to influence the course of this war."

He speaks the truth, but I feel no better. How do I trade one group of lives for another? How do I endorse a plan that only *might* work? These are the decisions my father and sister have been making for years, the decisions Alejandro has been avoiding. Maybe I should distance myself, think of everyone as game pieces on a board. It's too hard to think of them as people.

Father Alentín shakes his head and mutters, "This will be unbelievably dangerous. Cosmé, do you think the conde would welcome you back?"

"Ah, you mean if we declare ourselves rather than traveling in stealth?" I ask.

He nods. "As far as the conde knows, Cosmé disappeared from the palace at the same time you did."

"We have to assume the condesa contacted him regarding our disappearance," Cosmé adds. "It would be very strange indeed for me to show up on his doorstep." Her voice drops a register. "But he would welcome me back. He always does." I peer into her conflicted face, trying to discern what it is I'm missing. For the first time since I've known her, she flinches away from my gaze.

It's not important for me to understand the history between Cosmé and the conde, so long as she can help us. "So you think you can get the information about the supply train that we'll need?" I ask her.

She looks up at me in surprise—or maybe gratitude—that I've chosen not to pry. "From the conde, no. But if my contacts are still in place, and if they'll talk to me, then yes. The difficult part will be getting the information before the conde can spring his own trap."

"Then we should arrive unannounced," Humberto says. "Give ourselves a few days to ask around before presenting ourselves to Treviño."

I nod. "We'll leave in two days. How much duerma leaf have we harvested?"

Humberto grins, his face cheerful once again, and I find myself grinning right back. "Enough to poison an army," he says.

"If we travel along the desert border," Jacián says, "we won't need to move in stealth. We can take the camels."

I nod with false enthusiasm. It's the best plan we have. But I dread the prospect of another painful journey with uncertain outcomes.

We agree to a small contingent. If things go wrong, if it is a trap, the majority of the Malficio will remain behind to carry on. After much discussion, we settle on a group of ten. Twice the number of perfection.

Father Alentín decides not to join us. "I fear the priests of the Monastery-at-Basajuan would be disinclined to welcome me back," he tells me.

"Why?" I ask, from curiosity rather than disappointment, for there is no other person I'd rather entrust the Malficio to in my absence.

"We had some acute doctrinal differences. In regards to the bearer, mostly. They are pro-Godstone. I am pro-bearer. Had they found you, they would have ripped the stone from your navel."

I narrow my eyes. "You're afraid to see them again because of a doctrinal difference?"

"Well, there was the small matter of my absconding with their oldest copy of the *Afflatus*—"

I laugh and clap him on the back. When I turn to leave the

cavern in search of volunteers, a tall, thin figure blocks my path.

"Take me with you," Mara says, her voice soft but insistent. I peer up at her, noticing the soot stains on her cheek, the wisps of still-ragged black hair escaping the leather tie at her nape. Her face has healed nicely, though a shimmery scar from a much older injury weighs down her left eyelid. The drooped effect makes her appear perpetually sad. She has a faint scent about her, as always, of garlic and roasting meat. I imagine she's weary of preparing food for eighty people. "I've always wanted to see a big city," she continues hurriedly. "My family, they're all . . . gone, so you see, I wouldn't be leaving anyone behind anymore. . . ." Her voice shakes as her eyes plead with mine.

"Would you be willing to cook for us?"

"Yes."

"Will you make jerboa soup every single night of our journey?"

She wrinkles her nose. "I'd prefer not to, but if—"

"Please come."

She smiles in relief, opens her mouth to say something, then snaps it closed and hurries away. I smile sadly at her back, hoping I've done her a favor by letting her come.

I hear shouting. A flurry of motion draws my gaze to the cavern's opening. *"Find Elisa!"* someone hollers. I rush outside, squinting in the daylight. Below, where adobe buildings begin to creep up the slope toward our caves, a group of boys hauls a filthy, ragged creature my way. Through the puzzle of heaving arms and billowing robes, I can make out greasy hair, skeletal fingers, the ripple of burned flesh.

I step down the sloping path, heart pounding, though I'm not sure why. As I approach, my throat constricts. The man is emaciated, his knees shredded from being dragged along by our villagers. His torn robe hangs lopsided, revealing lumpy, barely healed burns on his bare shoulder. His head swings limply from his neck, and I can't help wincing at the pasty patches of scalp showing through clumped hair. His head rolls upward. I look into a crusty crater of an eye socket. He peers at me sideways through his remaining eye, and I gasp.

It is Belén.

"Oh, God," I whisper, hand to mouth. "Belén, what happened to you?"

He exhales raggedly. "Elisa." His shoulders shake. He might be sobbing. "Elisa, I came to warn—" His eye closes tight, with pain or concentration. He takes a deep breath and tries again. "Warn you. Go back to the king. Leave this place. Before the animagi find you."

The Godstone warms to his words. Because he speaks truth? "Belén, you need water and food. I'll have Cosmé tend—"

"No! Not Cosmé. Oh, God, anyone but her." He continues to mutter, but his words unravel into nonsense.

Tears prick at my eyes. I bite my lip and clench a fist until I feel steady. I gesture to the two holding his arms. "Take him inside. Be gentle. We need him fit enough to tell us what he knows." They move off immediately, lifting the bedraggled man between them. I turn to the other three. "Was he followed, do you think?"

They look at each other, shrug, turn back to me. "We'll scout around, Highness," says a boy with bright eyes.

"Thank you. I fear he may have led Invierne right to us."

"We should extend the guard perimeter for a few days," he suggests. "Just in case."

"Good thinking. What is your name? I'm so sorry, but I've forgotten."

He beams. "Adán. I was a trapper like my father before I joined the Malficio."

I hope he doesn't notice how reluctant my smile is; he can't be more than thirteen. "I'm placing you in charge of scouting for possible pursuers, Adán."

He nods solemnly. "We'll report back by nightfall." Together they rush off, so eager to risk their lives.

But I can't worry about them. I swallow and take a deep breath before heading back to the half-cavern. I find Belén slumped against the curving wall. Cosmé is already there, sponging his face. They don't speak. When she tilts his chin to look for wounds, his eye darts to the side to avoid her gaze. The young men who brought him watch from a quiet distance.

"Cosmé."

"He is no traitor," she snaps without turning.

"That may be. When will I be able to talk to him?"

She blots at a crusted gash along his hairline with a wet cloth. "He's delirious from fever. He needs rest and water. Talk to him in a day or so."

"He spoke of a warning. He was quite frantic about it."

"He needs rest."

I sigh, remembering the way Papá and Alodia used to talk over my head. "Belén."

Cosmé whirls and stands. Tears shimmer in her eyes. "I said, he needs rest. Before he does anything else. Or he might not recover."

I ignore her. "Belén, when *you* feel ready to talk, have Cosmé or one of the guards send for me."

"Elisa." The voice is so cracked and low that I'm not sure he really spoke. "Elisa!"

I rush forward and crouch beside him. He smells of rot, but I lean toward his face anyway. "I'm here, Belén." He may be a traitor, but before that he was my friend, and my chest stings to see him this way.

"You must get away. You and the Godstone. They know, Elisa."

"They know what?"

Cosmé squats beside me, ready to interfere on Belén's behalf if necessary.

"They know you're the bearer. They want your Godstone." His hand darts out from within tattered robes and clutches my wrist with desperate strength. "They must not get your stone, Elisa. All of Joya will be destroyed if they do. You must flee. Now. Today!" He gasps, and his eye rolls back. Cosmé lunges forward to catch his head before it impacts the limestone wall.

I stand slowly, pondering his words, while Cosmé gently lays him out. He tries to speak, but she hushes him and continues to bathe his injuries. Her motions are careful and slow, as if Belén is made of precious glass. All the while she murmurs to him, runs fingers through his hair, caresses his face.

"I'll find out what I can," Cosmé says in a resigned voice.

"Thank you." Looking down at them, I hug myself against a stab of cold. Then I flee the cavern in search of Humberto. I'm suddenly desperate to see him. I need his cheerful smile and laughing eyes, his steady counsel.

25

WE delay our journey to Basajuan to allow ourselves time to learn all we can from Belén. The first day, he spews thoughts in panicked bits, and we cannot string them together in a way that makes sense except to understand that he fears for my life and for the fate of all of Joya d'Arena. I feel oddly detached from his ravings. Fear has been my steady companion for so long now. What is another warning? Merely the words of a madman, harmless and deflected as easily as a will-o'-the-wisp.

Humberto, however, cannot share my calm. He is never far, and every time I glance in his direction, I see huge brown eyes lingering on me, bright with feeling. He is aware of me in a way Alejandro never was, and it gives me a little thrill each time I notice him noticing me. I wonder if he thinks about our kiss as often as I do.

I don't dissuade him from looking after me. He's the most determined and capable person I know, equally adept at snaring rabbits or finding water or making people laugh. I know he'll do everything he can to keep me safe.

On the afternoon of the next day, I sit on a pebbly mound, my back against the sun-warmed side of the butte. I spread Homer's *Afflatus* across my lap and read it over again, hoping to find something that will help me, something missed by centuries of devout scholarship. The village is only steps away but out of sight. Never in my life have I been so sought after for my opinion, my approval, my presence, than in these last days. I have power over these people, power they freely gave to me. It's frightening and strange and a little bit wonderful. It's also exhausting, and I'm relieved to be alone.

I hear the crunch of footsteps and sigh. But my disappointment gives way to delight when Humberto's head bobs above the rise. I smile in greeting.

"You shouldn't be alone," he says.

My grin widens. "I'm not alone anymore, am I?"

Our shoulders touch as he settles beside me. He rests his forearms across bended knees and stares out toward the desert. "I need to talk to you about something."

My smile fades. I swallow. "About what?"

He doesn't look at me, just digs at the shale with the heel of his boot. "That day. In the cave. Before you were captured."

Heat floods my neck at the memory of his kiss. I've started to invent this conversation a dozen times in my mind but never pursued it, as if talking about it—even thinking about it—would make it ordinary and final. It's a kiss that can't ever have a happy ending, and I'd prefer that it stay dreamlike in my memory, full of possibility.

"Elisa, I'm sorry."

I whip my head around to study his profile. "Why?"

"I thought . . ." He looks skyward and breathes deeply. "I thought I'd never see you again. I was scared and sad, and . . . and I'd been wanting to kiss you so badly. It made me stupid. I promise I won't be . . . inappropriate with you again."

This was not how I imagined our exchange would go. I press my lips together, determined not to cry. "Do you regret it, then?" I whisper.

A half smile flits across his lips. "No. I mean yes. I mean—"

"I'm not sure I want to be married to Alejandro."

His head whirls, and I jump, startled as much by my own words as his quick motion. It's true, I realize, my heart pounding in panic. Alejandro is the handsomest man I've ever known. But it's not enough.

"What do you mean?" he asks softly, and the hope in his eyes makes my throat hurt.

"I have to be married to him. I've made promises to the Malficio and I must be Alejandro's wife to keep those promises, but . . ."

"But what?"

The truth is huge and heavy. "He doesn't love me. I used to wish he would learn to. But now that I've been gone . . . I guess I don't respect him very much." *Not the way I respect you.* "He's handsome. Very charming. But he can be indecisive." I think of his refusal to acknowledge me as his wife, his neglect of Rosario, even his disregard of his mistress. "And he's unkind sometimes, thoughtless."

Humberto's gaze holds mine. I love the lines of his face—so

proud and strong. I ache to trace the curve of his stubbled cheek with my fingertips. My lips part.

"Elisa," he whispers.

I lean closer. My lips buzz; my heart pounds.

"I won't kiss you again," he says.

I snap my mouth closed.

"Not that I wouldn't like to, understand," he says with a lopsided grin. He returns his gaze to the safety of the desert landscape. He is silent a moment. Then: "You are the bravest person I know. And smart. And..." He shifts his feet. "And beautiful. The king is a fool for not loving you."

My next breath is more like a sob. I should laugh off his words, or thank him for saying so, but my throat won't open.

Instead, I join him in careful study of the dry scrub and its occasional lizard. We sit together a long time, shoulders barely touching, and watch the sun paint the land in pink and coral as it dips below the jagged horizon.

The air is dim and cool when Cosmé finds us.

"Belén is ready to talk," she says.

We scramble to our feet and hurry after her. Humberto doesn't say anything to me, doesn't even look in my direction. But as we walk I feel his arm brush mine, then his fingers. He grabs my hand and squeezes, too briefly, before letting go. My hand is unbearably cold as we enter the village.

Belén repeats his warning first. "Elisa, please leave. Go back to Brisadulce. Or better, go far away. Somewhere no one would expect to find you."

Humberto and Father Alentín exchange an uneasy glance, but I ignore them. "Start at the beginning, Belén." I try to keep my voice gentle. "Tell us how they knew about our cave." He wears a patch now, so I'm spared the view of his wasted eye.

He hangs his head. "I told them."

Cosmé looks away. Jacián just glowers.

"Why?" I ask.

He rocks back and forth. "They told me they'd spare my village." But his eye is unsteady. Continued fatigue, perhaps. Or maybe he's hiding something.

I shake my head. "That doesn't sound like you, Belén. You wouldn't betray Cosmé that way." I feel the young woman's glare at my back as I crouch down and lean toward Belén's ruined face. "Why did you do it?"

He continues rocking.

"Belén?"

"I brought you to the gates of the enemy!" he spits. "I thought it was the right thing!"

I lurch backward on my heels, stunned. "You thought you were fulfilling Homer's prophecy."

He nods, still refusing to look at my face. "I knew the others could get away. I thought you needed to be in the enemy camp. I thought it was God's will."

God's will. How many times have I heard someone declare their understanding of this thing I find so indefinable?

Humberto steps forward. "Something changed your mind," he says. His face has nothing of the sad desperation that fills his sister's. Instead, he seems furious.

Belén ceases rocking. "She escaped," he says simply. "And the whole army of Invierne had a mad celebration. One of their own was killed, an animagus, yet they celebrated."

"I don't understand," I say.

"They celebrated because they found you, Elisa. The bearer. Only the bearer could have escaped an animagus. Could have used fire against him. They've been searching for you for years, and you came right to their camp."

"What do they want with her?" Alentín demands.

"They want her Godstone. They have nine already. Almost twice the number of perfection. They only need one more, a living one."

"They need two more," I say fiercely. I pull the amulet from under my robe and hold it out for all to see. "I took this one from the animagus."

But Alentín doesn't seem to hear. "How in God's name did they acquire nine Godstones?"

Humberto shrugs. "Maybe they robbed the graves of dead bearers."

Cosmé sends her brother a disgusted look.

"Many bearers never completed their service," Jacián points out. "Or were never recognized. Maybe it's because Inviernos killed them and took their Godstones."

Alentín raises an eyebrow. "If that's true, they've been collecting Godstones for centuries."

"Or maybe," I say slowly, "some of the bearers were chosen from Invierne."

I'm rewarded with faces of laughing skepticism. Even Belén

wrinkles his nose in contempt of the idea. But they don't understand. I'd rather believe Godstones came to them freely. Otherwise, we'd have to conclude that Inviernos have walked among us, stolen from us, and are now on the verge of realizing a centuries-old plot.

But what plot? "What can they accomplish with ten Godstones?" I ask, my voice quavering.

He looks up at me, finally. Dead on. "Sorcery. Right now, they use their amulets to channel a bit of the magic that crawls beneath the earth. With ten Godstones, they can free it entirely."

"Why?" The *Scriptura Sancta* forbids the use of magic. There must be a reason.

But Belén only shrugs. "I'm not sure. I don't speak the Lengua Classica fluently. And they speak with such strange accents. After a while, the burning was so bad, and when they took my eye, I couldn't think anymore. . . ." His head falls to the side again, and his cheek twitches while he loses himself in memory.

"Belén?" Cosmé whispers.

He blinks, refocuses. "They wanted to find out about *her*. About the bearer."

Humberto strides forward and grabs Belén's chin. "What did you tell them?"

Belén rolls his head, grimacing. "I don't know. I really don't know."

"Did you tell them about this place? About the Malficio?"

A tear leaks from Belén's eye. "I don't know, Humberto! I

don't think so. All I could think of was that I'd made a mistake. A horrible mistake."

"And then you miraculously escaped." It's Jacián's dark, drawling voice. He echoes my own fear, that Belén has led Invierne to us, perhaps even purposefully.

"Oh, it was no miracle," Belén says. "They let me escape. They tried to follow me here."

I ask, "How can you be sure they didn't?"

Belén closes his eye and leans against the wall of the cavern. "I traveled in circles for days. I didn't come here until I was sure they had lost the trail."

"You were badly injured," Jacián says. "I can't imagine that you were able to elude them."

"It was not a pleasant journey," Belén says, his eye still closed. "But I did elude them." I'm inclined to believe him, for young Adán and his friends have not been able to find any sign of lurking Inviernos. I managed to avoid pursuit myself, inexperienced and clumsy as I am, so I know it's possible. And neither was mine a pleasant journey.

"These ten Godstones you speak of," Alentín says. "Do you really think Invierne can use them to loose magic on the world?"

"The Inviernos believe it. They believe it powerfully. Now everyone searches for Elisa."

We ask more questions while Cosmé hovers like a suspicious mother cat, but Belén has little more to offer. We decide his betrayal has nothing to do with the conde's summons, and everyone leaves to get some sleep before tomorrow's journey.

I linger awhile, unable to tear myself away from the sight of Belén's gaunt cheeks, the burns on his neck and shoulder, his quivering limbs. I never knew him as well as I do Humberto or Cosmé. Still, I mourn his easy smile and the way his steady stride vanquished the desert terrain. I steel myself against pity. By his own admission, Belén is a traitor, though a reluctant one. If Alodia were here, she would have him executed for treason.

But I am not my sister.

I thank Cosmé for looking after him and tell Belén to rest well before I stumble off to my bedroll. I lie awake a long time, thinking of Humberto, of Belén, wondering about Invierne's mysterious purpose. Just before drifting off to sleep, I realize I forgot to eat dinner.

The air is dark and chilly when Humberto awakens me. I wrap up my bedroll and shoulder my pack before following him outside into the predawn chill. To the east, the blue-black sky cedes to a yellow glow that huddles over the darkly distant peaks of the Sierra Sangre. I glare at the mountains, thinking of the vast army sheltered in their shadow.

We step softly among adobe huts. Our plan to sabotage Invierne's tithe depends on our unannounced arrival. The messenger who brought the conde's summons is not to know of our departure, lest he take word to Basajuan. Adán and others have been instructed to keep him busy and distracted—even if that means making him a prisoner—to ensure that we have several days' head start.

A soft nickering greets us as we round the butte. Jacián is

already there, holding the reins of two horses; they are huge and colorless in the dark. I recoil when one shakes its head, rattling metal cheek pieces.

"Horses?" I whisper to Humberto, though it sounds more like a squeak. "I thought we were going to take the camels."

My face burns at his quiet chuckle. "Horses are faster. And we're not going deep enough into the desert to require the camels. Don't worry. We won't make you ride one."

I sigh in relief and determine to keep my distance.

The others come in quiet twos and threes, and within moments our traveling party is complete. Led by Jacián, we head westward at a brisk walk. We are a perfect grouping of ten, including quiet Cosmé and tall Mara. I place my fingertips to the Godstone and pray that this journey will not be so ill-fated as my last.

We cut northward and take advantage of the flat terrain with a steady, ground-consuming pace. To my delight, my legs churn effortlessly. My ankles don't ache, my lungs don't burn, the skin of my legs remains smooth and unchafed. The horses allow us to carry more varied foodstuffs than on our last journey, and every night, Mara cooks for us all, alternating flatbread and lightly stewed jerky with freshly caught rabbit or wild turkey. She has even brought her own satchel of spices that she puts to expert use.

While we travel, Cosmé is distant and quiet, her delicate features sculpted in steel. Humberto tells me she was reluctant to leave Belén behind, that only a combined appeal from himself,

Jacián, and Father Alentín caused her to agree to this journey. He says this is common behavior for her, that she pouts in isolated silence for days when she doesn't get her way. Humberto knows her much better than I do, but I am reluctant to dismiss her so easily. I fear that her withdrawal is more deeply rooted than he realizes.

After a week of unbroken travel, Jacián leads us eastward, back into the hills. The sun is high and hot, and sweat is trickling down my neck and soaking the collar of my robes when I smell smoke. At first, I think it must be the cook fire of a fellow traveler. But as we continue on, the scent grows stronger, then unbearably acrid. We exchange uneasy glances. I put my fingers to the Godstone, trying to detect a hint of its icy warning, or even a pulse of warmth, any activity that would give me a clue as to what lies ahead. But it is as indifferent as a common stone.

We crest a ridge and are finally able to see, ahead and slightly north, a mantle of smoke on the horizon. It is no lazy campfire, but a wide swath the sickly brown color of devastation.

Jacián spins to face us. "The village of Cerrolindo burns," he says. "I was going to guide us around it, but—"

"There may be survivors," Cosmé cuts in.

We look at each other, and I know what our decision will be by the determined faces of my companions.

"Elisa," Humberto says. "Your Godstone. Is it telling you anything?"

I shake my head. "Nothing."

"Then the enemy is gone," Jacián declares, and we need no

further prodding to hurry down the hill after him.

By the time we reach the village, I'm almost sobbing from the unrelenting smoke and from my own dread. I can hardly keep my eyes open for the sting, but even through the blurry haze of tears and hot fog I see the blackened skeletons of buildings. Wooden posts that end in charred jaggedness, rock walls layered in soot, remains of tables and chairs caved in on themselves and glowing red.

"Look for survivors!" Humberto yells. He pulls his cowl over his head and ties his shawl to cover his nose and mouth. Quickly I mirror his actions. "And be careful," he hollers. "Any of the remaining structures could collapse."

I hurry through smoldering streets and curving alleys, blinking to keep my eyes moist, desperate to find life. I nearly stumble over the charred body of an animal—I can't tell if it's a sheep or a dog—and I almost vomit over the smell of burned meat, the reddish ooze leaking through cracks in its charred skin.

"Over here!"

I can't tell who cried out or where the voice comes from, but it fills me with hope. "Where are you?" I shout back.

"North end!" Humberto's voice.

I plunge back into the smoke, my forearm raised as if it could shield my eyes from the nebulous stuff, and head in the direction I think is northward. I see a tall figure on my left. It's Mara. She hurries to my side, and we rush ahead together.

My lungs burn by the time we reach them, a huddled mass of soot-smeared skin and hacking lungs, a family of four.

Humberto is squatted down next to the smallest, offering comfort. He looks up at me as Mara and I approach, tears shimmering in his eyes.

"They were locked inside that building," he says in a wavery voice. "They were left to burn."

"Oh, God." The cruelty of it is unfathomable. "Who did this to you?" I demand, as if I don't know. The Godstone sends raging heat into my chest in response to my anger.

A face peers into mine. Wide-eyed, blistered, female. "The animagi," she whispers. "They said they were taking their revenge on us. They said they would destroy a village each time the Malficio struck."

She doubles over with coughing, but I hardly notice. The earth below me sways too much.

26

WE can only hope most inhabitants managed to flee, for we find no other survivors and only a few blackened bodies. I crouch a safe distance away on a barren rise, hugging knees to chest. My companions poke through the smoldering ruins to salvage what they can. I should be helping them, but my stomach churns, tears pour down my cheeks, and I am so, so tired.

These last weeks, I have presumed to feel useful. I have treasured the success of the Malficio in my heart, taken pride in the way my tiny group of rebels looks to me for guidance and inspiration. I have allowed myself to feel so accomplished, so grown up. But I have been a fool.

Jacián will tell me that all wars have casualties. Humberto will assure me that none of this is my fault. They will both be right. But in this moment, I close my eyes and feel the weight of death on my shoulders.

"Elisa!"

My eyes snap open. Humberto is hurrying toward me.

"Are you breathing easier now?" he asks, eyes round.

I nod. "The family?"

He plunks down beside me. "They have cousins nearby. Cosmé offered to let them accompany us to Basajuan, but they'd rather stay in the area and look for survivors. We gave them food and water."

I say nothing. He puts a gentle arm across my shoulders and pulls me against him. "It's not your fault," he murmurs into my hair.

"I know." But new tears spring, stinging, to my eyes.

"What worries me is how far west we are. I didn't expect Invierne to have a presence this near the desert. Not yet anyway."

"Perhaps they will march on Alejandro even sooner than we expected." I rub my nose against the fabric of his robe, giving a flitting thought to the inappropriateness of our actions. I should distance myself from Humberto. I should prepare myself to be the wife of a king.

"That's what Jacián said. We can't linger. We must leave for Basajuan immediately."

"If they are willing to burn a village because of one of our silly raids, what will they do when we poison their food?"

I feel his chest rise and fall with a sigh. "That's why we're doing this, Elisa," he says gently. "Remember? We *want* Invierne to retaliate against the conde."

"We're going to get people killed."

"Yes."

There's something about his honest regard of the situation that clears my head. He has accepted our choice. Believes in it. But he cannot mask the sorrow in his voice.

I stand and stretch, putting distance between us. "Let's go, then," I say.

The lighthearted banter that characterized the first leg of our journey has been replaced by brooding silence. I don't feel like talking either. Instead, I use the time to experiment with my Godstones.

My own has never seemed magical. Alive, certainly. A conduit for communication, perhaps—a link between me and God. Yet the animagi use Godstones that no longer pulse in their bearers' bodies to call up the magic that slithers beneath the earth. I remember the way the animagus clutched his amulet to freeze us in place, how it glowed fiery blue with his intent to burn me.

Thinking of the *Scriptura Sancta*'s many warnings against sorcery, I reach beneath the collar of my robe and clasp the amulet's cage. *God, please keep me safe*, I pray. My own stone flares its response.

Gripping the caged stone, I think hard about the magic beneath the surface of the world. I reach down with my mind, plunging my thoughts into the dry earth. I imagine the stone warming in my hand; I imagine fire bursting forth to burn the crooked juniper on my left. I imagine so hard that I trip on a jutting stone and tumble to my knees.

"Elisa!" Humberto yanks me upward and steadies me. "Are you hurt?"

His grip on my armpit is too tight, but I don't care. I lean into him. "Thank you," I whisper against his ear. But I see his reaction to my nearness—eyes closed, breath inhaled—and my whole body responds with aching warmth. I want to wrap my arms around his neck, tangle my fingers in his soft hair.

But I can't keep letting myself think such things. "I'm fine," I mumble, wiping grit from the front of my robe to give my hands something safe to do. My heart twists at the hurt on his face, but I resume our journey resolutely.

It takes two days to reach Basajuan, two days of failing to elicit any kind of response in the strange Godstone.

Conde Treviño's city nestles snug in the crook of two meeting mountain ranges, the Sierra Sangre to the east and the jungle-tangled Hinders to the north. It's cooler here, the air moist enough to feel like a blanket against my skin. Humberto laughs when I tell him so and assures me my own country's air would feel much the same now that I am accustomed to the deep desert.

We wander among quaint two-storied buildings with generous windows and flowering ledges. I'm charmed by the bright-washed walls of color; corals and yellows dominate, with splashes of soft blue and lavender. Iron scrollwork curls around windows and doorways, bright tiles—the same odd yellow-and-blue flower design from my atrium in Alejandro's palace—line archways and stair steps. It's a cozy, bright place, and my chest twinges as I realize it reminds me of my home in Amalur.

Jacián rents stable berths for the horses, then leads us to a wide three-story building fronted by a breezy café. Long tables spread beneath a red-tiled overhang, and a counter in the back is painted with colorful promises of crepe-wrapped meat and savory stew. Behind it, cooks scurry to fill orders. Our group takes two of the tables while Jacián orders food at the counter.

If asked, we will claim to be refugees from Cerrolindo, come to trade our remaining belongings for coin and then flee this place before the war begins. It was Mara's idea, and we all agreed. Such a story is not only plausible, it speaks powerfully of the conde's inability—or maybe unwillingness—to protect his people.

Jacián returns and settles beside us to wait. "They board guests upstairs," he says. "I reserved two rooms." He lowers his voice. "We'll stay here until we find the information we need. It's far enough from the conde's palace to attract little attention."

He turns to me. "Elisa, I inquired at the pigeon post for you. No response from your nurse yet."

"Oh." There has hardly been enough time, I tell myself. At least by now she knows I'm safe. "Thank you."

Distant monastery bells ring their midday triplets as a small, barefoot boy brings two platters of spiced, shredded beef and accompanying flatbread. We stare at Jacián in surprise.

He grins, and I'm equally shocked at the merriment in his usually dark eyes. "I splurged," he confesses. "I know we've little coin between us, but we've been out in the desert so long. It's probably been a year or more since I've had beef."

We need no prodding to help ourselves. We eat noisily and greedily, smiling around full mouths, giggling at the mess we make trying to scoop the dripping meat onto our flatbread. But Cosmé's and Humberto's eyes are clouded, and I wonder if they've had the same sobering thought I have about the real reason Jacián has chosen to treat us to a final, glorious meal.

Our rooms are spare but clean, and the owner of the boarding-house helps us drag several sleeping pallets from storage to supplement the meager cots. Cosmé, Mara, and I are the only girls in our group of ten, so Jacián and Humberto share our room. I've slept beside Humberto countless nights, even had him bodily guard the threshold of my hut back in Alentín's village. Somehow, though, this enclosed space feels more inti-mate, and I'm acutely aware of him as we unload our packs and stretch out our pallets.

Once we are settled, Cosmé and Jacián leave to wander through the city in search of old acquaintances. I offer to accompany them, but Cosmé just smiles. "You would slow me down," she says. "I'm trained to gather information. Rest here; I'll be back soon enough."

As they close the door behind them, I say to no one in par-ticular, "How can one so young know so many things?"

"What do you mean?" asks Mara.

"Cosmé was my maid, briefly, in Brisadulce. Then I learned she is a traveling escort. And a healer. And of course, a spy." I whirl on Humberto. "Is everyone this side of the desert so multifaceted?"

He chuckles. "Just inconvenient daughters of wayward condes."

My eyes widen. So that's it. The missing link between Cosmé and Treviño. "But I thought Cosmé was your sister?"

"She is. Same mother, different father."

Mara takes a step back. "I'm not sure I should hear—"

"Cosmé wouldn't mind your knowing," he assures her. "Not now. But it's not something we talk about often. My papá became a true father to her, and she feels it would dishonor him to be blatant about her relationship with the conde."

"Cosmé told me Inviernos killed her parents," I remember aloud.

He nods. "About five years ago. It was a bad time for us." He settles onto a cot and runs a hand across the soft stubble on his chin. "Cosmé went to the conde for help. She wanted vengeance, but—"

"Treviño never had any intention of fighting Invierne."

"Not since the armies started amassing, no. My sister was very insistent. The conde did nothing, of course, but he decided to keep her in his household. At first he just wanted her closely watched. But he grew fond of her. Too fond of her. It made her very uncomfortable.

"He had her trained in all sorts of skills and gave her a position as lady-in-waiting to her older half-sister, Ariña. The two girls got on well enough, I suppose. They even struck a deal. Ariña promised Cosmé that if King Alejandro married her, she'd let Cosmé inherit the conde's holdings."

I gape at him. "She could have stayed in Brisadulce. She could have helped Ariña become queen and then become a condesa herself."

Humberto nods. "She could have. But she came to believe her father and sister would sell their souls to Invierne to accomplish their ends. Maybe they did." His eyes glaze over and his brow hardens. "We watched the faces of Mamá and Papá melt away in the fire of an animagus. She never forgot that. So when Uncle Alentín fled the monastery and started his little rebellion, we supported him in secret and vowed to seek out the bearer."

I plunk down beside Humberto to absorb what he said. "If this works, Humberto, if I can keep my promise and free this land from Joya, then Cosmé can be a condesa after all. Maybe even a queen."

He nudges my shoulder with his and grins. "That's why I told you."

Mara is a statue of discomfort near the far wall, eyes wide like an animal caught in a trap. "I'm going to find some water," she says. "I need to wash my hair."

After she flees, Humberto and I regard each other awkwardly.

"You've been avoiding me the last two days," he says in a careful, even tone.

I look down at my hands. "Yes."

He leans forward, elbows to knees. "It's all right. I understand."

Our thighs are very close. Were one of us to shift slightly, we would accidentally touch. "I'm so sorry, Humberto. But I have to be married to Alejandro for this to work."

"You never shared a bed with him." A statement rather than a question.

I swallow, unsure about discussing such things with him. "I did not."

He turns on me, eyes narrowed. "Elisa, if there were a way, any way, for you to escape marriage with the king, would you do it?"

"Any way?"

"Nothing you'd be ashamed of, I mean."

I try to imagine my husband's face. I used to picture him with such clarity. But time and distance haze my memory.

I look up at Humberto, at high cheekbones that testify to his desert heritage, the determined jaw, lips always on the verge of a smile. And I realize that my memory of Alejandro is not hazed by time and distance, but by this other, better, dearer face that now fills my thoughts.

Humberto's eyes shine with desperate hope, and I ache to run my fingers through his rioting hair and tell him that things could work out between us. I offer him what I can. "If there were a way, then yes, I'd choose to be free of Alejandro."

He smiles. "I'm glad to know it."

We sit side by side in companionable silence, both of us careful not to touch. I look down at my skirt to avoid his gaze and note how my thighs spread wide across the firm cot. My skin mocks this new slenderness, lying flaccidly in wait for the bulk to return. I steal a glance at Humberto, marveling at the sure knowledge that he would still care for me—even if I started eating pastries again every day.

"What are you smiling at?" he demands.

I'm saved having to respond when Mara returns with news that she has traded a sheepskin for soap and hot water service.

Mara is braiding my damp hair when Cosmé and Jacián return. I know something is wrong by the sharp planes of Cosmé's face, the shadow in Jacián's dark eyes.

"What is it? Would no one speak to you?" I ask.

"We found what we needed to know," Cosmé spits. She begins pacing.

I look at Humberto in alarm. He just shrugs as if to say, Give her a moment.

Cosmé purses her lips, then blurts, "The supply carriages leave first thing tomorrow morning. We must act tonight."

Tonight! I was hoping to adjust to the idea, maybe spend some time in prayer, gather a store of courage.

"The tribute is collected by the priests," she continues. "And held in trust at the monastery."

My stomach falls away at her words. That priests would sanction such an act is unfathomable. No wonder Cosmé and Jacián are so darkly livid.

"Can we figure out a way inside?" I ask.

Jacián nods. "They are conducting the sacrament of pain tonight. All ten of us will go, then slip toward the kitchens after the ceremony while the crowd is leaving. We will all carry the duerma poison. Hopefully, at least two or three of us will be able to find the stash."

"And if we are captured?" Mara asks in a small voice.

"If anyone is captured, it will be up to Elisa to set us free," Cosmé says pointedly.

"Me?"

"That's when you reveal that you are the leader of the Malficio. You agree to discussions only if your people are freed."

I narrow my eyes. "That could just as easily get you killed," I say. "We can't be sure what the conde intends."

Cosmé raises her chin in challenge. "No one said our undertaking would be without risk."

I sigh, hating this moment. "In other words, we have no real plan for escape."

It is Mara who quietly whispers, "If we can force the conde to defend himself, it will be worth it. His resources are so much greater than that of our tiny Malficio."

"It could be the advantage *your husband* needs to win this war," Humberto adds.

I wince. "Cosmé, could you use your connection with the conde to get us out of trouble?"

The young woman frowns.

"I told her everything," Humberto says apologetically.

"I would try," she says in a stiff voice. "Though it feels wrong to use my relationship with him for anything. Very wrong. Asking favors of him is . . . unpleasant. There is always a price."

I study her thoughtfully. "Then we'll try to avoid that. Let's inform our companions of the plan and be on our way."

The monastery is a smaller version of the one presided over by Father Nicandro at Brisadulce. The same adobe walls, the same prayer candles and long wooden benches. And just like Brisadulce, the number of worshippers is thin indeed, the benches far from full. I had hoped for a large crowd to get lost in.

Our desert robes are nondescript, appropriate for penitents seeking a boon through the sacrament of pain. Cosmé and Humberto pull up their cowls to avoid recognition as we file in with pious decorum. We spread out to avoid suspicion, and the low murmuring of prayer begins to fill the room, rising and falling in soft cadence. My Godstone buzzes with warmth.

Near the waiting altar, a priest's bowed head snaps up. He scans the growing crowd.

I lower my head and huddle behind Cosmé as she works her way forward, cursing myself for forgetting something so important. Hiding at her back is a futile gesture, for she is dainty and I am not, but the priest continues his scan, unable to pinpoint my location. With as understated a motion as possible, I grab her elbow and force her into the nearest bench row. We sit down as one, our thighs brushing.

She whispers, head lowered, "We were supposed to separate and—"

"The priest can sense my Godstone. Just like Alentín and Nicandro. I dare not get any closer."

A slight intake of breath. Then: "You should go. Leave as soon as people rise to accept the invitation."

I start to nod, but I then I get a better idea. "We could use my Godstone as a distraction."

"You think you can do that?" she mutters.

"I can. At the end of the ceremony, you and the others will

head toward the kitchens. I'll go out the rear door toward the dormitory and pray to draw their attention."

Her cowled head leans closer and her forehead brushes mine when she whispers, "You're sure you want to do this?"

"I do. I'll meet you back at the boardinghouse." I'm almost sure I can find my way alone.

"They'll know the bearer is here."

"It's already too late to hide the fact from them."

A sobering thought, and we wait in nervous silence through the preservice rituals. The priest leads us in the "Glorifica," and it takes all my willpower to not raise my soul in worship at the lyrical beauty of it. Any thought of worship or prayer will cause the stone inside me to flare in joyous response, so I concentrate instead on coconut scones with cream filling, trying to remember the exact taste and texture on my tongue.

I thrum my fingers against the bench as the priest raises a sacred rose, with its enormous thorns, above his head and launches into a hymn of deliverance. At last he invites all who wish to partake in the sacrament of pain to step forward. Mara rises from her spot a few benches ahead. I recognize several others from our group. Cosmé and Humberto remain seated, for fear of recognition. In this prayerless moment, I feel bereft and darkly wrong.

Finally the ceremony concludes. The remaining petitioners have their bleeding fingers tended to while the head priest—still scanning the crowd in obvious agitation—offers extra prayer and counseling to the needy. Some of our group move forward to corner the priest with bogus appeals, while others inch toward the side door leading to the kitchen and stables.

I stand, my mind firmly on pastries, and edge toward the dormitories. From the corner of my eye, I see Mara's tall form shrouding the nearest priest with clever solicitude. I can't help but grin as I duck into a cool, dark archway.

But my grin disappears when I see a branching corridor. Two directions to choose from, both gloomy. Heart pounding, I decide on the one that doubles back toward the entrance. Though I said nothing of it to Cosmé, getting caught here could mean my life. Father Alentín told me the priests of this monastery are supporters of the Godstone rather than of the bearer, and it's possible they would rip the stone from my navel given the chance.

I hurry down the corridor, straining to see through the murkiness. Footsteps patter in the distance; I hope they are nothing more than petitioners exiting the receiving room, but it's impossible to know. At last I reach a wood beam door with iron hinges and an arched apex. The handle is cold in my palm as I begin to pray.

God, please help me distract the priests.

The Godstone leaps in greeting, shooting sparks of warmth. I pull the door open.

Please keep my friends safe. Let them be successful.

A rush of fresh, warm air bathes my face. I step outside onto a brick street. Torches pour bronzed light onto the walkway at regular intervals. Ahead is a cluster of robed petitioners, laughing together with that familiar sound of release that so often follows the sacrament of pain. I'm even nearer the original entrance than I thought.

Thank you, God, for this lovely city. If it be your will, please spare it from destruction.

"I feel it again!" A male voice, distant but urgent. "This way!"

I squat down behind a low bush lining the wall—blooming hibiscus, my nose tells me—and try to think of scones again. But the Godstone persists as if I am still praying.

I think about the animagus, his white blond hair and blue eyes, the way he slithered, catlike, around his candle-smothered altar.

The Godstone freezes.

Hinges squeal as the door I just exited flies open. Feet patter by, at least two pairs, though I do not dare raise my head to look.

"I felt it," one says. "I swear it."

Eyes like ice, the amulet in his long, lovely hand glowing with wicked fire . . .

"I believe you. I felt it too." More footsteps. "Nothing now, though."

"Maybe we went the wrong direction?"

White-quartz robes, face smoother than a child's . . .

"Maybe." But doubt fills the voice. "Let's try the dormitory."

They patter away, the door closes, and still I remain hunched behind the hibiscus bush, my nose tickled by what I hope is not a spiderweb. I very nearly pray with relief.

I squat until the arches of my feet are numb and my neck

aches. Then I rise, slowly and carefully, and walk down the street with forced carelessness, toward the boardinghouse. It's the longest walk of my life.

I'm the first to arrive. I spend the next hour luxuriating in fervent prayer for the safety of my companions. Gradually they trickle in—Mara first, then our two young bowmen. Jacián arrives, harried but gleeful. Carlo, the trapper, and his little brother, Benito, follow. We wait long, tense moments before Bertín's smiling face fills the doorway. And finally, just when we are beginning to lose hope, Cosmé and Humberto stumble in, exhausted but grinning.

All ten of us, returned safely. And successful, judging from the looks of triumph. It is so much more than I had hoped for. We collapse together in a muddle of laughter and tears, overwhelmed with relief.

It is far from over. The supply train must reach Invierne successfully. It must poison enough of their warriors that they connect their illness to the conde's tribute and enact retribution. We must parlay with Treviño.

And the priests of Basajuan have felt the presence of the bearer.

But tonight, we glory in our little success.

27

WE wait three days before declaring ourselves to the conde—time enough for the tribute to reach the amassed army of Invierne. We debate the best way to present ourselves to Treviño.

"What if we went publicly?" Mara suggests.

Cosmé nods thoughtfully. "If we announced ourselves publicly, it would make killing or capturing us very awkward for him."

"Only at first," I say. "He could always do it later. At a time when his court isn't watching."

Cosmé smirks. "At first is all we need. Once word reaches him of the bad shipment, it will be too late for him."

"So we surprise him during the receiving hour," Jacián says, pursing his lips. "We must do it in a way that builds sympathy for our cause."

Humberto frowns. "This is out of my realm of experience," he says. "I'm a shepherd's son."

Mara holds up a hand. "I'm just a village cook."

"Times like this," Cosmé points out, "a princess comes in handy."

As one, they all turn to me. I smile weakly, thinking of the times I skipped out on court functions, assured that Alodia would handle everything.

"Er . . . well, I think it's important to make a show of confidence and strength." A safe, general observation.

"You mean like dressing nicely?" Mara asks.

Why didn't I think of that? "Yes, exactly."

"I really need to fix your hair," Mara adds, "so it's not so . . ." She makes an obscure gesture with her hands.

I glower at her.

Cosmé considers. "And we need to get you *something* else to wear."

I glower at her too. "I hate corsets," I mumble.

"Not a corset," Cosmé says. "Riding leathers, like the guards wear. Maybe a cloak. We can't go in armed, but an empty quiver across your back would be very telling. A sword belt."

I stare at her.

"You must look like a warrior, Elisa." But Cosmé's lip trembles with trying to keep a straight face. "You must make enough of an impression that it will be very difficult for the conde to make you disappear."

The rest of our companions look on in shrinking silence.

I throw up my hands. "Do what you think is best."

The conde's palace is much smaller than Alejandro's, but finely crafted in pastel-hued limestone and the familiar tile pattern of yellow-and-blue flowers. All of us have come, save Carlo, who will return to the Malficio if he does not hear from us before a week has passed. We are dressed in the finest weaves our sheepskins and coin could buy. My riding leathers creak with every step. They are tight against my chest, the curve of my waist, my thighs. Only the skin of my neck and arms remains uncovered, yet I feel exposed and vulnerable without my shapeless robes.

The petitioners in line around us keep a cautious distance. I look at my companions, trying to see them through the eyes of a stranger. Though we are all young, our skin is tanned and weathered, our hair bleached with red streaks from the sun. We stand straight, with resolve and with the strength that comes from being able to walk for days on end. Still sated with our recent victory at the monastery, my friends return the surreptitious looks cast their way with unflinching cool.

"What are you smiling at?" Humberto whispers in my ear.

"Look at us. We seem far more fearsome than we actually are."

He grins. "Cosmé and Mara did an excellent job outfitting us. But think about it—we *are* fearsome. We are the Malficio."

The crowd's motion propels us forward a few steps through the corridor. "I'm glad the line is moving quickly," I tell him.

"And I'm glad the crowd behind us blocks my escape," he responds in perfect understanding.

"It's easier," I say. "With you here."

He says nothing, just studies my eyes, my lips, my neck. With the buzzing crowd so thick around us, it's almost like being alone. "Elisa," he murmurs. The soft pad of his thumb brushes my shoulder. "I think there is a way."

"What do you mean?" I could stand here forever with him.

"You said if there were a way to be free of him"—his thumb skims my collarbone, reaches the hollow of my throat—"you would do it."

I feel a little dizzy. Is it possible? Could I be free of Alejandro? The line of petitioners pushes us forward. "I can't think about this now!" I put my palm—so briefly—to his face. "But we will discuss it. I promise."

He gifts me with that easy smile of his, so familiar now, and so dear. Something unfurls inside of me, like a blooming sacrament rose. And I realize I love him.

"What?" he whispers. "What is it?"

My heart is so full it aches. "I'll tell you later!"

I turn my back on him and the topic, but my chest stings with delightful hope. So when it is finally our turn to enter the receiving hall and the bored herald asks who he should announce next, my tone is high and sure as I say, "I am Lady Elisa of the Malficio, here by His Grace's invitation."

The herald's eyes spark with sudden interest. He taps on the double doors with his staff. They open inward, and we stride into a wide receiving hall while he repeats my words for the assembled court.

I hear gasps from both sides, feel the hot stares on my shoulders. My confidence dribbles away as the pressure of so many people bears down on me. How can an enclosed space contain so many bodies? I smell them acutely, their floral perfumes, the twice-breathed air. I've been in the desert far too long.

"So, Lady Elisa of the Malficio," says a high, clear voice. The Godstone cools.

I peer in the direction of the sound. At the end of the aisle, several fierce retainers step aside, revealing a small, fair-skinned man on a throne. His black hair is plastered shiny on his skull, with flat-sculpted curls that wrap around his ears and spiral against his brow. His eyes are sharp and dark, his chin dainty, like a girl's. Like Cosmé's. He looks so much younger than I imagined.

He wears a gaudy golden pendant from a chain around his neck, large as my spread hand. It's a peculiar and grotesque design, like a rotting flower, yet it's familiar somehow.

"Your Grace," I say loudly, remembering at the last instant to bow. Behind me, the others do the same. I wonder if the conde will recognize Cosmé, but she is cowled and his regard is focused on me. I pull his rolled parchment from my leather belt and brandish it high. "We come at your summons, Your Grace. To discuss an alliance, as you requested."

His cheek twitches and his hands turn white as they clutch the armrests. "It would be untoward to discuss such things here, of course. I'll have the guards show you to the guest rooms." He flicks his fingers at one of the stony-faced retainers, then rewards us with a syrupy smile. "Please rest. Make yourselves comfortable. Order food and drink from the kitchens if you like. I will send for you after the lunch hour."

I'm about to protest, but the guards surround us and herd

away. From the corner of my eye, I see Conde Treviño whisper something to an attendant; then the crowd parts before us, revealing a side door. We enter a dark hallway as the throng behind us relaxes into humming speculation.

Worry knots in my chest as we are led down the hall, up a flight of creaking stairs. The guard opens a door to a large suite of eggshell-colored adobe walls and wood-beam braces. It's windowless and unadorned, but adequate enough for four or five, with its rounded fireplace and wide beds. But the guard ushers all nine of us inside and slams the door. Then we hear the grind and thud of the bolt shoved into place.

We stand there, stunned, until Cosmé lowers her cowl. She is laughing.

We gape at her.

"What did you expect?" she asks. "We definitely surprised him. I haven't seen him twitch like that since the day I informed him of our unfortunate relationship." She plops onto the nearest bed, a smug grin on her face.

"He didn't recognize you," Humberto says.

"I just kept my head down and covered. He had eyes only for our princess."

"What will he do next?" young Benito asks in a tight voice.

"Once he's had a chance to collect his thoughts, he'll send for Elisa and one or two others. He'll question you, first together, then separately. The rest of us will be held as leverage."

"You know him well," I say.

She avoids my gaze. "Yes."

So we settle in to wait, trying not to panic over our sudden captivity. I hope she is correct, that I'll have a chance to talk to him before he turns us over to Invierne.

We nap in shifts. The guards outside ignore our repeated requests for food, and I ache with hunger by the time we hear the rasp of the sliding bolt. Those lying down jump to their feet. Together, we face the doorway. Cosmé huddles in the back, cowl raised.

Two thickset men enter. Short swords slant away from their hips; daggers hug their boots, sheathed in buckled leather. "Lady Elisa of the Malficio?" one says.

I step forward. "I am Lady Elisa."

"Come with us. You also." He points to Humberto and Benito.

One guard angles behind us, and I hear the distinct rasp of steel on stone as he unsheathes his sword. Humberto grasps my hand as they herd us through several hallways. I squeeze back gratefully.

By the time we arrive at an ornate mahogany door, I am praying furiously. The door opens, and we are prodded inside. It's an office of sorts, with a polished desk and a huge fireplace. I'm slightly nauseated by the lushness of the room, with its brightly gilded edges, plush carpet, and scalloped curtains. It reeks of spicy incense, like the animagus's tent. I barely swallow my cough. The guards lead us to one of several couches facing the desk and shoves us down.

A smaller door behind the desk opens. A tall, wrinkled man in plain robes glides through, followed by Conde Treviño. The conde seems slight next to his towering companion, but sharp faced. Quick of motion.

"Lady Elisa," the conde says in a musical voice. "I'm so glad you came."

"Why have you taken us captive?" I demand, then add, "Your Grace."

His smile is slick and lovely. "For your own protection, of course."

I let him have his lie. "That was very kind of you, then." But Humberto stiffens beside me, and his quiet anger gives me the strength to say, "I was pleased to receive your message, Your Grace. I think an alliance between my people and yours would be very beneficial."

"Oh?" His lips quirk as if it's a great joke, and he raises an eyebrow, a startlingly familiar gesture. It must have been no trouble at all for Cosmé to convince him of his paternity.

The wrinkled man standing at his shoulder remains unflappable.

"Certainly," I affirm, even more suspicious now. "The skill of my people, combined with your resources, would give His Majesty the advantage he needs to win the war against Invierne."

He sighs dramatically. "I'm afraid there will be no alliance, for there will be no war."

Benito gasps. My hands clench into fists. "What do you mean?" I whisper.

"I have brokered a deal for peace." His voice rings with pride. "Thousands of lives will be saved."

Humberto shakes his head. "Invierne will burn your city to the ground," he spits. "No matter what promises they have made to you."

"No, no, you are wrong," Treviño says, advancing on us. The tawdry amulet at his neck slithers on its chain, like a whisper, and I flinch at the Godstone's hot response. "I have found them to be most reasonable. A pleasure to treat with. Why, just yesterday I received word from their ambassador of a poison spreading through the camp. They thought I had instigated this egregious act of war. Of course I assured them I had not. Then the ambassador suggested that perhaps the Malficio were responsible. Imagine my surprise to find you on my doorstep this very morning!" He paces now, red-and-gold cloak swishing at his ankles, revealing daggers sheathed against his boots. "All I have to do to preserve my city and my people is turn you over to them. All of you. I regret it, I really do. But peace is worth it, don't you think?" He whirls on me and bends over until his nose is a handsbreadth from mine. "So, my lady, you will tell me exactly where your hidden camp is."

I swallow, searching frantically for some clever strategy, some brilliant rhetoric that will save us or at least buy us time. All I manage is, "I'll never tell you."

The conde steps back and shrugs. "You will. Then you will be sent to Invierne's camp as a measure of good faith. They're desperate to have you, for some reason." He flicks his fingers at one of the guards. A heavy hand grips my shoulder, and fingertips dig deep under my collarbone.

"No!" Humberto launches to his feet. "Take me. I am the leader of the Malficio. The girl is just a decoy."

The air in my lungs takes on the weight of a boulder. *No, Humberto. Please, no.* I'm shaking my head, trying to catch his eye, but his gaze remains fixed on the conde.

Treviño turns to the wrinkled man, a question in his eyes.

"He lies," the old man rasps. "She is the leader. And the bearer. I felt her Godstone earlier. This boy is nothing."

A priest! Together, the conde and the priest stare at Humberto as if they are coyotes sizing up a juicy rabbit.

Dread curls in my gut.

Humberto's face is a frozen sculpture of fear. But then it relaxes into resignation. He turns to me, regards me steadily, his eyes so full of warmth, his smile so brave. "My Elisa," he whispers. "Surely you know how much I—"

"Kill him," Treviño says.

"No!" I lurch from the couch to shelter his body with my own. But the guard's hand tangles in Humberto's hair, wrenches his head backward.

I'm reaching for him as steel glints, cold and swift, against his neck. The flesh parts smoothly into a crimson smile.

He tumbles forward, and I grab him. In spite of his shuddering, in spite of his liquid breath, his arms slide around my waist, and he clasps me fiercely to himself. He chokes out something guttural. My name. He's trying to say my name.

Humberto's legs give way, and we crumple together to the rug. I bury my face in his hair as he drowns against me. The arms around my waist go slack. Too late, I whisper, "I love you."

I could hold him forever, but hands seize him, pull him from my grasp. I sit back on my heels, shaking, staring at his limp body as it is dragged away. His eyes are still wide, but the boy I knew does not live in them anymore.

I hear a keening sound. High-pitched, wild. I realize it's me.

I'm lifted to my feet by pressure at my armpits. The conde stands before me. I lunge for him. The guard yanks me backward and I whirl on him too, but I am weak. In moments my arms are pinned at my side and I'm facing the conde again. Treviño has a spatter of blood across his cheek, a line of drops arching up to his brow. From my hair, I realize. When I whirled.

He whispers in a low voice, "You will tell me all about the Malficio. Each day you are silent will result in the death of one of your companions. I will send for you again tomorrow afternoon. If you do not reveal the location of the Malficio's camp, this boy dies."

Benito. I had forgotten he was there.

The guards drag us through the corridors, back to our room. I have no strength left. No resolve. Not even rage. Just grief so huge that I think I'll drown in it.

The others understand as soon as the guard opens the door. They have only to note Humberto's absence, see my hair and my riding leathers, steeped in blood already sticky and cold.

Except for Cosmé, who demands, "What happened? Where's Humberto?"

The door slams, locking us in again.

I can't speak. I'm shaking too badly. The faces of my companions blur as a sharp pain streaks through my temples. *Oh,*

God, oh, God . . . The Godstone warms to my grief.

The Godstone.

That's what Invierne wants. Not me, not the Malficio. Just the stone inside me to complete their perfect grouping of ten.

"I need a knife," I say.

They gape at me.

"A knife!" I scream. "Doesn't someone have a knife?"

Jacián advances on me, his face darker than ever. He reaches into his boot and pulls out a tiny blade no longer than my forefinger, then flips it around and offers it, handle first. He steps back and crosses his arms, unspoken questions in his eyes.

I rip off my leather vest and pull up the undershirt to reveal my stomach, taut now and flashing with blue fire.

"What are you doing?" someone asks.

I push the blade's tip into my navel, right where the edge of my skin overlaps the embedded stone. I dig inside, feeling around the side of the jewel. Astonishing pain shoots through my abdomen, down into my buttocks, whisking my breath away. It's like lightning, quick and fiery. But it's not as bad as grief, so I dig and pry. Blood dribbles down my skin into my pants, mingling with Humberto's. But the Godstone won't budge. I try using my fingers, but I can't get a good grip. I try shoving the knife in from a different direction. The pain is too much. I'm growing weak; I can't feel my legs anymore.

I give up trying to dislodge it and decide to cut around it instead. I'll have to cut deep. *Don't think, Elisa, just do.* I raise the knife.

A hand on my wrist, small but strong. Fingers digging in

at the base of my palm. The knife clatters to the floor. "It's all right, Elisa." Cosmé's voice. Arms wrap around me. Dark hair caresses my cheek.

"But I don't want it," I whisper in her ear. "I'm done. He never should have chosen me. He was wrong and I'm done."

"Maybe he's not done with you." Together we sink to our knees. She's holding me so tight I think I might die of it.

"But, Cosmé . . ."

"I know." Her body quakes softly against mine, and my cheek is wet with her tears. "I know."

28

COSMÉ and Mara do their best to help me clean up in the bathing room. They strip my blood-soaked leathers and toss them into a corner. Our austere suite does not have running water, so they wipe at my skin with a strip torn from a bedsheet. My abdomen throbs, and the knife wounds I inflicted upon myself continue to ooze, but I'm a little less crusty, a little less cold, when Mara drapes the remaining portion of sheet around me and ties it cleverly at my shoulder.

"When the guards come next, I'll ask for water buckets," she says.

We gather in the sleeping chamber. Most of us sit on the beds, feet dangling over the edge. Only Jacián and Mara stand. We fit so easily now, with one less person.

Jacián is the one to break the silence. "We can overpower the guards. There are eight of us. We have my knife."

Cosmé shakes her head. "It's too small a doorway. We would have to overwhelm them, whereas they need only keep us inside. And without weapons . . ." Her voice is steady, her eyes free of tears. I grind my teeth at the wrongness of it, that she is able to ignore her brother's loss with such ease when I can hardly draw breath.

"Maybe we could lure one of the guards inside?" Benito suggests.

Jacián nods. "Or even two. I don't think we're guarded by more than four at a time. So half of us draw the guards in, the other half storm the doorway."

"There would be casualties," Cosmé says. "They have weapons. We don't."

We look at each other in dismay. She's right, of course, and after today, the prospect of casualties is devastatingly real.

"It's time," Cosmé whispers, "for me to declare myself to the conde." But her head is lowered, and her fist clutching the bedcover turns white. She hates him, I realize. It's not dislike or discomfort or shame, but raging hatred with a dash of fear.

"It might make things worse," Jacián says. "What will he do when he learns his daughter has betrayed him and joined the Malficio?"

"Don't, Cosmé," I whisper. I'm looking at the floor, at my bare toes wriggling along the fringe of a threadbare rug, but I can feel their collective gaze on my face. "Treviño is bluffing. Invierne will march against him because of our poison, I'm sure of it. He hopes to save himself by offering the Malficio. But they don't care about that. They only want my Godstone."

Cosmé crouches before me and peers up into my face. "You cannot give yourself to them."

I almost laugh. "When you first stole me away, you weren't

sure if I would prove useful to your cause. You wanted to tear the stone from my navel yourself. Remember?"

Her breath catches. She whispers, "Humberto defended you. Remember? Don't let that be for nothing."

For a moment, the grief is a roiling black cloud. It's going to smother me, sweep me away. My vision darkens.

"Elisa!"

I give a start, then I rise from the bed to pace, for stillness is dangerous. The walking motion pounds my injured stomach, and my Godstone feels heavier and harder than ever. But the pain is clearing my head. "I won't give myself up," I assure them.

"Then what do we do?" asks shy Bertín. He is no more than thirteen, and still gangly, with too-large hands.

"Benito and I will go to the conde tomorrow as expected." Strange that I have been so loathe to use a knife on a man. Now, I relish the prospect. "Tomorrow, I kill Treviño."

The conde sends us a meager breakfast of thin oats and weak wine. I eat with everyone else, knowing I'll need the strength. Moments later, I heave it all up into the garderobe.

The conde summons us earlier than we expect.

Our requests for water resulted in three bucketsful. We used one to rinse the blood from my vest and pants. So I am clothed in riding leather once again when the guards come to retrieve a terrified Benito and me. I look down at my vest as they shove me through the corridor. Damp leather is disgusting—musty and impenetrable as a second skin. But the stains, brownish black now, remind me of my purpose and brace me for what I must do.

The conde is already in his office when we arrive, sitting at his lavish desk. He wears green with gold velvet trim today. The colors sallow his skin, but his hair is as luxuriantly black as ever. The same gaudy amulet dangles at his chest. My Godstone warms in response to it.

"Lady Elisa, have you brought your friend to die?"

I need him to move away from the desk, out into the open.

"No, of course not." I hang my head in surrender. A stain on his rug stares back at me, a pool of ochre-brown marking the spot Humberto died in my arms.

"Excellent." He rises from his chair. My heart hammers. "I know I sent for you early, and I apologize. I do prefer to be a man of my word."

I refuse to look him in the eye for fear he'll read the subterfuge there. "I was concerned that you had changed your mind, Your Grace."

"About what?"

"About not killing my companions if I told you the location of the Malficio's camp."

He steps toward me, a fatherly smile on his pretty face. "As I said, I prefer to be a man of my word. I summoned you early because I am expecting a very special guest, and I hope to be done with our business by then. You will be my proof, you see. Proof that I have bargained for peace." His grin widens; his black eyes spark with delight. "Is it not God's will that all men live at peace? So says the *Scriptura Sancta!*"

All of this is yet another act in service to God. I shudder, staring at the rug stains again to hide my reaction. I wonder what they did with the body. Tears spring to my eyes, and I let them flow. I must appear unbalanced. Weak.

He takes another step forward. "So now you will tell me where you have been hiding all these months."

I think of Jacián's tiny dagger, hidden in my boot. Treviño is almost near enough.

"Lady Elisa? If you say nothing, your friend will die."

I realize with dismay that he's not going to approach any closer. So I lurch forward and drop to my knees at his feet. Behind me, I hear the sound of a sword drawn. "Oh, Your Grace!" I sob. The tears flow so easily. "I need to hear it from your lips."

"Hear what from my lips?" At least he doesn't back away.

And now I notice the daggers sheathed on the outsides of his boots. Longer blades than my own. "Tell me that if you learn what you need to know, you will spare the lives of my friends." I clutch his ankles in desperation. I slide my right foot forward for leverage.

A knock sounds at the door. The guard tells Treviño something, but I'm not listening. I'm raising my arms toward his calves, toward the hilts of his daggers.

"Yes, yes," says the conde gleefully. "Show him in. He'll want to witness this moment, I'm sure."

I rip the daggers from their sheaths and launch upward. The blades are at his throat, just beneath his lovely chin, before he can blink.

"Do not move," I snarl. "Do not even consider moving. Tell your guards to back away from Benito or I will slit your throat." His huge pendant winks back at me. Solid gold and crudely crafted. It's hard to tear my gaze away.

"You are no warrior," he says, but I see the fear in his eyes, for I have him trapped against his desk.

"Do you remember the way my friend bled all over your rug? Do you remember the way his eyes turned glassy, like a flawed jewel?" Treviño is of medium height, like me, and dainty.

I am not dainty. I press my knee into his groin and push the blades against his skin.

His mouth opens. Closes. Then: "Do as she says. Back away from the boy." His upper lip quivers; his eyes widen. I should be glad to see him cower. But I'm merely disgusted.

"Order the guards to free my friends."

"Do it," he hisses. "Do it now!" I hear footsteps as at least one guard exits the office.

I know the guard will not really release my companions. And I know I don't have much time; he'll return soon with help, and an arrow will pierce my back. Or maybe a long-sword.

"The Inviernos already know you're here," the conde says pleasantly. "I could help you escape."

Maybe I should pretend to hear him out, just until I can figure out a way to free the others before I die.

Another voice cuts in from behind me. "That won't be necessary."

I'm startled enough that the daggers wobble in my hands. I

know that voice. Deep and confident. So familiar . . .

"Is this the mutinous leader you spoke of?" says the voice. I don't dare release the conde to face this new threat.

Treviño swallows, the knob in his throat lurching beneath my blades. "Yes."

I hear the whisper-slide of a sword pulled from a honing scabbard. This is it, I think. I should kill the conde now before I've lost the chance.

"I'll take it from here, Your Highness," says the voice. A sword point lands atop my daggers with a soft *plink*. A tiny bubble of crimson rises where the blade meets the conde's fair skin.

My heart hammers in my throat, my breath comes too fast, but I force my hands to relax, to lower the daggers. Someone is saving me. Someone who called me "Your Highness."

I step back, daggers at my side, and turn to my rescuer.

"Hello, Elisa," Lord Hector says, and his gaze on Treviño is unrelenting. "I've been searching for an excuse to put a sword to His Grace's throat for years now, so I am in your debt."

All the rage and grief and fear flow out of me until my body is limp. I stumble toward Lord Hector, wrap my arms around him.

"Watch the daggers, Highness," he says, patting my back awkwardly with his free hand.

"Why are you doing this?" the conde exclaims. "The girl is a traitor!"

Lord Hector's hand has reached my unraveling braid. His fingers pause as they note the drying stickiness there. "Elisa is no traitor," he says. "In fact, I think His Majesty will be much dismayed to learn you have been keeping *his wife* captive."

Only then does it occur to me to wonder why my husband's personal guard is here, so far from Brisadulce.

I want to lock Conde Treviño in his own prison. Lord Hector patiently explains how it would be better to place him under house arrest, confining him to his suite. "Though we act with His Majesty's authority, we still require the cooperation of Treviño's people."

"We will treat him with respect, then," Benito adds. The look he turns on Lord Hector glows with hero worship.

I know they are right. But just before the door closes on the conde's livid face, I have an almost overwhelming desire to stab him after all. I settle for ripping the ugly amulet from his neck.

Hector gives me a strange look. "This amulet," I explain. "It feels familiar. My Godstone heats up every time I look at it."

"It's ugly," Benito says.

"Yes. I can't imagine why our foppish conde chose to wear it." It's heavy in my hand, and the four scallops feel rough, unfinished. My blood tingles.

Lord Hector gives instructions to the guards. Then he takes my arm while Benito falls behind, and I'm reminded of that day long ago when he guided me and Ximena on a tour of my new husband's palace. "So, Highness, you must tell me exactly how you came to be here," he insists. "And how you came to be so . . . bold with the conde." It's been so long since we've talked, and I can't tell whether or not admiration tinges his voice.

I hesitate at first, for I don't care to see my companions punished for kidnapping me. But I'm bereft and exhausted, and I know he'll learn the truth eventually. So I tell him about the kidnapping, our desert journey, and my discovery that the war had already begun. I explain how I came to trust and respect my companions, how I studied Homer's *Afflatus* and formed the Malficio of wounded refugees and orphaned children. His eyes widen when I tell him about my capture by Inviernos. His jaw hangs slack when I describe how I killed the animagus, stole his amulet, climbed the cliff to escape, and used the Godstone to navigate to safety. And when I start to explain our plan to poison Treviño's traitorous tribute, he stops short in the hallway.

"That was you?"

I make a careful study of the floor's geometric stonework.

"Elisa?"

I sigh. "It was. We hoped to force Treviño into marshaling troops. It didn't work out the way we planned. We were captured. Humb—my friend was killed." My voice is too flat to fool anyone. I glance up, looking for that sure-burning intelligence I remember. Sure enough, his eyes seem to whirl as he mulls over my words, draws conclusions.

We start walking again. "Ximena and Nicandro never gave up, you know," he says gently. It's kind of him to change the subject, but hearing my nurse's name makes it hard to hold my tears in check. "They insisted you were alive. Ximena was certain Ariña had something to do with your disappearance."

Oh, I have so many questions! I want to hear all about Ximena and Father Nicandro and little Rosario. Even Alejandro. But we have reached the suite where my companions are being held captive. The guards peer at us in suspicion until they notice the crown seal that gathers Hector's red cloak in folds across his shoulder. They straighten to immediate attention just as the Royal Guard declares, "Release the prisoners by order of His Majesty, King Alejandro de Vega!"

They scramble all over one another to comply. The door opens. At the sight of Benito and me, the apprehension on the faces of my companions softens into wary hope.

I make quick introductions. Everyone is perfectly polite in spite of the obvious questions in their eyes, though Cosmé looks ready to escape out the doorway at any moment. She did kidnap me, after all. Hector just smiles at her. "It's nice to see you again, Cosmé," he says.

She wilts with visible relief and mumbles something in response.

Hector looks around at our dour accommodations, then leans out the doorway. "Find suitable rooms for everyone in the guest wing," he orders. "I want them located as near to my own suite as possible." He turns back to us. "Once everyone is settled and refreshed, we will meet. There is much to discuss and plan."

Hector escorts me himself. "I already have a room picked out for you," he says.

I shrug. After traveling through the desert, any room would serve. "Hector, when we were in the conde's office, you told him I was Alejandro's wife."

"Yes."

"It's not a secret anymore?"

"The king made an announcement. Once the storm season was over and trade with Orovalle resumed, he had no choice."

I ought to feel glad that he is finally acknowledging our marriage. But I feel nothing. I ask in a quiet voice, "And . . . how is he?" It seems proper that a wife should inquire about her husband.

We stop outside a thick door. Hector looks down at me in sympathy. "He is well, Elisa. Occupied with planning for a war. Worried about you, I'm sure. But he's well." He knocks.

I stare at him, wondering why he'd knock on the door of the room he chose for me.

He smiles. "She insisted on coming. So certain was she that Ariña and her father had something to do with your disappearance."

I am beginning to process his words when the door opens and Ximena peers out.

My heart is a warm, wet puddle as my nurse gawks at me. Her gray hair has whitened at the temples, her cheeks are more prominent, the lines around her eyes deeper. Fingers fly to her lips as tears spill from her eyes.

"Oh, Elisa," she breathes. "Oh, my sky." She wraps me in her arms and pulls me inside.

I had forgotten what it was like to be so pampered. It's an amazing thing to lean back in muscle-penetrating warmth while someone kneads your shoulders, lathers your scalp, caresses your skin with moistening herbs. She towels me off and wraps me in a soft robe before settling me on the edge of the bed to work through my hair.

I close my eyes, savoring the occasional brushstroke that grazes my neck.

"Did you get my message?" I ask.

"What message?" I feel a tug as she rubs a dab of sunflower oil into the ends of my hair.

"A few weeks ago, I sent you a note to let you know I was safe."

"I left Brisadulce more than a month ago."

"Oh."

"Those clothes you were wearing," Ximena says calmly. "They had blood all over them." She continues to brush steadily.

I don't dare open my eyes, and it's a moment before I can speak. "Yes," I manage. "Ximena, can I tell you about all of that another time, maybe?"

"Of course, my sky." Her strokes are so gentle, drawn out as if she is relishing the feel of my hair in her hands. "You are different," she says, though her tone holds no accusation.

Yes. In so many ways. I decide to focus on the obvious. "The desert sucked some of the flesh right off of me."

"No." Her brushing stalls. "I mean, yes. But it's not that. It's the way you hold yourself. The way you *move*."

She braids my hair quickly, then dresses me in a soft green gown ordered from the storeroom. It's a little too big at the waist, a bit snug around the breasts, and chilly compared to my desert robes or my riding leathers. But the look on Ximena's face when she sees me in it silences any complaint.

A guard comes to escort me to Lord Hector's suite. Before I can walk out the door, Ximena grabs me and hugs me tight to her breast. I smile into her hair. "We have all night to catch up. All day tomorrow," I whisper.

She releases me and backs away, chin held high. "And I want to hear every detail. While you're gone, I'll find more clothes for you."

I cast a glance at my pack, discarded against the fireplace. Everything I need is inside: an extra outer robe, a knife, a tinderbox, some underthings. But I suppose I'll have to be a princess again. "Thank you, Ximena. I'll see you soon."

Hector's room is only two doors down from mine. My desert companions and several of his own guards are already arrayed on cushions scattered throughout the suite when I arrive. They gape at me as I stand in the doorway, for I'm the only one in court finery. The rest chose newer, cleaner versions of their usual desert costume. Mara's eyes go blank; Jacián looks down at his lap. I step inside, feeling a pang I'm not sure I understand.

Hector inclines his head in greeting. "Now that the princess is here, we can begin."

I settle on a cushion beside Cosmé before asking, "Lord Hector, could you start by explaining why you are here in Basajaun? I thought the king's personal guard never left his side."

"Not usually. His Majesty ordered the evacuation of Treviño's holdings soon after you disappeared," he says, his face grave. "He offered sanctuary behind the walls of

Brisadulce to all the hill folk. But the conde refused."

"Treviño believed he had bargained for peace," Cosmé says.

Hector nods. "So he said in the message we received. Condesa Ariña worked very hard to convince the king her father's words were true. His Majesty hesitated to act a long time. Finally, other counsel won him over, and he ordered me here to oversee the evacuation firsthand. He had to send a member of the Quorum, someone who had the authority to seize the conde's holdings if necessary. Ariña and I were the only members available. I arrived just yesterday."

"And yesterday, the conde told you he had found a way to leverage for peace, once and for all," I say.

"Yes. He said he'd captured the leader of a treasonous rebellion." A darting smile quirks the edges of his mustache. "Someone the animagi were desperate to acquire. He thought if he offered you to Invierne as a gesture of good faith, they could resume trade and negotiations. Apparently, there was an incident that nullified their earlier agreement. Something about poisoned food stores."

My companions glance at one another in discomfort, not understanding the merriment that flickers in Hector's eyes.

"A brilliant plan, brilliantly executed," he finally concedes, nodding in respect. "I think it will work to our advantage after all."

"So what next?" Cosmé asks. "I think we should get a message to Alentín and the Malficio and tell—"

A knock resonates on the door. "Lord Hector!" calls a muffled voice. "It's Captain Lucio."

Concern edges his brow. He strides to the door and flings it open. "Captain?"

I can't see past the bulk of Hector's shoulders, but I hear the captain's voice loud and clear when he announces, "We've just received word, my lord. The army of Invierne marches against Joya d'Arena."

PART III

29

HECTOR asks me to return with him to Brisadulce. My mind is such a jumble, it's hard to know what's right. *The Malficio need me*, I tell myself, even though it's not true. My people are perfectly capable of continuing on without me. But maybe I need them. I created them. They are *mine*, wholly separate from my sister or my husband. Something to be proud of. If I leave them, I'm only Elisa again.

I try to imagine what it would be like to see Alejandro after all this time. If I close my eyes, I remember hair that curled at the nape of his neck, eyes that shone ruddy brown, but I still can't summon the exact lines of his face to mind. The harder I try, the more my memory of him slips into fog. Different lines materialize then, a specter of swarthy skin and laughing eyes, a strong chin dusted with the beginnings of a beard.

I don't cry anymore. I'm too tired. Ximena knows something hurts my heart, but I can't bring myself to talk about Humberto. Not yet.

Cosmé is the one who convinces me to go. "If what Belén

said was true . . ." She swallows hard and tries again. She grieves for Belén, for what he has become. "If what he said was true, the animagi want your Godstone." She has her usual control now, face hard, voice flat. "We cannot begin to guess what sorcery they'll bring to bear with a final, living Godstone in their possession. You must flee this place. Give your husband a chance to defend you." Her words are strong. They should have passion in them, but she is like iron. Or ice. It occurs to me that she has lost more than I can imagine. I never had parents to lose—my mother died when I was born and my father was always too busy for me—so I can't begin to understand her pain. Then she lost Belén. Countless friends and relatives. And now her brother.

Cosmé is right. I know it in a deep place of understanding. Invierne cannot be allowed to possess my Godstone. Neither can they be allowed to discover the amulet I now wear around my neck or the Godstones buried with my potted palm in Brisadulce.

We leave Cosmé in charge of Basajuan, supported by Jacián and most of Lord Hector's retainers. She will evacuate as many as she can, then use the conde's troops to harass Invierne's northern army from behind as it marches toward the coastal holdings. Carlo will return to the Malficio with news of what has transpired.

I want a reminder of the life and purpose I created for myself. So Mara agrees to fill the lady-in-waiting position that has been vacant since Aneaxi's death. Benito also decides to accompany us when Hector promises him a post in the palace guard.

We leave the next day, early in the morning when dawn's light is merely grayish. In spite of the hour, everyone comes to the stables to see us off. Walking away from my desert companions feels like cutting off a limb. How does one say goodbye to an arm? One doesn't, I suppose. One pretends it isn't happening. I steel myself, make a rock of my heart. My friends seem disappointed that I don't make more of a fuss. Carlo, in particular, looks at me with such hurt, his eyes liquid and searching. I clasp his hand briefly and turn away.

Someone grabs me, spins me around. It's Cosmé. She hugs me then, just long enough to say, "Don't be so cold, Elisa. Don't be like me."

I stumble back. "But . . . it helps."

She shakes her head. "No. You think it does, but it doesn't."

I'm skeptical, but I nod.

Then Hector helps me into my carriage. Ximena and Mara are already inside, still and stoic, hands folded in their laps. Someone barks orders, reigns snap, and we lurch away.

But thinking of Cosmé's words, I rip aside the back curtain to wave one last time.

Armies move slowly, Hector tells me. Still, everyone feels the unspoken urgency. We must reach Brisadulce well before Invierne does.

We cannot cross the deep desert with horses and carriages, so we skirt it to the north, keeping an even distance from the jungle line of the Hinders to avoid ambush by the Perditos. The carriage pitches and sways at our bruising pace, so I spend a part of each day jogging beside it. It's hard to believe I ever preferred clunky carriage travel to my own two feet.

Fortunately, no one tries to coerce me into mounting a horse.

We don't even pause to rest when we reach the road that would take us through the Hinders and back to the country of my birth. By the time we pass the place where Aneaxi died of infection, Ximena has thoroughly adopted my new lady-in-waiting into our strange family. I smile to see them laughing together, one gray haired and thickset, the other young and scarred and tall as a palm. Their easy friendship relaxes me. Gradually, through many hair brushings and carriage rides, I tell them both about Humberto. I can't say a lot at once; the whole picture of him is still too precious. But neither of them press the matter, and slowly his story leaks out of me.

Nighttime brings horrifying dreams of icy-eyed sorcerers and glowing amulets. Sometimes I'm fleeing from clawed hands that grasp for my navel. Other times, I'm searching for something, searching so desperately because everyone I care about will die if I don't find it. When I wake, I can't remember what I was looking for. But I know in those first moments of stirring that there are things I've yet to comprehend. I clutch my amulets—the animagus's caged Godstone and the conde's ugly golden flower—to remind myself that I've been victorious twice.

I know it is not enough. Something still eludes me.

In desperation, I close my eyes. *"Pray through your doubts,"* Father Alentín told me. So I do.

We push hard, and our caravan makes the trip from Basajuan

to Brisadulce in a little over a month. Like before, we pass a line of palms and suddenly a giant wall rises into the sky, a perfect companion to the yellow-orange sand it springs from. It is so like my first view of the city that my throat squeezes closed. How long have I been gone? Five months? More? I've lost track.

Hector calls a halt and rides toward me. I peer up at him, hand shielding my eyes from the desert sun.

"How would you like to enter the city, Elisa? Announced at the main gates? Or do you want to go in through the merchants' alley again?"

His horse, a blood bay, tosses his head and flares his nostrils. I recoil from the creature, saying, "Not the main gate, please."

Lord Hector nods. "The merchants' alley, then."

He leads us south, along the wall. Up close, I see the changes that have occurred in my absence. Small fortifications extend outside in an even perimeter: dark pits in the sand, hastily constructed walls of brick and clay with arrow slits, mounds of sand covered in tent cloth and hide. High above, figures pace back and forth along the wall's crest, tiny toy guardsmen with spears and bows.

Inside, the fortifications are even more apparent. Arrows lie in neat piles along the inner wall, and the first buildings we encounter are silent and still, a barrier of abandoned lifelessness ringing the city. Sadness twinges in my chest when we finally encounter the citizens of Brisadulce. They walk hurriedly, heads down, unsmiling. So different from the vibrant society I left behind.

I pull Hector aside when we reach Alejandro's stables. "You're certain no one is expecting us?" I ask.

"We did not dare send a message," he confirms. "Given how the jungle Perditos were able to ambush us on our last journey together. You're a target now that you are known to be Alejandro's wife."

I was a target already just by bearing the Godstone, but I don't bother to correct him. "And Alejandro does not know what has become of me?"

"He does not."

I am suddenly glad Ximena never received my coded note. Now I will use the surprise to our advantage.

"Please do not announce us just yet. I would like to make an entrance."

His eyes narrow. "What do you mean?"

"I want to be announced as—as the Lady of the Malficio. In public."

He considers for a moment. "In that case, I can't take you to your suite. We'll have to find another place for you to freshen up. The servants' quarters, perhaps."

"That would be perfect."

We hide in the carriage with curtains drawn while Hector makes arrangements. In no time, Ximena, Mara, and I are ensconced in a plain whitewashed room with a bunked bed. Mara volunteers to sleep on the floor.

King Alejandro will not be holding court until tomorrow afternoon. We order food and stay inside, exchanging stories, pacing. It's a strange time, for I keep wondering about my husband, about how many walls separate us. This castle should feel familiar and homelike. Here, I am a princess again, a future queen. But I feel distant and cold. I miss the open air, the streaked light-and-shadow combination of our village by the butte.

I miss Humberto.

The next day, Ximena prepares me expertly. She braids a chunk of hair and wraps it around my head like a circlet. The rest falls in waves past my waist. The day we left Basajuan, she threw away my blood-soaked riding leathers and scouted the storerooms for suitable gowns. Today she pulls them out of a traveling trunk one by one for my approval. The first is soft green linen with sheer panels that flow from the gathered waist. "Too feminine," I tell her. "I need to look like I could have led the Malficio these last months."

She retrieves a velvet gown next, thick with geometric lines and black trim. But the color, a deep desert red, looks like blood in certain light. I tell her the dress will do if we find nothing more suitable.

Ximena sets aside a riding skirt to reach for the next gown.

"Wait," I tell her. "What is that?"

She holds up the riding skirt. It splits down the center, and the fabric is a dense, black wool broadcloth. It has a matching corset and vest of forest green with black buttons and trim. It's strong and ambitious. It looks too small.

"I like it," Mara says.

It settles over my hips with surprising grace. Ximena laces the corset, amid dire warnings of what will befall her if she yanks too tight. My nurse then rubs a bit of rouge on my lips and below each cheekbone, smears kohl along my eyelashes. Mara watches the process carefully, fascinated.

Lord Hector retrieves us and leads us toward the center of the castle. "King Alejandro knows I'll be introducing the leader of the Malficio," he tells me. "But he does not know it is you. You realize, of course, that this slight deception could displease him?"

I smile humorlessly. "I'll protect you." Though whether or not I have any influence with my husband has yet to be determined.

I turn to my ladies. "When I am introduced, I need you to watch the crowd for their reaction. I want to understand the sentiment here toward the Malficio. Likewise, when everyone figures out who I am, I want to know if that sentiment changes at all."

They nod understanding while Lord Hector reflects darkly.

We're there too soon. I look up at the double doors and feel very small. The last time I entered this audience hall, I stood at the receiving end while a child declared my corpulence to the world.

The doors open to a long walkway hemmed in on both sides by dense humanity. Chandeliers drip heavy from the ceiling above in a perfect line that leads toward the dais and the throne. My husband, King Alejandro de Vega, slumps there in a pose of glorious boredom, shoulders cocked, one long leg sprawled well across the dais floor, his beautiful face barely registering my presence.

"Your Majesty," Lord Hector intones. "I present the Lady of the Malficio, who has recently slain an animagus by her own hand."

I glance at him sharply. I hadn't asked him to say that.

The members of the court peer at me with unabashed interest. Alejandro straightens a little, his eyes narrow. It's still hard to breathe while he looks at me so intently. Hector gives my elbow a gentle push. I stumble forward, my ladies right behind me.

The king's face becomes clearer as I approach the dais. It's strangely void, with only a hint of curiosity. I've traversed half the length of the hall when I see his expression change. His eyes travel the length of my body from my feet to my head, lingering on my chest. His lips curve into a half smile. The curiosity remains, and it's more intense, somehow. Inviting. It's the face of a stranger.

Heat fills my cheeks. Pleasure sparks inside me, sharp as an arrow. No, it's not pleasure, it's power—a kind I've never felt before.

Alejandro stands, smiling. "Welcome, Lady of the Malficio," he says, his voice formal, eyes appreciative.

I almost panic then. The pleasure-power feeling flees, replaced by humiliation. It's obvious my husband doesn't recognize his own wife. Yet even in this public place, he can't be bothered to hide his admiration for a woman he finds attractive.

He used to stare at me so intently, like I was the only thing in the world. Have I changed so much? Or maybe that mesmerizing gaze was just a weapon in his arsenal of appeal. Maybe he never actually *saw*.

Anger carries me the remaining distance. He is the one who should feel grimy with shame, not me. I reach the dais steps and drop into a curtsy.

"Your Majesty," I intone, my eyes downcast.

Then, a little voice to Alejandro's left says, "Elisa? Er, I mean, Your Highness?"

I look up, startled. A young boy is peering wide-eyed from around someone's ample skirt. Tousled black hair, cinnamon eyes. It's Prince Rosario, grinning hugely. "It *is* you!"

I reach out my arms just as he topples forward. He clings to my waist as I bend over and kiss the top of his head. I blink back tears, embarrassed at how much his enthusiastic greeting means to me.

"Oh, my God." Alejandro steps toward us. "I didn't rec—we thought you might be . . ."

It's unforgivable, really. Rosario had no problem recognizing me, in spite of the fact that we spent mere hours together. And Ximena at my back should have been clue enough. But I decide to be kind. "It's nice to see you again, Alejandro."

"Yes, yes, you too." He presses his lips to my forehead, then studies my face. He looks so perplexed that I almost laugh. "What's this about the Lady of the Malficio?" he asks.

"We have much to discuss."

He blinks a few times. Then he turns to the crowd and announces, "Court is dismissed for the day." He grins—that boyish grin that used to melt my toes—and says in a softer voice, "My wife has returned."

He wraps an arm across my shoulders and pulls me against

him, then escorts me from the audience hall while the court mills and murmurs behind us. He seems delighted, now that the initial shock is wearing off.

I wish I knew how *I* felt.

I tell him a little about my time in the desert, our capture by the conde. But being around him is confusing. Though my ladies and I have been cooped up in the servants' quarters, I plead hunger and exhaustion and take my leave of Alejandro as soon as I can.

He agrees to give me some time to myself. "We'll have dinner together tonight," he insists. "In my rooms. You can finish telling me then."

I murmur some kind of agreement and let him guide me to my old suite. The queen's suite. While walking along the stone and plaster corridors—Ximena and Mara trailing behind—I realize the castle seems different. Brighter or fresher. I peer into passageways and alcoves, trying to pinpoint the change. We turn a corner, and my hand brushes palm fronds.

Plants! That's the difference. They are everywhere. Palms and ferns, mostly, with a smattering of jungle flowers.

"Why are you suddenly smiling so much?" Alejandro asks.

"Potted plants!"

He chuckles. "Yes. It started just after you disappeared. Word got out that you had ordered plants for your suite. Everyone wanted one after that."

We reach the door. Like the first time Alejandro escorted me here, I feel like a guest staying the night.

He leans down and brushes my lips with his. "Until dinner tonight," he whispers.

I swallow as he takes his leave. Ximena and Mara rush into the suite ahead of me.

"Oh, it's lovely!" Mara squeals.

I shut the door. "The Godstones," I say. "We have to find them. Before we do anything else." I scan the room, looking for a young palm.

"What are you talking about?" Ximena asks.

"Father Nicandro gave me some Godstones. Old ones. I buried them at the root of a palm tree."

My nurse appears shocked. She's still unaccustomed to speaking so openly about such matters. But she no longer frightens me, and I ignore her, striding to the balcony to whip the curtain aside. The balcony is empty.

"There's a palm in here," Mara calls from the echoing atrium.

I rush inside and look where she's pointing. "That's not it," I say. It's too small, too dense. "My palm was taller." I turn back toward the bedroom, but something catches my eye. The tiles around the tub, the tiny yellow flowers painted on them. Odd four-petaled flowers with splotches of blue. My Godstone jumps in response.

"My sky, that's the only plant in the suite," Ximena says. "Are you sure it's not the one?"

My heart begins to pound with the gravity of the situation. "Oh, Ximena, they're not here. The Godstones are missing." Someone must have raided my suite to keep up with the new demand for decorative greenery.

"I'm sure we'll find them eventually," Ximena says, her brow knit in perplexity over my panic.

"You don't understand. We have to find them now, maybe destroy them, before the army gets here. If the animagi get their hands on them before we do, we will lose the war."

30

HOURS later, I am forced to abandon the search to have dinner with the king.

Alejandro's suite is just as I imagined it would be—dimly lit with deep reds and browns, a bed and dressing table of dark, raw wood, the air spicy and warm. I sit cross-legged on a huge fringed cushion, facing him. Platters of steaming food on the rug serve as a comforting barrier between us.

I start with the pollo pibil—Alejandro's favorite, I remember—and wash my first bite down with a sip of chilled wine. I study the platters carefully, planning my next selection as if the fate of Joya depends on the wisdom of my decision. It's better than noticing how he watches me with such unwavering interest.

His delighted-child grin from earlier is gone, replaced by fatigue and worry. "I spoke with the Quorum today," he says carefully as I take a hot mushroom stuffed with garlic breading.

"Oh?"

"They feel we should hold your coronation as soon as

possible. With the war . . ." His voice trails off, and the light of his eyes turns in on itself. He blinks and starts again as I bite into the mushroom. "With the war coming, they feel it would boost morale to have a newly crowned queen."

"And what do *you* think?" I say around a mouthful.

"I agree."

I take my time chewing and swallowing so I can collect my thoughts. "When I first came here, you asked me to keep our marriage secret. Now you seem eager to acknowledge me as your wife and make me your queen. Why?"

He picks up his wine before answering. "Before, there was too much political advantage to be gained by making everyone believe the queen's throne was still empty." But his eyes are unsteady, and he gulps his wine as if it were a life-giving tonic.

"And now that everyone knows, they think I should be crowned right away."

"Yes."

"Even Ariña?" The condesa must have had apoplexy when she learned of our marriage. And finally it occurs to me that, though political leveraging may have been a factor, the real reason we kept our marriage a secret was because Alejandro could not bear to face his mistress with the news.

The hand on his wineglass has turned white, but his voice is steady when he says, "Even Ariña. Especially in light of the fact that it is you who has been leading the mysterious Malficio all this time. It will be a great boon to the people of Joya to know that their queen is not only the bearer, but a legendary hero in her own right."

Hero? It sounds preposterous. "I had some ideas. That's all. Your people did the rest." Then I frown at him. "You must realize, Alejandro, that Condesa Ariña is a traitor."

His eyes narrow. "She won't be in my bed, if that's what you're worried about."

"I'm worried about the minor matter of treason," I snap at him. This is not going how I imagined. I can't believe I just spoke to him that way.

He shrugs, looking vulnerable again. "We can't be sure—"

"She knew what her father was doing. She knew he sold out to Invierne. But she said nothing. Think of all those war councils, Alejandro. All those Quorum meetings when she could have told you the truth."

Hesitation flickers across his face. "If it makes you feel better, I'll have her watched."

I want her imprisoned, out of my—and Cosmé's—way, should we survive this war. "That would help. Thank you."

"So, the Quorum would like to hold the coronation in two days."

So soon! I remember a time—so long ago, it seems—when I lay on the bed next door, fingertips to my Godstone, praying about whether I should become queen. Now I must play the game, if only to fulfill a promise to a brave group of people who want the freedom to make their own place.

While the wine swims warm in my blood and feels something like courage, while Alejandro's softly yearning gaze on me feels something like power, I make my first move. "You were right about one thing," I say, my tone respectful again.

Almost flattering. "The people of the Malficio are heroes. They are the bravest warriors I've ever known, and they would give their lives if it gave you victory."

"You are right to be proud of them."

"If we survive this war—" Fear flits across his features at my words. "Then I would take it as a personal favor to see them honored."

"Of course," he concedes quickly, but his brow is furrowed, his gaze distant.

"What is it, Alejandro?"

He sighs. "Can I tell you something in confidence, Elisa?"

"Of course."

He gulps the rest of his wine and sets his glass down. "I'm afraid of this war." His smile is self-deprecating. "My father was killed by an Invierne arrow. Right before my eyes. I still have nightmares about it. And my next true battlefield experience left me bleeding badly."

"The Perditos," I whisper. Is this why he is always so indecisive? Because he is terrified?

"Yes, the Perditos. See how unheroic I am? *You* saved me that day, remember?"

I hadn't realized having one's life saved could be so humiliating. I barely refrain from rolling my eyes at him. "I promise to spare you future embarrassment. Next time, I'll let you die."

He winces, and I wish I could take the words back. Where does this new, cruel Elisa come from? "I understand," I say by way of a peace offering. "Several times during the last months, I became so frightened I thought I'd die of it. But time passed, decisions were made and acted upon, and I didn't have to be afraid again for a while."

"Does that make it easier?"

I smile sadly. "I'm more frightened than ever. I've watched people die." *Die in my very arms.* I have to swallow before continuing. "I know how hard it will be to . . . keep going. After. Even if we win."

He wilts at my words, and I realize I've probably made things worse.

I stand and stretch. My appetite is gone, and I suddenly long to be with Ximena and Mara. "I hope you'll excuse my early departure, Alejandro, but if we are to have a coronation in two days, I must begin preparations." It's a lie. I couldn't care less about the coronation ceremony.

He rises and takes my hands. "I'm glad you're back." It's that lost look again, the one that used to make me want to hold him close and murmur words of comfort.

His eyes fall to my breasts. The corset and riding vest push them toward my chin. I almost feel that if I lowered my head enough, it could rest there, pillowed comfortably.

His arms snake around my waist, and he pulls me toward him until my breasts are smooshed against his chest. "Elisa," he whispers, staring at my lips.

I want him to kiss me, even though my heart squeezes with wrongness. I want to feel the victory of being desired by someone I once found desirable. With the way he looks at me now, I know I can be with a man for the first time tonight, if I choose to be.

He leans in; his lips brush mine. Gently first, then with insistence. His fingers tangle in my hair, he takes my bottom lip between his, his tongue whispers against my teeth. His indoor, gentleman's mouth is so soft. Softer than Humberto's.

With a gasp, I lurch away from him.

The confusion on his face is quickly replaced by a soothing smile. "I understand, Elisa. You're not ready for this. We have plenty of time to get to know each other." It's the same voice he'd use with little Rosario. Placating, condescending.

"Thank you for understanding." I smile sweetly. On the day he died, Humberto spoke of a way to be free of Alejandro. What did he discover?

But it is of no matter now. I must become queen if I'm to help the people I care about. I only hope that, months from now, there is something left to be queen of.

I enter through the door connecting our suites. Ximena is reading the *Scriptura Sancta*, Mara is mending her robe. They both look up in surprise.

"I didn't expect you so soon," Ximena says.

"Did you find that potted palm?"

Ximena sighs. "No. It wasn't in the monastery. Mara checked the servants' quarters."

"The kitchen master caught me digging into a pot of soil," Mara says, voice tinged with laughter.

I plop onto the bed, frustrated. "It's probably decorating some noblewoman's suite. I have to figure out a way to check every single room in the palace. Maybe Hector will help me."

"We'll ask him tomorrow," Ximena says. Searching for the Godstones is awkward for her, against her staunch Vía-Reforma belief that all such matters should be left to themselves. She only agreed to help when I pointed out how much worse it would be if Invierne's sorcerers found them first. I suppose I could order a search of the entire palace once I am crowned queen. The thought makes me scowl. What a lovely way to endear myself to my new subjects.

I take a deep breath and say, "I'm to be crowned queen in two days."

They stare at me. "That's wonderful, Elisa," Mara says.

Someone raps at the door. I jump, half expecting it to be Alejandro again. Ximena opens the door a crack, grabs something, closes it.

"A message for you via pigeon," she says, holding out her hand. A tiny canister is pinched between thumb and forefinger.

I grab it, unscrew the top, uncurl the tiny roll.

"It's from Cosmé!" I gasp. Tears spring to my eyes. "Basajuan is overrun, the conde's army scattered into the Hinders. All the nearby villages have been burned. She organizes a group to harry the Inviernos from behind now that they march on Brisadulce." I look up at them, waving the tiny parchment. "It says to expect refugees. Maybe thousands."

"That's good, right?" Mara says. "That means she was able to evacuate a lot of people."

I nod. "It's good."

Pray through your doubts. I drop to my knees on the hard stone floor. I prostrate myself and pray for Cosmé, for Jacián, even for traitorous Belén. I plead for the lives of Alentín and the people of his hidden village. I beg God to show me how to combat the sorcery of the animagi. Surely, with so much at stake, He will heed my prayers.

By the time I collapse into bed, my body shimmers with sweat from the Godstone's burning response.

The next day is a whirlwind of monotony. Everyone wants my opinion, but only on the most minor of matters. "How would you like to make your entrance, Your Highness?" "Which dishes would you prefer for the feast afterward?" "Do you want stargazer lilies or allamanda?" "Should the orchestra play the 'Glorifica' or the 'Entrada Triunfal'?"

Don't they realize a war is coming?

"It is precisely the coming war that makes them so desperate to lose themselves in the details of this celebration," Ximena explains. "So be a good queen-to-be and smile a lot and let them have their bit of happiness."

She's right, and guilt twinges in my chest. I have been forgetting to be kind.

"Now tell me," she says. "Which of these gowns do you like best?"

We settle on a silk gown with a sheer overlay. It's an airy wine gold color, with dainty yellow vines embroidered along the hem. Next to the shimmery fabric, my sun-darkened skin fairly glows. We used to hem all my dresses, but I'm a little taller now than when I was taken into the desert. Surely that will be the last of my growth spurts.

"It will be perfect once I let it out a little in the bust," Ximena says. "Alejandro will think you're beautiful when he sees it." Her eyes shine with something powerful. She is the mother I never had, and like a mother, she is going to soak up the day of my coronation, treasuring each moment in her heart. I reach forward and give her a squeeze.

"Thank you, Ximena."

Early the next morning, my nurse awakens me by opening the balcony curtains to let the sunrise stream copper across my face. Mara helps me across the slippery tile into the bathing pool while Ximena prepares an herbal soak.

"Mara, these tiles." I run my fingers across the glazed surface. Each one is individually painted, but they all show the same thing: a bouquet, four yellow petals to a flower, each petal with a single blue spot, like a blot of ink or maybe an eye. My Godstone responds so strangely when I look at them up close, like it's greeting an old friend. "Can you ask around today? Learn something about them?"

"Of course." She lathers my hair and I lean back, closing my eyes.

Hours later, I'm standing outside the audience hall for the second time in three days. I hear the buzz behind the double doors as I wait, suffocating in my creamy silk. Another rushed ceremony, like my wedding. And once again, Alejandro waits for me at the end of a very long walk. This time, though, my father is not here to escort me. Lord Hector has that honor, by my request.

I look up at his handsome, weathered face. He is taller even than Alejandro, a sturdy, comforting presence.

He studies me thoughtfully. "You are a beautiful queen, Elisa," he says, voice pitched low.

I never expected he would say such a thing. "A month or two of pastries will fix that," I say. Then I smile to show him I mean it flippantly.

His expression does not change. "Even then."

It is kind of him to say so. "Thank you for doing this, Hector. I'm glad you're here."

He squeezes my arm. "Always." He looks toward the doors now, his face a stone, but I know him a little better now. Like Cosmé, he becomes ice to keep from feeling too much.

The first wisps of the "Glorifica" filter through the walls. Hector and I straighten. The music ascends in steady arpeggios, the doors open inward. I hold my head high as Hector escorts me down the newly carpeted aisle. Alejandro stands transfixed by my approach, Rosario a slender shadow beside him.

It all happens very quickly. Alejandro kisses my cheek; Father Nicandro intones an oath about honor and responsibility that I repeat back to him. The priest lifts the crown from a cushioned pedestal—a thick golden thing that makes my head hurt just to look at—and lodges it firmly against my scalp with a wink.

He gestures for me to face the court, then announces, "Queen Lucero-Elisa de Vega né Riqueza!"

The entire nobility drops to its knees. Alejandro grasps my hand, and together we sit side by side on our thrones. I watch enviously as Rosario is whisked away by a nurse. My rear grows cold and stiff as every single noble in the audience hall is presented to me. I remember Ximena's words about allowing them the veil of happiness they desperately desire. So I greet each one with a confident smile and mumble words of encouragement whenever anyone brings up the subject of war.

But it is all an act, for as the afternoon wears on, my navel begins to pulse with telltale cold. It's faint, nothing a quick prayer can't erase. But it means that Invierne is coming for me, that they are even closer than we thought.

31

WHEN the coronation ends I expect to return my attention to the serious matter of war preparation. Instead, it seems as though half the citizens of Joya d'Arena need a royal consultation or a queenly favor. The other half is anxious to place me in their debt, and they inundate me with nuggets of wisdom regarding certain pertinent matters, shower me with gifts, introduce me to people of crucial importance. I spend the first two days as queen bobbing my head like a chicken and saying "Thank you."

On the second afternoon, while the petite but unlovely Lady Jada chatters at me in my suite, frustration builds like an avalanche in my gut. There are so many things I could be doing. I need to be searching for the Godstones, going over battle strategy with General Luz-Manuel, preparing for refugees, having a talk with Condesa Ariña, maybe spending time with Rosario.

Rosario. No one notices him. No one cares what he does.

I interrupt Lady Jada's aspersion of inferior laundering

practices by raising my hand. "I just realized I've forgotten to attend to something very important." I smile blandly. "I hope you can forgive me."

She wrinkles her tiny nose in confusion but recovers quickly. "We'll have to talk again soon," she says, curtsying.

"I look forward to it."

As soon as she leaves, I turn to Ximena. "Rosario is going to stay in our suite for a few days. I need an extra bed brought in, some clothes for playing in, maybe a few toys. Tell his nurse she has a week off. In fact, tell her she doesn't have to come back until the war is over."

Her smile is broad. "I'll go at once."

I send Mara to retrieve the boy himself, then spend a few minutes pacing through my suite, thinking. Every time I glance at the tiles rimming my bathing pool, the Godstone hums in response.

Mara returns, Rosario in tow. His eyes are wide, his gaze bordering on suspicious.

I grin. "I thought you might like to stay with us for a while."

His eyes narrow. "How come?"

I open my mouth to tell him something comforting and innocuous. *I want us to get acquainted,* or *I need a companion for a few outings.* But I remember growing up in Papá's palace hacienda while adults talked over my head, and what I say is, "I need your help."

His lips purse with serious consideration. "I told Papá I could help. With the war. But he said I had to wait until I was older."

"Well, I need your help right now. With the war. How would you like to do a little spying?"

His lips curve into a shy grin.

Late in the afternoon, the first wave of refugees arrives. They are mostly young and healthy—the ones who could travel quickly. We accommodate several hundred in the palace, a hundred more at surrounding estates. I spend the early evening making them as comfortable as possible, sifting through their tales of hardship and escape for any possible mention of the friends I left behind. I learn that the Malficio continues to make its presence felt, that thousands of people, mostly refugees, now contribute to its purpose. But my Godstone grows colder, and I worry for the those who will not reach us ahead of Invierne's advancing army.

That night in the dining hall, I share a private meal with my husband and General Luz-Manuel. We're finishing off a platter of wild turkey glazed with honey and shredded orange peel when a breathless scout tumbles in, Lord Hector on his heels. He reports sighting a huge line of cavalry, less than a day away.

"Just cavalry?" Alejandro asks.

The scout confirms and is dismissed.

"That doesn't make sense," he muses as Lord Hector plunks down beside him.

"It's just an advance guard," Luz-Manuel says. "They're here to cut us off. The bulk of the army will arrive during the next month or so."

Alejandro sighs. "Then we must cover the pits and close the gates."

I put a hand to his arm. "Refugees will trickle in all night. Can we keep the gates open that long, at least?"

He hesitates until Lord Hector nods. "Every person will be needed on the walls," the guard points out.

"True. The gates will stay open, then." Alejandro kisses my forehead and takes his leave, accompanied by Lord Hector.

The General and I regard each other for a moment, and I see the strain of the last months in the sag of his eyes, the gauntness of his cheeks. Besides Hector and Alejandro, he is the only member of the Quorum I've encountered since I returned. Conde Eduardo left months ago to defend his holdings from Invierne's southern army, and Ariña has kept to her quarters.

"I'm glad you're here, Your Majesty," he says, a slight frown creasing his brow.

My eyes widen. Luz-Manuel has never shown me the least bit of welcome.

"I may need your help," he explains. "His Majesty is . . . well, he is not a man to make quick decisions. A lovely trait when it comes to matters of state. But during battle . . ."

It's because the king is afraid. I nod. "I'll help any way I can."

He rubs at his bald spot. "Thank you. Another voice of encouragement in his ear may be all he needs."

"You should know, General, that Invierne would love to get their hands on the stone I bear. There may come a time when it would be best to make myself scarce."

He nods. "Yes, Hector told me how they believe they can harness its power."

I say nothing.

He continues, "We'll protect you as best we can, but if they take Brisadulce, they win the war, with or without your Godstone."

"They're going to burn their way in. Through the gate."

His face becomes graver. "The refugees spoke of a strange fire. Some even bear the scars. We've been hoarding water at the walls, but our gate is strong. Thick."

"General, I've seen the devastation caused by this fire and I assure you, the animagi are perfectly capable of burning the gate down."

"The portcullis outside will hold," he assures me.

"If the gate bursts into flame, what else might catch fire? The siege towers, certainly." We have built several along the wall at steady intervals. Most are used to keep weapons within easy access. "And surely there is wood-work inside the walls themselves? What about the nearby buildings?"

"How close must they approach to use this . . . fire?"

"I don't know. I'm sorry, but I just don't know. Maybe one of the refugees—"

"I'll ask," he says. "And we'll station our strongest bowmen here at the gate. Hope for the best."

"Oh, and tell those bowmen to keep themselves hidden. No peeking over the walls."

"Why?"

"The animagi can freeze a man where he stands. Just by looking at him."

Mara almost flings herself into my arms when I return to my suite. "I asked everyone I saw today, but no one knew. I mean, everyone knew which tiles I was talking about, but no one knew anything about them." She's nearly dancing from excitement.

Rosario huddles on my bed, grappling with his toes while watching my maid's exuberance with wary curiosity.

"I suppose you discovered something?" I ask.

She grins. "Rosario knew about them."

"Oh?" I turn to the little prince.

"Father Nicandro told me." He scrunches his nose in distaste. "During history lesson."

My breath catches in my chest. This is going to be something important. The thrumming of my Godstone attests. "What exactly did Father Nicandro tell you?"

"He said a very important person made the tiles. A person no one cares about anymore, but Father Nicandro thinks people might care again soon."

It makes no sense. "That's it? That's all he said?"

Rosario sinks into himself, becoming a tight ball. "I don't remember," he says in a small voice.

I'm frightening him. I take a relaxing breath. "Rosario, this is such a big help. Thank you."

He beams.

I don't ask him if he tried to find the Godstones. A quick glimpse at his hands, at the crescent of dirt under each fingernail, tells me all I need to know. I excuse myself to visit the monastery.

Father Nicandro is delighted to see me. I stifle a grin when he hugs me, for he barely reaches my cheek and is as slight as a child. He ushers me by candlelight into the scribing alcove, and we settle on stools around the table.

"Majesty, I'm so glad you came. We haven't had a chance for a proper conversation since you returned. Now tell me . . ." He leans forward, nose twitching. "Is it true that you were taken to the gates of the enemy?"

I shrug. "I don't know, Father. I was in the enemy camp for a short time, but not in the country of Invierne itself."

"Very interesting. And it's true that—"

"Father, I'm sorry to be in a hurry, but I need to know about the tiles in my atrium."

"What tiles?"

"Prince Rosario said you knew about them. Little yellow flowers with blue spots. Actually, they're quite unattractive—"

"Oh, yes! I should have realized you'd want to know about them."

"What do you mean?"

"Almost every tile with that design was painted by Mistress Jacoma herself. Her father owned a tile factory. Since the time she could walk, she amused herself by painting her father's tiles." At my confused look, he adds, "She bore the Godstone, Your Majesty."

I gasp. I knew this. Somehow, I knew.

"She died when she was about your age. Barely seventeen. Written accounts reveal that she never completed her service. But she painted over two thousand tiles with that obnoxious yellow flower. Artists copied the pattern for generations. You can find it in every castle and monastery in Joya d'Arena. Sadly, the only people who remember her now are a handful of priests and artists."

"Mistress Jacoma," I echo in wonder. "A bearer."

The priest leans forward and peers at me with round black eyes. "Remember when I showed you that passage in the *Afflatus*?"

"I remember."

"I have a theory about it. You know how it speaks of individual bearers at one point, and then seems to change? How it suddenly refers to all bearers in general?"

I nod, remembering the hours I spent pouring over Alentín's copy of the *Afflatus*, wondering if I would be the one to face the gates of the enemy.

"Well, I think we've been looking at it the wrong way. What if it does refer to each bearer—and to all bearers—at the same time? What if this act of service is something that all bearers throughout time accomplish together?"

"What are you saying?"

He shakes his head. "I don't know," he says wearily. "I don't know what I'm saying. It's just the spark of an idea. I feel like there's something larger here, and I'm only grasping the edges."

"I will give the idea some thought. Thank you, Father Nicandro. I may have more questions for you."

"Of course." He smiles. "I'm glad you're back safe, my queen."

I refrain from pointing out that I don't feel safe at all.

The next morning, Alejandro orders the gates sealed, leaving any remaining refugees without asylum. It's the right thing to do. Hector's captain reports dust whorls along the eastern horizon, heralding the coming army. Still, my chest aches for the thousands who didn't make it inside.

I spend a good part of the afternoon staring at the tiles in my atrium. There is a message here. I'm sure of it. I study the color and shape of the flowers, trace the edges of curving petals with my fingertips. I feel a kinship with this ancient tile painter. Another girl, like me. *Jacoma, what are you trying to tell me?* She doesn't answer, of course, but God whispers warmth into my belly as if I'm talking to *Him*. I will need more than warmth from Him if we are to win the day.

I'm still in the atrium when I hear the cry go up. Feet patter by in the hallway; panicked shouting drifts through my open balcony. Then the monastery bells toll a slow, deep warning.

I leave Rosario in Ximena's care and rush from my suite. Alejandro is already in the hallway. As soon as he sees me, he grabs my hand and pulls me down the corridor, past the kitchens and into the stables.

I freeze at the sight of enormous horse heads overhanging their stall doors. "Alejandro," I squeak. "I don't ride."

He frowns. "It's just to the wall and back." Already the stable hands are saddling a big dun stallion. "It will take too long to walk," he insists.

"I'll take her." I whirl at Lord Hector's voice. "Your army needs you, sire," the guard continues. "I'll escort Her Majesty to the wall. We'll join you shortly."

Alejandro nods, then swings up onto his horse and trots away.

The streets are full of people rushing to get a first glance at the enemy. Lord Hector and I weave through buildings, around panicked citizens, and reach one of the many crudely erected bits of scaffolding that now press against the inner wall. Hector hauls me up a set of rickety stairs to the top. Instantly the wind beats at my hair; sand stings my eyes. I sniff the dry desert cleanness and feel a pang of loneliness for my desert rebels.

Movement draws my gaze downward. A line of cavalry stretches in both directions as far as I can see, the late afternoon sun glinting from mouth pieces and sweating hides, obsidian arrowheads and white face paint.

White face paint.

I wonder how they brought so many horses through the desert. Even if they took the long route, hugging the greener line of the Hinders, they must have been hard-pressed to provision the animals for such a long journey. They can't expect them to survive a long siege in this barren place.

A group breaks off from the rest and gallops forward. They curve into a circle and ride around and around, brandishing spears, screaming like mountain cats. Even at this distance, the swirling pattern of black and white on their limbs makes me shudder.

"Hector," I gasp frantically. The horses didn't make the trek all the way from Invierne.

He bends down so I can whisper in his ear.

"Those aren't Inviernos," I tell him. "They're Perditos."

He nods solemnly. "Yes. We've long suspected an alliance between them."

"They're here to begin starving us out in advance of Invierne's real army."

"I'm afraid so."

We stand there a long while. Lord Hector's eyes harden to a dangerous glint, his face a sculpture of resolve. It's as if he's in deep meditation of purpose, storing something up within himself. I just pray.

The Perditos trap us in our own city. Alejandro, Hector, and General Luz-Manuel spend the next days strategizing about food rations and building up a store of water to combat the Inviernos' fire. While they are occupied, Rosario and I hunt for the Godstones.

Word reaches me that His Highness suffers an unnatural obsession with dirt. At least once per day someone catches him next to an overturned potted plant and a river of moist soil. I treat each complaint with proper gravity, then shower my little prince with praise as soon as the door is closed. Still, his enthusiasm for the task begins to wane. I almost order a palacewide search. But the memory of Belén's betrayal holds me back. I still don't know whom to trust. I cannot allow the wrong person to learn about the missing Godstones.

The troops my father promised as a condition of my marriage arrive in three great ships. Hector and Captain Lucio guide them in groups through the sewer tunnels that lead from the sea cliffs into the city. I tear through the barracks that day, looking for familiar faces. So many things remind me of Orovalle: the spicy scent of oiled leather, the de Riqueza sunburst embroidered into sashes, the loose-fitting blouse worn by all of Orovalle's soldiers when not in full battle gear. But I recognize no one. For that matter, no one recognizes me. After a while, I have to admit to myself that I'm looking for Papá, or even Alodia, and I walk away feeling foolish.

Their arrival is none too precipitous. The very next day, the first wave of Invierne's massive army materializes against the shimmering desert horizon. The Perditos greet them with feral celebration, screaming and riding in circles, shooting arrows into the sky. I stand beside Hector at the top of the wall to watch their approach. In those first moments, the combined forces of Orovalle and Joya d'Arena fall into awed silence. The enemy are so many, and they are barefoot, colorful, not quite human.

I too am silent, but for a different reason. I'm remembering my own first view of Invierne's massive army, the way their campfires lit the dark hills in either direction as far as the eye could see. So I know this first wave is just a fraction of the forces to come.

Beside me, Hector hammers his fist on the stone. "I wish we knew what they wanted."

"They believe this is God's will," I say softly.

"Acquiring a seaport? Invading another country? Killing innocent people? Which of their actions, exactly, are they going to blame God for?"

Something about his edged tone pleases me. "They want me, or the stone I bear."

"Yes, but why?"

"I wish I knew."

He regards me dead on. "They won't have you, Elisa. Not as long as I'm alive." He whirls and walks away, down the wall until he disappears behind a group of bowmen.

Another message comes via pigeon from Cosmé. My fingers shake as I unroll it, and Mara peers over my shoulder as I read.

Elisa,

Section of Invierne's southern army broke off and joined march toward Brisadulce. Five animagi heading your direction; only three were sent against southern holdings. I think they know you're there.

We continue to harass army's rear, but Perditos make our task difficult. They have begun shooting our pigeons. This will be my last message.

Take care,

Cosmé

32

As the Inviernos come, the line of enemies thickens into a dark ribbon across the desert, then a great river. The river expands until, from the vantage point of the wall's highest tower, they seem like an ocean of fleas writhing in the sand.

I huddle inside the wall with the bowmen, the Godstone chilling me, unable to tear myself away from the strange scene below us. The slitted loopholes between bricks splay to the inside, allowing a huge viewing range. Like everyone else, I stare through a loophole until my eyes water with heat and glare, looking for any subtle shift that could hint of their attack plan.

Finally the animagi show themselves. I see the unlikely white-gold of their heads first, bobbing through the ranks of Inviernos. They break free of the army to stand facing our main gate. Five of them, just as Cosmé said, all wearing supple, whitish robes, their amulets darkly caged at their breasts. When they raise their eyes to the wall—their Godstone-blue eyes—I double over in icy agony.

"Your Majesty!"

I peer up into the sun-browned face of Captain Lucio. "I'm fine, thank you." I manage a smile and straighten, my insides already warming from the prayer that flew from my heart with instinctive ease. I can pray in any circumstance, now.

I remember what the general said about offering an encouraging word to the king, so I take my leave of the captain and descend to the road, where my husband is overseeing the accumulation of water barrels.

Alejandro is relieved to see me. He puts an arm around my waist and pulls me close, but he's not giving comfort so much as taking it. "The portcullis outside will hold," he assures me. "Even if they burn the gate."

Soldiers passing by on the road don't bother to hide their grins. They don't know that we have yet to share a bed, and they like to see their king and queen embracing. So I hug Alejandro back, even though I can't offer encouraging words in return.

Never in my life have I so desired to be proved wrong. But the next morning, when our soaking gate steams under the onslaught of the rising desert sun, the animagi attack exactly as I foretold. They stand shoulder to shoulder, slender as palm trees, just outside the range of our weapons. I pray harder than ever to breathe life into my frozen limbs.

Five others, clumpy haired and barefoot, slip from the crowd to face the animagi, one on one. They kneel to the ground and throw their heads back. A trumpet sounds, but it is eerie and keening, like no instrument I've ever heard. As one, the animagi whip daggers from within their lovely robes. I don't see the flash of blades against flesh, but the bodies topple over and blood, crimson and sparkling in the sun, pools too quickly to disappear into the sand.

At the sacrifice of their own people, the amulets around the animagi's necks begin to glow.

The Godstone is a knife of icy rage.

Five more Inviernos come forward and surrender to the animagi. And five more after that. They continue the passionless process of slitting throats until twenty-five bodies lie crumpled in the sand, their blood feeding the magic that squirms beneath the earth.

Five times five.

And the amulets glow brighter.

"More water!" I yell past the bile in my throat. I don't know how well my voice carries inside the crowded wall, so I yell again. "More water on the gate *now*!"

I don't bother to see if anyone follows through with my command. My eye is drawn back through the arrow slit and to the caged Godstones that glow blindingly in the distance. The animagi tilt their heads toward the sky, mouths agape in effort or ecstasy. My nails dig at the sandstone in front of me as streaming light, blue-white, brilliant and arrow straight, thrusts from the amulets and pounds against the gate.

I smell acrid smoke. The walls around me tremble.

"Water!" someone yells. *"Water, water!"* The others take up the cry.

Agonizing moments pass in a haze of icy warnings and warming prayers as we pit our buckets and pots and ladles against their sorcery. At last the streaming light fizzles away. The animagi stagger back and are absorbed into the writhing wall of Inviernos.

A cheer thunders through our wall, shaking it as much as the animagi's magic did. I join in the cheer because they need me to.

Lord Hector finds me moments later. "Do you think they'll try again?" he whispers in my ear.

"Yes. They will rest. Then they'll find twenty-five more who are willing to be sacrificed, and they'll come at us again."

He grips my upper arm so hard I gasp. "Elisa, you shouldn't be here. There's probably a black crater the size of Alejandro's banner crown on the other side of that gate. We can last through three more attacks at the most."

"I'm the queen!" I protest. "I should be here to—"

"You said it yourself. They must not find your Godstone. Did you see what they just did with only five?"

I swallow and nod.

"Good. I'll find someone to escort you back. Be prepared to flee through the tunnels if the wall is breached."

"And . . . Alejandro?"

"I'll try to convince him to return, so watch for him. He is more a nuisance here anyway."

Only the stress of battle would make him say such a thing aloud. His eyes flash with regret and surprise, but I put a hand to his shoulder, grateful for his honesty. "Hector, be safe."

But instead of going back to my suite, I rush to the monastery to see Father Nicandro.

He huddles in the empty gathering hall, on his knees before the candlelit altar. I kneel beside him.

"Oh, dear girl, there should be so many more of us here," he breathes. My heart catches at the sorrow in his voice. "Have the people of Joya d'Arena strayed so far from the path of God that we do not turn to him even in such times?"

"Perhaps things are not desperate enough," I say. "Perhaps they will come soon."

"Perhaps."

"Father, I have not come to pray either."

He looks up startled. I tell him about the streaming fire that beat against our gate. "You see, Nicandro? It's the blood. Something about the blood feeding the earth that allows them to use their amulets."

He glares at me in warning, his dark eyes becoming very sharp. "You want to try something with the amulet you took."

"I do. Father, I have to try something."

He slumps against the altar. "What did you have in mind?"

It only takes moments to prepare. I pull the amulet from beneath my vest and stare at it while Father Nicandro collects a ceremonial rose. He gestures me toward the altar.

"No," I tell him. "We should do this in the garden. Where no one will chance upon us."

He hesitates only a moment before leading me behind the altar and out the door. The monastery garden is tiny, with a three-tiered marble fountain and a bench that fits no more than two. We sit together, beneath a trellis woven with the vines of a creeping sacrament rosebush. The roses are not in bloom, which exposes the long thorns in sharp clarity.

In unison, we chant the "Glorifica." I put the fingertips of my right hand to the Godstone, the fingertips of my left to the amulet. Also a Godstone, I remind myself. Not for the first time, I wonder about the one who bore it. Did it detach from her body at the moment of her death? Did she part with it willingly, or did an animagus rip it from her belly while she lay screaming in agony?

Nicandro pulls my head forward until our noses almost touch. "What is it you seek, dear girl?"

I take a deep breath, then I pour all the longing of my soul into my request. "I seek victory over my enemies."

The prick is deep and painful. The first drop wells too quickly on the thorn, and when the priest pulls his rose away from my finger, three more quickly follow. They drop and bead against the hard-packed earth.

While the dry ground drinks my blood, I pray. I reach with my mind deep into the earth's crust. I imagine the amulet at my chest glowing with sorcery. I concentrate so hard that I lose my surroundings; the grotto garden, Father Nicandro, the clear desert sky above, all fade into a miasma of need and of prayer-induced heat.

But nothing happens.

I open one eye to peek at the priest.

"Maybe you need more blood?" he asks skeptically.

All the air inside me leaves in a disappointed rush. "If this was the way, I would have sensed *something*. I know I'm no sorcerer, but I have a Godstone living inside me! I should be able to *do* something."

He puts an arm around my shoulders. "Maybe the prophecy isn't about *you* doing something," he murmurs. "Maybe it's all the bearers."

I lean my head against his shoulder. "Is this that strange idea you were telling me about? The one you couldn't explain?"

He sighs into my hair. "Yes. Yes, that's the one."

I am sick with helplessness as I rush back to my suite. The halls are empty and silent, my footsteps loud. What Hector said was true; we cannot risk Invierne finding my Godstone. But I hate feeling useless. I want to be at the wall with everyone else, hauling buckets of water, preparing for the wounded.

How long will it take for the animagi to regain their strength and attack again? An hour? A day? The siege will be short-lived, of that I'm sure. My heart clenches to think of the brave people of my Malficio, of the risks they took, the lives we lost. All for nothing, since my brilliant strategy assumed a drawn-out siege that would make our enemy vulnerable.

The possibility that Humberto died for nothing is unbearable.

Rosario and Mara are huddled on my bed when I enter. Ximena sits next to the empty fireplace, sewing a skirt.

"What happened, Elisa," Mara says flatly as soon as she sees my face.

"The animagi attacked. We held them off."

"Papá will kill them all," Rosario says.

Ximena and I exchange a sad look. Then I plop next to him and hug him tight, but he squirms away, giving me a disgusted look.

I finger my amulets—the dead Godstone and the ugly pendant—and think about the empty victories they symbolize. I failed to accomplish anything with the Malficio. I failed to use my Godstone against the enemy, the way Homer foretold. Perhaps, centuries from now, a priest will show the list of God's chosen to another young bearer. Perhaps he will point at my name and say, "Ah, yes. Lucero-Elisa. Yet another failed bearer."

I gaze at Alejandro's tiny son. Just maybe I'll have one last chance to do something right. When the animagi break through our gate, someone must get the prince to safety. I may have failed to save Joya d'Arena, but maybe I can still save its heir.

"Ximena! No, wait. Mara." Mara will know what to bring, how to pack. "Go to the kitchens and storage rooms to find traveling food. Enough for all four of us for two weeks. Hurry!" There should be plenty of dry goods to choose from; Alejandro's household has been stocking up for months.

"Are we going on a journey?" Rosario asks.

"As soon as possible. But I need to stay a little longer."

He sighs. "Because you haven't found your Godstones yet."

"Yes."

"I think the condesa has them."

"What?" I exclaim. Ximena's head whips up.

"I tried to go in her rooms three times. But her lady says she needs rest. What are monthly courses?"

I almost bite my lip. "Er . . . that's when a woman doesn't feel very well for a while."

"Oh. Well, Condesa Ariña has been having them for a long time."

Ariña has definitely been scarce. She made a brief appearance at my coronation, but I haven't seen her since. I wonder if Alejandro kept his promise to have her watched.

"Why do you think she has them?"

"I looked everywhere else."

It makes sense. When Cosmé and I disappeared, Ariña undoubtedly took the opportunity to search my suite. I just wonder if she commandeered the palm out of pique, or if she knew the Godstones were hidden there.

"Well, Your Highness, I think we should pay a visit to the condesa immediately." I lean toward him conspiratorially. "I'll keep her distracted so you can dig."

A sallow woman with gray-brown hair opens the door. "The condesa is not seeing visitors right—oh, Your Majesty." Her curtsy is awkward and quick.

"May we come in?" I give Rosario's hand a reassuring squeeze. Or maybe it's to reassure myself.

Her body is firmly lodged in the opening, preventing me from seeing inside. "Well, Your Majesty, I'm afraid the condesa truly feels—"

We don't have time for this. I stare evenly at the maid. "I insist."

She steps back, head down. "Yes, Majesty."

I push inside. Ariña's suite is very similar to mine, with a large bedroom and adjoining bath area. She prefers darker, jeweled tones, though, which surprises me. I imagined her surrounded by whites and airy pastels.

Ariña lounges on her poster bed in a nightgown of deep plum, one arm wrapped around a shiny emerald throw pillow. She raises a wineglass to me as I enter. "Your Majesty!" It sounds like an expletive in her mouth in spite of her childlike voice.

"Hello, Ariña." She is less beautiful than I remember. The same slender limbs, the same startling honey-gold eyes. But she's like an old corn husk, all dried out and empty inside.

"Have you come to gloat?" she asks.

I actually hadn't considered gloating, so intent am I on finding the Godstones. I smile sweetly. "I came to check up on an old friend."

She giggles, and I finally realize she's drunk.

"Actually, I'd like to discuss something with you. Alone." I need to get the maid out of the suite so Rosario can start searching.

Ariña flicks her fingers, and the maid scurries out the door.

"You don't mind if the prince uses your garderobe, do you?" I ask. I don't give her a chance to respond before giving the boy's hand another gentle squeeze and sending him into the bathing room with a wink.

Uninvited, I take a seat beside her on the bed. "I have some questions for you about your father. I need to understand why Conde Treviño—"

Her eyes widen. She stares at my chest, blinking erratically. "What is it?"

"That. How did you get that?" She gestures with her glass, and a bit of golden wine sloshes over the side and across her fingertips. She doesn't seem to notice.

I put my hand to my chest and feel the amulets there. "Which one are you—"

"Roldán's amulet. It's my father's. You should not be wearing it."

"It became mine when your father tried to sell me to the enemy."

"Ah, yes. Because you bear the Godstone. That was very clever of you, by the way, to keep it a secret when you first came here."

"Tell me about the amulet."

She shrugs. It's hard for her to focus.

I snap my fingers in front of her nose. "Ariña!"

She blinks. "Roldán's amulet. It's the first piece he ever made. Roldán became a famous master jeweler, and collectors pay very high prices for his early work. That piece"—she sloshes the wineglass toward me again—"is crude but priceless. It's been in my family for centuries."

I put my hand to the amulet. It's not easy to grasp, with its rough lines and awkward protrusions, but as soon as my skin brushes cold metal, the Godstone flares bright and warm.

"This jeweler, Roldán." It's hard to keep the shaking out of my voice. "Was he a bearer?"

She peers at me in obvious contempt. "Of course."

I feel hot and constricted, like the walls are closing in. No, it's the history of the Godstone that presses around me with such unwavering insistence. It's a rich, living thing that surprises me at every turn.

"All the bearers throughout time," Father Nicandro said. *All the bearers.*

A tiny, filthy hand creeps into mine and tugs. "Can we go now?"

I look down into Rosario's excited face. He waggles his eyebrows rather obviously. I hope Ariña is too drunk to notice.

"We'll let you get some rest, Condesa. I hope you feel better soon."

I turn to go, Rosario in tow. Ariña says, "Didn't you have questions for me? Don't you want a glass of wine?"

"Maybe later." I open the door.

"*He* doesn't want to talk to me either, you know. Since you came back. And now, someone follows me everywhere I—what happened to my palm tree?"

Just then, the monastery bells begin to toll in deep, steady triplets. It is not time for services. The bells can only mean one thing: Our gate has been breached.

We slam Ariña's door behind us and flee down the hall.

33

WE tumble into my suite. Rosario reaches into his pocket and pulls out the leather bag, brown near to black now, and already dusting the floor below it in fine soil. I clap and hug him and kiss him on the cheek.

"We'll take them with us," I breathe. "Invierne will never have them."

"Now are we going on a journey?" Rosario asks.

"Yes." If Mara doesn't return soon, we'll have to leave without her. With the walls breached, we can't have more than a few minutes.

"Will Papá go with us?"

I had forgotten Alejandro! "Remember, your papá may be needed at the wall." If anything, the opposite is true, but there's no need for Rosario to know that.

The door flies open, and Alejandro bursts in. His eyes are wide, and soot streaks his face. "They burned through the gate," he whispers. "Only two attacks, and they were able to burn it down."

"Are they on their way here?" I demand.

He gulps. "In minutes. Elisa, what do we do?" Rosario creeps from behind me to swallow his father's legs in an embrace.

"We flee. Mara will be back any moment with supplies. We'll leave through the sewer tunnels and hope the tide is not too high."

"But the cliffs . . . we'll have to climb part of the way, and Rosario doesn't swim well, and—"

"We can make it." I glare at him. "I'm leaving, and I'm taking Joya d'Arena's heir with me so at least one of you survives." My tone is harsher than I intend, but I swallow my twinge of guilt. Cosmé was harsh with me once or twice. It made me stronger.

It's like a slap in his face. His eyes clear; he nods once.

Ximena has been quiet this whole time, steadily stitching at my new skirt as if a normal tomorrow were a foregone conclusion. She looks up from the fabric in her lap. "Someone needs to guard your back as you leave," she says gently. "Someone needs to stay behind."

Her face is dark and calm and beautiful, and I know what she intends. "No," I whisper. I shake my head, unable to bear the thought. "No, Ximena."

"I could buy you several minutes' time. Precious time. I know just what to do. It is the only way."

"I can't lose you too."

She smiles. "I'll find you later." But she and I both know it's not true. Ximena could buy us time, but she wouldn't survive a confrontation with a sorcerer.

I won't let it happen. She doesn't yet understand how determined I've become.

I rush into the atrium, where we have stashed Rosario's things. He will need sturdy shoes for our journey, a change of clothes, the signet ring he wears on a cord around his neck that will always prove his identity.

I pass the bathing pool, and the Godstone pulses such heat that I whirl. The tiles with their four-petaled flowers stare back at me.

My hand flies to Roldán's amulet. Four rounded protrusions, just like the flowers. I whip the chain over my head and turn it around to stare at it. Is it supposed to be a flower?

I hear pounding. The squeak of hinges as the door is thrown open. Gasps.

"This is the correct room?" I can't see the speaker from my huddled crouch beside the bathing pool, but the voice makes me shiver.

I creep forward on all fours, peer into the bedroom, then yank my head back.

My heart pounds with the knowledge that there can be no escape. Three animagi stand just inside the door, their whitish hair gleaming, their Godstone amulets already glowing with recent bloodshed. Condesa Ariña stands with them.

"This is the room. I swear it," she says. She has led them right to me. I should have realized she'd betray me at the soonest opportunity. I should have—

"Where is the one who bears the mark of sorcery?"

No one answers.

Another voice bellows, "If you do not tell us who bears the mark of sorcery, you will burn."

The Godstone hammers at my navel with angry heat.

Heat. It should be cold. Icy cold. I stare at the amulet in my hand, at the tiles next to me. *All the bearers* . . . Little yellow flowers with blue spots, one blue inky blot on each petal. Bright, gorgeous blue. Godstone blue.

God, tell me what to do.

The amulet's petals are curved. Concave. Godstone sized. The stone in my navel leaps as my mind makes the connection. I grope at the caged stone at my neck, trying to lift the latch and open it, but my fingers fumble.

"I am the bearer." Mara's voice, from farther away. She must have come up behind them. "I'm the one you seek."

Oh, Mara, no. I whip the amulet over my head. I flick the latch open with a fingernail and upend it; the ancient Godstone tumbles into my palm.

Angry questions, too muffled to understand. Soft crying. "Né es ella." She's not the one.

I place the dead Godstone against the ugly amulet, snug into one of the concave petals. *Is this what I'm supposed to do, God?* Something clicks, the pendant vibrates, and I snatch my fingers back. The Godstone is embedded in the flower amulet now, as if a jeweler soldered it in. My heart pounds with fear and hope. I need the three Rosario has.

I shove the amulet into my belt sash and rise from my hiding place. I have to catch Rosario's eye somehow, communicate what I need. If he's frozen in place, I'll have to find a way to approach him.

The Godstone pulses warm encouragement, but my heart

races in my throat and my fingers are icy. I step into the bedroom.

Mara kneels at the feet of an animagus, her head down. His fingers tangle in her hair.

Their amulets glow. Condesa Ariña lies off to the side. Her legs are unnaturally cricked, and her blood pools on the stone floor. They're going to use the condesa's blood to burn answers out of my lady-in-waiting.

"Wait." I step forward. Ximena is closest to the door, frozen in a half step toward Rosario. The little boy looks at me pleadingly. "I'm the one you want." My voice is getting stronger. I'm doing the right thing. Even if I can't get to the Godstones, there's a chance that if I give myself up, they'll spare my friends.

An animagus brushes past Mara. "You bear the mark?"

"If you mean do I have a stone like that"—I indicate his amulet—"living in my gut, then yes. I bear the mark."

The animagus's impossible eyes widen. I ignore him, glancing around for Alejandro, wondering if he escaped somehow. But no, that's his head peeking over the edge of my bed. He's on the floor beside Ariña, forced to stare, frozen, at her broken body.

Their amulets brighten as the blood soaks into the stone. Not much time left before they burn us all. "Free my companions, and I'll let you live," I say.

The animagus nearest me smiles. I shudder at the sight of his pointed, brown-stained teeth. "Oh, you are no threat," he says pleasantly.

My legs shiver with the desire to run. "I have a *living* Godstone inside of me. That dead thing around your neck is no match for it." It's a ridiculous bluff. It will fool no one.

But he hesitates, eyes narrowing.

"Maybe," I continue brazenly, "I should take *yours*." I look meaningfully at Rosario.

Rosario starts, his chin lifting just slightly in my direction. He isn't frozen after all. He was pretending, the way I did months ago in the animagus's tent. Precious, clever boy! The Godstones must have protected him.

But the animagus is not convinced. "You lie," he snaps. "If you were able to call on the earth fire, you would have done so long ago."

I grasp for a convincing retort. My hands shake. I take a step forward, toward the animagus and Rosario. I hold my head high, my gaze steady. *"The champion must not fear,"* Homer said in his prophecy.

"I've been waiting," I say. "Waiting until I could gather more than a single stone. And look! Here you are. Three of you." One more step takes me just past Rosario. The animagus before me holds his ground. I hope I block his view of the boy behind me. "Surely you've heard what happened to your brother. The one camped with your northern army." I slip my right hand behind my back while I speak, curl my wrist so my palm faces upward. "I burned him. I used his own amulet against him and I burned him."

Concern flickers in the animagus's porcelain features for just a moment. It's replaced by a feral smile. "I think you love your friends too much, little girl," he hisses. He turns to the other two. "Burn the tall one."

"No!" I can't see Mara's face, but I imagine it. I picture the droopy scar across her eyelid, her lips pressed together in determination.

Rosario drops the Godstones into my hand.

The animagi's amulets are blazing now; I can hardly look at them. The one clutching Mara's hair hauls her to her feet.

The champion must not waver.

I yank the golden flower from my sash and thrust the Godstones into the indentations on the petals. They click into place, fused there by sorcery. Streaming light from the animagus's amulet plunges into Mara's torso as I raise my own amulet toward him.

Please help me. God has never intervened to save the life of a person I care about. Still, I pray, willing the amulet to do something, anything. Just this once.

Nothing happens. The amulet does not even warm in my hand.

Mara's screams rend the air. Something breaks inside me. "Wait! Stop!" I cry. "I'll give you my Godstone. Just stop."

The animagus thrusts Mara away. She crumples to the ground. Smoke rises from her clothes. *Oh, Mara. You've already suffered so much.*

As one, the three animagi advance on me, blue eyes on the strange object in my hand, their long fingers twitching like spider legs. Tears stream down my cheeks. I have failed so utterly. Rosario will not escape. The animagi will have their ten Godstones, and more. My hands fall to my sides, my chin drops. Four Godstones should have accomplished something.

Shouting, heavy bootsteps, the ring of steel. Joya's soldiers pour through the doorway. The animagi turn from me, startled. I back away quickly, hand still grasping my failed amulet.

An animagus seizes Ximena by the shoulders and places her body in front of his; the other two grab Rosario and Alejandro. The presence of the soldiers makes no difference. Invierne's sorcerers will still have what they want from me.

"Let them go," a dark voice commands. Lord Hector! Foolish hope glimmers inside me. No, it's the Godstone, sparking warmth.

"Leave this room at once, or we burn your king and queen."

The Godstone pulses in manic excitement, like it's going to burst from my belly. I look down, half expecting to see it glowing through my sash. I realize I have clutched the amulet to my stomach.

My mind is a fog of heat and certainty, my body awash with blistering power.

Four Godstones is not enough. Five is the perfect number, the divine grouping.

I turn the amulet over in my hand. There, in the back, almost hidden. Another indentation, perfectly centered.

Of course. A *living* Godstone should complete the holy grouping. *My* Godstone.

I tear the sash from my waist, pull up the edge of my blouse and hold it in my teeth. The Godstone gleams at me, and I gasp. Light swirls inside it. No, *thousands* of tiny lights, from white to midnight blue, whirl in a lazy, glittering maelstrom.

I press Roldán's ugly amulet to my stomach. The muscles

in my body tighten as it clicks into place. The sorcerer holding Ximena thrusts her to the ground and strides toward me, his eyes fixed on the amulet. He reaches for it.

"No!" Alejandro screams. He wrenches free of the animagus's grasp and launches toward the one approaching me, yanking a dagger from his boot. He plunges it into the sorceror's back.

The animagus freezes midstride, icy eyes opened wide. He drops to his knees, and blood bubbles on his lips.

The remaining two lift their amulets toward the king; light streams forth, crashes into his body. Alejandro collapses to the floor, shrieking in pain.

"Papá!" Rosario screams.

And then my amulet begins to spin like a pinwheel on the axis of my navel.

Everything tingles. The maelstrom of light from my Godstone is all around me now, swirling and beautiful and terrifying. My skin breathes in the energy of the earth, of the air around me, and feeds it to my living Godstone.

So much power! I'm panting, shaking. It's all too big for my skin, too huge for me to hold. I will burst if I don't do something soon. My amulet spins faster.

Instinctively, I do what I have practiced unceasingly for months: I pray, harder and more desperately than ever.

Dear God almighty, please deliver my enemies into my hands.

The maelstrom of light coalesces into a tight ball, a small blue sun hovering at my navel. I place my hands below it. Though the air crackles around me, it is cool in my palms. Wonderingly, I lift it toward the animagi.

Words stream unbidden from my lips. "My God is with me; I will not waver. My God is with me; His power is mine."

The animagi gape at me in horror. I realize I'm quoting scripture in the Lengua Classica. I cannot stem the flow of words, and my voice grows stronger. "I will look in triumph on my enemies. They will scatter to the ends of the earth, and God's righteous right hand will endure forever!"

The ball of light whirls. My body tingles with power. I'm shouting now.

"*I* am God's righteous right hand! And I will. Not. Waver."

I splay my feet wide and toss my tiny, whirling sun high above my head.

It hovers near the vaulted ceiling a moment, spinning faster and faster, sending sparks in all directions.

A massive boom rocks the world as it explodes into a wave of heat and shimmering air. My hair blows back from my face; my skirt plasters against my legs. Windows shatter, and glass falls in a glittering wash all around me.

The animagi scream. I watch in horror and relief as their bodies wrinkle and wither and dissolve into blackened dust.

And suddenly, I am empty. Powerless. A drained husk of a girl.

My knees can no longer support my weight. I crumple to the floor as the amulet detaches from my stomach, plinks to the ground, slides under my bed.

I'm lying on my side, cheek pressed into my sheepskin rug, my eyes drifting shut. The amulet flares once where it lies, and winks out. I follow it into blessed darkness.

34

I wake to sun streaming harsh against my eyelids.

"Elisa?" A head hovers above me. I blink rapidly, but my mind clings to sleep. "Elisa! You're awake."

"Rosario?"

"Ximena! She's awake."

Another head. My vision is clearer now. My body aches everywhere, like I was beaten with wooden swords. "Ximena?" I croak, almost choking on the dryness in my throat. "What happened?"

She places a cool hand to my forehead and chuckles. "Elisa, my sky, you destroyed the animagi."

I gasp out a sob of relief, remembering. "Yes. Yes, I did."

"That amulet of yours. It sent a wave, like light or heat, all through the city. Every mirror and window in Brisadulce shattered. Then the animagi just . . . grew old right before our eyes. It was the strangest thing I've ever seen. They say the same thing happened to the two who remained on the battlefield."

It's overwhelming. The animagi are dead. Tears squeeze

from the corners of my eyes. From habit, I put my fingertips to my Godstone and send a prayer of thanks. It responds with balmy warmth.

I gasp. "My Godstone. It lives."

"Yes. I suppose God isn't done with you yet." I'm not sure I appreciate the amusement in her voice. The possibility that God has a further use for my stone could make me ill if I thought about it too much.

"Your amulet didn't fare so well, I'm afraid," she says. "When it fell away from your body, it blackened and shattered."

"Invierne's army?" I ask in a shaky voice.

Ximena strokes my hair. "Lord Hector and the general pursue them. He says the army was already falling apart, demoralized by your Malficio. Without the animagi, the Inviernos can't sustain a fighting front."

I swallow. "And the southern holdings?"

"Invierne is in retreat there too. Your strange wave reached all the way to the southern coast. But . . ." Her hand freezes. She takes a deep breath. "There's something else."

I sit straight up. I remember hearing screams, smelling burning flesh. "What? Is it Mara? Or Cosmé? Have you heard from her?"

Her brows slope with sorrow. "Mara and Cosmé are well enough. Mara rests while her burns heal."

"Then—"

"Papá is sick," Rosario says.

Alejandro. I swing my legs around to the edge of the bed. Ximena grabs my robe from its bedpost and hands it to me.

"Sick?" I ask her quietly, heart pounding with dread. He saved my life, I remember now, the same way I saved his months ago. He killed an animagus with a dagger, and they burned him for it.

"Badly injured," she whispers back. Everything in her expression speaks to the seriousness of his wounds.

"I'll be back soon."

My bones ache as I limp to the door connecting our suites. I pause to take calming breaths. My hesitant knock is answered quickly by Captain Lucio.

"Your Majesty." He bows.

"How is he?"

He rubs at weary eyes with a fist. "The animagus burned him severely, and he was badly cut by your window. We stopped the bleeding, but he is weak now, and—"

I brush past him, remembering the way my window shattered. How many more of Brisadulce's citizens were as unfortunately located when my shock wave hit? How many died?

Alejandro lies on his back. Linen swaddles half of his beautiful face, including his mouth. The rest of his body hides beneath his blankets, and I'm glad for it because I could not bear to see his wounds. His unbandaged eye crinkles when he sees me.

"Elisa." His muffled whisper sounds so painful.

I bend over and kiss his forehead. "I'm so sorry, Alejandro."

A rattling sigh slips through the linen. "Don't be. This was my choice."

I run my fingertips across his eyebrow, let them trail into

his hairline where they tangle in his hair, the way I used to imagine doing. "What do you mean?"

He leans into my caress. "The animagus holding me was distracted." He takes another ragged breath. "I didn't have time to think about it. *You* were more important."

I feel more fondness for him in this moment than ever before. "You are a hero," I say with conviction. "Thank you."

His eye closes, the lines of his face relax. I'm ready to tiptoe away when he says, "Elisa, we've become friends, haven't we?"

I'm not sure, but I'd like us to be, so I say, "Of course. Just like you said we would. On our wedding night."

"Good." He sighs. Then: "Ariña's dead, isn't she?"

"I'm not sure, Alejandro. I think so."

"I loved her." Sorrow creases his brow, then he seems to melt into himself. I feel a strange distance when he says, "Take care of Rosario."

"Take care of him yourself."

"Promise me. He loves you."

I should shower him with encouraging denial. I should say something to give him hope. Or I could be honest. "I promise."

"Elisa? I would have loved you too, given a little more time."

During Alejandro's final lucid moments, he summons me, Father Nicandro, and General Luz-Manuel to his bedside. With shaking hands, he signs an edict declaring me his heir and Queen Regnant of Joya d'Arena until such time as his son comes of age. "When I'm gone," he explains in a voice so soft I have to bend to hear, "no one can dispute your right to rule. Even though you weren't born here."

I would have raised Rosario to the throne, even without his help. I know that about myself now. Still, I'm touched by the gesture. I have to blink and swallow a bit before saying, "Thank you, my friend. Rosario will grow up knowing his father acted nobly till the very end."

My words seem to soothe him. The next morning, he slips into a coma and does not awaken from it.

Lord Hector pursues Invierne's huge but dispirited army well into the jagged arms of the Sierra Sangre before returning home. He reports to me in my new office—a sumptuous chamber of lush rugs and gleaming bookcases that I'm not yet comfortable in—and lays a letter of resignation on my desk.

I look up at him, confused. "What is this?"

"Your Majesty, I am the king's personal guard and man-at-arms. My king is dead. Therefore, I am unemployed. This letter just makes it official."

My heart hammers in my throat. I can't bear the thought of losing Hector. Sometime, when I wasn't paying attention, I grew unbearably fond of him.

I search his face, but his handsome features are cast in iron and unreadable. "You are so eager to retire, then?" I ask hesitatingly. "You really want to leave?"

His mouth opens. Closes. He shifts on his feet.

"Unless you're determined to escape me, I'd like you to consider staying. I . . . well, you have to forgive me . . ." My cheeks feel hot, and my hands are sweating. "I just assumed you would be Queen's Guard."

I wait an eternity for his answer.

Then his face relaxes, and his mustache twitches with the influence of a soft smile. "I would be honored, Your Majesty."

I exhale in relief. "Oh, thank God."

Three months after the death of Alejandro, on the day Brisadulce throws off its mourning rags, I crown Cosmé Queen of Basajuan, the new country extending from the desert's eastern edge to the foothills of the Sierra Sangre. Jacián is there, and Father Alentín. Even Conde Eduardo from the southern holdings makes the journey to welcome the new queen.

Only Papá and Alodia decline my invitation, though they send letters of congratulations.

In the same ceremony, I honor Prince Rosario with the Queen's Star for acts of bravery and heroism in circumstances of extreme danger. He stands so straight, and his little lip trembles as I pin the medal to his sash.

There are many deserving of the same honor. Hundreds, perhaps. But he is the perfect representative for the children of my Malficio—an orphan like them, and equally brave. He also represents hope for us, hope of a strong future and a strong king. When I step away and present him to the court, the applause is thunderous.

The dining room is too small to hold all our guests, so the kitchen staff brings food to the audience hall. I'm pleasantly ill from spiced, blackened chicken, creamy potato soup, and orange-peel scones when Cosmé glides up to me wearing her new crown. She leans forward and kisses my cheek. "Thank you, my friend," she says. "I am glad to have been proven wrong about you." She shifts uncomfortably; such declarations do not come easily to her. She hurries away before I can respond and disappears behind a wall of celebrants.

Ximena's arm sneaks around my waist. Together we survey the smiling, milling crowd.

"You see, my sky?" Ximena whispers. "God was right to choose you."

I grin. "Yes, he was right to choose me. He had a plan all along, just like Aneaxi said."

She gives me a squeeze. "I knew someday you would realize your worth. Your worthiness."

I shake my head. "Oh, Ximena, he was right to choose me, but not because of my worth." I gaze happily at my friends as they swirl through the hall, feasting and chatting. "You, Cosmé, Hector, even little Rosario, were already willing to be heroes." *And Humberto*, says a little voice in my head. "You didn't need to be chosen. But I would have done nothing, become nothing, were it not for this thing inside me. So you see, God picked me because I was *un*worthy."

"But you rose to the choosing. You gave hope to your people. Solved a divine puzzle that was centuries in the making. Defeated our enemies."

Understanding hits like a rock in my gut, and I gasp just a little. I know God selected me because I needed a push, but Ximena is right, too—I rose to the choosing. I didn't need faith in God so much as I needed faith in myself.

"Yes, *I* did all that, didn't I?" I breathe wonderingly. I loved and lost and survived. Me, not the stone in my navel. I place trembling fingertips to the Godstone.

It pulses with purpose.

God is not done with me yet, and I may be in more danger than ever, now that the whole world knows I bear his stone. But in this moment, I choose to revel in our victory, in the warmth of having made a place for myself, surrounded by friends. For the first time in a long time, I am not afraid.

ACKNOWLEDGMENTS

A novel, especially a first novel, is an enormous undertaking of faith and frustration, of learning and hope, of despair and triumph. And I could not have navigated the craziness if not for the following fabulous folks.

Thank you to:

My amazing editor, Martha Mihalick, for both falling in love with the story and being relentless about making it better. (Are you *sure* we don't have time for another revision round?)

The Greenwillow team, for their warmth, their enthusiasm, for my beautiful book jacket, and for so many little things.

My super-agent, Holly Root, for getting my work on a fundamental level, for endless patience and humor, and for taking care of all the details.

My friends at the Online Writing Workshop for Science Fiction, Fantasy, and Horror; including but not limited to Jenni Smith-Gaynor (yes, you were first), Ian, Heidi, Deb, Marsha, Amber, Aaron, Brad, Jo, and Heather.

Elizabeth Bear, for taking a newbie under her wing and giving some formative advice for no other reason than to pay it forward. I promise to continue the tradition.

Amanda Downum, Leah Bobet, Vernieda Vergara, and Chance Morrison, who read early drafts and gave much needed encouragement.

Jodi Meadows, Jaime Lee Moyer, and Jill Myles, early-draft victims whose friendship has meant the world to me.

Sarah Prineas, for responding helpfully to a panicked e-mail, for understanding my need for ruthless practicality, and for being an honest and thoughtful reader and friend.

Holly McDowell, for friendship and advice, but mostly for wonderful times.

Rebekah Piedad, my sister and best friend, for being the perfect cheerleader.

And, most importantly, my husband, C. C. Finlay, the best man I know, for editing genius that makes my writing better, for dreaming right along with me and never complaining when the dishes aren't done. I like you a lot. Let's get married.

THE
GIRL OF FIRE
AND
THORNS

RAE CARSON

"Weighing In on Weight"

A Q&A with Rae Carson

A Recipe for Honey-Coconut Scones

An Excerpt from Book Two, *The Crown of Embers*

WEIGHING IN ON WEIGHT

BY RAE CARSON

A long time ago, in a galaxy far, far away, I worked for a technology company as an inside sales rep. I'd already experienced the "glass ceiling" and wage inequality, but working at—let's call it Misogyny, Inc.—was my first encounter with that special brand of endemic discrimination that borders on harassment.

A few quick examples:

1. I had an idea that I felt would save our company tens of thousands of dollars per month. So for our weekly company meeting, I prepared all my data, dressed in my best suit, and confidently proposed a new inventory system.

I wasn't even halfway done with my spiel before everyone started laughing. They told me it would never work. *But,* they said, I did look very cute in my suit.

At the next weekly meeting, our manufacturing manager presented the exact same proposal. He was lauded as a genius. We implemented it right away, and he got a big bonus for saving the company so much money.

2. After two years, I got a raise and a tiny promotion. My sales numbers were the highest in the company. Not by much, and not all the time, but it was an impressive feat, considering the other reps were seven-year-plus veterans.

After the news got around, one of my female coworkers said, in a biting tone, "I'm sick to death of people thinking you do a good job just because you're hot."

She worked hard to promote this perception among our coworkers. In no time, I had a reputation as "the lazy one who gets away with stuff because she's cute."

3. I got very sick with food poisoning or a stomach bug or . . . something. I'll spare you the details. But after two miserable days, I clawed my way back to work. I still couldn't eat, so I brought a large supply of Pedialyte to keep me on my feet. Naturally, I lost a ton of weight very quickly.

The rumor quickly got back to me that I was bulimic. Another female coworker had told everyone that *for months*, I had been eating meals on the company dime and throwing them up to lose weight.

Looking back, a couple of things stand out to me. In all three of these instances, a) my body was tied to my performance, and b) women were involved.

My experience is not unusual. Thousands, maybe millions of women have their accomplishments waved away or ignored daily, even as their bodies suffer devastating scrutiny—from both men and women.

These experiences were very much on my mind when I sat down to write *The Girl of Fire and Thorns*. The protagonist, you see, is fat. Elisa has an unhealthy relationship with food. No one believes she'll accomplish anything, and her lifelong social conditioning has caused her to believe this harmful perception.

She begins to change right away. In chapter two, she stands up for herself and takes control of her wedding night. In chapter three, she saves a man's life by grabbing the weapon of a dead enemy and stabbing with it. In chapter four, she has an epiphany about her own self-absorption and makes a point to focus on others—and on and on through the end of the book. My goal was to show Elisa gaining confidence through a gradual process of taking control of her own life and destiny.

But with Misogyny, Inc., so fresh in my mind, it occurred to me that some people in Elisa's world might be unable to see past her body to her accomplishments and personal growth. So, for instance, without knowing Elisa at all, her maid finds her unworthy of being the chosen one, and despises her. And later, when (minor spoiler . . .) Elisa loses some weight, a certain man finds her attractive for the first time—but is unable to acknowledge that she has become a great leader in her own right.

One sees her as fat. One sees her as beautiful. Neither can see beyond her outward appearance to the truth of who Elisa really is.

I know how easy it is to look at a woman and see nothing but a body. I'm guilty of it, too. How many times do we look at a beautiful, blond woman in a short skirt and think *airhead* or *bimbo* or *shallow*? Maybe she's a rocket scientist with multiple PhDs. Maybe a battered paperback of her favorite Coetzee is shoved inside that Prada bag.

We just don't know.

You can't tell by looking at a woman's body how much she exercises, how much she eats, whether or not she's lazy, whether she is confident or depressed or accomplished.

When I drafted *The Girl of Fire and Thorns*, I was an athletic size 6. I felt beautiful then. I'm sixty pounds heavier now, and aside from my wardrobe, little has changed. I'm still smart. I'm still writing books. I'm still in love with my life. I still feel beautiful.

I grant that there have been some gradual shifts in maturity and confidence. But like Elisa, I've earned the heck out of these changes through life experience and introspection—not through changing the way I look.

A woman has a right to have and *enjoy* whatever body her choices or circumstances give her. But Misogyny, Inc., showed me how crushing it is to feel that the sum whole of your worth is wrapped up in your flesh.

So, to my fellow women I make this resolution: I will commit to seeing beyond your breasts or fat or beauty to the essence of who you are. And I will vociferously defend your right to have your accomplishments acknowledged and lauded—no matter what you look like.

Originally posted on *Under the Greenwillow*,
the official blog of Greenwillow Books: greenwillowblog.com.

An Interview with Rae Carson

Sharon Rawlins interviewed Rae Carson on the Young Adult Library Services Association (YALSA)'s blog *The Hub* after *The Girl of Fire and Thorns* was nominated for the William C. Morris Award. You can find the interview online at this link: http://www.yalsa.ala.org/thehub/2012/01/16/author-interview-rae-carson/

Congratulations on your nomination as a Morris Award Finalist! What was your reaction to being nominated?

There was some shaking involved. A few tears. An awkward-author happy dance. And then champagne!

Paranormal fantasy books are all the rage right now. Your book doesn't include vampires or other supernatural creatures but there is a fantastical element in the book: the mysterious Godstone that the main character Elisa has permanently imbedded in her navel. How would you categorize this book?

I would call it "high fantasy," like *Lord of the Rings*, with some of the political underpinnings of George R.R. Martin's *Game of Thrones*— except for teens.

Religion, spirituality, and faith is not often addressed in YA books but here it's an important element. What was your intent in including it in the book?

I live in a country where 83% of the population still professes affiliation with some kind of religious faith. It seemed to me that deciding what one believes about religion in the face of so many conflicting messages is a much more important part of the coming-of-age experience than is necessarily represented in current teen lit. So I wanted to write a book that did justice to this struggle without condemning or condoning any particular faith.

The main character Elisa undergoes a physical transformation in the book from being overweight to losing a lot of weight after undergoing an arduous, physically challenging journey. Did you worry that readers might object that you're implying that there was something wrong with Elisa when she was heavier?

Oh, yes, I worried about that a lot. And for that reason, I considered having her not lose weight. But I realized it would be narratively ludicrous for her to experience everything she does without profound physical consequences. Also, I got a lot of mileage out of my secondary characters because of it. I was able to use their contrasting responses to her—both before and after the weight loss—to reveal important things about them and their relationships to Elisa. I tried very hard to show her personal growth in each chapter prior to her weight loss. For instance, saving a man's life, defying her nurse, deciding to play the game of politics to win, all result from her gradually increasing confidence and have nothing to do with her size.

I love reading about strong female characters, especially those who are smart. Elisa is a particularly clever girl, as adept at military strategy as any of the guys. Is that the kind of book you also like to read yourself?

Definitely! I think smart is very sexy—in guys and girls.

I appreciated the fact that the plot wasn't predictable. In fact, there were several surprising plot twists that I didn't see coming. It was really refreshing to read a book where you didn't see what

was coming. I think even the teens are savvy enough to find a lot of books too predictable that way. Will we see a lot more in the other books in the trilogy? Maybe you can elaborate on the plot twists?

Thanks! Yes, more twists are coming. I'll just hint broadly and say that the true love of Elisa's life is someone she never saw coming, everything she was taught about the mysterious Inviernos is wrong, and the Godstone has more power than she ever imagined.

This book has a number of romantic relationships but things don't necessarily turn out the way you think they might. Can you give your fans (including this one) any hints about whether Elisa will find happiness in the end of this projected trilogy? Maybe you can give a few details about the next book in the series?

That is the question, isn't it? In *The Crown of Embers*, Elisa now rules the vastest kingdom in the world. Is it possible to find true love when you are so powerful? When every man in the world is subservient to you? Can that even be sexy? I believe it can be incredibly sexy. But Elisa—and her one true love—will have lots of obstacles to overcome to get there.

Who are some of the other authors who have influenced you as a writer?

Scott O'Dell was one of my favorite authors when I was a child. I must have read *Island of the Blue Dolphins* and *Sing Down the Moon* a dozen times each. Later, I fell in love with Robin McKinley, and though I didn't reread her work the same way, it must have made an impression because I've been told at least eleventy gazillion times that my writing reminds people of hers. More recently, I've enjoyed Paolo Bacigalupi, Margaret Atwood, and Patrick Rothfuss.

What's the strangest thing anyone has said to you as you've been on tour promoting your book?

I don't know that I've heard anything strange (give me time!) but I've had people say some pretty awesome things such as, "I feel like you wrote this book just for me," or "Elisa is my hero." Hearing this stuff fills my author-heart with ridiculous, giddy joy.

What's the most surprising thing that has happened to you since your book was published?

Getting shortlisted for the Morris Award has been my hugest surprise to date. I did not see that coming!

To borrow a question from James Lipton from *Inside the Actors Studio*, as originally posited by Bernard Pivot from the French series *Bouillon de culture*, What's your favorite word? and What's your least favorite word?

I loathe "orientate." Also, "fudge." (Seriously, say "fudge" five times in a row. Starts to feel odd, doesn't it? Kind of guttural and mean.) But I love "viscosity" and "luminous." Of course, I hope to never, ever, ever encounter a substance that is both viscous and luminous, because *ew*

HONEY-COCONUT SCONES

INGREDIENTS:

2 cups flour

¼ cup brown sugar

1 tablespoon baking powder

¼ teaspoon salt

¼ teaspoon powdered ginger

4 tablespoons cold unsalted butter, cut up

½ cup shredded coconut

1/3 cup heavy or whipping cream

1/3 cup coconut milk

1 large egg, beaten

2 tablespoons honey

½ teaspoon finely grated lemon peel

parchment paper

cookie sheet

DIRECTIONS:

1. Preheat the oven to 375 degrees.

2. In a large bowl, mix the flour, brown sugar, baking powder, salt, and ginger.

3. Add the butter. Either with a pastry cutter or using two knives in a scissoring motion, cut the butter into the dry ingredients until the mixture resembles coarse crumbs.

4. Toss in the coconut.

5. In a small bowl, mix together the remaining ingredients (cream, coconut milk, egg, honey, lemon peel).

6. Slowly pour the wet mixture into the dry and stir with a rubber spatula until the dough forms.

7. With a floured hand, knead in the bowl for several minutes, until the dough comes together. It will still be sticky.

8. Line a cookie sheet with parchment paper. Using your hands, separate an approximately two tablespoon–sized dollop of dough and place on cookie sheet. Repeat until dough is gone. The batch will make about a dozen scones.

9. Bake for 12–13 minutes. Let cool on a towel or wire rack.

Particularly delicious served with whipped cream (use a bit of whatever you have left over with a dash of vanilla and powdered sugar to taste and beat it till stiff) or your favorite jam.

Read on for a preview
from the sequel to THE GIRL OF FIRE AND THORNS

THE CROWN OF EMBERS

RAE CARSON

MY entourage of guards struggles to keep pace as I fly down the corridors of my palace. Servants in starched frocks and shined shoes line the way, bowing like dominoes as I pass. From far away comes a low thrum, filtering even through walls of stone and mortar, steady as falling water, hollow as distant thunder. It's the crowd outside, chanting my name.

I barrel around a corner and collide with a gleaming breastplate. Firm hands grasp my shoulders, saving me from tumbling backward. My crown is not so lucky. The monstrous thing clatters to the ground, yanking strands of hair painfully with it.

He releases my shoulders and rubs at red spot on his neck. "That crown of yours is a mighty weapon," says Lord-Commander Hector of the Royal Guard.

"Sorry," I say, blinking up at him. He and the other guards shaved their mustaches to mark our recent victory, and I've yet to adjust to this new, younger-looking Hector.

Ximena, my gray-haired nurse, bends to retrieve the crown and brushes it off. It's thick with gold and inlaid with a single cabochon ruby. No dainty queen's diadem for me. By tradition, I wear the crown of a fully empowered monarch.

"I expected you an hour ago," he says as I take his offered arm. We travel the corridor at a bruising pace.

"General Luz-Manuel kept me. He wanted to change the parade route again."

He stops cold, and I nearly trip. "Again?"

"He wants to avoid the bottleneck where the Avenida de la Serpiente crosses the merchant's alley. He says a stranger in the crowd could spear me too easily."

Ximena takes advantage of our stillness to reposition the crown on my head. I grimace as she shoves hairpins through the velvet loops to hold it in place.

Hector is shaking his head. "But the rooftops are low in that area. You'll be safer from arrows, which is the greater danger."

"Exactly what I said. He was . . . displeased." I tug on his arm to keep us moving.

"He should know better."

"I may have told him as much."

"I'm sure he appreciated that," he says dryly.

"I've no idea what advantage he thought to gain by it," I say. "Whatever it was, I was not going to give it to him."

Hector glances around at the people lining the corridors, then adds in a lowered voice, "Elisa, as your personal defender, I must beg you one last time to reconsider. The whole world knows you bear the Godstone."

I sigh against the truth of his words. Yes, I'm now the target of religious fanatics, Invierne spies, even black market gem traders. But my birthday parade is the one day each year when everyone—from laundress to stable boy to weather-worn sailor—can glimpse their ruling monarch. It's a national holiday, one they've been looking forward to for months. I won't deny them the opportunity.

And I refuse to be governed by fear. The life stretching before me is that of a queen. It's a life I chose. Fought for, even. I cannot—will not—squander it on dread.

"Hector, I won't hide in the sand like a frightened jerboa."

"Sometimes," Ximena cuts in, with her soft but deliberate voice, "protecting Elisa means protecting her interests. Elisa must show herself publicly. These early months are important as she consolidates her power. We'll keep her safe, you and I. And God. She has a great destiny. . . ."

I turn a deaf ear to her words. So much has happened in the last year, but I feel no closer to my appointment with destiny than I did when God first lodged his stone in my navel seventeen years ago. It still pulses with power, warms in response to my prayers, reminds me that I have not done *enough*, that God has plans for me yet.

And I am sick to death of hearing about it.

"I understand, my lady," Hector is saying. "But it would be safer—"

"Hector!" I snap. "I've made up my mind."

He stiffens. "Yes, Your Majesty."

Shame tightens my throat. Why did I snap at Hector? Ximena is the one I'm frustrated with.

Moments later we reach the carriage house, which reeks of steaming manure and moldy straw on this especially hot day. My open carriage awaits, a marvel of polished mahogany and swirling bronze scrollwork. Banners of royal blue stream from the posts. The door panels display my royal crest—a ruby crown resting on a bed of sacrament roses.

Fernando, my best archer, stands on the rear platform, bow slung over his shoulder. He bows from the waist, his face grave. Four horses flick their tails and dance in their jeweled traces. I eye them warily while Hector helps me up.

Then he offers a hand to Ximena, and in spite of their recent disagreement, a look of fierce understanding passes between them. They are a formidable team, my guard and my guardian. Sometimes it's as though they plot my safety behind my back.

Hector gives the order, my driver whips the reins, and the carriage lurches forward. My Royal Guard, in its gleaming ceremonial armor, falls in around us. They march a deep one-two-one-two as we leave the shade of the carriage house for desert sunshine.

The moment we turn onto the Colonnade, the air erupts with cheering.

Thousands line the way, packed shoulder to shoulder, waving their hands, flags, tattered linens. Children sit on shoulders, tossing birdseed and rose petals into the air. A banner stretches the length of six people and reads, HAPPY BIRTHDAY TO HER MAJESTY QUEEN LUCERO-ELISA!

"Oh," I breathe.

Ximena grasps my hand and squeezes. "You're a war hero, remember?"

But I'm also a foreigner queen, ruling by an accident of marriage and war. Warmth and pride blossom in my chest, to see my people accepting me with their whole hearts.

Then Ximena's face sobers, and she leans over and whispers, "Remember this moment and treasure it, my sky. No sovereign remains popular forever."

I nod from respectful habit, but I can't keep the frown from creeping onto my face. My people are giving me a gift, and she takes it away so soon.

The steep Colonnade is lined on either side by decadent three-story townhomes. Their sculpted sandstone cornices sparkle in the sun, and silk standards swing from flat garden rooftops. But as we descend from the height of the city, cheered all the way, the townhomes gradually become less stately, until finally we reach the city's outer circle, where only a few humble buildings rise from the war rubble.

I ignore the destruction as long as I can, gazing instead at the city's great wall. It rises the height of several men, protecting us from the swirling desert beyond. I crane my neck and glimpse the soldiers posted between the wall's crenellations, bows held at the ready.

The main gate stands open for daytime commerce. Framed by the barbed portcullis is our cobbled highway. Beyond it are the sweeping dunes of my beautiful desert, wind smoothed and deceptively soft in the yellow light of midday. My gaze lingers too long on the sand as we turn onto the Avenida de la Serpiente.

When I can avoid it no longer, I finally take in the view that twists my heart. For Brisadulce's outer circle is a scar on the face of the world, blackened and crumbled and reeking of wet char. This is where the Invierne army broke through our gate, where their sorcerous animagi burned everything in sight with the blue-hot fire of their Godstone amulets.

A ceiling beam catches my eye, toppled across a pile of adobe rubble. At one end the wood grain shows pristine, but it blackens along its length, shrinking and shriveling until it ends in a ragged stump glowing red with embers. A wisp of smoke curls into the air.

The outer ring is rife with these glowing reminders of the war we won at such a cost. Months later, we still cannot wholly quench their fire. Father Nicandro, my head priest, says that since magic caused these fires, only magic can cool them. Either magic or time.

My city may burn for a hundred years.